P9-CDE-729

A

Master Plan

for

Rescue

ALSO BY JANIS COOKE NEWMAN

Mary: Mrs. A. Lincoln

The Russian Word for Snow

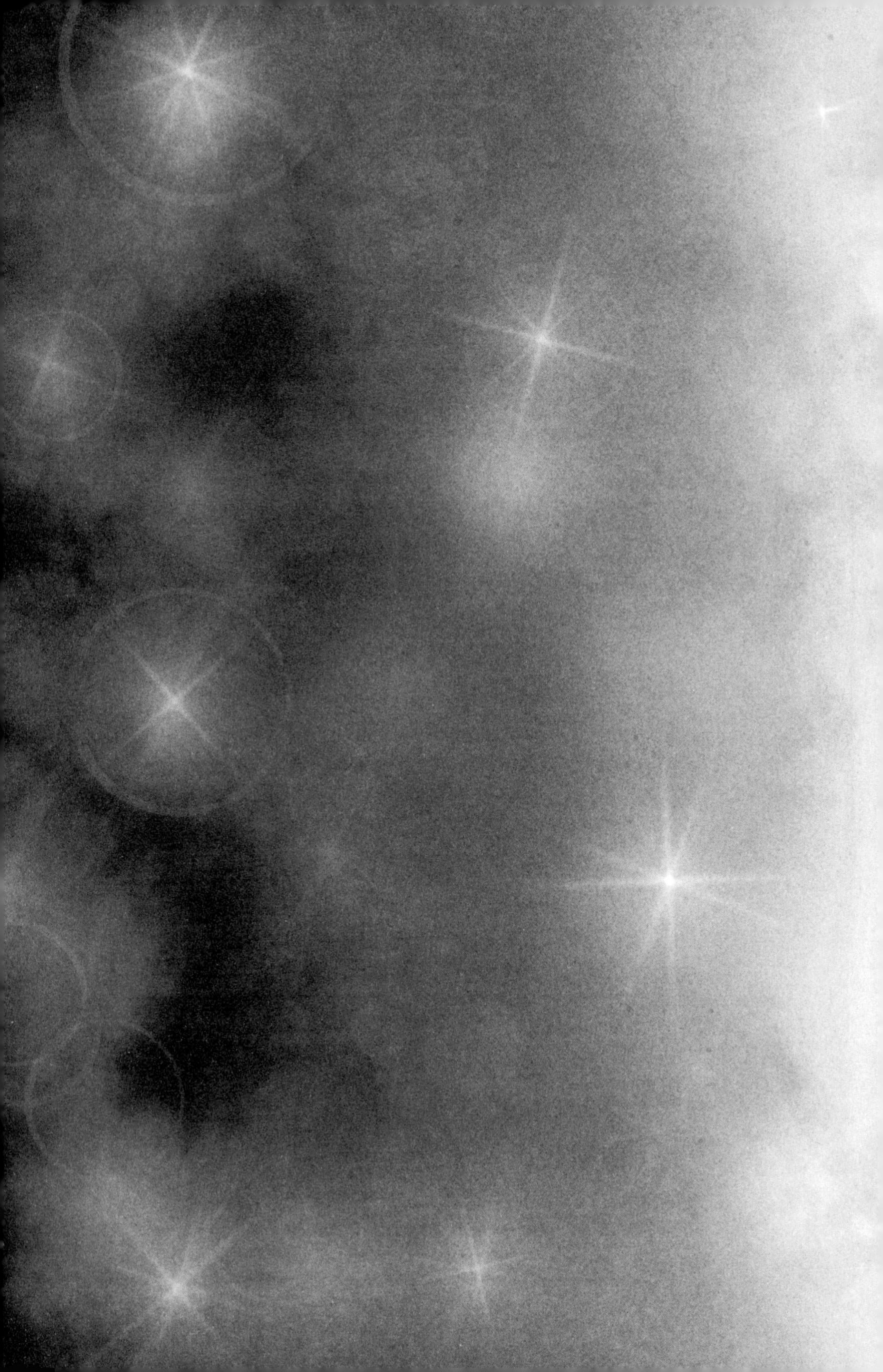

A Master Plan for Rescue

JANIS COOKE NEWMAN

RIVERHEAD BOOKS
New York
2015

Riverhead Books
An imprint of Penguin Random House LLC
375 Hudson Street
New York, New York 10014

Library of Congress Cataloging-in-Publication Data

Newman, Janis Cooke.
A master plan for rescue : a novel / Janis Cooke Newman.
p. cm.
ISBN 978-1-59463-361-4
I. Title.
PS3614.E626M38 2015 2015004284
813'.6—dc23

Printed in the United States of America
1 3 5 7 9 10 8 6 4 2

BOOK DESIGN BY AMANDA DEWEY

To my father,

who told me his stories

A

Master Plan

for

Rescue

One

This is the moment I spend the rest of my life trying to return to:

The three of us sitting around the table my father and I have painted red to match The Flash's cape. A shade, I now know, that doesn't belong in a kitchen, but it was my father who suggested bringing the comic book to the paint store on Dyckman Street.

It's early December, and the clanging of the radiator mixes with the violins that spill from the speakers of the Silvertone radio. I know the Silvertone is on, because it is always on. My grandfather, a man once known as the Gentleman Bootlegger, a man who is dead by this time, claimed that music during meals is what separates man from beast, and so my mother—his daughter—puts on music. But we never listen to it. Instead, we sit above bowls that smell of gravy and spices and talk over each other, sometimes banging our silverware on the red table for attention. The three of us—my father, mother, and me—in our small apartment at the northern tip of Manhattan.

In this moment, though, there is only the clanging of the radiator and the violins. We have stopped talking so my father and I can watch my mother add up numbers inside her head.

Because that is what she can do. Her ability.

Though to be more accurate, it's my father who is watching her. I am watching him. And I'm realizing, for the first time—and probably because I am so close to turning twelve—that it isn't the feat of her adding up those numbers he enjoys so much. It's the way she's sliding the tip of a No. 2 pencil into and out of the gap between her front teeth.

And now that I've noticed this, I cannot remember a single time my father has taken that pencil back and checked her answer. I can only remember him doing exactly what he's doing now. Gazing at her mouth, her eyes—the exact shade of green the Hudson River gets on a clear day—her long swoops of black hair.

In the pocket of the black Mass pants I have not yet had time to change out of is something rare I am waiting to show my father. This morning, during Father Barry's sermon, I found the stub of a Mass candle caught under my kneeler, and I've spent the past hour melting its wax into the hollow of a perfectly round beer bottle cap, creating an object I believe will make me unbeatable at the game of skully.

I'm, at best, a mediocre skully player. However, with this new skully cap—this Holy Skully Cap—it will be as if God Himself is directing my thumb every time I flick my cap across the chalked squares of the board. As if His Mighty Force is propelling my cap into that of another player, one filled merely with the wax of a melted crayon.

As I wait, I imagine myself dropping the Holy Skully Cap into my father's hand, telling him the story of finding the candle, melting the wax. I know that when I've finished this story, my father will lift his eyes—brown like mine—and run them over me, reading me. I know, too, that he will understand all the powers I believe the Holy Skully Cap to possess without me having to say them aloud.

Because that is what he can do. His ability.

I do not yet have an ability. I am only an almost-twelve-year-old boy, small for my age, black-haired like my mother, wanting no more than for the life I have to keep going as it is.

All these things are held in that moment. Everything I am about to lose. My mother adding up numbers inside her head. My father watching as she slides the tip of a No. 2 pencil into and out of the gap between her teeth. Me with something rare I am waiting to show my father.

It has been a cold day, the temperature barely making it into the twenties. But the chill has thinned the air and the sky is clear. The last rays of sunlight slant through the front windows of our apartment, and though it is only mid-afternoon, there is a sense of the day ending. That nostalgic Sunday afternoon feeling of wishing to remain exactly where you are.

Those things, too, are held in that moment, the moment before the violins turn into words. Turn into

Surprise attack and *Japanese bombs* and *Pearl Harbor.*

It is my father's hand I'm looking at when my eyes go bad.

My father's hands are not like anyone else's. The skin in the creases has been bleached white by the chemicals he uses to develop his photographs. My father shoots portraits, and I think of these white marks as the ghosts of every picture he has ever taken.

It's these white marks that disappear first, blurring into nothingness, like ghosts vanishing. Then the hand itself. The edges melting away, dissolving into a table painted a red that doesn't belong in a kitchen.

My eyes dart around the room, but everything has turned into a mass of color, as if the outline of each object—the icebox, the stove, the window over the sink—has been erased, as if the boundaries that keep the color of one thing from invading another no longer exist. And what I think—what I can only think—is that it is the Japanese. That they, with their bombs, have knocked the entire world out of focus.

I search for my father, stare into the space where a second ago, he was sitting. But there's nothing there except the brownish-red smudge of the wallpaper, and it feels like those bombs have sucked all the air out of the room along with the outlines of things, because I cannot breathe, can only gasp.

I hurl my arm into the place where my father had been, stunned that the Japanese could have taken him from me, amazed at their evil magic. My hand collides with something, the bones of his chest, the worn fabric of his shirt. My father shifts in his chair, drops his hand over mine, and I realize that his reddish hair, the Sunday stubble on his face, his brown shirt have all merged with the wallpaper behind him, turning him invisible. I press the flat of my hand against his chest until I can feel his heart beating.

And that's better, but only a little. Because now Aunt May—my mother's sister—and Uncle Glenn are in our kitchen, which I know only by the sound of their voices. The two of them, up from their apartment one floor below. And I have the sense from the confident movement of their blurs—Uncle Glenn's pudgy and beer-colored, Aunt May's still in the navy blue suit she wore to Mass—that they do not see our kitchen as an unnavigable smudge of color. And I'm figuring out, by the way Aunt May is clattering what sounds like rosary beads on the table, and saying we should all go straight back to Good Shepherd and repeat a thousand Hail Marys for peace, saying to my father, "Yes, even you, Denis," my father having long declared that Ireland more than cured him of Catholicism; and by the way Uncle Glenn keeps repeating that first thing tomorrow morning he's going to Whitehall Street and joining up; and by how the black-haired blur of my mother is heading for the living room, shouting back that everybody needs to pipe down, because she can't hear the radio, that it is only me who is seeing the world this way.

And that is worse. Much worse.

I take my hand off my father's chest and press both palms into my eyes until I see sparks of light, and then I press harder, as if that light is a mechanism for fixing what has gone wrong. But when I open my eyes, nothing has changed. Or, I suppose, everything has.

I have to say something, I'm thinking. *Tell somebody.* But I can't pull enough air into my lungs for speech. And even if I could, everybody is talking. About the Japanese. And their bombs.

Except my father, who hasn't moved, hasn't spoken. Who, I believe, has been running his eyes over me, reading me.

"Jack," he says. "How many fingers?"

But I cannot tell he has raised his hand.

Two

The following day, my father took me to see Dr. Shaperstein, the optometrist on Broadway and 207th Street.

Dr. Shaperstein's office was nothing more than a brown blur, except for a model of an eyeball the size of a grapefruit that appeared to be floating in space and Dr. Shaperstein's white coat, which hovered over me.

"Tell me what you can read on the chart," Dr. Shaperstein said.

I squinted into the brownness.

Dr. Shaperstein dropped his hands on my shoulders and pushed me forward a foot.

"Better?"

I shook my head.

His hands fell onto my shoulders once more, and he pushed me again. Then he kept pushing me, asking every foot or so what I could see. Not until I was near enough to touch the chart, press my palms flat against it, did I finally say, "E. I can see E, the big letter at the top."

Dr. Shaperstein turned to my father. "Your son has the most remarkable case of myopia I have ever encountered."

He did not say *remarkable* as if I had developed a special skill like flying. He said it as if I might have wandered over from the Coney Island sideshow.

My father told him my eyes had been fine only a couple of days before, and Dr. Shaperstein said it wasn't uncommon for boys on the cusp of puberty to experience a sudden deterioration of vision. Then he moved me back and forth in front of the chart to see exactly what I could and couldn't read, and repeated *remarkable* a few more times, until my father said, in his voice that still contained enough Irish to push around the American, "How about you knock it off and see about making him some glasses."

After that, there was the noise of wooden drawers opening and shutting, and finally, Dr. Shaperstein said, "You're in luck. The luck of the Irish."

"I believe history has shown," my father said, "that the Irish have never been particularly lucky."

Dr. Shaperstein told us the glasses wouldn't be ready for a week. Because I couldn't go out without someone to guide me, I spent that week at home. Mostly, I listened to the radio, sitting on the green and brown checkerboard linoleum in front of our big cherrywood Silvertone, spinning the dial, searching for something familiar, some program that hadn't been preempted by war news. But like my eyes, everything that poured out of the Silvertone's speakers seemed to have been altered by those Japanese bombs.

I tried to put my faith in Dr. Shaperstein and whatever he'd found in those wooden drawers. Told myself that the glasses he was making would restore the world to order, reinstate the boundaries between objects, send the colors back within their borders.

I decided, too, that the Holy Skully Cap was a kind of relic, as potent as Holy Water, or the Communion Host after Father Barry had blessed it. During the day, I kept it in my pocket, running my fingers over its scalloped edges. Each evening, I placed it—always with two hands—on my night table next to my luminous-face alarm clock. Then I prayed to it—this beer bottle cap filled with melted wax—asking it to grant my request for the gift of sight.

I did not want to believe that something fundamental might have shifted. That for me, much like for the rest of the world, nothing would be the same.

When we returned to Dr. Shaperstein's office, he again placed me in front of the eye chart, this time settling the glasses on my nose. The weight of them was like coming down with a head cold.

"Well?" he asked.

Without hesitation, I read the rows of letters, my eyes stopping smartly against each sharp, black line.

Then I turned to my father, sitting on the other side of the room, wanting to see his expression. But his features—his eyes, his slightly freckled skin, his mouth—had gone soft-edged and smeared, as if somebody had rubbed an eraser over them.

Starting to feel breathless again, I ran my eyes around Dr. Shaperstein's office. Some of the things were clear. The floating eyeball, three feet away, the fountain pen next to it. But when I looked across the room at my father, he remained blurred.

I pushed the glasses closer to my eyes, slid them down my nose. But my father stayed out of focus, and the room was starting to feel airless.

"Something's wrong," I gasped.

"With myopia this bad, there's a trade-off," Dr. Shaperstein said. "Correct for distance, and you lose what's close up. Correct for what's close up, and you lose the distance."

I walked across Dr. Shaperstein's office, keeping my eyes on my father's face, bringing his features back into sharpness, turning them recognizable. But when I got too close, close enough to touch him, they began to drift out of focus again.

"What if I want to see something up close?"

Dr. Shaperstein lifted the glasses from my face and rested them on the top of my head.

"Now I can't see anything."

"Get closer," he said.

I stepped closer to my father, close enough to smell the chemicals he used to develop his photographs—a smell that was both bitter and sweet, a smell that made me think of science. His face moved back into focus.

"What exactly did you correct him for?" my father said.

"The best I could," Dr. Shaperstein told him. "Something in the middle."

He pushed the glasses back in front of my eyes and handed me a mirror. I stretched out my arm to put myself into better focus.

The glasses he'd made for me had black frames and lenses as thick as the bottom of a Nehi soda bottle. They looked like the X-Ray Specs advertised in the back of comic books. The ones that claimed they would let you see through walls and ladies' dresses. They took over my whole face.

I pushed the mirror back at Dr. Shaperstein.

"Any chance he'll grow out of this?" my father said.

"Anything's possible," Dr. Shaperstein told him. "But probably not that."

As my father and I walked back down Broadway, the people coming toward us—men in overcoats, women wearing hats—snapped into and out of focus without warning, as if they possessed the power to control how much of themselves they would allow the world to see.

I kept shutting my eyes, opening them again, willing everyone to stay still, stay in the three-foot distance where I could focus. But they kept moving, going from blurred to clear to blurred again.

"I'm thinking you'll get used to that," my father said.

"What about how they're staring?"

"That might take some time."

When we arrived home, my mother lifted the glasses off my face and held them in front of her own eyes.

It's possible what happened next was the power of the lenses, possible their strength was more than she'd been expecting. But the moment my mother looked through them, her head startled back, as if those thick lenses had shown her something she didn't want to see.

She took the glasses away from her face, set them back onto my nose.

"Your eyes won't stay bad," she told me.

"I suggested that same possibility to the doctor," my father said.

"And?"

My father repeated what Dr. Shaperstein had told us.

"What does he know?" My mother shrugged.

And what did he know—this doctor who could only correct me for something in the middle—against a woman who had no belief in her own bad luck. A woman who had witnessed her father—that man known as the Gentleman Bootlegger—shot point-blank on three separate occasions. And on three separate occasions, had seen him rise unharmed.

It was a story my mother repeated often. I suspect because it was about signs—in which my mother placed a good deal of faith—and also because I think she liked talking about the time she and her father lived in the warehouse full of illegal alcohol on Tenth Avenue. When it had been only the two of them, Aunt May having gone off to the convent school in Poughkeepsie, believing she possessed a vocation.

The first shooting had occurred at mid-morning, not a time a man expects to be shot. My grandfather had just finished his second cup of coffee and was about to head out the back door to the privy, when Red Nolan, a small-time nightclub owner, burst through the front door and shot him in the chest. My grandfather staggered back, exclaimed, "You should not have done that, sir," then took out his gun and shot the stunned nightclub owner in the center of his forehead. Not until he and my mother, who was fourteen at the time, dragged Red's lifeless body to the back of a saloon on West 37th Street did my grandfather show her the dented timepiece in his breast pocket.

The second shooting occurred in the early evening, while my mother and her father were setting out poison pellets for the rats that liked to nest in the straw that came packed around my grandfather's Canadian whiskey. This time the would-be murderer was called Johnny Nack, though his reason for wanting to kill my grandfather was much the same as Red Nolan's—a short shipment. On this occasion, my grandfather's life was saved by his great fondness for the poetry of William Butler Yeats. Indeed, he read one of Mr. Yeats's poems at Johnny Nack's funeral, reciting from a volume that had a bullet hole in its cover.

The third shooting took place at night. My mother and her father were on their way home from the Saturday pushcart market under the Ninth Avenue El. My mother was carrying a bag of peaches, and my grandfather was carrying nothing because he believed that gentlemen did not walk in public with groceries in their hands. The two of them turned the corner at West 39th Street and Billy Cremore, another speakeasy owner who'd been shorted, stepped out of the dark and fired his gun. Billy Cremore aimed for my grandfather's head, but it was dark and Billy Cremore wasn't much of a marksman. The police never did figure out why Billy's killer left a bruised peach perched on his chest.

"These shootings were a sign," is how she would finish this story. "God had taken my mother and wanted to make the point that He was done. Nothing bad would ever happen to anyone I loved."

"God sent Red Nolan, Johnny Nack, and Billy Cremore to shoot at your father to make a point?" my father would tease her.

But she'd only smile, showing him that gap between her teeth, and he'd have no further argument.

As for me, I would much rather believe my mother than Dr. Shaperstein. And that night, after I took off the glasses, I walked around my room, squinting at the objects there—the Holy Skully Cap on the night table, a model airplane on a shelf, the cowboys and Indians riding across my bedspread—attempting to pull the color of each thing back within its boundaries, trying to hurry along what my mother believed would happen. And it did seem after a while that the edges of things were growing more sharp.

But deep in the night, I woke to the sound of my glasses clinking against the lamp, and caught the scent of my mother—her unlikely smell of new cut grass. I sensed her standing beside my bed, looking at me, then I heard her bare feet crackle along the linoleum to the kitchen. After a moment there was the splashing of water, and I realized she was washing my glasses.

I lay there thinking about all the reasons my mother might have gotten up in the middle of the night to wash my glasses. Or perhaps I was thinking about all the reasons that weren't what I already suspected, what I might have already figured out, that washing the glasses was a ritual—practiced alone and in the dark—for luck. That my mother—who put so much faith in signs—had made a connection between clearing the lenses and clearing my vision.

I can't say if it had been those Japanese bombs, or what she'd seen through the thick lenses of my glasses, but whatever it was, I feared that the belief my mother had in our own good luck had been knocked out of focus as surely as my sight.

My mother's footsteps moved back along the linoleum toward my room. I tried to slow my breath, make it sound as if I was still asleep. But I could feel it moving fast and shallow in my chest, and I could only hope my mother would think I was in the middle of a nightmare. And somehow, as she set the glasses back on my night table, she didn't notice my breath, so I can only assume she was in the middle of her own nightmare.

The moment I stepped through the chain-link fence that surrounded P.S. 52 wearing the glasses, people who had been throwing balls stopped and held them motionless in the air, people who had been shouting ceased and stood openmouthed in the cold. I focused on my feet as I moved across the macadam, heading for the overheated building. *No one will notice me inside*, I was thinking. *It will be like I'm invisible.*

I slid into my seat and kept my head down, staring at the pencil-carved initials on the top of my desk, initials that were now soft-edged and blurry from the glasses. As the rest of the class rumbled in, bringing with them the smell of wool coats and bologna sandwiches, I felt everybody's eyes on me, crawling over my face, over the glasses—exactly like the X-Ray Specs in the back of comic books—making me feel exposed, like the Visible Man. The man on the poster Miss Steinhardt unrolled when we studied biology, a man with his skin peeled back and all his colorful organs exposed—blue lungs, orange kidneys, purple spleen.

Even Miss Steinhardt was not immune to the power of the glasses.

They revolved her from the chalkboard as if the thick lenses produced gravity, forcing a startled, "Well . . . Jack . . . glasses," from between her vermillion lips.

It was quiet for a moment, and then Miss Steinhardt asked me if I could see the board from where I was sitting.

"Yes," I told her, without lifting my head.

"Can you tell me what I've just written on it?"

I looked up and squinted. Miss Steinhardt's chalk marks resembled nothing except the snow clouds building up outside the window.

"The date?"

Miss Steinhardt used her piece of chalk to point to the front row.

"Why don't you bring your desk up here?" she said

Only the defective sat in the front row. Declan Moriarity, who could not bend his left leg all the way because of the polio brace buckled to it. Francis D'Amato, who had a lazy eye and was forced to wear a flesh-colored eye patch over the good one. And Rose LoPinto, who despite the complicated hearing aid she wore, still couldn't hear well enough to sit any farther back.

The legs of my desk made a horrible squealing sound as I pushed it up the aisle. Inside my head, I couldn't stop seeing the picture of Jesus from my *Child's First Catechism*, the one of him carrying his own cross up the dust-covered rise of Golgotha.

Miss Steinhardt pointed to an empty place next to Rose LoPinto. With more squealing, I pushed my desk into it.

"Rose," she said, "you can read for Jack anything he can't see. And Jack," she looked at me, "you can repeat for Rose anything she can't hear."

Then she turned back to the board.

This close, I could see what it was Miss Steinhardt had asked me to read.

Manifest Destiny.

I could also see Rose's hearing aid, which was called a RadioEar. It had three parts: a silver, lozenge-shaped receiver she wore pressed against the bone behind her ear on a metal headband; a microphone the size and shape of a box of matches, which she pinned to her collar; and a battery case the size of a pack of cigarettes she kept in a pocket. All of Rose's clothes, I guessed, had to have pockets.

The first thing I had to repeat for Rose was the *Annexation of Oregon*. I leaned over to whisper it into the lozenge-shaped receiver behind her ear, but Rose shook her head and pointed to the microphone box pinned at her collar.

I bent down and brought my mouth close to Rose's throat. The skin there was smooth and olive-colored, and smelled impossibly like chocolate and coconut. Like a candy bar.

It was a smell that stopped the *Annexation of Oregon* in my mouth.

"Are you talking?" Rose said, reaching into her pocket and shaking the battery case.

But I couldn't answer, too distracted by what felt like a cold stream that had started running just beneath the surface of my skin.

All that morning, I whispered important historical facts about the Monroe Doctrine and Mexican Cession into the microphone box pinned at the base of Rose's smooth, olive-colored throat. In return, she read various significant years off the chalkboard into my ear. And for the first time in more than a week, I didn't think about my eyes going bad.

Unless you count this. Listening to Rose, I noticed that none of her words had sharp edges. Her consonants were blurry, and her vowels out of focus. It was as if the way she spoke was the vocal equivalent of how I saw.

And also this. There was one piece of her black hair that kept breaking free of the metal headband, trying to curl itself around the silver lozenge of the RadioEar receiver. A piece of black hair I couldn't pull my eyes from.

That piece of black hair made me wish Dr. Shaperstein had corrected me better for things that were close up.

When the bell rang for lunch, I dashed out to the smooth stretch of playground where the skully boards were chalked. All morning, the Holy Skully Cap had sat in my pocket giving off emanations, assuring me I didn't belong in the front row with Declan Moriarity, whose polio brace prevented him from getting down on the ground low enough to flick a skully cap. Or Francis D'Amato, whose eye patch so interfered with his depth perception, his caps went veering off in bizarre directions.

Bobby Devine and a pack of boys were already standing around the chalked squares, the steam from their breath hanging in the frigid air. All of the girls—and possibly some of the boys—were in love with Bobby Devine, with his black hair and his blue eyes, and his breath that always smelled of Juicy Fruit, even when he wasn't chewing any.

They were deciding the rules—or more accurately, Bobby Devine was deciding the rules, and everyone else was waiting. A pack of boys, flipping their skully caps over in their palms, eager to start playing, poised for Bobby Devine to give the word.

I joined them, the Holy Skully Cap already in my hand, the steam from my breath mingling with theirs before settling to the ground.

"Sorry, Quinlan." Bobby Devine never called you by anything except your last name. "Too many players."

I counted the boys breathing steam into the frigid air. But I am not sure why. There were never too many players. And also, I'd heard something in Bobby Devine's voice. A kind of undertone, a humming beneath the words that bumped up against them, shading their meaning.

They say that when one sense is damaged another takes over. Develops an ability it never had before. And I suppose that is what happened with me. Over time, I would become skilled at hearing this undertone, this hum that exists beneath a person's words, that colors—at times, even contradicts—their meaning.

But that first time, standing in front of those boys flipping their skully caps, I heard enough of it in Bobby Devine's voice to understand now that I'd been moved to the front row, there would always be too many players.

A strange man was sitting in my father's chair when I got home. It couldn't be my father, though I was still too far away to see him clearly, because the man was wearing a white shirt, and my father only ever wore brown shirts. My father had a closet full of brown shirts. Shirts that smelled of the chemicals he used to develop his photographs. Chemicals that would have left small colonies of brown spots on shirts of any other color.

But when I stepped into the room, put the man in my three-foot range, I saw that of course it was my father. Just my father in a white shirt. A white shirt, I realized when I came close, close enough to sit on the wide, flat arm of his chair, that didn't smell of anything, that hadn't yet taken on the bitter and sweet smell of the developing chemicals. The smell that, along with the scent of the Wildroot Cream-Oil he used to flatten his hair—spiky, like mine—was the smell of my father. A white shirt that left him smelling only like Wildroot Cream-Oil, which could have been the smell of anybody.

"Hey, kiddo," my father said.

The words that would have told him to take off that white shirt, trade it for one of the brown ones hanging in his closet, crowded my throat, tried to scramble their way out of my mouth. But I couldn't stop thinking about how my father had figured out that I saw better when things were in contrast. Couldn't stop picturing him buying that shirt, which would be ruined the first time he developed any photographs, and the thought of that squeezed at my chest, making it impossible for me to let those words out, those words telling my father to take off the shirt that made him look and smell like somebody else.

I felt my father's eyes studying me, as if I were a book written in a language to which only he had the key. I did not want him to read the words in my throat, and I knew there was no way I could stop him. Because that was what he could do. His ability.

I got up and forced out some other words—something about homework—turned and went to my room. Leaving my father alone, his white shirt contrasting with the green chair.

I had never—not once—stopped my father from reading me. He had been doing it all my life, and I took his ability for granted—this father who always seemed to know what you were thinking or how you felt without you ever having to say anything out loud. Once, when we'd gone to Coney Island and seen a man in a turban who claimed to read minds, I asked my father if that was what he did, read people's minds.

"No," he'd told me. "It's the rest of them I read."

He first noticed he was doing it back in Ireland, growing up in St. Brendan's Home for Boys in an ugly seaside town north of Dublin. He'd see how Eamonn Plunkett could not prevent his hands from jerking during morning Mass, and stay out of his way, knowing that this would be the day he'd be looking to lay them on another boy. He'd note when Brother Garrity's eyes had the glaze of migraine, and keep his head down in class, so as not to be struck on the knuckles with the large wooden crucifix the brother kept on a rope about his waist.

The ability had gotten my father his first job in America. He'd been twenty years old and three hours off the boat from Liverpool, his clothes still smelling of seawater and his legs unsteady on the thick carpeting of a bootlegger known as the Duke of the West Side.

"I read how comfortable the man was in his fourteen-dollar suit," my father said. "Too comfortable. Like he'd studied on it."

As the Duke of the West Side read my father's letter of introduction from a Dublin pub owner, my father read the Duke of the West Side. He read something Irish beneath the bootlegger's English accent, and—like my father's own raising—a childhood spent parentless.

It was less the letter of introduction and more what my father read that got him the job as bodyguard to the Duke's illegal alcohol. The job that eventually sent my father to a warehouse on Tenth Avenue belonging to one of the Duke's best customers, the Gentleman Bootlegger.

One stormy afternoon in November, my father stepped inside that warehouse to get out of the rain and was struck by the sight of the Gentleman Bootlegger's sixteen-year-old daughter, Lily. She was seated at a high wooden desk, her dark head bent over her father's ledger books.

"It was the oddest thing," my father told me. "I know it was raining, but there was this one beam of sun falling through the skylight of that warehouse. Falling right on the head of that black-haired girl. As if someone—God Almighty, probably—set her there for me to look at."

My father stood a long time watching that sixteen-year-old girl slide the tip of a No. 2 pencil into and out of the gap between her front teeth. Long after all the Gentleman Bootlegger's illegal alcohol was unloaded.

When Prohibition ended, and my father needed to find legitimate employment, it was his ability, and the Gentleman Bootlegger—my grandfather by that time—that got him the job at Wasserman's Listening Emporium.

"That knack you have of reading people," my grandfather said, "that is going to make you the world's greatest radio salesman."

Wasserman's Listening Emporium was located inside a long, narrow storefront on a Times Square side street, tucked between a shoe repair shop and a pool hall. Every inch of it was filled with radios. The shelves were crammed with Philcos stacked on top of Zeniths stacked on top of Crosleys. The floor was so jammed with Silvertones and RCAs and Atwater Kents, most people had to walk through sideways.

My father read that his first customer—a lady in a homemade hat with a large feather—wished to be shopping somewhere grander than Wasserman's. He sold her a top-of-the-line Atwater Kent after telling her it was very much like the one Helena Rubinstein had in her Park Avenue apartment.

The fat man who came in after her had only entered the shop hoping for someone to talk to. My father sold him a Murphy tabletop model by implying that the constant sound of a radio left on was a good remedy for loneliness.

Shortly before closing, my father sold an enormous Philco to a middle-aged married couple, subtly suggesting it would allow them to spend their evenings listening to vaudeville comedians rather than each other.

This is much the way that first week went. Proving my grandfather right, my father's talent for reading people did make him the world's greatest radio salesman.

Over the weekend, Leo Wasserman took out a full-page ad in the *Mirror*. The following week, my father sold fifty-five radios. But that Friday evening, after Leo Wasserman locked up the store and said goodnight to my father, the stories of every person he had sold a radio to began pounding inside his head. It was as if all the radios in the Listening Emporium, every Zenith and Atwater Kent and Philco stacked on the shelves and crowded together on the floor, had been jammed into his skull and turned on at the same time. Each one tuned to a different station, each one broadcasting a different story of longing and desire and unfulfilled want.

And he couldn't turn any of them off.

My father couldn't bear to go down into the subway, couldn't stand to be anyplace that was enclosed. He turned away from the Listening Emporium and started walking, heading uptown, walking all the way up Broadway from 43rd Street to Dyckman Street—one hundred and fifty blocks. And still, when he got there, his head was so full of other people's stories—all those desires that had stuck there—he could barely tell my mother what was wrong, could only fall on the bed and think about desolate places. Places where there were no people wanting things. The moon. Antarctica.

He slept for thirty hours. When he woke, my mother was sitting on the edge of the mattress.

"Maybe you don't have to be the world's greatest radio salesman," she told him.

He sat up. "I'm thinking I only need to get used to it."

It was then he noticed the Speed Graphic camera in her lap.

"Where did you find that?"

"Remember Harry Jupiter?"

"The newspaper photographer?"

"Not anymore. Says he's shot his last picture of a dead body. Says he's giving up the newspaper business."

"And you're going into it?"

My mother shook her head. "You are taking up portraiture."

My father took the camera into his hands. It was boxy, and could be folded nearly flat. A newspaperman's camera.

"I've never taken a photograph in my life."

My mother pointed to the camera. "I'm thinking you can put some of those stories inside there instead of your head."

My father put the Speed Graphic up to his face, looked at my mother through the barrier of its lens.

"What if I'm not any good at it?"

"Just don't be too good."

But my father couldn't help being too good.

Mr. Lingeman's fiancée portrait for example.

I was there the day my father shot it, standing inside Lingeman's News & Novelties, next to a rack of new *Superman* comics. Mr. Lingeman wanted to show his fiancée in Stockholm how handsome and prosperous he was, and he'd insisted on being shot behind the glass case of cigarettes and chewing gum, next to a display of *Movietone* magazines. His blond hair had been so full of pomade, it appeared to be glowing.

But a couple of days later, when my father showed me the final photograph, I saw something I hadn't seen standing next to the *Superman* comics. I saw that Mr. Lingeman was wearing the smile he put on every time one of the young mothers in the neighborhood came into the News & Novelties. The smile that made it seem as if he wanted to eat them.

Mr. Lingeman's fiancée portrait ended up on a shelf in my father's closet, along with all the other portraits people had refused to pay him for, refused even to take.

But there were some photographs my father took that surprised all of us. Portraits of people we had always believed were unattractive—ugly, even—who looked radiant in his pictures. As if his lens had uncovered some hidden beauty in them, something the rest of us had overlooked.

I never thought of that stack of rejected portraits in the closet as failures, less impressive than the ones that had revealed some unexpected flash of radiance. All were equal displays of my father's remarkable talent, his ability to capture something true about a person and reproduce it on film.

A talent that, to me, has always seemed as remarkable as flying.

Yet the night I came home and found my father wearing the white shirt—something he would do from then on, no matter how many he ruined—I stayed in my room with the door shut, for the first time, preventing my father from practicing his remarkable talent on me.

Three

As I lay on the freezing sidewalk outside P.S. 52, empty-aired and panicked from Moon Shapiro's loose-fisted punch to the diaphragm, I wondered how I hadn't seen it coming. Perhaps, I thought, as I waited for my lungs to remember how to breathe, my head had been too full of the miraculous scent of Rose LoPinto's neck. Perhaps it was because he'd waited until the second day I turned up in the glasses to deliver it.

Moon Shapiro was a big, gangling boy who should have graduated by now to the junior high school on 211th Street. Instead, he remained at P.S. 52, stumbling over words like *slavery* whenever a teacher called on him. He was the only boy in the school with an Adam's apple, and wore a light blue yarmulke every day, which he kept fastened to his springy red hair with a circle of bobby pins. His real name was Marvin, but no one who didn't want to be punched in the head called him by it.

Moon dropped his weight onto my back, pushing air out of my lungs. He pounded at my sides, digging his hard knuckles into all the soft, vulnerable organs that lay beneath the skin—organs I imagined were the same bright colors as those inside the Visible Man. My cheek was pressed into the gravelly dirt around a sad, little tree, and I had the idea—I don't know why—that if Moon hit me in the face, if he knocked off the glasses, he'd knock my vision back into order.

Or maybe I just wanted him to hit the glasses.

I lifted my cheek, tried to put my face within range of Moon's fists. But his hard-knuckled punches never strayed above my shoulders, as if Moon Shapiro was operating from a code of instructions, a set of rules that prohibited him from interfering with the reason I was being beaten up in the first place.

At a point in time known only to him, Moon gave me one last punch in the side. Then he grunted in a tone of finality, as if we'd both completed some strenuous task, and his weight lifted off me. Cold, snow-smelling air rushed into my lungs.

I pushed myself to sitting. Moon Shapiro was already a blue-jacketed blur halfway up Academy Street. The people who'd stopped to watch began to drift away, the backs of their coats moving into and out of focus, as if I were discovering something about them, and then forgetting it.

I sat on the cold sidewalk brushing gravel off my cheek, thinking about the afternoons I'd come out of P.S. 52 and seen Declan Moriarity on the ground, the leg with the polio brace bent at an odd angle, or Francis D'Amato, his flesh-colored eye patch going grimy in the dirt. When you sat in the front row, a beating by Moon Shapiro was an inevitability. Fighting it would be like fighting fate.

I got to my feet, feeling the world tilt, then right itself. Yanking on the side of my jacket, trying to flatten the spot where it had bunched up from Moon sitting on me, I walked home, my sides aching with every inhale.

By the time I got there, it had started to snow. Aunt May was in our kitchen, still wearing her coat.

"Glenn went up to the roof an hour ago with a bottle of rye and my best bedspread," she was telling my mother. "Now he's just sitting there with it over his head and snow blowing in his face. Says he's not coming down."

My mother lit a cigarette and handed it to her sister. Aunt May was short where my mother was tall, curved where my mother was angular.

"Any idea why?" my mother said.

"Well, he finally got inside Whitehall Street."

Uncle Glenn had been going down to the induction center at Whitehall Street every day for a week. But the line of men trying to enlist had been so long—around the block most days—the office had closed before he'd managed to put one foot inside the door. That day, though, he'd gotten inside. Made it to the physical. Stood shirtless as an army doctor put a stethoscope to his chest and listened to his lungs, all the while Uncle Glenn talking about how eager he was to go overseas and kill Nazis.

"How long have you had asthma?" the army doctor had asked him.

"Pretty much all my life," Uncle Glenn told him.

My uncle's asthma would come on him like an ambush. More than once, I'd found him slumped on the stairs of our building, sucking on his inhaler, Aunt May's groceries spilled on the floor at his feet, a burst bag of flour drifting up around his ankles like snowfall.

"And what happened?" my mother said.

"They declared him 4-F," Aunt May told her. "Unfit for service."

I pressed my hands to my sides, pushing them against all the sore places. *Uncle Glenn must have been standing in front of that army doctor at the same time Moon Shapiro was sitting on my back, at exactly the same time.*

My mother noticed me in the doorway and asked me why I was touching my side like that, asked me if I needed anything. I told her no, nothing.

Then I went into the living room, turned on the radio and concentrated on *Superman*, pretended I lived in Metropolis, pretended I had nothing to do with anything that was going on here.

When my father got home and my mother told him about Uncle Glenn on the roof, he rummaged around the coat closet for an old horse blanket, got his own bottle of rye, and went up there himself. He didn't come down until after I'd gone to bed, bringing into my room the mingled scent of developing chemicals and whiskey.

"This 4-F business," he said. "That's only between Uncle Glenn and the U.S. Army."

His white shirt glowed in the darkness of my room.

"Nothing about it is the same as you."

I nodded in the dark.

"And about the other thing," he said, "I could take you down to Murray's gym tomorrow. Show you some moves."

"That's okay."

The white shirt stopped at the door. "You heard what I said? About it not being the same?"

This time I didn't bother to nod.

When I think of it now, I have to look for the logic. But then I was a boy, the son of a mother who had faith in signs. And in my mind, Moon Shapiro waiting until the second day I'd been moved to the front row to knock me to the dirt beneath that sad, little tree was a sign as clear as my grandfather's shootings. Moon's hard-knuckled fists had stamped 4-F into my flesh as assuredly as the army doctor had stamped it onto Uncle Glenn's paperwork. We were unfit for service. Whatever that service might turn out to be.

Over the next weeks, Moon Shapiro beat me up on a schedule only he could predict. Sometimes I'd come through the chain-link fence and find Declan's face in the dirt, or Francis flat on the sidewalk. Other days it would be only Moon, leaning against that tree, making it bend like he was a gale force wind. Then it would be my cheek pressed into the gravel, my colorful organs his fists would seek. And each time they landed, I'd think *4-F, 4-F, 4-F.*

Nearly every day, walking home, I'd see another blue star appear in another window of an apartment building. A Son in Service star, hung whenever someone in the family had enlisted, joined up to fight in Europe or the Pacific. Each time I spotted one of these stars, I felt more useless, more 4-F. Because they only reminded me that everybody—except me—was doing something for the war effort.

My father had taken a second job, working a graveyard shift at the Brooklyn Navy Yard—although he claimed he possessed no discernible mechanical skills. My mother was now doing the bookkeeping for the businesses of men who had gone to war. Aunt May got a job stitching together uniforms in a converted dress factory on 34th Street. And during the National Boy Scout Scrap Metal Drive, I'd had to walk around the block to avoid Bobby Devine—dressed in his uniform—who was on Dyckman Street collecting old signs and car bumpers.

Uncle Glenn had joined Civil Defense. After that night on the roof, he'd spent a couple of weekends training on Staten Island, and now he had a certificate signed by Fiorello La Guardia, a white Civil Defense helmet and armband, and a piercing silver Civil Defense whistle.

Every night, Uncle Glenn put on his white helmet and armband, and patrolled the neighborhood, blowing his whistle up at the window of anybody who hadn't pulled his blackout shades all the way down. One night, when we were on our way to see a Roy Rogers movie at the Alpine theater, Uncle Glenn made us miss the newsreel because he'd stopped to blow his whistle at somebody's window for five minutes.

"Can't you maybe take one night off from Civil Defense?" Aunt May had asked him.

"You don't see Hitler taking the night off," he told her.

I asked Uncle Glenn how old someone needed to be to join Civil Defense, and he said definitely older than twelve. But the next day, he brought me a pack of enemy aircraft spotter cards.

These were regular playing cards printed with the silhouettes of enemy planes—German and Japanese—and they were a coveted item at P.S. 52. Standing on the playground with your face turned to the sky, praying for the sight of a Focke-Wulf Kurier or a Mitsubishi Reconnaissance to come rumbling over the roof of the school so you could identify it, had replaced skully as the favored recess pastime.

That night, I sat on my bed and memorized the shape of all the German aircraft—the ones I thought most likely to find their way over New York City. I didn't worry too much about my eyes, how they had not been corrected as well for distance. The planes were big, and I only needed to recognize their forms.

The following afternoon, I took my place beside the other boys gazing into the sky.

It was one of those clear, blue-sky days New York sometimes gets in the wintertime. So clear, I couldn't tell how far up I was seeing, because it's difficult to gauge depth when everything is the same featureless blue.

Still, after ten minutes or so, I was certain I had seen the glint of something silver—possibly the wing of a plane—high in the sky.

"There," I called out.

"Where?" said Bobby Devine.

"Above the Chesterfield sign."

"That?" Bobby Devine breathed his Juicy Fruit breath onto my face. "Jesus, Quinlan, that's a pigeon." He shook his head. "Honestly, an entire battalion of Messerschmitts could come flying over Queens and you'd miss it completely."

That day, walking home, it seemed there were dozens of new Son in Service stars in the windows of the apartments on Academy Street and Nagle Avenue, dozens more on Dyckman Street. No matter where I looked, I was surrounded by them, entire constellations of blue stars.

As winter—and the war—wore on, sugar, meat, and rubber were rationed. One afternoon, Miss Steinhardt passed out colored ribbons for us to wear around our necks. Blue meant you lived near enough to P.S. 52 to risk running home during an enemy air strike. Red meant you had to take your chances of dying under a desk with Miss Steinhardt.

Those of us with blue ribbons spent most of the day praying for the shrill sound of the air raid siren—anything to break up the stuffy monotony of Miss Steinhardt's classroom. I prayed doubly hard, gazing at the twin bands of blue ribbon on either side of the microphone box pinned at Rose's throat, imagining myself leading her to safety as we ran down Academy Street, away from the strafing of a Heinkel 115. Away from the round face of Moon Shapiro, peering out of a P.S. 52 window, his red ribbon a noose around his neck.

Rose and the radio were my only consolations that winter.

Every afternoon, I went straight for it, draping my body over the top of its cherrywood console, as if that might cause the tubes inside to warm up faster. Then I stretched out on the floor in front of it, pressing my back against the green and brown checkerboard linoleum, pushing my glasses onto the top of my head, so that nothing in my real world would be in focus.

One of those afternoons, I was listening to *The Lone Ranger* in the dark. That was something I did. Pulling down the blackout shades and leaving off the lamps, so the only illumination would be the amber light shining from behind the small glass plate at the front of the Silvertone. It was late March, a sleeting day more like winter than spring. Moon had kept me pressed against the sidewalk a long time, and the front of my jacket was so soaked, I'd thrown it over the radiator to dry.

The Lone Ranger and Tonto were riding across the Texas plains, chasing after the Butch Cavendish gang, and suddenly I smelled those plains, a dry and dusty smell—though that might have been my jacket on the radiator. Still, a second later, I *saw* those plains, saw the flat, parched expanse of them, the long line where they met the horizon, and then the pale brown dust kicked up by the churning legs of Silver, the Lone Ranger's horse, moving in time with the hoofbeats coming out of the Silvertone's speakers.

I saw it all—in every distance, and more clearly than I could have in real life. The pearl handle of the Lone Ranger's gun, each strand of Silver's pure white mane, every feathery tip of Tonto's headdress fluttering in the wind.

I sat up, my head too full of these pictures to remain on my back, and stared into the amber light behind the glass plate. The light I'd always imagined was shining directly from whatever station the radio was tuned to, directly from the broadcasting studio into my living room.

Pictures kept tumbling from the speakers into my head, clearer than I'd seen anything in a while. The vast darkness of the western sky at night. The Lone Ranger's campfire, flaming up orange. I got to my knees, crawled to the radio, and pressed myself against the Silvertone's cherrywood bulk. Then I shut my eyes and let the amber light from the broadcasting station fall warm onto them.

I stayed pressed to the radio, its speakers vibrating against my chest, for all of the evening's serials. I saw the flakes of new snow catch in the thick fur of the malamute Yukon King. Watched the shimmers of blue-edged light play across the surface of Lamont Cranston's martini. Could see how when the Dragon Lady lit her cigarette, her shiny red fingernails reflected the flame like ten tiny mirrors.

Later—much later—I heard footfalls behind me.

"You're seeing that, aren't you?" my father said. "You're seeing the radio."

And what I heard, bumping up against his words, was that he did not think it as wondrous as I did.

Once I began to see the radio, I did nothing but listen to it. Every afternoon, before the glass tubes had warmed enough to catch sound, I'd be waiting on the checkerboard linoleum, waiting to see the purple and gold pennants of Jack Armstrong's All-American high school whipping in the wind, the knockout gas billowing from the end of the Green Hornet's gun like steam rising from subway gratings. I'd remain in front of the radio until my mother called me into the kitchen for dinner, but as soon as I could, I'd be back, the music from *Death Valley Days* filling my ears, my eyes trained on a distant line of covered wagons rolling across a sun-blasted landscape.

Saturdays, I spent the entire day in front of the Silvertone, beginning with *Rural Women's Day*, seeing perfectly the visit made to an Iowa farm by Mrs. Roosevelt, picking out every flower on the First Lady's hat as she stepped through a cow pasture. I followed that with *Calling All Stamp Collectors* and the *Interscholastic German Glee Club of New York*.

Sundays, I began with *Church of the Air* and *Let's Try Religion*, and only budged from the checkerboard linoleum when I was forced to put on my Mass pants and go with my mother and Aunt May to Good Shepherd. If I ran, I was always back in time for *Salt Lake City Tabernacle.*

My mother tried everything she could to separate me from the Silvertone. *There's a new Tarzan movie at the Alpine theater. Three inches of spring snow has just fallen in Fort Tryon Park.*

"I'm fine," I'd always tell her. And I would be. Because I could see those stamp collectors and glee clubbers and every member of that tabernacle choir.

Aunt May would come upstairs with a hundred separate errands for me. *Run down to Mandelbaum's for some evaporated milk. See if the butcher has any lamb.*

But I might as well have been a radio wave myself. No matter how often they sent me away, I continued to return to the big receiver in the living room.

Only my father didn't try to pull me from the radio. At least, not in the same way as the others. Instead, he listened with me, dragging his green armchair across the room, placing it near to where I was stretched out on the floor. And I suspect that if I hadn't been so wrapped up in the world of the radio, if I hadn't been watching the Green Hornet's car pass like a shadow through the velvety darkness, I likely would have felt his eyes moving over me.

Even on the days he worked the graveyard shift at the Navy Yard, he would wake himself when I returned from P.S. 52 to come and sit in the green armchair and listen with me, the scent of his coffee lending something familiar to the exotic world of *Terry and the Pirates.*

Sometimes I'd leave my spot on the linoleum and sit on one of the wide, flat arms of his chair, lean my head against the shoulder of his ruined white shirt, the front colonized by small brown spots. That close, I could see the dark circles under his eyes, the way he concentrated on what was coming out of the Silvertone's speakers, as if the answer he was looking for lay between the lines of dialogue and the advertisements for Palmolive dish soap and Blue Coal.

It was May when I began to want the Captain Midnight Code-O-Graph.

The code-o-graph I would use to help Captain Midnight capture the scores of Nazi sympathizers the War Department had convinced us were lurking around every corner of New York City. The Nazi sympathizers who had prompted them to put up posters saying things like *The Walls Have Ears* and *Because Somebody Talked* over a picture of a flaming battleship sinking into a dark sea.

Other people might use their Captain Midnight Code-O-Graphs for deciphering the messages the announcer gave at the end of the *Captain Midnight* radio program. But those people did not have the ability to hear the undertone in someone's voice, they couldn't tell just by listening if somebody was lying.

Me, I would use my ability—the thing I could do—to find a Nazi sympathizer, and then send a secret message to Captain Midnight, who would fly straight here and capture him.

I can only say that I had spent so much time in front of the Silvertone's speakers, this seemed a realistic plan. I can only imagine that by then, the line between the real world and the radio world had become as blurred as most things were to me.

But a Captain Midnight Code-O-Graph required a dime and the lids from two jars of Ovaltine, and my mother refused to buy Ovaltine, because she insisted chocolate-flavored dirt would taste better.

Also, all the spare change we had was going into the little half-moon-shaped slots in the *My First War Bond* book Miss Steinhardt had handed out back in February.

Still, each week as the announcer spoke the secret message, spelling out the letters for the members of Captain Midnight's Secret Squadron, my fingers itched with the desire to write them down.

Then, one hot Saturday afternoon in June—the first of summer vacation—my father came into the living room and dropped a package onto my chest.

Inside was a Captain Midnight Code-O-Graph.

It was made of brass, the size and shape of a policeman's badge. In the center was an airplane propeller that could be spun to point at the ring of letters and numbers stamped around the code-o-graph's face. And at the top, there was a little window for a photograph of yourself, though at the moment, it held a picture of Captain Midnight wearing his leather flying cap.

I sat staring at it, this piece of the radio world that had magically appeared in my hands.

"How?" I said to my father.

"Turns out Harry Jupiter likes Ovaltine. Said it's the only way he can get down all the milk he has to drink for the ulcer thirty years in the newspaper business gave him."

"And the dime?"

"Let's just say Hitler isn't going to lose the war any quicker if we buy that bond a little later."

The code-o-graph wasn't especially heavy. Yet its weight traveled straight into my bones, making them seem more solid. I wished it had come earlier, when I could have taken it to P.S. 52, and whispered into Rose's throat, *I am a member of the Secret Squadron*, instead of, *The heart has four chambers*.

My father took me up to the roof to shoot my picture for the little window. He said he wanted nothing except the wide, blue sky behind me. I stood on the west side of the building, with only the trees of Fort Tryon Park and the cliffs of the Palisades between me and the whole rest of the country. I could have been anywhere.

The Texas plains.

The Canadian forest.

The far horizon of Death Valley.

I took off the glasses and held them in my hand for the photograph, tried to look like the kind of person who would be in something like the Secret Squadron.

When my father called across the roof to say we were finished, I asked him how I'd looked inside his camera.

"Exactly like you," he told me.

I slept that night with the code-o-graph tucked into the chest pocket of my pajamas, feeling it lift and lower with each breath. The next morning, I slipped it into the pocket of my Mass pants, where it could remind me of its presence with every step.

On the way to Good Shepherd, I stayed a couple of paces behind Aunt May and my mother, tuning my ears to the conversations of the people around me, pulling in their frequencies. I was listening for the off-kilter hum of lying, the unbalanced sound of someone pretending to be somebody he wasn't.

Even after I stepped out of the heat and into the oceany blue coolness of Good Shepherd, I continued to listen. All through Mass, I sorted through the voices, dipped beneath their Latin phrasing. But I heard nothing more subversive than boredom and distraction.

Heading back, I hurried ahead of my mother and Aunt May, eager to get home, change out of the Mass pants and return to the streets. But when we got there, Uncle Glenn was in our kitchen, waving around a copy of *The New York Times*, which no one in our family bought unless the news was important.

Uncle Glenn was saying something about Nazi saboteurs landing on Amagansett beach. Saying it first to my father, who was sitting at the red table, still wearing his Navy Yard clothes, his denim overalls and heavy, round-toed factory shoes. Then saying it to Aunt May and my mother and me, showing us the front page of *The New York Times*, but before we could read any of it, taking the paper back and telling us the story instead.

Several weeks ago a German submarine had surfaced five hundred yards off the coast of Long Island. It had been a foggy night, but it had been clear enough for the four Nazi saboteurs onboard to inflate a couple of rubber boats and paddle to shore. Once there, they'd dug a hole on the beach and buried a cache of explosives. When they were finished, they headed to the road, and walked the two miles to the nearest Long Island Railroad Station. After that, they'd disappeared into Manhattan.

"Not, however," Uncle Glenn said, "before being observed by a suspicious young coastguardsman."

It was the call the coastguardsman made to the FBI that led to the saboteurs' capture.

Uncle Glenn carefully folded his copy of *The New York Times*, as if he intended to save it. Then he said some things about how many lives the young coastguardsman had likely saved, and that Fiorello La Guardia should give him a medal, because this was proof that it was just as important to fight the war at home.

It was some moments before I realized my father had been trying to get my attention.

"You okay, there?" he said.

I nodded.

But inside my head, as clearly as if it was coming out of the radio, I saw the young coastguardsman making that phone call to the FBI. Making it on a *real* telephone, to a *real* person. Not to some made-up character on a radio serial program.

I saw myself, too. Sitting in the ocean-y blueness of Good Shepherd listening to the people saying Mass, as if being a member of the Secret Squadron was something that existed outside of the radio world.

It was a picture that made me not want to be inside my own skin.

I turned from the kitchen and rushed to my room. Got to my knees and yanked out the box of sweaters I kept under my bed—sweaters I never wore because they itched in a way I couldn't stand. I reached into my pocket and took out the code-o-graph. I caught the image of Captain Midnight's face in the little window, smiling at me, and I shut my hand over it, so I wouldn't see him anymore. Then I buried the code-o-graph as far under those sweaters as I could.

I heard the linoleum creak behind me.

My father, still in his Navy Yard clothes, was standing in the doorway. Even I could see how tired he looked.

"Change out of your Mass pants and meet me at the door in fifteen minutes," he said.

"Why?"

"We're going to Paradise."

Four

My father and I took the subway to 42nd Street, then walked the hot, unshaded sidewalks of Hell's Kitchen to Paradise Photo, the photography studio Harry Jupiter opened after he quit the newspaper business. Harry Jupiter had named it Paradise because thirty years in the newspaper business had not only given him an ulcer, it had also given him a highly developed sense of irony.

I stood scowling up at the portraits of brides hanging in the Paradise windows, wishing I was back in front of the Silvertone, while my father went to retrieve the key Harry left for him behind a loose brick in the stairs. Before Harry Jupiter took over the building, it had been a butcher shop, and on hot days like this one, the smell of blood rose up inside Paradise, like an undertone beneath the bitter and sweet scent of the developing chemicals.

I smelled it along with the open bottle of whiskey on Harry Jupiter's desk, as my father and I passed through the cluttered front office. Harry Jupiter had still not flipped his girlie calendar from May 1936. Once, when I'd asked him about it, he told me he liked looking at that redhead more than he liked knowing the date.

We went through the dusty curtain that separated the front office from the studio in the back. Harry's studio was filled with painted backdrops that pulled down like window shades. People could stand in front of these backdrops and have their picture taken, pretend they were someplace other than the middle of Hell's Kitchen.

Niagara Falls.

The Coliseum in Rome.

Mount Rushmore.

Even with my eyesight, they didn't look very realistic.

I asked my father what we were doing there.

He pointed to the door of the Paradise darkroom. There was a sign taped to it. *Knock or die*, it said.

"In there."

For as long as I could remember, I'd imagined my father inside the Paradise darkroom, performing the miraculous experiments that made his clothes—possibly his very skin—smell like science, working the secret magic that transferred the ghosts of his photographs into the creases of his hands. In those imaginings, the Paradise darkroom was a supernatural place, a movie scientist's laboratory where electricity fizzed in jagged sparks and great clouds of colored smoke rose without warning.

But the actual room behind the *Knock or die* sign was cramped and narrow, with a long metal table that held two steel tanks and a high shelf crowded with bottles. It was cooler, though, and right away I felt the sweat drying on my skin.

"What are we doing in here?" I asked my father.

"You are going to develop the Silverman twins."

I wanted to run back out through that door with the *Knock or die* sign, past the redhead hanging above Harry Jupiter's desk, and out onto the hot, unshaded streets of Hell's Kitchen. Babies were my father's sure thing. All his pictures of them turned out to be exactly what everybody else saw. Nothing more. Perhaps because they hadn't lived long enough for there to be anything for him to read.

What if I ruin them, I said, what if they all turn out wrong? But my father was already preparing, taking out the plastic frames from the black box he used to carry his film—each frame holding two exposed film sheets of a Silverman twin, each sheet the size the finished print would be, and each one protected by a thin piece of metal that fit inside the frame. My father piled all the plastic frames on the table—there must have been a dozen of them—then piled an equal number of empty metal frames beside them. Next, he filled one of the steel tanks with the developing chemicals, another with fixer, and set them on the table. Last, he grabbed a wind-up timer from the shelf.

"I'm going to show you how to do one in the light, so you'll know how to do the rest in the dark."

"The dark?"

My father picked up one of the plastic frames and pulled on a handle at the bottom to slide out one of the pieces of metal, exposing the film sheet to light.

"What if that was the best one?"

"Let's just say that it wasn't."

He set my fingers on the other end of the frame so I could feel how the top edge flipped open and the film sheet slid out. Then he showed me how to slip it into one of the metal frames.

"When they're all frames, you hang them on this rod and drop them into the tank with developer."

I looked up at my father. There were dark circles under his eyes; he hadn't slept in more than a day. He was not going to let me out of doing this.

"Look at the table and memorize where everything is, so you'll know it when I turn out the light."

Plastic frames, metal frames, tank with developer, tank with fixer, timer. And then we were in darkness. Darkness so thick you could press your hand against it. So thick it made the air unbreathable. I couldn't seem to pull its blackness into my lungs, could only stand in the unnatural coolness of the Paradise darkroom, choking.

My father's hand fell over mine. So surely, he must have memorized me.

"First thing, figure out what type of film you've got. That will tell you how long to leave it in the developer."

The edge of a film sheet appeared under my fingers.

"Tell me what you feel."

I ran my finger along the razor-thin edge, expecting an unbroken line, but finding a gap.

"An upside-down triangle, then a square."

"That's the notch code. Triangle and square is Kodak Ektapan."

The film sheet under my fingers vanished and was replaced by another. "Try this one."

"Only triangles."

"Perfect. Fortepan 200."

My father rummaged around the Paradise darkroom, replacing one film sheet with another. Each time I ran my finger along the top, feeling for the notches, and each time I read them correctly, deciphering the language of the film sheets as precisely as if my finger was a type of code-o-graph.

"I'm ready now," I said, and I was sure I felt my father nod.

I pictured the metal table the way I pictured the table next to my bed when I woke in the night and needed to find my glasses, then put my hand out for one of the plastic frames, feeling my fingers brush the raised diamonds molded onto its face.

There was something familiar about working in the dark. About knowing exactly how far to extend my arm to find the metal frames or the tank of developer, about sending a signal from my brain to my body without any information from my eyes. It was like taking your sled over tracks you'd already made in the snow.

When all the film sheets of the Silverman twins were hanging from the metal rod, I dipped them into the tank filled with developer.

"How long?" I asked my father.

"Seven minutes."

I picked up the timer and felt for seven raised lines.

My father talked me through developing the Silverman twins, his voice coming at me in the dark like a voice on the radio, telling me when to move the metal rod into the tank filled with fixer, how many minutes to add to the timer. When it went off the second time, sounding bright in the blackness, he snapped on the light and pulled the metal rod out of the tank, handed me one of the dripping film sheets.

I pushed my glasses onto the top of my head and brought the piece of film—a negative now—close to my face. There like a black ghost propped up on a white sofa was one of the Silverman twins. My own miraculous experiment.

One by one, the Silverman twins emerged from the metal frames. Blackish bundles with fine white wisps of hair on their heads. And one by one, I hung them on a line strung across the back of the darkroom, these reverse images of the Silverman twins, made by me in the dark.

But the last negative was not a picture of the Silverman twins. It was the photograph my father had taken of me on the roof, the one that was meant for the little window in the code-o-graph.

In it, I had nothing except the wide, blue sky behind me. My face was smooth, uninterrupted by the round, black frames of the glasses. I looked like a person who could be anywhere, a person who might do anything.

I hung this negative—this picture that was the reverse of me—on the line with the Silverman twins.

. . .

Back out in Hell's Kitchen, the sun was still high and the streets were broiling. Streets that were filled with people pushed out of their apartments in search of a breeze—men in sleeveless T-shirts, suspenders cutting into their fleshy shoulders, women in housedresses and hair-curlers. And kids. There were always a hundred kids on the sidewalks of Hell's Kitchen. Kids who spit on the ground close to your Keds as you passed them, heading to the 42nd Street subway with your father.

The station was more stifling than the streets. My father and I stood on the uptown platform, pressed in on all sides by families on their way home from Coney Island and the Rockaways, a sea of sunburnt arms, and sandy blankets, and picnic baskets that dripped pink-colored water smelling of liverwurst around our ankles.

Behind us, soldiers with their arms wrapped around the waists of laughing girls poured down the stairs in twos and fours, girls in light dresses that moved about their legs in unfelt breezes, as if these girls carried their own weather. They joined the hot, sweating families, nudging us closer to the edge of the platform.

My father stepped aside for a woman who was tugging the sun-reddened arm of a crying boy. Two soldiers and their girls passed behind us, sharp elbows brushing my back. The girls' laughter echoed off the tiles.

We stood in the heat of the station for what seemed like an hour, our faces running with sweat, my glasses sliding down my nose. I began to believe the train would never come, and then, the air changed. All the particles of it, all the smells stirring—the sweat, and the liverwurst, and the perfume of the soldiers' girls. I felt a heavy rumbling beneath the soles of my shoes, as if a thunderstorm might be brewing under the ground. Everybody on the platform straightened, began to move—although there was no place to move to—because at last, the uptown A was coming.

My father and I were at the very edge of the platform. Hot, mouse-scented air, forced through the tunnel by the oncoming train, blew on our faces, ruffled through our sweat-soaked hair. The rumbling under my feet grew stronger, traveled up to my chest, shaking loose something I'd been thinking about, worrying over, all the way here.

My father watching me bury the code-o-graph in the box with the sweaters.

After everything he'd just taught me at Paradise—how to read the edges of film, the secret to making negatives while blinded by darkness—I needed him to know the reason I'd taken that object he'd gone to so much trouble over and shoved it under my bed. I needed him to know it had nothing to do with him, everything to do with me. I wanted there to be no chance he hadn't been able to read it for himself, no matter how unlikely.

"The code-o-graph," I began.

My father had been pushed so close to me, his face was out of focus.

"I know," he told me. And then, I suppose, because he wanted me to see his expression, he stepped back.

The bald-headed man should have turned that inner tube in for the rubber months ago. Should have let it be made into jeep tires or airplane tires, and then sent off to fight the Germans. Should never have let it remain the kind of inner tube that could be taken out to Coney Island for the day. Taken out, then brought back on the subway, where he could rush along the crowded platform, carrying it in front of his face, so he couldn't see that he was bumping into somebody's father.

In the glare of the uptown A train's headlamp, I saw my father's face, and I searched for the expression he had meant to show me. But whatever it had been, it had vanished. Replaced by surprise, and then by something else. Something darker. Because my father had begun to lean over the tracks in a way nobody could recover from.

The station filled with the sound of screaming—the train trying to stop itself, the brakes grabbing for the metal tracks. A sound that could cut through skin.

My father was arcing off the edge of the platform in pieces. His expression. His ruined white shirt. His camera. The newspaperman's camera, slung from his shoulder on a strap, making its own separate arc as he toppled.

He was timing it perfectly—his fall and the oncoming train. The train that, despite the terrible sound of the brakes, did not stop.

And then, another arc. My hand reaching up and pulling off the glasses.

But it did not matter if I turned the entire world into a blur.

The train, nothing more than green motion, flew past me. Right through the spot where my father had been.

When it came to a stop, everything went silent, as if the sunburnt families, the soldiers and their girls, me, were waiting for a signal. And then, I heard a screaming that might have been the echo of the brakes inside my head, might have been the soldiers' girls, might have been me.

The rest I recall in pieces. The families and soldiers' girls staring at me. A sweating, red-faced transit cop, getting down on one knee, his face too close to be in focus, asking if my father had jumped.

"It was a bald-headed man with an inner tube," I told him. "An inner tube he should have turned in for the war."

The red-faced transit cop asked me for my address, and when I said nothing, he suggested I think on it for a while, and went to talk to a couple of soldiers.

Instead, I thought about a flattened Chuckles wrapper that was next to my Keds. Wondered whether the person who'd thrown it there had saved the black one for last—the way I did—because it was his favorite. I thought about that black Chuckle long and hard, hoping to erase my address from my mind, so I would never have to walk out of this subway station without my father.

But sooner or later, I must have told the transit cop my address, because I remember walking up the stairs of the station with him, everybody else stepping back like I was some kind of bad luck.

I knocked on our door, because my father had had the keys. When my mother opened it, she looked at the transit cop, and then at me. She was wearing a white shirt with no sleeves, and her black hair was brushing across the top of her shoulders at the place where her shirt ended and her tanned skin began. She was smiling, showing us the gap between her front teeth, but already, her smile was losing some of its tension.

I wanted to push the transit cop back into the hallway, shut the door on him, as if that would stop what he had to say from coming into the house. But I could hear him speaking my mother's name over my head.

I couldn't watch what would happen to my mother's face when the rest of what he had to say traveled across the air to her. I pushed my way into the apartment, ran down the hallway, past the living room, where my father's green armchair sat, still pushed close to the radio. I went into my room and shut the door.

Then, as if the only thing that had been keeping me upright had been the presence of other people, I collapsed to the floor as if I was Superman knocked down by Kryptonite.

I squeezed myself under the bed and pulled out the box of sweaters, tore through them until I found the code-o-graph. I wrapped my fingers around its thin, metal edge, clutched it as tightly as I could, as if this thing from the radio, this object my father had gone to so much trouble over, possessed the power to bring him back.

I lay on the floor, hot cheek pressed to the linoleum, taking shallow breaths. All my colorful organs—blue lungs, orange kidneys, red heart—were turning black and withering inside me. All of them, one by one, as if I was dying from the inside out.

Five

My father was waked with an empty coffin. Two men from Dunleavy's Funeral Home carried it in, then balanced it on sawhorses in front of the Silvertone. The coffin was made of the same cherrywood as the radio, and it and the Silvertone looked like a matched set. I had to stop myself from believing that from now on it would live in our apartment instead of my father.

After the men from Dunleavy's left, Aunt May curled a rosary made out of wooden beads inside the coffin, placing it on the purple satin in the place where my father's hands would have been if the coffin hadn't been empty, if he'd been inside it. Then she told me to go put on my Mass pants and a shirt with sleeves.

It was too hot for the Mass pants and too hot for a shirt with sleeves, but I put them on. Before I left my room, I slipped the code-o-graph into my pants pocket.

In the two days since the transit cop brought me home, I hadn't been without the code-o-graph. I slept with it in the chest pocket of my pajamas, dropped it into the pocket of whatever pants I decided to wear each day—which was never the shorts I'd been wearing the afternoon my father took me to Paradise. My hand was always in my pocket, feeling for the thin metal edge of the code-o-graph, spinning the propeller that would turn the letters of a secret code into something comprehensible.

When I came into the kitchen, I saw that Aunt May had made my mother put on something that was black and too hot, too. She was sitting at the table in a black dress with long sleeves, holding a coffee cup with both hands as if she believed it was about to shatter into pieces. Aunt May was leaning into the oven, poking a fork into a casserole filled with something bubbling and orange.

My mother said my name, which was more or less all she'd had to say to me in the past two days. But I didn't need her to say many words in a row to hear the broken sound under them. A sound that let me know all her colorful organs had turned as black as mine.

She set down her coffee cup and got to her feet. She was wearing the black shoes she only wore to Mass and she walked over to me like she was unfamiliar with the floor. She came near enough to turn blurry and unfamiliar—my mother in that black dress I'd never seen before. With no warning, she wrapped her black-sleeved arms around my shoulders and pulled me against her angular chest.

My mother did not hug in this way. More often she surprised me with an arm flung across my collarbone from behind, a quick brush of her lips on the top of my head. Now I felt her breathing, her lungs—once blue—rising and falling against the side of my face. I smelled her cigarette, the cedar from the closet where she kept this awful dress, and beneath it, the improbable cut-grass scent of her skin.

I wanted to tell her it was my fault there was a coffin in our living room, that it was I who had changed our luck. But the many consonants of that confession, which out of my mouth would have been sharp and clear and not the least bit blurry, were caught in my throat.

I opened my mouth, tried to push the words into the space between my mother and me.

The oven door slammed shut. My mother flinched and let me go.

. . .

Our apartment filled up with people who had come to talk about my father and drink whiskey and stand in our living room with an empty coffin.

Harry Jupiter was there, his fat face sagging with sorrow. He walked in wide circles around the cherrywood coffin, clutching a glass of rye as if it were the one thing keeping him upright. Father Barry was there as well. Father Barry who belonged at Good Shepherd now standing in our living room with all his bright white hair and his black suit that smelled of Mass incense. Father Barry making me think about the Body of Christ disappearing from the tomb on Easter morning, leaving it as empty as the coffin balanced in front of our radio.

"We drove up," somebody said. "We couldn't face the subway," making *subway* sound like polio.

So many of these people I'd seen only in the portraits my father had shot of them, seen only in black and white. Now they stood in our living room sweating and drinking, looking in color much too lifelike.

I do not know if the Keener was invited, or if perhaps she was so old and close to dying herself, she knew when someone had passed and turned up on her own. She wasn't there, and then she was there, standing in the middle of our living room, her face so collapsed into itself, it could as well have been a forgotten apple from several winters ago as a human face. So few strands of white hair covering her scalp, the only way to tell she was a woman was by the black dress that hung from her shoulders. One of her legs must have been shorter than the other, because she walked toward the empty coffin with a hitched, rolling gait, as if she was traversing an invisible boat.

No one else noticed her. Not my mother, standing close to Father Barry, her pale hands trapped inside his waxy ones. Not Aunt May, bustling about the room collecting half-empty whiskey glasses. Not one of the too-lifelike people who had come by car to stand around and not stare at the coffin in front of the Silvertone. The Keener, though, she looked at it.

She looked at nothing else, gazing at its purple satin interior and the rosary curled up like a snake where my father's hands would have been. Looked at it as if she saw my father inside. She made her hitching way through the crowded room to its cherrywood side, circling it until she stood at the top, at the place where my father's head would be, as though we'd been saving the spot for her.

The old woman drew a breath that seemed to gather in more than air, that pulled at something that wasn't in the room at all. She opened her mouth, a dark hole empty of teeth, and produced a low-pitched wailing in that ancient language, the Gaeilge language of the Irish.

My father had once told me it was the language of Irish heroes. But coming out of the old woman's black hole of a mouth, it sounded like the knocking together of bones. As if the Keener was a radio for the dead. I stared across the empty coffin at her, certain she had been sent to broadcast the voices of ghosts, transmit their undertones through the dark speaker of her mouth. Transmit them to me. The one she was looking at. The one who was guilty.

And then, I heard it, *Donnchadh*, my father's Gaeilge name. And all the air in that chokingly hot room began to disappear into the dark hole of the Keener's mouth.

I had to get out, get away. Before everybody knew. Before they learned it was me.

I hammered my fists on their black-clad backs. Told them all to go home, get out of here. Finish your whiskey and drive away in your cars! It was only Uncle Glenn's hands coming down on my arms that calmed me. Only his voice suggesting everybody step back and give the boy some air. Leaning down and saying in my ear, "I've never been much for Keeners either, all that Irish melancholy."

Then he put an arm around my shoulders and the two of us went down to his and Aunt May's apartment and sat at a table covered in ruffled place mats and drank a couple of cold glasses of milk.

After a while Uncle Glenn said my name, and his undertone was so thick with sympathy I didn't deserve, the consonant-filled confession that had been caught in my throat broke loose and came pouring out of my mouth. I told my uncle everything about the sunburnt families and the soldiers with their laughing girls and the man running along the platform with the inner tube that should have been turned in for the rubber. Then I told him about how I'd needed to explain to my father about the code-o-graph, the object he had gone to so much trouble over.

But before I could get any further, Uncle Glenn said, a Captain Midnight code-o-graph? And when I nodded, he got up, pulled open a kitchen drawer, and tossed a Captain Midnight code-o-graph onto the table.

"Where did you get that?"

"Found it in the backseat of the taxi last time I took it out."

I reached into the pocket of my Mass pants and set my code-o-graph on the table next to his. They were identical except that Uncle Glenn's didn't have anybody's photograph in the little window. Not even Captain Midnight's.

"I was saving it for you," he said, "but I guess you've already got one." He sat back down. "From what you say, I don't see how anything was your fault."

"Then I didn't explain it right."

"You want to tell it over again?"

But telling it once had put too many pictures inside my head.

I slipped my code-o-graph back into my pocket, let my fingers spin the propeller around.

"You'll just have to take my word for it."

. . .

The first message arrived the following morning. It had been tucked inside our mailbox, which was never locked, because the lock had been broken a long time ago, a folded piece of paper with

FGVH

written on the outside.

And

YO PGLRY ITEN JGESO

written on the inside.

It was mixed in with the electricity bill and the sympathy cards, which had been coming every day now. Cards that just from the way our names were written on the envelopes made me sorry to be us.

I took the message upstairs and deciphered it using the code-o-graph. I didn't doubt—not for one instant—that the message could be translated with the code-o-graph. Perhaps it was because I'd already spent so many of my waking minutes spinning that propeller, running my fingers over the device's circle of raised letters and numbers, as if I could change history if only I did it the correct number of times.

FGVH

turned out to be

JACK.

And

YO PGLRY ITEN JGESO

was

IT WASNT YOUR FAULT.

And here is the other thing I didn't doubt—that the message had come from my father. Such an idea made no sense, was illogical. Then again, there was the message in my hands. And what was written there was precisely what I most needed to hear. My father, with his ability to read people, would have known that. Would have sensed it from wherever he was.

Which was where? And how had he ended up there?

I put my hands on the piece of paper that had come from my father, pressing it into my cowboy and Indian bedspread, and tried to imagine what might have happened in the 42nd Street subway, after I'd taken off the glasses.

Perhaps, in the final moment of the arcs, my father had tumbled off the platform with enough time to roll out of the way. To squeeze himself into the narrow space between the track—where in less than an instant the metal wheels of the train would come screeching—and the third rail. Perhaps that's where he'd been the entire time the red-faced transit cop had been leaning in too close to me. The entire time I'd been concentrating on the crumpled-up Chuckles wrapper. The entire time the uptown A train sat silent above him.

It was an improbable story—impossible, really—but I was a twelve-year-old boy who had lost his father. A twelve-year-old boy with a head full of radio serial dramas, dramas that depended on last-minute escapes. And perhaps more important, I wanted very much to believe it.

There was a mentalist at Coney Island who claimed to be able to tell your future. You would write a question on a piece of paper, and then he'd ask you to hold it in your hand for a few seconds to put your magnetism on it. I pressed my hand harder against the paper on my bedspread, sure I could feel my father's magnetism, a buzzing beneath my hand.

Then I smoothed my father's message flat and slipped it under my T-shirt, tucking in the hem to keep it from falling out. The paper felt stiff and scratchy against my chest. I got up and ripped a page from one of my old composition books, wrote

I NEED TO SEE YOU

which I turned into

Y RUUB OT LUU ITE.

Because I had to know why, once the uptown A train had pulled out of the 42nd Street subway station, once my father had stood up and brushed himself off, why he hadn't come straight home to Dyckman Street, where I was waiting, certain he was dead.

I folded the paper in half and wrote

BGB

on the outside, which was

DAD.

Then I ran downstairs and slipped it into the mailbox.

. . .

I waited all day for my father's answer. Leaving the Silvertone every fifteen minutes to run down to the mailboxes. Running my hand along the row of brass doors, each with a circle of holes punched into it, as if mail needed to breathe. Lifting the door of ours to see if my message had disappeared, if it had been replaced with one from my father.

It had not come by the time my mother left the apartment for five o'clock Mass, wearing the black dress that was too hot for days like this, a piece of black lace bobby-pinned to the top of her head. My mother had been going to five o'clock Mass every afternoon since Father Barry had turned up in our living room with his black suit smelling of incense.

It had not come by the time she returned, heading straight for her bedroom, as if she was worn out from standing and kneeling and repeating things in Latin.

My father's answer had not come by the time Aunt May came up to make the apartment hotter with her cooking. Aunt May had taken over all the cooking for us. Nearly everything she made came from *Victory Meat Extenders*, a cookbook that had come out since the war began, since meat had started being rationed. Aunt May served us dishes like Pork-U-Pines and Emergency Steak, dishes that tasted like cereal and gravy. Most nights, I pushed these gray-looking meals around on my plate until she went back downstairs.

I never saw my mother eat any of Aunt May's cooking. Except for her trips to Good Shepherd, she was always locked in her bedroom, so silent, I only knew she was in the apartment by the sense I had of her heart beating.

My father's answer still had not come after dinner, when I bumped into Uncle Glenn near the mailboxes. He was on his way out, wearing his white Civil Defense helmet and armband, the silver whistle strung around his neck.

Only later, after all these things happened, did I find a new message replacing mine.

When I brought it upstairs and decoded it, what my father had written back was

Y VGRO LUU ITE

which meant

I CANT SEE YOU.

If the piece of paper sitting on my bed, the paper with those four coded words, had not been full of my father's magnetism, I would have torn it into a hundred pieces. But it—and the paper crackling inside my shirt—were the only things I had left of him. The only things that had gone from his hand to mine. I slipped this latest message inside my shirt and instead tore up the paper from my composition book I'd used to decipher it. Ripped it into pieces, let it fall like a blizzard on the cowboys and Indians riding across my bedspread.

When I was done, I went into the living room and turned on the Silvertone, needing to fill up my head with noise, fill it with something that wasn't my father's voice—his mix of American and Irish I was already starting to forget—repeating the words

I CANT SEE YOU

over and over, as if every one of those pieces of ripped paper could talk.

I lay on the checkerboard linoleum with my head next to the Silvertone's big speakers. But I couldn't focus on what was pouring out of them, not the baritone of the announcer's voice, not the crashing of the orchestra.

My father was alive and somewhere out in the world and didn't want to see me. I couldn't believe that was true. Not unless he had a good reason. A life-or-death reason. A reason that had to do with the war, because everything in those days had to do with the war.

I lay there, trying to come up with a reason that my father—my father who had survived his fall from the subway platform—could not come to me.

It is no surprise that what I came up with was something straight out of a radio serial drama. A story built on a faked death and a secret identity and a plan for spying. What else would I have thought of? All I'd done for the past months was let radio serial dramas pour into my ears. A radio serial drama was pouring into my ears at the very moment I was dreaming up the story.

Here is how I told it to myself.

My father rises from that narrow space between the track and the third rail, that rail full of electricity. He leans down to pick up the Speed Graphic—miraculously undamaged—and looks up into the surprised faces of a couple of transit cops, the only people left in the station. Then he tells them to take him to the mayor.

Inside Gracie Mansion, my father and Fiorello La Guardia have a long talk about my father's ability to read people, about how useful it would be to have somebody like that on the streets of New York keeping an eye out for Nazi spies and saboteurs. Then my father drops his hand on the Speed Graphic. *Now let me tell you what I can do with this*, he says. Fiorello La Guardia smiles and shakes my father's hand. And my father tells him, *One last thing. The transit cops, everybody, they have to pretend I'm dead. Otherwise it will be too dangerous for my family.*

Was it an unlikely story? Perhaps. But it was backed up by evidence. The empty coffin that had sat balanced on sawhorses in front of the Silvertone. The fact that no one had brought my father's camera back from the 42nd Street subway station. The two messages crinkling inside my shirt.

I pushed my glasses back onto my face and rose from the floor. Turned off the radio and went into my bedroom. I tore another page from my composition book and wrote a new message for my father.

Y ERBERLOGRB

I UNDERSTAND

Then before it turned light, before it became another day, I went downstairs and slipped it into the mailbox.

For the first time since the red-faced transit cop brought me home, it felt like nothing inside me was dying.

Six

It was hot that summer and stifling inside our apartment, but my mother and I rarely left those four rooms. My mother spent the time she wasn't at five o'clock Mass lying on her bed with the lights out and her blackout shades pulled down, smoking and staring at the ceiling as if a better movie of her life was playing there. I got dressed every morning, tucking both of my father's messages inside my T-shirt and putting the code-o-graph in my pants pocket. Then I sat in front of the window with the radio on, staring out onto Dyckman Street, hoping for a glimpse of my father.

I was certain he came every day, though I believed it might be at night, when no one would see him. I imagined him standing on the opposite side of the street, gazing up at my window. Some nights, I was sure I could feel him there, his magnetism moving through the bricks like radio waves washing over me.

Because of the Dim-Out orders, I was afraid to lift the edge of my blackout shades and search for him. Although one night, I tucked the luminous-face alarm clock under my blankets, trapping its green light, and went to the window, lifted a corner of the shade. Only one corner, and only high enough to look down on Dyckman Street.

I saw darkness and a circle of light shining on the sidewalk from the downward-casting bulbs that were in all the streetlamps now. A taxi, the top half of its headlights covered with black paint, moved slowly up the street, and I imagined it had let my father off at the corner.

It was a hot night and my window was open. I breathed in the humid air full of garbage and the scent of distant rain, searching for the bitter and sweet smell of the developing chemicals, the smell of Wildroot Cream-Oil. Maybe it was there.

I went back to my bed and retrieved the luminous-face clock, brought it back to the window and lifted the corner of the shade once more. Only for a second, not long enough for any Germans who might be floating in the water off the coastline to see anything important. Only long enough for my father to know I was up here.

I let the shade drop and sat on the floor with the green glowing clock in my lap. Put my back against the wall, as if my father could reach up and touch it.

The rest of the time, I watched for him during the day, dragging an ottoman to the living room window, leaning against the wooden frame for so many hours, I frequently went to bed with a crease pushed into my forehead. After a week of this, on an afternoon when the air was full of ozone from brewing thunderstorms and I felt too jittery to sit at the window, I went out looking for my father.

It was the first time I'd gone into the subway since the transit cop brought me out of it, and the smell going down the steps—dead mice, urine, the sweetish scent of electricity—almost knocked me flat, made me grab for the railings to keep myself from crumpling to the ground like a drunk. I had to take one hand off the sticky railings and press my father's messages against my chest, remind myself they were there, to make myself walk to the bottom of the steps.

When the hot wind from the oncoming train blew into my face, and the brakes began screaming, metal on metal, I replayed the story of what had happened to my father after he'd arced off the platform—making myself see it clear inside my head—his incredible story of escape and rescue.

I came out onto Times Square, stood beneath the billboard advertising Camel cigarettes, the smoking man made into a soldier for the war. As his clouds of artificial smoke drifted over me, I studied the faces of the men rushing past, faces that snapped into focus, as if I were turning the pages of a book of photographs. I imagined my father in a disguise, a belted overcoat like a movie detective, a hat pulled low on his forehead, although the temperature that day must have been in the nineties.

After an hour or so, I walked down 43rd Street to Paradise Photo. I had decided that this was where my father came to develop the photographs he took of the people he suspected of being Nazi spies or saboteurs, that each night, he removed the key from behind the loose brick and went through the door with the sign that said *Knock or die.*

Later, when I returned to Dyckman Street, my mother was sitting at the kitchen table with Aunt May hovering over her.

"I told you he was safe," Aunt May said.

But my mother flew out of her chair and pressed her hands against my chest as if she was checking that I was solid, crushing my father's messages.

"You cannot ever leave this apartment," she told me.

"Lily," Aunt May said, "he's a boy. You have to let him out."

"Take this then." My mother pressed a rosary into my hand. "Carry it with you always."

The rosary was exactly like the one that had been coiled up inside the empty coffin. The moment I was inside my bedroom, I dropped it like it could bite me.

Later that night after Aunt May left, I walked down the hallway to my mother's room, stood outside her door with my father's messages in my hand, breathing in the smoke from her cigarette.

I should tell her, I was thinking, remembering the panicked feel of her hands moving over my chest. But my father had written only my name on the outside of those messages, and I believe there was a part of me that wanted this to be a secret between the two of us, to be something only we knew.

I stood in the hallway breathing in cigarette smoke for a while, then I slid the papers inside my shirt and went back to my room.

The following Sunday, when I returned to Good Shepherd with my mother, we did not go to the later Mass with Aunt May as we generally did, and we did not sit in our usual place in the middle pew. Instead, my mother walked me to the very front of the church, close enough to see the pots of wilted marigolds on the altar, to sit with the Desperate Catholics.

It was my mother who had given them the name. Whispering it into my ear one bright Sunday, as we watched them spring to their feet ahead of the rest of the congregation, as if Mass were a competition, drop to their knees as if struck down.

The Desperate Catholics repeated each phrase of the Mass after Father Barry in loud voices, their Latin disturbing the calm blue light of church. They did not pray with their heads bowed, the way the rest of us did, but craned their necks upward to stare at the ceiling of Good Shepherd, as if they believed the Holy Spirit might be hiding behind the burnt-out lightbulbs and cobwebs of the building's chandelier.

And now we were seated with them. My mother wearing the black dress that was too hot, even for this early in the morning, and me in my black Mass pants and a long-sleeved shirt, the code-o-graph in my pocket, my father's messages sticking to my sweating chest.

Father Barry came up the aisle swinging the censer, filling the already hot church with the smell of incense—that sweetish scent like candy you think will taste better than it does. He moved behind the row of wilting carnations to the altar and began the Mass, and though I tried not to hear it, my mother's voice rose above even the loudest of the Desperate Catholics.

It was not so much her voice, but what lay beneath it that disturbed me. The undertone that was asking—no, not asking, begging—God to protect me from German bombs dropping from the sky, and subway trains screaming into stations. Spare me from polio and tuberculosis and pneumonia, and a score of other diseases that had probably long since disappeared. And already my mother was looking up at that burnt-out chandelier with such concentration, I wanted to shake her and tell her there was nothing up there except spiders and dust.

It was time to kneel, but I couldn't move. I was paralyzed by my mother's voice. I sat in the row of Desperate Catholics, the only one silent, the only one motionless. And the more my mother beseeched God to watch over me, the more the terrible hum of her undertone worked its way beneath my skin, slipped into my bloodstream like one of the illnesses from which she was trying to protect me. Until I was sure that if I did not stop her, everything she was attempting to save me from would happen.

I felt the skin of my mother's lips under my fingers, rough and chapped from so many days spent smoking and staring at the ceiling, so many days of begging God for favors. The raised bits of dry skin were like the peaks and valleys on the edges of my father's film strips, the secret code I'd deciphered in the blackness of the Paradise darkroom. *Kodak Ektapan*, I thought. *Ilford Delta.* It was as if I was determining how long my mother would have to stay in the dark with the developing chemicals. But my mother had already spent her time in the dark, already done the work of becoming herself in reverse.

My mother placed her hand over mine and gently removed it from her mouth. She touched the side of my face with her fingertips. But her lips were already back to saying the Mass, already caught up with Father Barry, as if she'd never stopped saying it inside her head.

I was in the aisle before I knew I'd stood. Running past the early morning Mass-goers, my footsteps a pounding heartbeat beneath their holy repetitions. I burst through the church's double doors into the bright hot day like someone coming up for air, ran all the way home, rubbing my hand against the side of my pants to scrape away the feeling of my mother's mouth.

Once inside the apartment, I went straight to my mother's room and opened the door to my father's closet. I wanted to touch my father's clothes. Bury my face in those brown shirts he used to wear, shirts that smelled so strongly of the developing chemicals, it was like standing inside the Paradise darkroom. I wanted to run my hands over the white shirts, too. Those shirts with their colonies of brown spots. Shirts he'd bought, knowing they'd be ruined, just to make it easier for me to find him.

But my father's closet was empty.

Everything had vanished. Even his hats—tan for summer, brown for winter. Hats that smelled of Wildroot Cream-Oil and my father's head.

I craned my neck and searched the shelf. The photographs were gone. The portraits people had refused because he'd captured something about them they hadn't wanted to look at. The photographs that showed off my father's ability, the ability that was as remarkable as flying.

I turned to my father's dresser and pulled open all the drawers.

They were empty, too.

Not one piece of my father's clothing was left.

My mother had done this. She'd given my father's clothes to the church. To Father Barry, who every Sunday asked the congregation for donations for the Catholic missionaries saving pagan souls in darkest Africa. She must have done it the one day I'd gone out, the day I'd stood in the artificial smoke of the Camel cigarette soldier. She'd taken advantage of my absence to give away all his clothes, and once the war was over and my father could come home, he'd have nothing to wear. Not one white shirt. Not even a sock.

I went to my mother's closet and pulled open the door, thinking maybe she'd forgotten something, something put in here by accident. I grabbed an armful of her clothes. Blouses and skirts and dresses in bright colors she was never going to wear again. Reds and blues I couldn't imagine her putting on because I couldn't imagine her in anything except that black dress that was always going to be too hot for the day. I yanked the clothes out of the closet, tore them off their hangers, and threw them to the floor. Then I went back for more, pulling my mother's colorful clothes out of her closet until there was nothing left. Until her closet was as empty as his. When I'd finished with the closet, I did the same to her dresser drawers.

I waited for my mother in her room, my father's messages clutched in my hand. When she returned from Good Shepherd, she stood in the doorway, the clothes from her closet—those colorful clothes she would never wear again—piled up around her ankles like leaves dropped from a hundred trees.

"He's not dead," I told her.

My mother reeled back like I'd hit her, but I kept going, my words digging into all the soft, vulnerable organs that lay beneath the black dress. I described for her how he'd rolled out of the way of the metal wheels in the nick of time, how he'd talked himself inside Gracie Mansion, how he was, at this very minute probably, prowling the streets of Manhattan in search of Nazi spies and saboteurs.

When she widened her green eyes at me in doubt, I waded through the colorful clothes and showed her the messages, put her fingers on the code-o-graph and demonstrated how to decipher my father's code, turning

FGVH

into

JACK.

I can only now imagine what my mother thought, seeing me with those messages. Messages, she told me, that did not resemble my father's handwriting.

"That's part of the secret code."

But my mother was not a twelve-year-old boy who had spent months filling up his head with things that came out of the radio. She was a twenty-eight-year-old widow who had lost the ability to believe in anything resembling the nick of time.

She pushed her black shoes through the piles of colorful clothes to the bed, lay down on it and lit a cigarette. Her eyes followed the smoke up to the ceiling, where the better movie of her life was playing. Then she said my name in a voice full of sorrow.

What I heard was that my mother believed I had written those messages. That she believed I was fooling myself.

I left her room and went into mine. Then I wrote my father a new message that said

OUSS XU LTXUOKYRA TRSI ITE GRB LKU HRTP

which meant

TELL ME SOMETHING ONLY YOU AND SHE KNOW.

I folded the paper and held it in my hand, instilling it with my magnetism. When I was certain my father would be able to feel every bit of my need when he unfolded the paper, feel it right through his fingertips, I went downstairs and put it in the mailbox. Then I came back up and waited.

The next morning, my father left me this

ITEN XTOKUN VGRO HRTP

which meant

YOUR MOTHER CANT KNOW.

I sat in the early light of my bedroom, still in my pajamas, and stared at my father's message.

How could someone who could read strangers, who could look at a person and know something about him, how could that person have held my message in his hands and not understood how important this was?

But my father read people, not magnetism on paper. He hadn't seen my mother in her dress with the black sleeves, hadn't seen her leaving the apartment every day with the piece of lace bobby-pinned to her black hair, as if she was afraid to let God see the top of her head only walking down Dyckman Street.

He would have to see for himself, have to be dragged up to our apartment, made to stand in the doorway of the bedroom that was once his and watch her exhale cigarette smoke at the cracks in the ceiling as if she was letting go of some essential part of herself. And he would have to do it soon, before it was too late and there was nothing left of the black-haired bootlegger's daughter who had once been my mother.

That night I stood outside my mother's room listening for the sound of her sleeping. When my mother was awake, her breath stayed shallow, as if she was afraid to send it deep into her chest, afraid she'd disturb something that was lying there. Only when she slept did she take a full breath.

Once I heard it, I left the apartment, stepping out into the hot darkness. I crossed the street and slipped into a narrow alley. The supers of the adjacent buildings stored their garbage cans here, and the air was close and filled with the nose-biting smell of ammonia and the sickly sweetness of something rotting, but I was worried my father wouldn't come if he saw me, and I could see our steps perfectly from here.

Uncle Glenn came out wearing his white Civil Defense helmet and armband, and headed down the street. Then some of our neighbors who had war factory jobs, the sharp shine of their metal lunch pails glinting as they passed beneath the downward-casting light of the streetlamp. When my legs got tired, I found a wooden crate halfway down the alley, kicked it to the front and sat on it.

As it got later, a scrabbling started up from deeper in the alley, as if the garbage were coming to life. The sound made the skin on the back of my neck twitch, and I inched the crate closer to the sidewalk.

Then, suddenly, the alley was lit up with the pale gray light of dawn, and the side of my face was stuck to the cool bricks of the apartment building to my right.

The next night, I brought out my luminous-face alarm clock and set it to go off every hour. The green glow of the clock kept me company as I sat on the crate watching for my father. My eyes weren't good in the dark, but I was sure I would know it was him when he came, even if he was wearing a disguise, as if I were a radio tuned to his particular frequency.

Each hour, I woke to the hard brass ringing of the clock.

The next night, I set the alarm for every half hour.

I did this for two weeks. Leaving the apartment in darkness to sit in the alley with the clock shining green in my face. Staying out until the sky lightened enough for me to make out the shapes of the cars parked in the street. Only then would I go inside and change out of clothes that had taken on the ammonia and sweet rotting smell of the alley—or maybe it wasn't the clothes, maybe the smell had worked its way inside my nose—getting into bed and falling into a deep sleep that lasted until early afternoon.

I was living the schedule my father had lived when he worked the graveyard shift at the Navy Yard, the schedule he'd kept in those months before we went to Paradise together. Waking and sleeping the same hours, except for the time he'd spent with me, sitting in the green armchair listening to the Silvertone.

Over time, I began to believe that my father could sense when I was asleep, that this was one of the things he could read. I pictured him walking past the alley within reach of my hand, pausing to watch me sleep with my cheek pressed against the bricks, the luminous clock reflecting green off my glasses. I began to believe, too, that maybe he'd stopped coming, deciding it was too dangerous, deciding not to come back until I'd given up waiting for him.

And then, one night, I saw him going up the steps to our building.

It was a hot, humid night. A night with low thunder that rumbled over Long Island, making me believe I was hearing the war. A night full of heat lightning that flashed in the narrow band of sky over my head. A night too agitating for sleep. Twice already, I'd turned off the alarm before it rang. Even whatever it was that made that scrabbling sound at the back of the alley was feeling it. Earlier a garbage can lid had come clanging to the ground back there, and now it was being scraped from one side of the alley to the other.

A bus lumbered down the street, the top of its headlights painted black. It passed in front of me, blocking my view, then continued on toward Broadway. I looked back at the steps. A shadowy figure was hurrying up them. He was nothing more than darkness brought together into something denser. But I knew it was my father. Those gathered shadows were too familiar.

I darted out of the alley and across the street.

He wasn't wearing an overcoat. He was dressed in black pants and a black jacket, despite the hot night. I followed him through the front door. I meant to be silent, but I was in too much of a hurry, and the door banged shut after me.

He spun around.

Not my father.

Uncle Glenn. Looking surprised, and possibly like he'd been caught at something.

My uncle put a finger to his lips as if we were in on some secret together and gestured for me to follow him back outside. We sat side by side on the steps, the concrete still warm under my legs from the heat of the day.

I began to explain what I was doing out in the middle of the night, saying something about how I couldn't sleep, and it wouldn't be until much later that I'd realize he hadn't asked for any explanation. I was still holding onto the luminous-face clock, and I told him I'd wanted to keep track of the time.

"You can imagine your mother," Uncle Glenn said, "if she woke and found you missing."

I didn't want to imagine that, so I asked him why he wasn't wearing his white Civil Defense helmet or armband.

"I'm on a different kind of Civil Defense patrol."

I took in his black pants and jacket. "Are you spying on the neighborhood?"

Uncle Glenn put his finger to his lips again.

I lowered my voice. "Do you think somebody on Dyckman Street could be a Nazi?"

"That might be saying too much."

But that didn't mean the neighborhood wasn't full of Nazi sympathizers, he continued. People who could be talking to the wrong person about what they were doing at the Navy Yard, people who might be telling the wrong person something they shouldn't about what was being loaded onto the ships in New York Harbor.

I could hear the wheeze of my uncle's asthma humming beneath his breath. The humid air of New York summer was not good for his lungs.

"And you're going to catch them?" I said.

"If they're out there."

"How will you know if you find one?"

Uncle Glenn might have had Civil Defense training and a certificate from Fiorello La Guardia, but he did not have my father's ability to read people.

"How will I know if I find a Nazi sympathizer?" Uncle Glenn said.

Heat lightning flashed in the eastern sky and there was the rumble of thunder. Uncle Glenn looked into the darkness of the street.

"I grew up with one."

Seven

GLENN

My father had a Cauet hand. An aluminum replacement for the appendage he'd lost fighting for the Kaiser in what they called the Great War. The Cauet hand had been made in France, and my father loved the symmetry of this. That he had lost the original fighting the French, then had tricked—at least in his mind tricked—his enemy into making him a substitute.

The Cauet hand was shiny and hard, and attached with a shoulder harness that sprouted pull cords running the length of my father's arm to the aluminum wrist. These cords made it possible for him to move the fingers of the hand, but my father preferred to bang its hard metal side against whatever was closest, the kitchen table, the stovetop, the soft spot where my neck and shoulder met.

I was a terrible disappointment to my father. He couldn't understand how the son of the great war hero Gustav Hauck could have difficulty with something so simple as breathing. The first time I had an asthma attack with my father in public, we were on Lexington Avenue. We lived in Yorkville then, where all good Germans lived in New York City. All good Germans who had fled the Fatherland during the years of economic hardship that came after having lost the Great War. It was a freezing cold day, and we were on our way back from grocery shopping, an activity my father considered beneath the dignity of a man. But this was shortly after my mother disappeared and he would have to endure this indignity for another couple of years, until I was old enough to do it for him.

My father was walking fast, perhaps so no one would see him with his bags of food, and as I hurried to keep up with him, all the breathable air turned to concrete. I stopped and stood on the sidewalk with my mouth wide and gasping, trying to force solid air into my frozen lungs. After some steps, my father stopped as well. He turned his head and looked at me. Then, as if he didn't know me, he continued walking.

I watched his broad shoulders and the back of his blond head moving up Lexington Avenue. As he turned the corner at 92nd Street, the cold winter sun glinted off the fingers of the Cauet hand.

The second my father vanished, I remembered the nebulizer in my coat pocket. The nebulizer I had to remember to take with me every day, now that my mother was no longer there to remember it for me. I felt for the rubber bulb with numb fingers, and when I found it, I stood on the sidewalk of Lexington Avenue pumping bittersweet chemicals down my throat.

When I arrived home, the door to our apartment was locked. I knew my father would be on the roof with his pigeons, and I could have gone up there to ask for the key, but instead I sat on the floor with my back against the door to wait for him.

I hated watching my father with his pigeons. Hated how he took them out of their coop and let them climb onto his aluminum hand, their clawed feet making obscene scratching sounds. I couldn't watch him look into their red eyes, speak to them in a musical German I never heard, calling them *Liebchen* and *Schatzchen*. Couldn't bear how he put his thick lips close to the birds' heads before he sent them into the sky. It was disgusting to kiss pigeons. I hated especially how my father held out the Cauet hand to call the birds back, as if they were also war heroes, and how as each would land on the shiny aluminum hand, he'd stroke its head with his real one, the one made of flesh, the one he never put on me.

The only real hand I remember being touched by belonged to my mother, and it was a thing of unbelievable softness. It was plump and cushioned like a pillow, and it often smelled of cinnamon and sugar and cloves. My father was always shouting at her, calling her something in German that I believed translated into *swine.* One day she was gone. Vanished like the middle of a magic trick. And when I asked my father where she was and when she was coming back, he told me we were never to speak of her again.

It was inevitable that I would follow my father into the German American Bund. I was happy in the Bund. Not because I loved Hitler, who by this time—1936—was already in control of Germany, and not because I hated the Jews. At twenty, I had no opinion on either subject. No opinion that was not my father's. I was happy because my father couldn't dress up his pigeons in the shiny black boots and gray shirt of the Bund. He couldn't march them around the open fields of Long Island, or take them drinking with him in the beer gardens of Yorkville.

When summer came, my father and I—and hundreds of Bundists—spent weekends at Camp Siegfried, in the small lakeside town of Yaphank, Long Island. So many of us left Pennsylvania Station each Friday afternoon; the Long Island Rail Road arranged a special train, which we filled. As leafy branches slid past the windows of the cars, we roamed the aisles, singing Nazi songs about Jewish blood dripping from our knives.

When the train arrived at the tiny, wooden station house in Yaphank, hundreds of us poured from the doors, all wearing our starched gray shirts and black boots. We formed ranks, as if preparing to march on the town, raised our fists into the blue summer sky in the Nazi salute, then goose-stepped to camp, where most of us spent our time swimming in the lake and drinking warm beer. It was the elite of the Bund, a group that included my father, who met in a secluded bungalow on the far side of the lake. It was whispered that they were plotting acts of sabotage against America.

I once asked my father what he and the other men discussed in the bungalow on the far side of the lake. It was late, and the two of us were in our sleeping bags beneath the stars. My father never allowed us to sleep in the Camp Siegfried cabins, though his war hero status entitled us to one of the best. He also never brought a tent, the way most of the other campers did, despite the fact that sleeping in an open field usually triggered one of my asthma attacks. I always dreamed I was suffocating at Camp Siegfried. But it was worth it to sleep next to my father.

"Are you thinking to blow up a shipyard?" I whispered into the cricket-filled night. "A railroad line?"

Like a punishment from God, my father's Cauet hand came out of the darkness and struck me in that soft place between shoulder and neck. I do not know how he found it so easily in all that country blackness.

That summer was the summer of the Olympic Games in Berlin, and in honor of the occasion, Camp Siegfried planned to hold its own version of the Games with relay races and broad jumps and a swim meet across the green lake.

I was aware of the excitement surrounding the Camp Siegfried Games, but I was much more aware of Grete, who was tall and blond, and had skin that shone in the sun as if she were made out of gold. And if someone had told me that was true, I would have believed it, for she seemed that precious. Grete was a natural swimmer, and for her sake I'd started spending more time in the lake, though I was not a swimmer. I had never seen the point of purposely holding your breath. But for Grete, I would do it, and did do it. Chasing her beneath the surface of that green lake, willfully stopping my breath if it meant spending time beside that golden girl.

Grete was a full-fledged Nazi sympathizer and a raging anti-Semite. She loved the Fatherland and the Führer, and after dinner, she ran on her long golden legs into the camp's open-air pavilion to listen to Walther Kappe, Camp Siegfried's propaganda chief, give his nightly talk. And I ran after her. Sat in the folding chair beside her and studied her parted lips, tracked the breath lifting and lowering her swimmer's chest, knowing that if at any point she turned and asked me to go out and lynch a Jew, bring her back the limp body as a trophy, I would have done it in an instant.

It was Grete who informed me I was competing in the swimming race. She came rushing into the dining hall in her red bathing suit and pressed her golden body against mine, telling me it was for luck. I had not signed myself up, and I couldn't picture my father writing my name on the list. But perhaps he'd seen me swimming in the lake beside Grete and saw only what he wanted to see. Or perhaps he wanted to watch me fail. I never could guess anything my father wanted. The larger point was that this was the first time I'd touched more than Grete's hand, and I was certain it was a promise of more if I won. For Grete was a true Nazi, willing to reward perfection. No one could have forced me to scratch my name off that list.

Like so many days that August, the day of the Camp Siegfried Games was hot and humid with threatening thunderstorms. The ozone in the air made the hair on my arms and legs stand away from my skin, and the humidity made it difficult to pull into my lungs, even when my asthma was quiet. The sky was white and bright, and a rumbling of thunder traveled slowly across the opaque lake.

Lanes had been made with rope and floats. We racers stood together, looking across to a distant raft, still as death on the green water. I felt Grete's cool blue eyes on my back. I did not know how to feel for my father's eyes, for he had never come to watch me do anything.

A gun went off, and I dove low and straight into the cool water. Slicing through it clean and fast. I controlled my breath in a way I'd never done before, breathing in and out on command, holding it deliberately as I swam with long strokes across the green lake. Master of the race.

I heard the rumbling of thunder, but that might have been my heartbeat. My fingers touched the rough edge of the raft at the end of my lane. I flipped over, pressed my feet against the raft, and sprang away. Swimming back, back to where Grete waited, my golden prize.

Back to where my father waited, his aluminum hand shining silver in the hot sun.

The thunder was louder. The storm must be getting closer. Or maybe it was my heart, because I could feel it now inside my chest, rumbling there. The water was colder, too, sliding over my skin. I breathed out, commanded myself to breathe in, but the water had frozen my lungs, making it impossible to move them, to take in any air.

My mouth filled with water. I pushed my head above the green surface of the lake and began to flounder, my arms splashing against the ropes at the sides of my lane. I shook my head wildly, trying to clear the water from my mouth, and reached into the pocket of my swim trunks for the nebulizer. One part of my brain was telling me it would be better to drown here. But there is always that other part that wants to live, the part that will put the tip of the nebulizer into your mouth even while you are imagining what is going on behind Grete's cool blue eyes. The part that will make your legs kick hard enough to keep your head above water, while you consider how relieved she must be to have discovered this now, before she's put herself at risk of producing imperfect children.

I stayed in the lake until everyone had left its banks for the grassy field and the broad-jumping competition. Then I went to the meadow where my father kept our rucksacks and changed into a T-shirt and khaki-colored pants. As I walked to the gates of Camp Siegfried, I heard cheering coming from the field.

I hitchhiked back to the city. At the apartment, I stuffed some clothes and the money I'd earned sweeping in a beer garden for a friend of my father's in the rucksack. I would have liked to take something that had belonged to my mother, but there wasn't anything.

Before I left, I went up to the roof and opened the door to my father's pigeon coop, grabbed hold of the bird he had lavished the most affection on, the one whose head his thick lips had kissed the most often, an almost pure white bird. With a quick twist, I wrung its neck, telling myself it was to keep from being tempted to return.

I came up to Inwood, because my father hated the Irish only slightly less than he hated the Jews. I knew he wouldn't look for me here. Though if I was honest, I knew he wouldn't look for me at all—unless it was to get revenge for the pigeon. But he never came looking. And I never looked for him.

Your father suggested going after him once. The night the army made me 4-F and he came up to the roof to drink that bottle of rye. I told him this story, and when I was finished he asked me if I wanted to go down to Yorkville and beat up the son of a bitch. We were almost drunk enough to do it.

If we had, I would have taken that damned Cauet hand as a trophy.

Eight

As the wind picked up and the storm that had been threatening began to move across the river into the city, my uncle asked me if I was planning on coming outside again when I couldn't sleep.

"No," I told him, shaking my head. "I'm done."

And I was.

For as Uncle Glenn had been talking, I'd been remembering the day after I got the code-o-graph, the day I'd listened for the sound of Nazi sympathizers in the ocean-y blueness of Good Shepherd. The day I'd believed that if I found one, I would send a message to a made-up person on the radio.

But that was then. I pressed a hand to my chest, feeling how damp the papers had turned in the humidity, how soft they were against my skin. Now I would be sending a message to a real person.

A real person who would surely send a message back. One that said

Y RUUB OT LUU ITE,

I NEED TO SEE YOU.

. . .

Next morning, as soon as it was light, I got up and left the apartment. I had my code-o-graph in my pocket and also some paper, in case I found a Nazi right away. I'd also slipped some change out of *My First War Bond* for the subway.

It was hot, and the subway was full of people going to work. I moved through the car, listening for something suspicious—a voice that had beneath it a vibration that jarred me, like music played off-key.

When I finished with one car, I pulled open the door and moved to the next, stopping to stand on the metal platform as the train sped through the warm dark tunnel beneath the city streets. Under my feet, visible in the gap, was the narrow space between the track and the third rail where my father had squeezed himself, a space almost too narrow for a man.

I came aboveground in the places I knew I'd find people. In the street-side crush of Times Square. Beneath the blue-painted dome of Grand Central Station. Among the marble columns of Pennsylvania Station. When I got hungry, I went to the Automat on Eighth Avenue and used up one of my war bond dimes on a piece of coconut custard pie. I sat at a small table in the cold whiteness of the Automat taking the smallest bites I could of the pie and listening to the conversations going on at the tables around me. It was lunchtime and the Automat was filled with workers from nearby offices. Men in summer suits made of seersucker, women in dresses with narrowed skirts, because cotton had to be saved for uniforms.

When the Automat emptied, I went back into the subway. I rode it all the way out to Queens, as far as the stop for the World's Fair. All through the summer of 1939, my father and I had come out here to take pictures of Johnny Weissmuller swimming through the man-made waterfall inside the Aquacade, watch a robot smoke cigarettes in the Futurama exhibit. On Superman Day, my father had taken me to shake Superman's hand.

I did all of these things and was back by the time my mother returned from five o'clock Mass, pushing open our apartment door as if it weighed a hundred pounds. She did not ask me where I'd been all day, but I was certain she'd been praying to the chandelier for my safety.

This is what I did the next day, and the next, and every day of that summer.

Not always, but now and then, I heard something in a voice that made me follow someone. The man who stole a copy of *Life* magazine from the newsstand outside Grand Central Station, sliding it under his jacket when the vendor turned away to make change for a woman in a hat, all the while keeping up his conversation about Tiny Bonham's pitching arm. The man and the woman who exited the Eighth Avenue subway line as if they didn't know each other, waiting to come together until they were inside the pedestrian tunnel under 59th Street, the man pressing his body against the woman's, bending hers into the C shape of the wall.

But it was always people with secrets, never Nazis.

Still, I kept looking. When I ran out of money in the *My First War Bond* book, I went down to Aunt May and asked if she needed me to go to Mandelbaum's for her. Aunt May was still cooking for us, still making those horrible recipes out of *Victory Meat Extenders*—Codfish Casserole and English Monkey, which thankfully did not have any actual meat in it. If Aunt May had already been to the store, I took the change out of my mother's purse, which she left on a chair near the front door, ready for five o'clock Mass. Since my mother never went anywhere except Good Shepherd, she never seemed to notice.

. . .

I was still looking at the end of the summer, when my mother went back to her work as bookkeeper for the now-legitimate restaurants and supper clubs that belonged to her father's former customers. I don't believe she would have gone back at all, if Mr. Puccini hadn't knocked on our door every day for two weeks in August, asking about the rent.

For the first few days, she headed out wearing the black dress. Finally, Aunt May came by and said it would do everybody good if she put on something more cheerful.

"I don't feel cheerful," my mother told her.

"None of us do," Aunt May said. "But most of us are at least pretending."

The next morning when my mother left the apartment in the black dress, Aunt May was waiting for her on Dyckman Street. She took hold of my mother's black sleeve and made her look up at all the windows where blue Son in Service stars had once hung, blue stars that had more recently been replaced with gold ones.

"You're not the only widow on the block," she said, spinning my mother around on the sidewalk. "You're not even the only one in the building."

The next morning, my mother put on a brown skirt and a brown blouse. They were the color the leaves on the trees in Fort Tryon Park turn before they give up and fall to the ground at the end of autumn. Aunt May told her it was an improvement, though not much of one.

My mother said it was as much pretending as she was capable of.

She wore some version of that color every day for the rest of the week. Some version of that color for the rest of the month. My mother must have gone out and bought a small wardrobe of clothes the color of dead leaves. It was as if fall had come early to our apartment.

The Tuesday after Labor Day, Aunt May handed me five dollars and sent me to the Thom McAn on Broadway to buy new shoes for school. Buying shoes for school was something I'd always done with my father, the two of us taking our time to examine the paired-up samples in the window, standing together on the tiles that spelled out THOM MCAN while I made up my mind, going through the glass door to sit in the velvet seats joined at the arms like the seats at the Alpine movie theater. The Thom McAn shoe salesman always had a mustache and would take off my dirty sneaker with two hands, as if it was something precious, as if he were afraid of dropping it. My father knew that the metal instrument the shoe salesman used to measure my foot was called a Brannock Device. Once, even the Thom McAn shoe salesman hadn't known that.

Now I walked down Broadway by myself, stood alone on the tiled letters examining the paired shoes, sat in the joined-up chairs with no one next to me. When the shoe salesman, whose upper lip was clean-shaven, placed my baggy-socked foot on the metal plate to measure it, the words *Brannock Device* boomed so loud in my head, I couldn't hear myself say the style number.

Perhaps the shoe salesman hadn't heard me right, or perhaps I'd been too distracted thinking about how I didn't want to be standing out on Broadway with only my two feet on those THOM MCAN tiles, but the shoes the salesman brought me were the same terrible tan color as Aunt May's Victory Pudding, which was made with molasses and evaporated milk.

"These the ones?" Even the bare-lipped salesman sounded doubtful.

But by that time my throat was so closed up, I could only nod.

He slipped the shoes over my socks, and I walked around on the thick Thom McAn carpet. The shoes were stiff and rubbed against my heels.

"How do they feel?"

"Fine," I croaked.

When I got home, I left the shoes in my room, buried beneath the folded layers of tissue paper. Then I turned on the radio and tried filling my head with cowboys and flying men in capes. But I couldn't picture anything except myself sitting in the front row of a sixth-grade classroom wearing the tan-colored Thom McAns, squinting at the blackboard as a version of Miss Steinhardt chalked down facts about the Emancipation Proclamation, while finally—finally!—a Nazi spy slipped into the Automat for a piece of cream pie, or a Nazi saboteur hurried across Grand Central Station on his way to Croton to poison the water supply.

I pushed around the food Aunt May left us—Boiled Tongue with Horseradish Sauce—and then threw myself in front of the Silvertone again, radio serials unspooling from the speakers beside my head, unable to conjure up a picture of anything except me, trapped inside P.S. 52 as the Nazis I'd been searching for all summer strolled by the windows.

Around nine o'clock, somebody knocked on our door.

It was Harry Jupiter, wearing a rumpled jacket and a hat that looked as if he'd sat on it. I hadn't seen Harry Jupiter since my father's wake, since he'd stumbled around our apartment looking as if it was only his glass of rye whiskey keeping him upright.

I asked him if he wanted to come in, but he shook his jowls like he was afraid there might still be an empty coffin in our living room.

"I have something for you."

He dug around in both pockets of his rumpled jacket until he came up with a photograph.

"I'm sorry it took me so long."

He passed it over to me.

I pushed my glasses onto the top of my head and brought the photograph close to my face. It was the picture of me standing on the roof with nothing but the wide, blue sky behind me.

"I found it when I got around to printing the Silverman twins."

It had been a long time since I'd seen my entire face without glasses. Every now and then I tried to see it, standing in front of the bathroom mirror with the glasses in my hand. But to see anything clear without glasses, I had to put my face so close to the glass, I could only catch pieces of myself.

Yet here in this photograph was my whole face—without glasses.

I pushed the glasses back onto my face and looked up at Harry Jupiter. His blue eyes were watery.

"Thanks," I told him.

He nodded, and began to shuffle down the dim hallway.

"Why now?" I said to his back.

He turned.

"Why did you finally get around to printing the Silverman twins now?"

Harry Jupiter shrugged. "I came across the note from your father asking me about the darkroom. Must have been buried under the negatives on my desk."

I looked down at the photograph in my hand. The photograph delivered by Harry Jupiter, who had not been up here in all the weeks since we'd waked my father with an empty coffin. Harry Jupiter, who never came across anything buried under the negatives on his desk.

I shut the door. This photograph was a message.

My father *knew.*

Likely he'd followed me. Perhaps watched me in the cold brightness of the Automat eating a slice of coconut custard pie in small bites, or sat in the next subway car as I rode the train to Flushing, where the two of us had gone to shake Superman's hand. It would only have taken one time. One time for my father—who could read strangers, after all—to understand what I'd been doing all summer, and why.

And once I'd deciphered this part of my father's message, I knew why he'd left the note that sent Harry Jupiter up to Dyckman Street with it at the exact time he had.

I went to the kitchen and got the scissors, cut away just enough of the wide, blue sky to make the photograph fit into the little window of my code-o-graph. Then I slid out Captain Midnight's face and replaced it with my own.

The next morning, I walked out into the September wind wearing the stiff, new Thom McAns that were the color of Aunt May's Victory Pudding, and carrying my leather schoolbag as if I was on my way to P.S. 52. At the corner, I turned in the opposite direction and headed toward the subway.

Weeks went by and nobody from P.S. 52 tried to get in touch with us.

Once I ran into Mrs. Krinsky from apartment 1A, coming out of Mandelbaum's with an armful of groceries, and she asked me where I was going in such a hurry.

"School," I told her.

"Isn't it that way?" She pointed with her chin.

"I'm going to a special school. For people with bad eyes."

"You'd better hurry then," she said, clutching her bags to her chest, as if they might cover her embarrassment.

And a couple of times, I thought I spotted a very small man smoking a cigarette following me as I slipped into the subway at the corner of Broadway and Dyckman Street. But I could never trust my eyes, and he seemed very small for a man, so I figured I'd imagined him.

It's possible a call came when no one was in the apartment—or that my mother never picked up the phone—because every time it rang, she hurried away from it, as if that would prevent any bad news from finding her. And if a letter had been sent, it's possible it was lost in the mail. It was wartime after all, and there was a lot of mail. It's also possible that nobody at P.S. 52 wanted to talk to us about the reason I hadn't returned to school. Nobody wanted to come to our apartment and knock on our door and ask if it was about what had happened in the 42nd Street subway station.

As the leaves turned and the weather grew colder, I searched all five boroughs of New York City for a Nazi to bring to my father. I broke in the Thom McAns walking the stone floors of Pennsylvania Station and Grand Central, ate countless pieces of Automat coconut custard pie, and used up every one of my mother's nickels. One day I rode the subway all the way out to Coney Island and stood on the boardwalk in the salted wind staring at the gray sea, hoping to spot the periscope of a Nazi submarine. Another day I wandered Central Park in the slanted light of late autumn, crunching leaves the color of my mother's clothes, eavesdropping on every park bench conversation.

When I got discouraged, I pulled out the code-o-graph and looked at the photograph of myself in the little window.

It began to get truly cold and I spent less time on the street and in the park, and more time on the subway and in the Automat and the train stations. I followed a man in an overcoat who was following another man, a man in a suit. I followed them out of the West Fourth

Street subway station and around a corner, where the man in the overcoat punched the man in the suit, knocking him to the sidewalk, getting blood on the front of his jacket. The man in the suit did not seem surprised to have been hit by the man in the overcoat. He shook his head and wiped at the blood with a handkerchief. Another day, I followed a tall woman in a fur coat to a brownstone near Gramercy Park. While I was standing outside, debating whether to write down her address, she came back through the door, dressed as a man.

I was always right about the people I followed not being what they presented themselves to be. But I was never right about them being a Nazi spy or saboteur. And some nights, even with the code-o-graph in my hand, even staring down at that photograph, I began to believe that the war would go on forever and I would never find a Nazi for my father.

At the end of October a transit cop cornered me on the platform below Pennsylvania Station, grabbing me by the shoulders, asking me for the address of this special school for kids with glasses, saying he would take me there himself, make sure I got there okay. It took a wrenching twist to get free of his hands, and once I did, I bolted under the turnstile and ran up the steps to 33rd Street, the pounding of his heavy shoes behind me.

That night after dinner, after I knew Aunt May had left for her war job—an evening shift sewing uniforms at a converted factory down on 30th Street—I knocked on Uncle Glenn's door. When he opened it, I asked him if he would tell me how to spot a Nazi.

Uncle Glenn looked up and down the empty hallway. "Maybe we should talk about this inside."

My uncle had covered the ruffled place mats on Aunt May's kitchen table with newspapers, all opened to stories about the war. Uncle

Glenn followed the war news closely. I believed he bought nearly every newspaper sold in New York City, and read every one. He probably knew as much about the European theater as General Eisenhower.

My uncle sat me down, then took the seat across from me.

"What are you doing looking for Nazis?"

"Same as you. For the war effort."

He leaned back in his chair and smiled. "Why don't you take up something a little more harmless?"

"Just tell me."

He shook his head. I had the sense he was reading the story in front of him, a report about the bombing of Genoa.

"*You're* doing it."

"I've had Civil Defense training."

"Then tell me what they told you."

"It's not just Civil Defense, I know how Nazis think."

"Then tell me that."

My uncle's eyes were on the newspaper, full of photographs of the burning Italian city.

"I can hear what people are really saying," I told him.

Uncle Glenn glanced up.

"When they talk," I continued, "I can hear what they really mean."

"Like if they're lying?"

"Sometimes. Or if they mean something else."

My uncle shook his head. "That's not possible."

"Maybe. But I can do it."

He sat back in his chair, studied me with his pale blue eyes. "Can you show me?"

"I guess."

"Go get your jacket."

My uncle took me to Lou Brown's Pool Parlor. I had never been up to this second-floor establishment—no kid had—but I'd imagined it dozens of times. A male sanctuary of thick carpets and velvet curtains filled with billiard tables that stood on curved mahogany legs. In truth, Lou Brown's was a cavernous room with painted tin walls and a cracked linoleum floor, and the felt on the pool tables was ripped in places. The men playing moved through a layered haze of cigarette smoke like people caught in a fog.

Uncle Glenn sat me on a wooden bar stool and bought me a metallic-tasting ginger ale. Then he asked me to tell him who in the room was the biggest liar.

I squinted through the haze, tuning my ears to conversations punctuated by the hard clacking of billiard balls.

A short man who was playing with his hat squashed onto his head was predicting the outcome of his shots before he made them. *Seven into the corner pocket. Nine into the side.* His undertone said that even he didn't believe any of these were likely to happen.

A fat man in suspenders who hadn't stopped chalking the end of his cue since Uncle Glenn and I walked in was telling a story about a blond-haired waitress. I didn't entirely understand the story, but there was so much unsatisfied longing in his voice, I knew whatever he was telling the men around him had never happened.

And then there was the man I nearly missed, would have missed if the fat man in suspenders hadn't finished his story about the waitress and turned to him. Later, thinking on it, I wondered if I almost missed the man because his gray suit had blended in with the haze of cigarette smoke, or if it was something else, something more intentional.

The fat man turned, still chalking the end of his cue, and asked the man in the gray suit if he wanted to shoot some pool, and the man said, "No, but thanks anyway."

"Him." I nodded my head toward the man in the gray suit, the man I'd nearly missed.

Uncle Glenn looked over at the corner where the fat man had finally stopped chalking his cue. He was asking the man in the gray suit if he was sure about that, saying something about there still being plenty of night left.

My uncle turned back to me. "What makes you say that?"

"He really wants to play."

Uncle Glenn told me he'd been coming to Lou Brown's for a year before he'd noticed the man in the gray suit, and even after he'd started noticing him, he was never entirely sure about it. Sometimes he'd think he was seeing him, but it would only be some of the cigarette smoke clinging together.

He'd heard from someone—he couldn't recall who—that the man's name was Gary Adamson. But even the person who'd told him this wasn't certain that was true, because whoever had told him hadn't been certain of it himself. The important thing, though, was that the man in the gray suit was a pool hustler, probably the biggest one north of 125th Street.

"And that means?" I said.

"You can hear what people are really saying."

Uncle Glenn bought me another metallic-tasting ginger ale. Then he told me how to spot a Nazi. He said now that we were at war with them, they couldn't fill up trains and sing songs about Jewish blood and march all over Long Island in their shiny boots. They had to be unnoticeable, easy to miss, like the man in the gray suit.

"What you want to do is keep your eye out for somebody who's trying not to be noticed."

"I'm already doing that," I said.

My uncle shook his head. "Not the person you can see who's doing it. The person who is so good at it, it would take a year for you to notice he's there."

I looked through the haze at the man whose name might be Gary

Adamson. A gray suit moving through the cigarette smoke as if he was part of it.

"One thing," my uncle said.

I turned back to him.

"If you find this Nazi, you'll let me know?"

I nodded. Because who could tell if Uncle Glenn read voices.

My uncle asked me if I wanted another of the metallic-tasting ginger ales, and when I said no, he took me home.

The next day I found my Nazi.

Nine

I found him on the BMT line coming back from Brighton. He was sitting near the end of the subway car, and if I hadn't been looking for someone entirely unnoticeable, someone practiced at reining in his own energy to prevent it from disturbing the air around him, I would have missed him altogether.

He was wearing heavy shoes with reinforced toes, the kind of shoes you wore if you worked in a factory—the kind of shoes my father had worn when he worked at the Navy Yard—and a brown jacket that zipped up the front. He was younger than my father, probably the same age as Uncle Glenn, though the shadows that circled his eyes made him seem older. His hair was black and straight and too long. It fell over his forehead and caught in his eyes when he blinked. But what I noticed most about him was his hands. Inside all the creases, in the places where my father's hands were white, his were filled with black, as if all the evil he'd done—all the evil he was planning—had come to rest there.

At the stop for Greenwood Cemetery, a woman in a fur jacket got on the train. She peered out the window, though there was nothing to see by then except the dark tunnel, then she turned and asked the Nazi if this train went to Union Square.

I don't believe the woman would have spoken to the Nazi—don't think she would have even noticed him—if he and I had not been the only two people at this end of the subway car.

The Nazi nodded and the woman in the fur jacket sat across from him. Then she asked him what he thought about Wendell Willkie's harebrained scheme to fly around the globe while the world was at war. The Nazi replied that Mr. Willkie must have his reasons.

It wasn't much of an answer, but it was enough for me to hear his voice, which was unlike any I'd heard before.

Most people's undertones sound as if they are hiding one, maybe two things. But the Nazi's sounded as if he was hiding everything. As if every word that came out of his mouth had to be inspected, checked for the correct size and shape before it could be sent out into the world, as if he believed he was talking to an audience rather than only one person.

It reminded me of a radio announcer's voice, the way he might tell you to be sure to tune in next week for another exciting episode of *The Green Hornet*, or make certain not to forget to fill up your car with Skelly Oil. But on the radio, talking like this—like you'd rehearsed every syllable—sounded natural. In the real world, it made everything that came out of the Nazi's mouth sound like a lie.

The woman in the fur jacket said a few more things to the Nazi about Wendell Willkie's harebrained scheme, but the Nazi didn't say anything back that a conversation could stick to, and eventually she drifted into staring at the advertisements above his head, and I'm certain forgot he was there.

But I didn't. I couldn't stop thinking how after all these weeks of searching, I was now sitting one empty seat away from a Nazi. And I could not take my eyes off his hands, his hands that were the opposite of my father's, the reverse of them, like a negative.

When the Nazi got off the train, I followed him, up out of the subway and onto the corner of Essex Street and Delancey. This was the

Lower East Side, a neighborhood five times more crowded than Hell's Kitchen.

For several panicked seconds I lost him in the confusion of so many people popping into and out of focus—scrawny dark-haired kids waving copies of *The Forward*, men in calf-length black coats hurrying past, their side curls trailing behind in the wind, women in thick stockings who dragged two-wheeled carts filled with groceries dangerously close to the toes of my tan Thom McAns. By the time I spotted the back of the Nazi's brown jacket, it was already heading up Essex Street.

I ran after him, pushed my way up a sidewalk that was crowded with people, as if the narrow-fronted tenements had overfilled, and then spewed their tenants out onto the streets, streets that smelled of pickles and horse manure and garbage. I was sure I would lose him in this crush of horse wagons and aproned vendors and soldiers, lose him in the sheer mass of people.

I didn't see that all the men in black coats, all the women with carts, all the scrawny kids, everyone—including the Nazi—had halted at the corner of Rivington Street for the traffic, until I was within a foot of the brown jacket. I skidded to a halt, the rubber soles of the Thom McAns squealing against the sidewalk.

The Nazi turned and stared at me.

His eyes were of no definite color. They shifted in the slanted light of this late October afternoon from blue to green to gray and back again, as if everything about them was a lie as well. I had the uncomfortable sense he was trying to look inside my head, that he might be trying to figure out how I worked.

I forced myself to hold his gaze, my eyes watering behind my glasses. A cold wind blew across Rivington Street.

The people around us began to move. The Nazi turned away and hurried across the street.

I followed him up Essex and across Stanton to Ludlow Street. At a brick tenement a quarter of the way up the block, he stopped and looked back down the street. I stepped behind a vendor's pushcart and watched him from between the bolts of cloth. After a moment, the Nazi turned, then climbed a metal staircase to the front door.

I could have stopped there, could have written down the address—165 Ludlow—and put it in a message to my father. But I wanted to know which apartment was his, which set of grimy-looking windows belonged to the man who had evil living in the creases of his hands.

It was dark in the Nazi's hallway, and smelled like decades of other people's cooking—chicken soup and long-boiled cabbage—smelled also of the outhouse I spied through the half-open door at the end of the hallway. A woman bumped a grocery cart down the stairs, two girls came laughing past me as if I wasn't there, a pack of screaming boys clattered down the steps, while a man in an undershirt leaned over the banister shouting at them in Yiddish. And over all of it, I heard the heavy factory shoes of the Nazi climbing the tenement steps.

I kept thinking the Nazi would stop on one of the floors, but I followed his footsteps all the way to the final set of stairs—a narrow, wooden set that led to the roof. I crouched on the top one, pushing open the roof door an inch or two, enough to see the black tar of the Nazi's roof and the gray sky. Cold air blew in, and with it the sound of traffic on Houston Street and somebody on the sidewalk shouting about whitefish, and also something closer and quieter. Something that sounded like the cooing of babies, as if the Nazi had an entire roomful of them trapped up here.

I pushed the door open and squeezed through it. I still couldn't see the Nazi, only someone's laundry flapping around in the wind. Staying low, I crept around the door frame—a six-foot-high box with a slanted back, just something so somebody could stand while walking up the stairs—bits of gravel sticking to my palms.

The Nazi was standing not more than ten feet away from me. I could see the back of his brown jacket, his too-long black hair hanging over the collar. In front of him, propped up on wooden legs, was a coop filled with fluttering pigeons.

It felt as if those pale gray wings were fluttering against the inside of my chest. My ears filled up with the sound of Uncle Glenn's voice, telling me the story about his father and his pigeons. Telling me how he would take the birds out of their coop and let them walk across the aluminum surface of his Cauet hand, talk to them in the soft German Uncle Glenn never heard.

Especially how he would talk to them in the soft German Uncle Glenn never heard, because beneath the humming of the traffic on Houston Street and the shouting about whitefish, I could hear the Nazi talking to his pigeons. Talking to them in German. Leaning his dark head toward the chicken wire at the front of their coop and speaking sentence after sentence in the language of the enemy. And all the lies that had been lurking in the Nazi's undertone when he'd been talking to the woman in the fur jacket about Wendell Willkie's harebrained scheme, all the lies that had been there when he'd been speaking English, had vanished.

I stayed crouched behind the door frame with somebody's laundry flapping behind me and watched the Nazi feed his pigeons, watched him take a burlap bag of seed from some wooden shelves he'd knocked together and dump it into the side of the coop, all the while talking to the pale gray birds in the enemy's language, telling them the secrets he kept hidden when he spoke in English. When he was finished, the Nazi set the bag of seed back onto the shelf and stood looking up into the gray sky. Searching for what? A Messerschmidt? Rain?

Then he turned and began to walk toward me.

He was moving fast, and I didn't have time to slip back inside. I ducked around the side of the door frame—that six-foot-high box with the slanted back, that small thing that was only enough for someone to stand up in while walking up the stairs. The Nazi's heavy factory shoes came crunching across the gravel of the roof toward me, and all I could do was keep backing up in time with them, praying the Thom McAns wouldn't make any sound as I slid them over the same gravel.

When he was close, within an arm's reach, the footsteps stopped. I heard him breathing, the air going into and out of his lungs. He was so close, I smelled him, a scent that was acrid and oily. The smell of evil. I held my breath, as much so he wouldn't hear me, as so I wouldn't take in any more.

The door opened. The heavy factory shoes landed on the steps. Then the door slammed shut behind him.

I waited until I heard the Nazi's footsteps reach the bottom of the stairs before I put my hand on the door. The instant I heard him get to the end of the hallway, I ran after him.

I followed the Nazi back through the dim building, keeping one floor above him. When he stopped on the third floor, I waited on the fourth, trying not to be noticed by the people going into and out of their apartments, the people who had no idea they were living with a Nazi. I listened for the sound of a key going into a lock, a bolt turning, a door swinging open. I stood at the top of the stairs as long as I could make myself, then rushed down just in time to see the door to apartment 3D swinging shut.

Again, I could have stopped here. I had everything I needed to put in the message to my father.

But instead I crept down the hallway, pressed my ear against the Nazi's door, a door that was thick with brown paint, as if it had been painted a thousand times.

I do not know what I expected to hear through those layers of paint. I do know I did not expect to hear what I did. Voices. Familiar ones.

The Nazi was listening to *Superman*.

I wanted to pound my fist against the thick paint of the door, make the Nazi turn off his radio, make him vow never to listen to *Superman*—or any other radio serial—again. And who knows? Perhaps I would have done just that if I hadn't heard another voice—softer, like an undertone beneath the voices of *Superman*.

It was the Nazi's voice.

The Nazi is using Superman to cover up some conversation he's having with another Nazi, I thought. *He's using Superman to help Hitler win the war.*

And that was when I finally went to write the message to my father.

The message I sent said

OKUNU YL G RGQY GO 4 20 19 SEBSTP LONUUO GPO 16B

which meant

THERE IS A NAZI AT 1 6 5 LUDLOW STREET APT 3D.

I put it in our mailbox that night, and the next morning it was gone, replaced by a new message that read

GNU ITE LENU

which meant

ARE YOU SURE.

I sat on my bed and tallied the evidence—the lies in the Nazi's undertone, the pigeons, the German on the roof, the soft voice under

Superman. I also counted the black in the creases of the Nazi's hands, the creases that made them the opposite of my father's, though I supposed not everyone would.

I took out a piece of composition paper and began to put the word

YES

into code.

Then I stopped. What if my father went to 165 Ludlow Street and took a photograph of the man in apartment 3D, and he turned out only to be a person with a secret? If that happened, I could find a hundred, a thousand, an entire train full of Nazis, and my father wouldn't trust me enough to turn up at any of their apartments with his Speed Graphic.

I set aside the piece of composition paper I'd just taken out. Then I put this new message from my father—the one asking me if I was sure—with the others under my shirt, and went back to Ludlow Street.

For a while, I leaned against the glass of Moroshevsky's Kosher Meats across from the Nazi's tenement, staring up at the windows I was pretty sure were his, trying to tell if he was home. But the Nazi kept his blackout shades pulled all the way down, even in the daytime, and after half an hour, a man in a bloody apron came out of the butcher shop and told me to find someplace else to lounge around.

I took that as a sign to go inside the Nazi's building.

I checked the Nazi's mailbox to see if he had any mail or secret messages. It was empty. Taped to its door was a piece of paper with the name *Armstrong* written on it. I didn't believe this was the Nazi's real name. I was positive he'd stolen it from the radio, taken it from *Jack Armstrong the All-American Boy*, thinking he could hide behind it the way he was hiding behind *Superman*.

I tested the edge of the tape with my fingernail. When it came up,

I peeled the name off the door, rolling it into a little ball, and shoved it into my pocket.

I went up to the third floor and listened at the Nazi's door. All I could hear was the air moving around inside my own ear. *If I owned the kind of gun the Green Hornet did,* I thought, *the kind that could blow the locks off doors, I could break into the Nazi's apartment and find out what he was up to. Find out if he had any of the incendiary devices pictured on Uncle Glenn's Civil Defense pamphlets.*

A couple of men with bushy beards and velvet yarmulkes that were much fancier than the one Moon Shapiro wore came out of 3B, arguing about the Yankees. I didn't want to look suspicious, so pulled myself away from the Nazi's door and headed for the roof.

No one was up there. Only the Nazi's pigeons, fluttering around inside their coop.

I walked toward them, the gravel crunching under my shoes. It was a clear, bright day, the sky over my head open and blue. One of those rare fall days when wind blows so hard, the air in New York is as fresh as the air on the top of a mountain. As I approached the coop, the birds inside began to make that sound like a room full of babies, perhaps believing I was going to feed them. They flapped their wings and shrugged their shoulders as if putting on coats.

I turned from the pigeons and studied the knocked-together shelves where the Nazi kept bags of feed, certain the proof I needed was here among the rolls of chicken wire and glass jars filled with nails. I rummaged through the half-empty bags, rolls of knotted twine, and broken pliers until I found a Garcia y Vega cigar box.

I slid the cigar box out of the shelf and opened it. A few long, thin strips of paper flew across the roof.

I ducked down behind the shelves out of the wind, sat on the tar paper with my back against one of the wooden coop legs. I opened the box again. It was filled with those narrow strips of paper, all of them blank. I dug my fingers through them, and at the bottom of the box found two small metal canisters with tiny clips. The perfect size to fit around a pigeon's sticklike leg.

I searched through the box again, that feeling of birds' wings fluttering against the inside of my chest. All I needed was one message with words on it. Just one. My fingers brushed something at the bottom of the box. Something familiar.

I lifted it through the tangled pieces of paper. But I didn't need to see it to know what it was. My fingers spent all day reading its circle of raised letters like a kind of Braille, deciphering them in the darkness of my pocket the way I had my father's film.

I opened my hand in the clear light of that rare fall day. I was holding a Captain Midnight Code-O-Graph.

Which could not be possible.

Because why would a Nazi use a Captain Midnight Code-O-Graph for his secret messages? Why would he use something anyone with ten cents and the lids from two jars of Ovaltine could get from the radio?

Perhaps because nobody would believe it.

A waterfall of birdseed rained through the chicken wire into my lap. I looked closer at the Nazi's code-o-graph. There was a photograph in the little window. I pushed my glasses onto the top of my head and brought the device closer to my face.

It was of a woman. She had dark eyes and dark hair, and she wasn't smiling, though she didn't look sad or angry. She only looked as if she believed being photographed was something you should take seriously. She reminded me of my mother. It wasn't so much a physical resemblance, it was more the way the woman in the Nazi's code-o-graph was looking at the camera. Or perhaps the way she was looking at the person holding the camera.

It was how the light reflected back from her eyes, what it seemed her mouth was about to do next. It recalled my mother's expression when she would add up those numbers for my father, sliding the tip of that No. 2 pencil into and out of the gap between her teeth.

I'd always had a hunch that adding up those numbers only took a part of my mother's attention. And now, on the Nazi's roof, I had the feeling that the rest of it had been on my father, and that she had only agreed to add up those numbers so that he would watch her.

It was this, the way the woman in the photograph was looking at the person holding the camera, how her expression so recalled my mother's, that made me believe the Nazi had stolen the photograph of the woman, the way he'd stolen Jack Armstrong's name and the voices from *Superman*.

I closed my fingers around the Nazi's code-o-graph and put it in my pocket. Then I got to my feet and slid the Garcia y Vega box back onto the shelf.

The pigeons were eyeing me from the sides of their heads.

Nazi pigeons.

I flattened my hands on the chicken wire. It was sharp and cold. The gray birds behind it flapped their wings, sending stray feathers into the wind.

I imagined myself doing what Uncle Glenn had done, imagined the feel of a feathery neck snapping in my hands.

My hands seemed small on the chicken wire. And there were so many pigeons inside the coop.

I took my hands off the wire, rubbed them on my pants to warm them.

The latch on the door was a simple hook and eye, the kind of thing people use on a screen porch. I flipped it open, then I swung the door to the coop wide.

The birds tilted their heads to look at the sky.

I hit the side of the coop with the flat of my hand.

"Go!" I shouted.

Two pale gray birds flew out.

"Go! Go!" I banged again on the side of the coop.

Two more pigeons came swooping out.

"Auf wiedersehen!" I shouted in the only German I knew besides *Heil Hitler.*

As if to prove they were indeed Nazi pigeons, the rest of the birds came soaring out of the coop, the entire flock swirling above my head, two dozen or more gray birds following each other into the clear blue sky, leaving behind only a scattering of airy feathers that circled in the air before settling onto the black tar of the roof.

I shut and latched the door behind them.

As I ran down the stairs and out of the Nazi's tenement, I was already thinking about how I would translate

YES I AM SURE

into

IUL Y GX LENU.

How I would do it the moment, the second, the instant I got home.

But when the subway doors sighed open at Dyckman Street, I stayed in my seat.

The strips of paper. The metal canisters. The code-o-graph. Were they enough? If I was wrong, I wouldn't see my father until the war was over. And it seemed like the war was never going to be over.

I rode the subway all afternoon, taking the train to the end of the line, then crossing the platform and taking it back, all the while adding up the evidence in my head, as if I had inherited my mother's ability for calculation.

Pigeons. German. Black creases.

Paper. Canisters. Code-o-graph.

Then I remembered Uncle Glenn dressed in black to spy on the neighbors. Dressed in black because if they were going to do anything suspicious, they were going to do it at night.

By eleven o'clock, I was back in front of Moroshevsky's Kosher Meats, my eyes on the front door of the Nazi's tenement.

Ten

I'd planned to arrive in front of Moroshevsky's sooner, intended to eat whatever cereal and meat combination Aunt May made us from *Victory Meat Extenders*, then slip out the second my mother's breath reached the deepest part of her chest. But when my mother returned from five o'clock Mass that night, she went into the kitchen and began cooking.

My mother had not cooked anything since July, not since the day the transit cop brought me home from the 42nd Street subway station. I lay on the linoleum in front of the Silvertone, waiting for her to go into her bedroom and stare at the ceiling until she fell asleep the way she had every night, while instead, she filled the apartment with the smell of meat browning. And when I sat up and pushed my glasses back onto my nose, I saw that she was standing in front of the stove with the piece of lace she wore to Mass still bobby-pinned to the top of her head, stirring something in a pot.

My mother only cooked meals that could be made in one pot. A habit left over from her days cooking in her father's warehouse on Tenth Avenue, when their stove had been a single kerosene burner. Back then, my mother had gotten all of her groceries from the market under the Ninth Avenue El—turnips, parsnips, potatoes, small bags of spices from the Italian and Jewish pushcart vendors. She'd simmer everything with bits of ground pork or chicken parts until it turned into a velvety stew. My mother improvised these combinations, and according to her, some of them were so horrible, even the Hell's Kitchen dogs, legendary for eating anything—the dead, bloated bodies of cats, for example—wouldn't touch the remains of her discarded pots. But occasionally the stars aligned and some of her stews were miraculous. But my mother was never able to repeat any of these star-struck dishes, claiming that writing down recipes gave her headaches.

When the apartment was full of the smell of cooking—a smell unlike my Aunt May's *Victory Meat Extenders* meals, which always smelled of grains, a smell I'd begun to associate with the fight against Fascism—my mother called me into the kitchen. I sat down and she placed a bowl of something meaty and brown in front of me.

Then she served herself and sat across from me.

Most nights if she ate at all, my mother ate the meal Aunt May left us standing at the sink, holding the plate near her mouth, a cigarette caught between the fingers of her hand. The last time my mother had sat at the red table and had dinner with me there had been three of us.

"How is it?" she said.

The stew my mother made that night was one of her best, one of the ones where the planets and stars had lined up perfectly. She'd put steak in it—probably used up all our ration coupons—and after Aunt May's meat loaf bulked up with mashed potatoes and hamburgers made of ground beef and corn flakes, it was like biting into a cow. The gravy was thick and brown and smoky, and the spices were sweet and savory at the same time. But for all that, I could barely choke down the miraculous stew.

For beneath all its meaty, spicy richness, the stew had an undertone, and it was as complex as the combination of flavors swirling inside my mouth. It tasted too much of trying, of my mother having carefully placed each ingredient into the pot, which was something she had never done before, instead of tossing in herbs by the handful, throwing in spices with a kind of intuition. The stew tasted also of the brown clothes and the piece of lace on her head, of the fact that she'd just come from the front row of Good Shepherd, which made me think too much of how she'd looked at my father's messages, as if his magnetism was nowhere on them. And spicing all of it was the taste of how long I'd waited for her to begin cooking again, how long I'd waited for her to come out of her room, and how now that she had, I only wanted her to go back into it and fall asleep.

"It's fine," I told her.

"Do you want more?"

"No. No, thanks."

I pushed away from the table and went to my room, chose my spying clothes carefully. The black Mass pants to blend in with the dark and a heavy wool sweater with a reindeer knitted into the front that Aunt May had given me last Christmas, the warmest thing I owned. I put on a dark wool cap, pulling it to the frame of my glasses to hide as much of my pale forehead as possible.

In case the Nazi caught me—something I didn't want to think about—I left his code-o-graph and my father's messages in my bedroom. Without the paper messages up against my skin, the T-shirt I'd put on under the reindeer sweater to keep it from itching felt almost too soft. Before leaving my room, I slipped my own code-o-graph with the picture my father had taken of me into my pocket.

I wonder now at how sure I was that the Nazi would step out of that tenement door. How sure I was that he hadn't already gone to bed behind those blackout shades, or already left for whatever terrible purpose he intended. I can only put it down to those weeks in front of the Silvertone's big speakers, the weeks in which my life was made up of programs in which the Shadow or the Lone Ranger waited in a dark alley or behind a boulder for the saboteur or the cattle rustler to turn up—and he always did. This was what those weeks of living inside the radio world had taught me, and I wouldn't have believed you if you'd told me the real world worked otherwise.

It was especially dark on the Lower East Side. Half the streetlamps were dark, and whether they were broken or it was intentional, I didn't know. No one left their blackout shades up, and no one had left on an outside light. It was as if the people who lived down here were more afraid of the Germans. The figures passing me on the sidewalk were nothing but footsteps and shadows.

Moroshevsky's doorway was a couple of steps below the sidewalk and I huddled there, out of the way of a chill wind that was full of ice and the smell of the East River. I imagined my father doing the same thing, waiting in a doorway for a Nazi to show his face, and I sent my mind across the dark streets to find him, as if he and I were radio waves on a channel that was always open. I felt a shiver, as though we'd connected, but it might have been the cold.

I don't know how long I stood in Moroshevsky's doorway watching the Nazi's tenement. Long enough for my fingers, curled inside the sleeves of the sweater because I'd forgotten gloves, to start aching from the cold. Long enough for my feet to turn numb through the thick soles of the Thom McAns. But not long enough to doubt that the tenement door would eventually open and a shadowy figure would step out, that I would hear those heavy factory shoes coming down the metal staircase.

I knew it was him from across the street. The sound of his footfalls recognizable now. The way that even his shadowy self held its energy in check. When he reached the sidewalk, turned and began walking, I slipped up the steps and followed him.

He led me to the Canal Street subway station, where even in the middle of the night there were people waiting for the train. People who worked the graveyard shift, like my father had done—men whose overall pant legs poked out from beneath their winter coats, women who'd wound turbans around their hair to keep it out of the machinery. Turbans that made them look as if they could grant you any wish.

I hid near the turnstiles, peering around the corner at the Nazi, waiting for the train in the harsh light of the station. He wore heavy denim pants and his brown jacket, and around his neck he'd wrapped a brown scarf. He would have been easy to miss, standing so still on the platform.

A Brooklyn-bound train came screeching into the station. The men in overalls and the women in turbans moved toward the open doors, none of them noticing the Nazi in their midst. These people appeared as if they'd only just woken up, which perhaps they had, with the remnants of dreams playing behind their eyes. Still, I don't think they'd have noticed the Nazi if they'd been wide awake. He took up so little space, it was hard for me to keep focused on him.

I waited until the Nazi got on the train, and then I dashed for the car behind his, ducking under the turnstile and sprinting for the door. It began to close when I was halfway across the platform. I leaped the last couple of feet, feeling the edges of the door move across the back of my sweater like it was brushing off leaves.

"Nice timing, kid," said a man over his copy of the *Mirror*.

I nodded at him and went to sit at the end of the car.

It took me until almost the next station before I spotted the Nazi through the scratched-up windows between my subway car and his. He was sitting in the middle of the car with his hands in his lap.

The factory shoes, the heavy denim pants made me think the Nazi would get off at the stop for the Brooklyn Navy Yard. It was a good place for a Nazi to work. He could spend all day loosening bolts on battleships, then come home and talk about what was being loaded onto them on the shortwave radio while *Superman* played.

I counted the stops as we moved through Manhattan, and then

under the East River. When the train pulled into the station for the Navy Yard—the station that had been my father's—everyone in the Nazi's car stood. I tensed, ready to follow him out.

But the Nazi stayed in his seat.

The doors opened and the people in the Nazi's car—the men in overalls, the women in turbans—filed out. Then a new batch streamed through the doors, people who had finished their shifts, people on their way home to Bay Ridge and Bensonhurst. I kept my eye on the Nazi, sitting with his hands in his lap, wondering if he'd spotted me, if he was waiting until the last second to bolt, to run for the open door.

But the doors closed, and the Nazi was still sitting there.

The train jolted, and we began traveling deeper into Brooklyn.

Pacific Street.

Union Street.

Prospect Avenue.

At each stop, the people who'd gotten on near the Navy Yard stood, yawned, and got off the train.

By 45th Street, I was alone in my car, and the Nazi was alone in his, except for a skinny old man sitting across from him. The old man had fallen asleep two stops back, his head resting on a *Buy War Bonds* poster of a soldier about to throw a grenade. The old man had gotten on at the Navy Yard. A metal lunch pail sat in his lap and beneath his unbuttoned overcoat he was wearing overalls.

We were deep in the tunnel between stations when the Nazi stood and began to walk across the car toward the old man. I leaned forward to get a better angle. *What was the Nazi after? Something in the lunch pail? In the old man's pockets?* Then I noticed it, clipped to the front pocket of the old man's overalls, hanging there on his skinny chest. I didn't need the windows to be any clearer to make out what it was, didn't need to be any closer to recognize it. My father had had one just like it.

A Brooklyn Navy Yard war factory worker's badge.

It would have the old man's name on it, but the Nazi had already stolen the name of Jack Armstrong the All-American Boy. It would also have the old man's photograph, but anyone who would steal a woman's picture to put in his code-o-graph could probably figure out a way around that, too.

But you couldn't turn up at the Brooklyn Navy Yard wearing the badge of somebody who also might show up there. You would have to do something to keep that from happening.

The Nazi took another step toward the old man and raised his hand, his hand that had black in the creases, black from all the evil he'd done. He was reaching for the old man's neck, a skinny neck left exposed by the way the old man's head was resting on the *Buy War Bonds* poster.

I got to my feet and pressed my palms against the scratched-up windows of the subway car door.

The train rounded a curve, and the Nazi steadied himself.

I thought about banging my fists on the scratched-up glass and stopping the Nazi from doing what I was certain he was going to do—wrap his black-creased hands around that skinny neck and squeeze it until the old man was dead. But then I thought—and I remember this clearly—that if I don't bang my fists on the glass, and the Nazi does squeeze that skinny neck, if the Nazi takes that war factory badge, I could go home right now and leave my father a message that says

YES IM SURE.

And while I was hesitating, while I was feeling that scratched-up glass under my palms, the train slowed beneath my feet.

The Nazi's hand moved toward the old man's neck, and then past it, falling onto his shoulder and giving it a shake. The old man jerked his head, suddenly awake. The Nazi pointed past his ear at the signs for 59th Street, moving past the windows as we pulled into the station.

The train stopped. The skinny old man grabbed the handle of his lunch pail and stood, rubbing at his face. He gave the Nazi a small salute and walked off the train.

The Nazi turned and went back to his seat.

I sat back in mine.

The doors closed and the train began moving. We made a hard left turn onto the tracks for the Sea Beach Line.

The Nazi and I were going to Coney Island.

The Nazi and I rode the subway all the way to the end of the line. When the train stopped on the elevated platform, I followed him off, stepping into what seemed like another world, a world where everyone else had disappeared, and it was very cold, and very, very dark.

We were near the ocean, and because of the threat of German U-boats floating beneath the black waves, no lights were left on at Coney Island. I moved through the blackness, listening for the sound of the Nazi's factory shoes on the pavement, like following footsteps on the radio, my hands splayed in front of my face to keep myself from walking into anything. There was no one on the streets, no one driving on the road. There was only the Nazi's footfalls and the sound of the waves breaking on the beach, like endless card-shuffling.

I was surprised by how fast the Nazi could move in the dark, certain he'd come out here before. A gust of wind blew in from the ocean, full of salt that bit at my cheeks. It rattled something ahead, something that sounded like ice knocking together in hundreds of glasses, as if a horde of Nazis were ahead in the darkness sipping on cold drinks. I squinted into the black night and saw bits of light, glinting. As I came closer, they turned into a glittering wall of ice illuminated by the downward-casting bulb of a single lamp.

Another salty gust of wind blew in, and the glittering wall shook, sounding once again like ice in the drinks of a hundred Nazis. I squinted. It was not ice, but a chain-link fence catching light in the cold, clear night.

The Nazi continued toward the fence, not breaking stride, as if he believed he had the power to walk straight through it. At the last second the fence slid back only enough for him to pass through, and the instant he did, it slammed shut behind him. He raised his arm in what at first I thought was the Nazi salute, but was only a wave. I looked back at the fence, and only then noticed the small building—no more than a box—near where the Nazi had entered. A man's head was outlined in its dimly lit window.

The Nazi disappeared into the darkness beyond the fence.

But I knew these fences—some version of them were around every playground and schoolyard in New York City. Staying away from that small building and the man inside, I crept up to the fence, ran my hands along its icy diamonds. After a few feet, I found what I was looking for, the place where the sections of fence joined together, the narrow gap between the metal pipes.

I squeezed an arm and a leg through, but got stuck on the reindeer sweater. I didn't know how far ahead of me the Nazi was. *Far*, I thought. I slipped back through the fence and yanked off the sweater. Cold air blew through my T-shirt, but without the sweater, I fit easily through the fence. It wasn't until I was through and running in the dark that it occurred to me that I could have held the reindeer sweater in my hand.

I ran blindly into blackness. And then I wasn't running anymore. I was on the ground, tripped up by something colder than the air, something that was hard beneath my hands. Train tracks, crisscrossing the pavement in every direction.

I sat up and listened. The heavy footsteps of the Nazi were gone, but I heard buzzing, as if there were hives of bees somewhere out in the darkness. I got to my feet and ran toward the sound, feeling the tracks merge and split beneath the soles of my shoes.

The buzzing led me to a hulking building. The sound was deafening, even through its walls, even with its big sliding doors pulled closed. There was no light anywhere. If the building had windows, they'd been painted over. I moved along its side, looking for a way in. Turning a corner, I saw a narrow rectangle of light hitting the pavement. One of the wide doors hadn't been pulled all the way shut.

I crept closer to it. Here the buzzing was joined by loud clanging—metal against metal—and a low electrical humming that made me jittery. *This was a factory. A Nazi factory building things for Hitler right next to where the rest of New York came to ride the Cyclone and splash around in the ocean.*

I slipped through the opening in the door.

In the air before me hung a floating subway car.

Its metal wheels hovered above the floor at the height of my head, and shining out of the car's undercarriage was a blindingly bright white light. A light so powerful it had carved a deep hole into the cement floor beneath the car in its own shape. There was a man—a Nazi—moving around inside that hole. He wore a hard hat and had goggles over his eyes, and he knew some trick that let him stand in that powerful white light and not be harmed.

I pressed myself against the wall where the shadows were thickest and looked about the cavernous room. There were at least a dozen of these floating subway cars hovering in the air, all of them shooting out blinding white light, all of them with a Nazi who knew the trick of staying unharmed in it moving around beneath its undercarriage.

I was in 1942, at the very end of the age when it was possible for me to enter a place like this and imagine I'd entered a world that belonged more in a comic book than at the southernmost tip of Brooklyn. But as I say, I was at the very end of that age, and as I stood with my back pressed against the wall of that room, I began to notice that the wheels of all those subway cars were resting on raised tracks, and that all that blinding white light was more probably shining up into their undercarriages rather than down from them. And not long after those two realizations slid into my brain, I remembered my father telling me about the Coney Island Yards, the true end of the line for broken subway cars.

But in 1942, I was still young enough—and had lost enough—that the real world didn't possess a fair chance of impressing itself on me. And once I understood where I was, I also understood what the Nazi was doing there. He had come to sabotage the New York subway system. And all I had to do was catch him at it.

The islands of white light around the floating subway cars were the only light in the big room. The rest was in shadow. I pushed myself off the wall, heading toward the nearest raised-up car. One of these men in the hard hats and goggles was my Nazi; I would skirt the light and find him.

My feet tangled in a snarl of wire and I fell to my knees. But with the buzzing and the clanging and that electrical hum I was coming to believe was the vibration of my own nerve endings, even I didn't hear the fall. I got back up and moved closer to the white light.

A hand clamped over my mouth.

I knew this hand, recognized its scent—acrid and oily—from the roof on Ludlow Street. I could picture it as perfectly as if I was examining it beneath all that bright white light, black in the places where my father's hand was white, black in the creases where the ghosts of my father's photographs lived. But who could say what lived in the creases of the Nazi's hand?

I threw my body from side to side trying to get free; an arm wrapped itself around my chest like a snake. Then I was being dragged backward.

I dug my heels into the floor, but the cement was smooth and the soles of my shoes slid as if I was being pulled over ice. I yanked at the arm locked across my chest, but it might as well have been made out of iron. The Nazi dragged me until there was no more floor under my feet, until I was falling into one of the deep holes under the floating subway cars, this one dark and unlit. This one empty except for me and the Nazi, his hand on my mouth, his arm across my chest, and the bulk of him pressed against my back.

"I will take my hand away," he said, in that voice that made everything sound like a lie. "If you do not yell."

I nodded beneath his oily-smelling hand. It was so loud in this room, there was no point in yelling.

His hand left my mouth, and I backed away from him.

It was dark under the subway car, and my eyes weren't good in the dark. The Nazi was all shadows, like a person made out of smoke.

"You," he said, "from Rivington Street."

I shook my head, thinking if he believed I was only some kid who had wandered in, he might let me go.

"Why are you following me?"

In his undertone, working its way up between the lies, I heard fear, and that made me less afraid.

"I know what you are," I told him.

I saw him startle in the darkness.

"And what is that?"

"A Nazi."

He unwound the scarf from around his neck and sighed.

"One thing I am not is a Nazi," he told me.

I moved away, pressed my back against the cold cement wall.

"Why should I believe you?" I said.

"To begin, I am a Jew."

"Prove it."

From out of the darkness, I heard him laugh. Though if laughter had an undertone, his would be saying there was nothing here that was funny.

The Nazi shook his head. "Never before have I been asked to prove that I *was* a Jew."

"I'm asking you to prove it."

"Why?"

"I need you to."

"You have heard of the ship the *St. Louis*?" he said.

"The ship of Jewish refugees?"

From the still way his shadowy figure was standing, the Nazi must have been staring at me.

"I was one of them."

"That's impossible," I said.

"But it is true."

Over the years I have wondered why Jakob—for that was his name, at least all the name I ever learned—told me this. Why he told me any of what he said that night. For once he realized I knew nothing about him, he could have lifted me out from under that subway car and gotten somebody, perhaps another transit cop, to take me home without ever telling me any of the information it was so dangerous for other people to know. My only guess is that he needed to tell the story. That he had kept it inside for too long, and that I—a twelve-year-old boy out in the middle of the night on a mission of his own imagination—seemed the safest place to put it.

"Sit," he told me. "Because if I am going to tell you how I got onto the *St. Louis*, how I got here, I am going to have to tell you about Rebecca."

Eleven

JAKOB

That she had a bad heart was the first thing Rebecca told me about herself. This was on a warm afternoon of thunderstorms, after the two of us had waited for the hour Jews were allowed on the Friedrichstrasse underground. You, I think, are too young to know this, but most love stories begin in the rain. There is something about sunshine that makes people believe they can stand better being alone.

My clothes were soaked from waiting outside. Still I sat next to her and stared at her dark hair. Later, she said to me that she was making bets with herself on the number of stops we would make before I said something to her. But in the end, it was she who spoke first. That day, I thought it was because Rebecca had no patience. Later, I knew it was because she had no time.

"What do you suppose they did with the Romani?" she said.

"The Romani?"

"The gypsies. Have you noticed the way they have all vanished?"

I thought about how I had not seen the women who wore always three or four dirty skirts, one atop the other, begging for coins outside the cafe on Wassertorplatz the past few mornings.

"Where do you think they have gone?" I asked her.

"Somewhere they will not embarrass the Führer," she replied.

This was August of 1936, a week before the world would arrive in Berlin for the Olympic Games, and of course the Führer would not wish to be embarrassed.

As the train approached the station at Unter den Linden, Rebecca stood. "This stop is mine."

I got to my feet. "Mine as well," I said.

Rebecca smiled, and I am certain she knew that Unter den Linden was not my stop. For a reason I cannot tell you, I am certain she knew I rode the Friedrichstrasse underground all the way to Hallesches Tor.

We came out of the station into torrential rain. Rebecca is the first and only woman I ever knew who walked straight into rain. Let it fall on her like something natural. The two of us stood together looking across the wide avenue of Unter den Linden at a row of stunted lime trees, the rain soaking Rebecca's hair like it was trying to turn it blacker, which would have been impossible.

"I loved those trees." She said this more to herself than to me. "The old limes."

The trees, which had been planted by Friedrich Wilhelm in the sixteenth century, had been chopped under Hitler's orders, because they blocked his view of the Nazi soldiers marching toward the Brandenburg Gate.

Rebecca turned her face up into the pouring rain. "Hitler is a swine," she said.

I, too, had loved those big old trees. And I also thought that what Hitler had done to them was a terrible thing. But I would never have had the courage to do what Rebecca had just done, stand on one of Berlin's most well-traveled avenues with that very black hair, and those very dark eyes, and those very Semitic—yet very beautiful—features and call him a swine.

I tell you that this instant—with the rain falling on us with a force like God Himself was trying to wash us from the face of the earth—was when I fell in love with Rebecca.

We crossed the street with the water dropping on us to the railing where Rebecca had locked up an ancient bicycle. She bent to unlock it, and as she began to push it over the cobbles, I heard that the chain was not moving over the crank in the right way.

"Stop," I said.

I kneeled at her feet and examined the crank. With the rain pouring over my head, it was like working in a shower. I was so wet I could not tell my clothes from my skin. Still I took my time resetting the chain of her bicycle, stretching it evenly over each individual sprocket until it matched a picture I had inside my head.

When I finished, I stood and pushed the bicycle back and forth so she could hear how it sounded.

"I always wondered what was wrong with that chain."

"Unevenness."

"How did you know?"

"I can see how things are supposed to work inside my head. And also how to fix them."

I did not know which was more unbelievable, that I would stand in the pelting rain and talk to a girl about fixing bicycles, or that she would stand and listen.

"Can I take you for a coffee?" I asked her.

"Is that how you make your living, you fix something for somebody and then take them for a coffee?"

"I have a shop in Hallesches."

This made Rebecca laugh.

It is possible the two of us would have stood in the rain until we drowned before I thought of something further to say.

"Yes," Rebecca said when she had stopped laughing, "you can take me for a coffee."

We went to a cafe near the Universität where the windows were steamed over from the rain and the marble tables so narrow, our knees touched beneath them.

"I have a bad heart," she told me.

She gave me this information before she gave me her name. "You do not want to fall in love with me."

"'Bad' as in you will treat me badly?" I said this lightly, thinking she was being careless talking about love with a man she'd just met on the underground.

"'Bad' as in it's broken, which when you are not talking about love, means that it is not fixable."

Rebecca, I would learn, was never careless.

"The doctors tell me I will die early."

"If things in Germany continue as they are," I said, "I expect most of us will die early."

I meant for it to be a dark joke, the only kind of joke we Jews were making then. Although for the short time of the Olympic Games, our jokes—and our lives—seemed maybe less dark. For the Romani were not the only things that had vanished from Berlin's streets. Hitler had also ordered all the *No Jews Allowed* signs removed from the shop windows, and we Jews had decided to make ourselves as willing to be deceived as the rest of the world.

The following week, on the day the Games began, I invited Rebecca to meet me.

"You have remembered what I told you about my heart," she warned, not realizing it was too late for warnings.

I told her I did, and said I only wanted to check on how her bicycle was holding up.

We met in the plaza outside the Dietrich-Eckart-Bühne amphitheater, where the opening ceremonies were being held. Rebecca was taking photographs when I arrived. Shooting the old Berliners who came to the plaza to feed the pigeons that even Hitler couldn't banish.

"You do not want to wait by the entrance?" I asked her. "Try for a picture of the athletes as they pass?"

"I am not interested in Hitler's idea of perfection."

She pointed the lens of her Leica at an old woman standing in front of the massive statues outside the amphitheater. These statues—naked giants sculpted by Josef Wackerle—were a favorite of the Führer.

"See that woman with the shriveled leg leaning against the concrete thigh of the statue?" Rebecca said. "That they can both exist, and that they are both in this moment next to each other, that is my idea of perfection."

She raised the Leica to her eye. "And if for once I can make this camera focus, I will capture it in light and shadow. An image of perfection shot by a Jewish girl with a bad heart."

"Let me fix that for you."

"I've already told you, it's unfixable."

"The focus."

She pulled the camera away from her face. "You know about Leicas as well as bicycles?"

"I know about anything mechanical."

Rebecca shoved the camera into my hand, which maybe does prove she had no patience. Or maybe that she knew even with a shriveled leg, the old woman was not going to stand in front of Josef Wackerle's concrete thigh forever.

I twisted off the range finder at the front of Rebecca's camera and looked inside, and closed my eyes to see better the way it worked without anything distracting me, like Rebecca's very black hair. When I had a clear picture of how all the mechanisms fit together, I opened them again.

"Do you have a safety pin?" I asked Rebecca.

She turned over the hem of her skirt. Most of it was held up with safety pins.

"I hate sewing," she said.

She gave me a pin, and I felt around the inside of the camera with it until I found the small spring that had come loose. I reset it, spun the range finder back on, and handed the Leica back to her.

"Tomorrow I will bring you a new spring."

But I was speaking to her narrow back, Rebecca being already gone, shooting the picture of the woman with the shriveled leg. I think Rebecca fell in love with me the instant I fixed the focus on her camera. I think this because she said nothing about her bad heart when I spoke about meeting again the next day.

And because in the time we were together, she printed that photograph a hundred times, in a hundred ways. More grainy, then more blurred. With more shadows, then with more light. Small, so its world became condensed. Large, so that it became abstracted. After she moved in with me, I found versions of that photograph all over the flat, tucked into the corners of mirrors and windows, taped onto the backs of cabinet doors, sliding around in the bottom of drawers.

"Why so many?" I asked her.

"It is my definition of perfection."

"But all over the apartment?"

"Maybe I need reminding."

When she left me, it would be the only thing of hers I would find. One version, perfectly sharp, exactly the size to fit between the pages of a passport.

. . .

It was Rebecca's tooth that pushed her into my flat. A molar that developed an abscess because she could not find a dentist to treat her. Every Jewish dentist had left Berlin—had left Germany—once the rumors started that the Nazis would forbid Jews from practicing dentistry, even on other Jews.

"Cannot you find a German dentist who will see Jews?" I said to Rebecca when she turned up at the cafe near the Universität with the left side of her face swollen like a child with mumps.

It was autumn by then, the Olympic Games had ended and both the visitors and the *No Jews Allowed* signs had returned to their usual places. Oddly, the Romani remained vanished, and no one knew where they had gone.

"Just thinking about asking the question makes my tooth ache more."

What Rebecca did not tell me was that a tooth infection can travel to the heart. If she had, I would have forced her out of that small cafe and taken her to every dentist in Berlin—every dentist in Germany—until one agreed to treat her. Instead, she told me she was bathing the tooth in salt water and peroxide, and so it was a full week before I wound up banging on the door of the room she rented in the Alexanderplatz, rousing the prostitutes and drug addicts who liked to sleep late, but not waking Rebecca.

Unlike her neighbors, Rebecca was not a prostitute or a drug addict, but a teacher of French in a gymnasium. When I pointed out that she could afford to live in a better section of Berlin, she explained that then she would be spending her money on rent instead of film.

"Also here," she said, "almost nobody complains that I am a Jew."

If it had been someone other than Rebecca I had been waiting for in the Tiergarten that afternoon, I might have believed she'd forgotten we had arranged to meet so she could photograph the October light on the dead leaves and then explain to me why this golden sunlight shining on a dry and brittle leaf is the most perfect thing in the world. But it was Rebecca, so I broke down her door. Because Rebecca never kept a spare key hidden anywhere, and though I had known her for three months by then, she would not give me a key, "because then you will begin to think of me as someone you should get used to."

I found her feverish in bed. Twisted up in sweaty sheets, surrounded by rolls of exposed film, like she had been trying to develop them with the heat of her body. She was wearing a damp slip and a beret made out of wool felt that I never had the heart to tell her was too big for her head. Although she did not seem to know who I was, she also did not seem at all surprised to see me standing there with splinters from her shattered door on the shoulders of my coat.

She could, however, recall the name and address of the doctor who treated her for her bad heart. I wrapped her in a blanket and took her there in a taxi.

It was Dr. Lieberman who explained to me how easily an infection can travel from an abscessed tooth to a heart.

"That tooth must be pulled," he said.

"Can you do it?"

"I am a heart specialist."

"Have you tried to find a dentist who will treat Jews in Berlin?"

After Dr. Lieberman pulled Rebecca's tooth, I asked him to tell me what was wrong with her heart.

He ran a hand over his hairless head. "The simple explanation, which I suppose is as good as the complicated one since they amount to the same thing, is that no part of it is strong enough to last very long. Over time it will begin to work less efficiently. Then it will give out."

"How long?"

"Are you asking me how much time you will have together?"

I nodded.

"You are Jews in Hitler's Germany. The answer to that has nothing to do with anybody's heart."

Because her door was broken, I brought Rebecca to my flat and put her into my bed. When her fever came down some days later, I suggested she stay.

"So you do not have to break down any more doors?"

"That would be one reason."

Rebecca and I were all the other had. Except for the prostitutes and drug addicts in her building, Rebecca avoided other people. "If you have friends, you have to be willing to accept their sympathy," she told me. "That is a tiring proposition."

Her parents were alive. Still living, as far as she knew, in Frankfurt. She told me they were wealthy Jews with Communist leanings. "You know the type."

"No," I told her. "I have no idea."

"My father's department store makes considerable money, which he donates to Jewish charities. My mother is a surgeon who has a way of not performing the abortions the Nazis want, and then performing the ones they don't."

"I do not know what you mean by that either."

Rebecca explained that her mother refused to force abortions on women the Nazis determined had a chance of passing on a hereditary illness. And that she was willing to perform them on the healthy Aryan women who wanted them.

I told her they sounded like good people.

"It would be better if they were less good."

Rebecca had turned herself into an orphan. "It is best if the last memory they have of me is of a nineteen-year-old girl who is not much paler than she should be getting onto a train they believe is bound for Stuttgart."

I was a true orphan. My mother died the day after my sixth birthday, as if she had been holding out, waiting for me to reach an age where I would not miss her too much. We lived in Oranienburg then, a not-so-scenic town north of Berlin. It was winter and influenza swept through the town, taking someone from nearly every house. The person it took from our house was my mother.

This was the same winter my father taught me the trick of fixing things. That happened two months after my mother died. I was playing with an electric train set, making the cars go around on the tracks beneath our Christmas tree, which had been dropping needles for weeks. My father had tried taking the tree out—it was so dry, he could no longer risk turning on the lights, no matter how much I begged him—but the moment he put his hands on its trunk, I'd throw myself against it and push my face into the brittle needles, sending the glass balls my mother had hung with her own hands smashing to the floor.

"You must let me take the tree," my father said. "It is long dead."

But I would hold onto the rough trunk, unable to explain that as long as the tree stood dropping needles in the parlor, I could believe my mother was only out on an errand.

On the day two months after my mother died, the coal car that belonged to the electric train set stopped moving, and I went to the bedroom looking for my father. It was afternoon and the sun had already set in that northern city, but my father hadn't gotten up to turn on the light. He was sitting in the wooden chair placed beside the bed where my mother had died two months earlier, looking into the empty air as if he could still see her.

"Fix this, Papa." I dropped the coal car into his lap.

My father looked into his lap for a moment, then he picked up the coal car and handed it to me. "See if you can fix it, Jakob."

My father had not gone into his repair shop since my mother died, and I decided then that my mother's dying had taken away his ability to fix things, and that this had happened because they had fallen in love over a broken bicycle.

"It was a terrible bicycle, and not worth fixing," my father would always say when he told the story.

"Still I loved the thing," my mother would tell him. "Because it belonged to my aunt Ida, who was an anarchist."

"Which explains the condition of the bicycle."

I could never figure out the connection between anarchists and terrible bicycles, but even at six, I believed I could understand the connection between my father losing my mother and losing his desire to fix things.

"Picture what makes the coal car move around the tracks," my father said to me. "See it inside your head. Then look for what might be stopping it."

This was the method I used to find the dried pine needles caught in the wheels of the coal car. And the following day, in the wheels of the engine.

Two days later, I allowed my father to take the dead Christmas tree out into the yard and burn it.

My father died thirteen years after my mother. The day I buried him, I turned my back on the shop he left me in Oranienburg and took the train for Berlin, where I had a friend.

But he's gone now, too.

Rebecca and I were happy with only the two of us in Berlin. More than happy. Maybe this is not something I should say to you, it is something you are still too young to understand, but when we came together beneath the blankets of my small bed, I believed Rebecca made us into her version of perfection, that she turned us into the rarest combination of opposites. When we came together there was strength and heat and an overwhelming energy that made me want to cry out, *Let every single jack-booted officer of Hitler's Gestapo come bursting through the door and I will kill each one without rising from this bed, without lifting a finger. I will kill them all merely with the act of love.* And also because there was a feeling so vulnerable, I felt I had become Rebecca's fragile heart, that I'd been taken out of the protection of her chest and left in the open, where all it would have taken was the slightest breath for me to cease beating.

The December after Rebecca moved into my flat, she said she wanted to go to the Christmas Market in the square outside the Berliner Dom, the cathedral near the Spree River.

"Do you think that is a good idea for Jews?"

"I have been going to the Christmas Market since I was a child, and as far as I know, the Nazis have not made believing in Jesus Christ a prerequisite for drinking a glass of glüwein."

"Yet."

"All the more reason to go now."

It was true that the Christmas Market had always been more about drinking cups of hot spiced glüwein and eating handfuls of roasted almonds and baked cinnamon stars than celebrating the birth of the Christian Messiah. In Oranienburg, everyone except the most orthodox of Jews went to Christmas Market. I remembered as a child, seeing the men who prayed loudest in temple devouring slabs of pork knuckle at Christmas Market, rivulets of grease sliding into their beards like the River Nile. And tucked always away in the sellers' booths, among the hand-carved shepherds and baby Jesuses in their mangers, would be a few painted dreidels.

Still, if we Jews were not allowed on the underground during certain hours, or permitted to sit on a bench in the Tiergarten that was not painted yellow, how could we think we would be welcome at a market to celebrate the birth of the Christian Savior? On the other hand, I could not imagine that either the Nazis or I could keep Rebecca away from Christmas Market if she wished to go.

The day we went was cold, cold enough for me to blame it for the blue of Rebecca's lips. But still Rebecca made us leave the tram early, so that we could walk the last part over the Spree and watch the walls of the market rise up like a medieval castle.

"I see that the Nazis have gone and annexed Christmas," she said. And it was true, for pasted onto the turrets of the crenellated walls of the market, alternating with the smiling faces of St. Nicolas, were black swastikas.

The Nazis had annexed the inside of the market as well. Every stand selling hot wine and cinnamon stars, painted toys and roasted meats, had a *No Jews Allowed* sign fixed to the front of it.

"There is no point to us being here," I said.

"Because they say so?"

I turned to Rebecca, standing in the cold with the beret that was too big for her head, the only other Jew besides myself in the Christmas Market. If I left, I knew I would never see her again.

"What then?" I asked her.

Rebecca walked toward a stand where a stout woman with white-blond hair was waiting, half-hidden behind her *No Jews Allowed* sign. A sign that someone—perhaps she, herself—had written in letters that were thick and dark and pressed deep into the cardboard. As Rebecca and I came closer, the woman puffed herself up, preparing, I was sure, to shout us away. But Rebecca smiled at her, the kind of smile you reserve for someone you expect to do your bidding.

Rebecca pointed to the pot of glüwein steaming on an amateurishly embroidered cloth and asked in perfect French, *"Qu'est-ce que c'est?"*

The woman sputtered, unsure of how to answer.

Rebecca let her smile falter the smallest amount. *"Non parlez-vous pas francais?"* In her tone was amazement that any civilized person would be incapable of speaking French.

The stout woman shook her head. Rebecca sighed in a manner that even to me sounded very French. Then she said in careful German—as if the woman might not have a complete grasp of her own language—"We would like two glasses of this drink, please."

The stout woman filled two glasses with steaming glüwein. Rebecca counted out her money as if it was unfamiliar to her.

"Merci," said the stout woman, beaming.

"Je vous en prie," Rebecca replied, nodding her head only the slightest amount.

We disappeared into the crowded Christmas Market with our glüwein.

"The pleasure of deceiving her is tainted a bit by letting her have any of my money," Rebecca said. "And by reinforcing her notion that Jews couldn't possibly speak French."

"Do you think you could overlook your scruples with that man selling cinnamon stars?"

"Only because I am about to become your concubine and will have to get used to doing your bidding."

"As pleasant as that sounds, why?"

"I have to give up my job at the end of the year."

"Is that what Dr. Lieberman says?"

"It is what Hitler says." She said this as if Hitler was one of her least promising students, as if no matter how long she worked with him, he would never master the future tense. "As of January, Jews will no longer be allowed to teach Germans."

"What will you do?"

Rebecca put her hand in my pocket. She never remembered to wear gloves and her hands were always so cold I would believe she had slipped something else in there—a stone, a turnip, a lump of ice.

"First I will get you your cinnamon star. Then I will advertise for private students who do not mind learning French from a Jew."

Rebecca pulled me by my pocket toward the man selling cinnamon stars.

"What does it matter? All this teaching of French has only been to keep me in practice for when I go to Paris."

Going to Paris was the only lie Rebecca ever told herself. Though I do not think it began as a lie, I think it began as a dream. A dream that had made her go to university and study French. This, when she lived in Frankfurt and had parents and knew nothing about her heart. Now she lived in Berlin and had turned herself into an orphan, and knew enough about her heart to have killed off every dream except this one. The best she could with this one was turn it into a lie. A lie that needed to be fed from time to time.

She would begin, "When I go to Paris," and then she would tell me what she would do there, who she would see—most often the Jewish photographer Gisèle Freund, who had escaped from Berlin three years ago with her negatives strapped to her body. Always I would listen, even if she talked for an hour. Because the lie of going to Paris was the one thing Rebecca allowed herself that wasn't a brutal truth. It seemed so little to help her feed the lie.

. . .

That winter, Rebecca advertised for private students. But no private students were willing to learn French from a Jew, and Rebecca had no one with whom to speak French except herself.

And that turned the lie ravenous.

On a frigid night near the end of January, I came home from the shop and found Rebecca wrapped in blankets on the sofa. The heat in the building was unpredictable and she'd forgotten to light the fire in the tiled stove, which we used for a backup. It was nearly as cold inside as out, yet her face was flushed and feverish-looking.

"When I go to Paris," she said as I stepped through the door. Not, Hello. Not, Why are you late? Because I was late. Because five minutes before closing time, an officer of the Gestapo had come into the shop with a broken gramophone, and you do not tell an officer of the Gestapo that it is five minutes before closing time and would you mind very much coming back tomorrow. Not if the name on the door of your shop has a Semitic ring to it. No, you bow your head as if you are grateful for the business, and you accept the gramophone, and you stay as long as it takes to fix it, and then you arrive home late.

"The first place I go will be the Sorbonne," Rebecca was saying as I built the fire. "And I will sit there until Gisèle Freund agrees to see me."

"Is there food?" I asked her. "Have you thought about supper?"

"I will explain that I, too, have escaped Hitler, and that even though she does not know me, she does. Then I will show her my photographs."

"Stay here. I will go and see if the butcher on Fraenkelufer is still open."

The butcher's shop was shuttered, and I had to resort to making a watery soup from what I could find at the bottom of our vegetable box. I do not believe Rebecca noticed. She barely stopped talking long enough to put the spoon in her mouth, hardly ceased speaking long enough to swallow.

She told me about the photographs Gisèle Freund had taken for *Life* magazine, pictures she had heard of in rumor, because the Nazis would never have allowed *Life* magazine into Germany. "She has put photographs of the poorest of England's working class in the middle of a story on the British aristocracy," she told me, soup spilling down her chin. "She will understand my woman with the shriveled leg leaning against Josef Wackerle's concrete thigh."

While I tried to get her to eat the sorry soup, she explained how Gisèle Freund would take her to meet all of her bohemian friends—Jean-Paul Sartre, who Rebecca claimed was never cheerful, and Colette, who she believed always was. She told me this in such detail that I saw it all inside my head, the way I saw how mechanical objects worked, and I began to believe in it myself. Only when her voice became hoarse and started to crack did I remember that this was her lie.

I took the empty spoon out of her hand. "It's late," I said. "You can tell me the rest tomorrow."

Rebecca did. She told me about Paris the next day, and the day following. Until I realized that she never went out, never left the flat, only moved from the bed to the sofa, where she waited for me to come home from the shop so she could begin talking.

"When I go to Paris, I will live in the Latin Quarter on the Rue Saint-Jacques, and I will have an apartment where all the windows face west and south, and none of them face east, so I will never have to look toward Germany."

"Rebecca, have you eaten today?"

"I will invite over all the people I have met there, all the people Gisèle Freund has introduced me to. James Joyce and Jean Cocteau. Marcel Duchamp and Virginia Woolf."

"Let's go around to the cafe that serves the sheep stew you like."

"In Paris, I will eat *coq au vin*, and *cassoulet*, and *steak frites*, and I will eat them in any cafe I wish. Because no one on the Boulevard Saint-Germain or Rue de Rivoli or the Champs-Élysée will care that I am a Jew or an existentialist or a Hindu or a lesbian."

"Are you planning on becoming a lesbian in Paris?" I smiled.

"I might. In Paris, I might become something different every day. A lesbian on Monday, a Negress on Tuesday, a devout Catholic on Wednesday. In Paris, I shall become whatever I want and there won't be a single Nazi to tell me that I can't because a quota for it has already been filled."

"And what about me?"

"You?" She wrapped a thin arm around my neck. "You, my darling, will come and fix the typewriters and cameras and bicycles of all my famous bohemian friends. Because, of course, they are artists and incapable of fixing anything for themselves. And they will adore you and call you *indispensable*, which, of course, you will be."

Listening to Rebecca talk was like falling into an opium dream. It was much easier to stay with her inside the lie of Paris than to go outside into the reality of Berlin. But I saw how the lie was feeding off her. How purpled the skin beneath her eyes had turned—a color I could not blame on the early sunsets of February. And at night, after the nervous energy of feeding the lie had finally exhausted her, I would reach under the sweaters she wore to bed and count her ribs with my fingers, a task that got easier each time I tried it.

During the first week of March, I knocked on the door of our downstairs neighbor, Frau Nowak. Frau Nowak was a brown-haired, buxom woman with a tired face who disapproved of Rebecca and me. Not because we were Jewish, but because we were not married.

However, Frau Nowak had a twelve-year-old daughter who had impressed me as quick-witted and also, I suspected, many things in her flat that needed fixing, as Herr Nowak had taken off two years ago with Frau Nowak's younger sister.

As Frau Nowak would not let me past her doorstep, I offered her my bargain while standing in the street. I would come once a week and fix whatever was broken in her flat if she would send her daughter upstairs to Rebecca for French lessons.

Frau Nowak looked suspicious, but free labor and free French lessons proved more potent than her sense of morality.

"Under no circumstances can the Fräulein upstairs know of our exchange," I told her.

"I understand." Frau Nowak nodded. Although I cannot imagine what she believed she understood.

I must have been correct about Frau Nowak's twelve-year-old daughter, because Rebecca complained about her much less than she had about her gymnasium students, the bulk of whom she believed would be fortunate if they could convince anyone in France to bring them so much as a croissant. Although she did wonder where Frau Nowak had found the money to pay for French lessons.

"Perhaps Herr Nowak has had an attack of conscience."

"I very much doubt it."

"Then perhaps there is something to the rumor about Frau Nowak taking up with an officer of the Gestapo."

On the two days a week Frau Nowak's daughter came for her lessons, Rebecca did not talk to me of Paris. And on those days, she generally remembered about the fire and about eating.

During that time, I also scoured Berlin's pawnshops in the Kreuzberg until I found one that would sell me a shortwave radio.

"You can have that one cheap," the man behind the counter told me. "It does not work."

"I should have it free then."

"I have to make something."

I took the radio back to my shop and worked on it all afternoon. When it was fixed, I brought it home to Rebecca.

She was waiting for me on the sofa, wrapped up in blankets. "When I go to Paris," she began.

I ignored her, placing the radio on the table where there was nothing set out for our supper and turned it on. Static poured out, drowning Rebecca's voice. Then, because I'd tried it out in the shop and knew where to look for it, I turned the dial and the sound of French—no, the sound of France—filled our flat.

Rebecca stopped talking. She rose from the sofa and with the blankets still wrapped around her, walked to the radio. She was staring at it like it wasn't a box filled with tubes and transmitters and amplifiers. She was looking at it as if it was something magical, something that could take the lie and not turn it back into a dream—nothing could do that—but turn it less deadly maybe.

"What are they talking about?" I asked her.

"Soap powder."

I looked at her—pale and too thin—standing before the shortwave with the blankets wrapped around her fragile shoulders.

"It is an advertisement. And I can see it perfectly—a French woman hanging her husband's shirts on the line with the curved dome of Sacré-Coeur at the edge of her window. The husband's shirts, they're very white." She laughed. The sound of it was so rare and lovely, I had to turn away.

Two weeks later when a chest cold kept Frau Nowak's daughter from her lesson and bad weather prevented the radio from pulling France into our flat, Rebecca greeted me once more with, "When I go to Paris."

"But what about me?" I interrupted.

She looked up at me from her pile of blankets on the sofa.

"I cannot spend all my time fixing typewriters and cameras. What if I want to ask Jean-Paul Sartre for directions to the *bibliotheque*? Suppose I would like to talk to Colette about the train service to Marseilles? I cannot stand around Paris like a mute."

And so Rebecca began to teach me French. At first I was not as quick as her twelve-year-old student. But after a month, I was good enough for the two of us to occasionally go out and flaunt the *No Jews Allowed* sign in a cafe or butcher shop. While we were often chased away—even in French—it did not bother me as much as it should have. I had only to notice how the shadows beneath Rebecca's eyes had lightened to lavender, and think how long it had been since she had last begun a sentence with, "When I go to Paris."

In November of that year the Eternal Jew exhibit opened in Munich. This was the type of news I would have gone to lengths to avoid, but Rebecca would not let me. She dragged me to a kiosk on Unter den Linden to buy a copy of *Jüdische Rundschau*, the Jewish newspaper. *Jüdische Rundschau*, Rebecca claimed, was the only newspaper in Berlin that could be trusted, because the Ministry for Enlightenment and Propaganda did not interfere with it.

"How can that be?" I asked her.

"Because the only public opinion Herr Goebbels cares about is *German* public opinion."

We took our newspaper to the small cafe near the Universität to read over coffee. But since we had last been there, they had put up a *No Jews Allowed* sign.

"It is not too cold," I said. "We can go sit in the Tiergarten."

Rebecca looked up into the blue sky, as if checking the weather. It was a clear autumn day, the kind where one can see for miles.

"Hitler is probably happy for the weather. Clear enough for everybody in Germany to look toward Munich and see exactly what he thinks of the Jews."

I took her arm and led her toward the Tiergarten. At times I wondered if Rebecca was testing which would kill her first, her heart or the Gestapo.

We sat on one of the yellow benches reserved for Jews, and Rebecca—who insisted on reading all injustices in newspapers out loud to me—read from *Jüdische Rundschau*.

"Julius Streicher," she said, "a member of the Nazi Party, opened the exposition by declaring that Jews are children of the Devil."

According to the paper, three thousand German people had attended the opening day of the exhibit. They had wandered through its twenty rooms, reading posters with titles like *How Bolshevism Is the Jewish Desire to Rule the World* and *Usury and the Fencing of Goods Were Always Their Privilege*, then marveling at the displays of *Jewish Facial Features*—the hooked noses, thick lips, and enormous ears made of rubber.

"Herr Streicher told the story of the Eternal or Wandering Jew," Rebecca read into the clear autumn air, "the Jew who mocked Jesus on his way to the cross and was condemned to wander the earth until Judgment Day. A poor Jew, Streicher said, who would have considered it a favor to be put out of his misery."

She dropped the paper into her lap; her face was paler than usual.

"This is how they will begin to exterminate us."

An elderly German couple walking by turned their heads to stare at her.

"En francais," I said.

"They will turn us into something other than human," she continued in French. "And they will call it a favor."

She grabbed hold of my wrist with more strength than I would have imagined she possessed. "You have to leave."

"We both have to leave."

"There are only so many visas for Jews in countries outside of Germany. There is no point wasting one on me."

"I will not go without you."

"Do not make me responsible for you dying here."

I pointed to the newspaper. "This is only one exhibit in one city."

She picked it up, showed me the listings.

"After Munich it will go to Vienna, then it will come here to Berlin. The Ministry for Enlightenment and Propaganda is already preparing a documentary of it to show all over Germany."

"Still, from a documentary to extermination?"

Rebecca shook her head. She knew it would not be such a long journey.

I knew it as well, although I tried very hard not to know it.

But Rebecca would not let me. All that winter, she filled the flat with newspapers. Three years earlier, when Berlin had published more than fifty daily newspapers, this would have been easier. But Herr Goebbels had declared it illegal for Jews to work at non-Jewish newspapers, and since that time, Berlin's newspapers had shrunk to less than a dozen. Still, Rebecca bought every one of them and left them scattered around our flat. On the sofa—where she no longer sat wrapped up in blankets—spread out on the kitchen table, covering our bed. I even found them pressed against the window glass, as if it would be more difficult for me to disregard the news if there was more light shining through it.

Each day when I returned home from the shop, I gathered these newspapers and stacked them neatly beside the tiled stove to use for kindling. It is not easy to hold so many words in your hands and prevent your brain from turning them into meaning. To do so, I paid more attention to Rebecca, noting that her lips looked bluish even in the warmth of our apartment, that her skin had a permanent pallor.

When Rebecca understood that I could be surrounded by newspapers covered with words that if added together equaled an ominous outcome for anyone who was Jewish and still ignore them, she tried a different tactic.

"You have to leave" became the new phrase she greeted me with each evening. And each evening, I tried to find a way to convince her that she should leave as well.

"What about France?" I said. "Your French is good enough that maybe we can buy you a French passport."

"And you?"

"Maybe I can get a visa. Or maybe I can be smuggled in."

"What makes you think we will be safe in France?" she asked me. "You do not believe the Führer has plans for France?"

"Palestine, then. They actually want Jews."

"Jews who will live."

For each night of the length of that winter, Rebecca and I had some version of this argument, some version of her telling me to leave, reminding me she would die, until I wanted to run out of the flat and search the entire Kreuzberg, the whole of Berlin, until I found this hypothetical Jew she believed deserved to leave Germany instead of her. And when I did, I swore I would put my hands around his deserving neck and strangle him until he was the one who was dead and Rebecca could leave with me.

In March, there was news even I could not ignore. Hitler had invaded Austria, a country with two hundred thousand Jews.

I came home early and found Rebecca on the floor of the flat, surrounded by open newspapers, a country of newsprint she had decided to occupy.

"It says here that Hitler has established an Office for Jewish Emigration in Vienna."

"Do you think they will be allowed to leave?"

"With Eichmann in charge? Only if their destination is Herr Himmler's new concentration camp near Linz."

I sat on the floor beside her. "You are going to tell me to leave again."

"And you are going to tell me some new idea you have about me going with you."

I took her hand, telling myself the blueness at the end of her fingers was only ink from the newsprint.

"Here is what I think," I told her. "I think that shortly before you believe it is too late, you will find some way to make me leave."

She looked up at me. Her eyes were very dark. "That is probably true."

"So let us not use up any more of the time between now and then talking about it."

Rebecca nodded, and I no longer came home to newspapers.

But I was not agreeing to leave Rebecca in Germany, only to stop trying to persuade her to go. For if she would not go because her heart was bad, I would find a way to fix it.

I went to see Dr. Lieberman and asked to borrow a few of his medical texts. It would have been easier to get these from a library, but by this time Jews had been banned from libraries.

"Are you interested in taking up medicine?" His question, implying that any of us had a future in which to take up anything, almost made me laugh.

"I want to see how a heart works when it is healthy."

The doctor put his hand on my shoulder, as if he believed what he was going to tell me would be better communicated through touch. "You know Rebecca's heart is not fixable."

I nodded. But there are sometimes things we cannot be made to understand.

I brought Dr. Lieberman's books to my shop and opened them across the table where I fixed the things my customers brought me—the clocks and toasters and motorbike engines I could repair by seeing how they worked inside my head. I had learned little about the human body at the gymnasium in Oranienburg, and as I examined the diagrams in Dr. Lieberman's books, I was surprised to discover that the heart was nothing more than a pump, a machine made of muscle and tissue.

I pored over the doctor's medical books, learning the mechanism of how a heart worked, the way I had learned the mechanisms of radios and gramophones. I memorized each part—the chambers, the ventricles and valves, the aortas and arteries—all of which seemed familiar, like so many tubes and clamps. It was so familiar, I began to believe that if only I could get to it, if only I could crack open Rebecca's chest, remove her heart and take it apart as carefully as I had the shortwave radio, I would be able to make it work perfectly.

This idea of fixing Rebecca's heart became my version of going to Paris, and it began to feed off me. I stayed in the shop until long past the Jewish curfew, until I risked arrest or worse on my way home, studying the books I had long ago promised to return to Dr. Lieberman, picturing inside my head every step it would take to fix Rebecca's bad heart. When I did at last return to the flat, past the time Rebecca was able to keep herself awake for me, I would slip into our bed and rest my head on her chest—lightly, fearing that the weight of my head would be enough to stop her heart—and listen to the beating, trying to make it confirm what I had pictured back in the shop.

. . .

By spring, newer, deeper shadows had appeared beneath Rebecca's eyes, and I found myself always taking her by the shoulders and pulling her into the sunlight, as if that would make them disappear. Now when I returned to the flat at night, I lifted the sweaters Rebecca slept in—though the weather had warmed, she had not—and traced the line I would need to cut to uncover her heart. *Just here*, I would think, or perhaps I'd say it aloud, because this no longer felt like something that would stay inside my head. *You will not have to go very deep, there is so little between the skin and the bone. And even the bone is so thin it could all be done while she sleeps.*

I traced this line every night that spring. Allowed my finger to move over that place on her chest so often I began to know how her heart would feel cupped in my hand, how it would beat—I had listened to it enough—the weight and the warmth of it. Then one night, when the window was open and the air, even in Berlin, smelled of things that were blooming and coming to life, Rebecca's hand fell over mine.

"Go into the kitchen and get a knife."

I froze, my finger poised on her chest.

"Do you think I am always asleep?"

When I made no move, she slid out from under my hand and went to the kitchen. She returned with the big butcher's knife we used to cut apart the breastbones of chickens.

She put the knife into my hand and pulled off her sweaters. For a moment, she stood naked in the moonlight, her skin white as paper. Then she got back into bed, arranging herself under my hands.

"I have heard a deep cut is less painful than a shallow one," she told me.

It was the middle of the night, but I knew I was not dreaming. I put the point of the knife at the top of Rebecca's chest and felt the skin give beneath its sharpness. My fingers were electric with the desire to slide the knife along the line I had traced so often I was certain I could see it. I had never pictured anything I could not fix, and I had been picturing Rebecca's heart for months, spent so many nights listening to its beating, I could predict each irregularity.

I knew everything there was to know about Rebecca's heart.

Including this—what it wanted most was for me to leave Germany. Wanted it enough to let me murder her in our bed if that was what it would take to accomplish it.

I moved the knife from her chest and dropped it to the floor. Then I pulled the blankets over Rebecca.

"It was a very good effort," I told her.

She turned and pressed the length of her body against me. Her skin was very cold. "Maybe if I had waited longer?"

I wrapped my arms around her. "That much time neither of us has."

The next day I returned Dr. Lieberman's medical books.

In that summer the Nazis passed a law that required all Jewish-owned businesses to register with the government.

"Do not do it," Rebecca warned. "It is the first step of them taking the shop away from you."

"What else can I do?"

"Close the shop."

"And what will I do all day?"

"Sit in the shop and wait. Even the Nazis own things that break."

"But if I take their money, they can arrest me."

"That is why you will fix their things for favors, which are much more valuable than money."

I shook my head. "I opened the shop because I wanted to stay away from politics."

Rebecca laughed, the kind of laugh where nothing is funny. "You are a Jew. You are not allowed to stay away from politics."

It was politics that had brought me to Berlin, arriving on the same day that I buried my father in Oranienburg. The year was 1930, and I was nineteen years old and restless for revolution. Too restless to spend my days repairing the radios and motorbikes of the local bourgeois when each day the battle for the future of Germany was being acted out on the streets of Berlin between the Nazi brownshirts and the Communist red tide. That morning, I had walked away from my father's fresh gravesite, packed a small suitcase with a few clothes and a copy of *Das Kapital*, and turned my back on the repair shop that was my inheritance, leaving the door unlocked and all my father's precious tools unguarded, because I did not believe in private property.

I knew only one person in Berlin, Pietr Abend, who had been two years ahead of me at the gymnasium. Pietr had been the first of us to leave Oranienburg. The first of us to do anything—ride a motorbike, get drunk on the sour beer made at the Oranienburg brewery, become a Communist.

The day Pietr graduated from the gymnasium he invited all of us to the crumbling tavern at the edge of town that would serve anyone with enough pfennigs in his pocket, and stood us to a pitcher of beer. When we were all drunk but he still seemed sober, he brought us back to the leaning, windswept house he shared with his mother and we watched him pack a single suitcase. I do not know where Pietr's mother was while he was packing, most probably still at the tavern.

"The day that you graduate, you must come to Berlin and join the revolution," he told us. "I will send each one of you a postcard with my address, so you will know where to find me."

Over the next five years, while I finished my studies at the gymnasium and fixed sewing machines and gramophones with my father, I received fourteen postcards from Pietr Abend, each with a new address. At the bottom of every one was this sentence, *The revolution is waiting*.

The morning my father died, I sent a telegram to the most recent address, *Arriving Mitte station 3 pm tomorrow.* I did not know if Pietr Abend would turn up to meet me, or if I would recognize him if he did.

Five years in Berlin had not altered Pietr much. His blond hair had darkened a bit, as if it had absorbed some of the griminess of the city, and while he had always been slight, he was now more gaunt than I remembered.

"You have arrived on an auspicious day." Pietr waved his arms at the blue May sky, making me believe he was talking about the weather. "Twelve Nazi Storm Troopers have trampled a Communist to death at Innsbrucker Platz."

"What will happen to them?"

"The Minister of the Interior has already issued a swift and just punishment." Pietr was smiling. "He has banned the wearing of brown shirts."

I recalled then that Pietr's smile had always been like this—ironic—as if he never expected to find anything genuinely amusing.

"I understand some members of the SA have already begun wearing white shirts," he continued. "So much better for showing blood."

Pietr walked me down Friedrichstrasse toward Hallesches Tor, to give me a better sense of "this gorgeously terrible city." We passed packs of blond-haired SA members—"You will never see one walking alone"—who forced us off the sidewalk and into the street. And more promisingly, small groups of city girls dressed in airy skirts that swirled about their legs, that made me think it would only take the lightest breeze to raise them.

"Tell me all the news of Oranienburg," Pietr said. "Even there, something interesting must have happened in the past five years."

"Your mother has not sent you a letter?"

"I only know she is alive because no one has written me for the money to bury her."

The address on Pietr's fourteenth postcard was in the Wassertorstrasse, on a street of ruined buildings built so close together the street was in perpetual dusk. We were near to the Spree here, and the damp from the river made it feel as if the spring weather in the rest of the city intended to pass this neighborhood by.

A man dressed in a suit was standing outside one of the ruined buildings, whistling up at its cracked facade, as if he was calling for a dog. But rather than a shepherd or a dachshund bounding out of the open doorway, a window on the second floor opened wide enough for a feminine hand to toss out an old-fashioned skeleton key.

Pietr gave me his ironic smile. "The means of production are terrifically straightforward on this street. Remind me to show you which windows are worth whistling at."

The flat Pietr led me into was dark and close and smelled of something poisonous.

"Lung soup," said a voice in the dimness.

When my eyes adjusted, I saw a man wearing only a pair of boxer shorts standing before a stove. He stirred a pot filled with something thick and viscous.

Pietr slapped the man on one of his hairy shoulders. "I am sorry to say that Otto here is the best cook among us."

"Each according to his abilities," Otto declared.

In addition to the tiny kitchen where Otto was cooking the lung soup—a staple of the household, it would turn out—the flat on Wassertorstrasse possessed two other rooms which the inhabitants used for sitting, eating, and sleeping, as needed. There was also a WC at the end of the hallway that was for the use of the entire floor, although most of the time we either pissed in the sink—or if it was dark and not too cold, out the back window. If we needed a proper wash and did not have a girlfriend at the time, we went to one of the communal baths.

For the three years I lived in the flat in the Wassertorstrasse, I never once spied the floor in either of those two rooms. There was always a pile of dirty clothes, or someone's latest manifesto, or a snoring Communist—or more often all three—covering it. I could also never say with any certainty how many comrades I would find stretched out on the floor, or ravenously spooning up whatever foul-smelling concoction Otto had cooked in that tiny kitchen, as the number depended on who was hiding out from the SA, or his landlady, or his girlfriend, or some combination of these.

To help me earn my share of the rent money, Pietr got me a job at *Rote Fahne*, the newspaper where he worked. I told him I had given up fixing things until after the revolution, but Pietr convinced me I should make an exception for the ancient printing presses of a Communist newspaper.

Pietr worked at *Rote Fahne* as a photographer. He called it "documenting the Communist Revolution," although he was documenting it with a capitalist camera—a Speed Graphic he had talked a rich American girl into giving him. Pietr was good at talking girls into giving him things, and not only cameras. Pietr was also—for a Communist—very fond of all things American. American girls. American jazz. American movies. American movie stars. Especially Gloria Swanson, who we had seen in the movie *Male and Female* in a scene with a caged lion—a scene he claimed was now burned into his memory alongside the quotes of Karl Marx.

Pietr never told any of the other comrades in the flat in the Wassertorstrasse about his fondness for American things. I think that he trusted me with this knowledge because we were from the same town, and maybe also because I knew about his mother—and perhaps because I agreed with him about Gloria Swanson. How he justified the Speed Graphic to our colleagues at *Rote Fahne* was that he was utilizing a product of capitalism in the service of the Communist cause.

In those years the struggle that was going on in the Reichstag—the German government—between the Communists and the Nazis was also taking place in the streets. But in the streets, instead of words, it was being fought with rubber truncheons and lead pipes, and also with bullets. It was this fight that Pietr went out to photograph, and I never knew how he did not come back with more cuts and bruises than he did. Could not figure how he did not come back with his precious American newspaperman's camera smashed into many pieces.

I had watched Pietr walk straight into a band of SA men who were throwing bricks through the windows of Jewish-owned department stores in the Leipzigerstrasse—because in their minds Jews and Communists were the same thing. Seen him photograph these same SA men as they smashed more bricks into the faces of any passersby whose features they thought too Semitic. When a riot erupted between a group of Nazis and Communists in Hallesches Tor, right around the corner from our flat, rather than stay inside the way any sane person would, Pietr grabbed his American camera and ran out, capturing the streams of blood that ran between the cobbles. He roamed the streets of Berlin late at night, photographing the bodies of comrades shot in the face and the back of the head, preserving their images before the SA men could drag them away, go back and tell their families they'd been sent to a work camp, or pressed into service in the army.

Pietr photographed all of it, then hurried back to the darkroom at the *Rote Fahne* offices because he did not trust anyone else to develop his pictures. Once they were developed, he would follow Herr Brackman, the editor, around, the way a dog will chase after a car it cannot catch, insisting he run every single picture, preferably on the front page.

"If you show people the truth," Pietr would tell him, "they will have to look at it."

Herr Brackman, hunched from all his years bending over photographs and reporters' copy, would look at all of Pietr's pictures. Then he would shake his head and say that he would like to continue publishing his newspaper. And when Pietr repeated his comment about the truth, Herr Brackman would tell him, "If people do not want to see something, they will not. Even if you put it on the front page of a newspaper."

Pietr would then gather up his pictures and tell Herr Brackman that neither he nor *Rote Fahne* deserved his photographs. Herr Brackman would attempt to unbend his spine and nod. "But if you find you've changed your mind tomorrow, I would be happy to have you and your photographs." The next day, Pietr would return with a new batch of photographs, because at least you could count on *Rote Fahne* to run one or two of your pictures, which was more than you could say for the rest of Berlin's newspapers.

I also wound up as one of Pietr's photographs one afternoon when three SA men in street clothes beat me unconscious on the Kurfürstendamm for the crime of appearing too Jewish. I was one of a half dozen perpetrators of the same crime, all of us lying bleeding on the pavement when Pietr turned up with his camera. He told me he had shot six or seven pictures of my swollen face before he recognized me.

"You looked wonderfully horrible. I was counting on you for the front page."

For once Herr Brackman agreed with him, and to show his appreciation, Pietr treated me to a session behind what he considered the best window on Wassertorstrasse.

The spring Pietr met Lena—the spring of 1932—was the spring the Nazis killed ninety-nine people in four weeks. It was also one of those unusual soft springs that do not usually come to a northern city like Berlin—an Italian spring.

I cannot tell you if it was raining on the day they met, but let us say that it was. I can say that they met near the Wassertorstrasse archway, and that it was just before dawn because Pietr was shooting a fight that had begun in a nearby tavern between a gang of Nazis and some drunken Communists. By this time—just before dawn on a soft Italian-like spring morning, with a bit of rain falling—the fight had moved to the Wassertorstrasse archway and the Nazis were not merely trying to beat the drunken Communists to death, they were also trying to kill a couple of policemen who had come to stop the fight.

Lena, who was neither a Communist nor a Nazi, but—as Pietr would later learn—an anarchist, was trying to get to her job as a seamstress over in the Mitte. A task that was being hampered by the fight outside her door.

"The moment I saw her standing in the street with her bicycle," Pietr told me later that morning, "I didn't care so much about shooting any more pictures."

"Seriously?"

"Maybe it was all that red hair."

"Maybe you realized Herr Brackman would not print them."

"No," he insisted, "it was the hair."

Using the unnatural luck that had gotten him through countless street battles with only minor cuts and bruises, Pietr strolled through the pipe-wielding Nazis and led the red-haired anarchist to safety. Then—as if forgetting his bag was filled with exposed film—he accompanied her all the way to the factory in the Mitte. Running alongside as she pedaled her bicycle, as she was already late for work—anarchists, as it turns out, are habitually late for work—the Speed Graphic camera bouncing against his side.

Lena Rubinowitz did indeed have hair that could make you forget what you were meant to be doing. It was red like something set on fire. So thick and full of untamable curls, you knew no matter how deep you sank your hands into it, you would never reach the bottom. Pietr called it anarchist hair and claimed she had only become an anarchist so she would have an excuse for it. This made Lena laugh, as if Pietr was right about this. Although the two of us were also sure that this small, red-haired girl kept a cache of Molotov cocktails stashed under her bed.

I think this was the reason Pietr loved Lena, that she could laugh when he accused her of playing at being an anarchist. I know it was one of the reasons I was half in love with her. Or if I am being honest, I would tell you that I was all in love with her. Because although I had vowed to fix nothing until after the revolution, I fixed Lena's bicycle at least once a week. Proving two things, I suppose, my feelings for her and the connection between anarchists and terrible bicycles.

Because there were two seamstresses who shared Lena's flat, and so many comrades in ours, it was impossible for Pietr and Lena to be alone. To solve this problem, Pietr would whistle up at one or another of the windows in Wassertorstrasse and pay the woman behind it to spend the evening at the cinema. I think maybe I loved Lena even more for her willingness to visit these small flats without asking about Pietr's friendship with their owners, and because she always brought a gift of still-warm bread from the bakery near her flat, explaining, "When the bread comes out, the prostitutes are always working."

Sometimes Lena and Pietr would take me with them to small underground bars that were the haunts of bohemians and homosexuals—and mercifully, never Nazis—to hear American jazz. Not being a Communist, Lena was free to love things that were American. One night at the Tingle Tangle Club, as Herr Mike Plottnik *aus Neu York* played saxophone, we drank gin, then watched Lena dance around Pietr's chair, in an imitation of Josephine Baker's banana skirt dance.

Lena danced like an anarchist, with no design or purpose, letting the sinuous bass notes of Herr Plottnik's saxophone move her small body around Pietr's chair like a snake. When the music ended, she threw back her head full of red hair and laughed with more uncomplicated joy than I have seen before or since.

I am certain Lena knew that I was in love with her. She treated me like a favorite younger brother, bringing me white shirts from the factory where she worked in the Mitte—shirts I am sure she stole—teasing me about girlfriends I did not have. She cut my hair when she decided it was too long. Lena gave the worst haircuts in the world—anarchist haircuts—but I let her keep doing it because I liked the feeling of her fingers in my hair.

I am certain also that Pietr knew I was in love with her, and I believe it made him happy. For he was a true Communist.

On New Year's Day 1933, on her way back to the flat she shared with the two seamstresses, after spending the evening with Pietr and me drinking cheap champagne and listening to German-born musicians play American jazz at the Tingle Tangle Club, Lena Rubinowitz was shot dead by an SA man on a bicycle. As he rode away into the gray dawn, the SA man shouted, *"Heil Hitler!"* to no one in particular.

We learned about it from one of the seamstresses who had also been on her way home and had seen it happen. She came into the office later that morning with blood on her dress and told Pietr and me together. I do not think she had ever been clear which of us belonged to Lena.

After the seamstress—whose name I realized I had never known—left the office, Pietr grabbed his Speed Graphic and ran out. I was certain he had gone to look for the SA man on the bicycle, the one who had shot Lena for no reason other than she'd been a Jewish girl walking home on New Year's morning and he had a gun in his hand he felt like using.

I wanted to go with him, although I knew we would not be able to find the same SA man. But then, were not all SA men the same? Would they not all shoot a Jewish girl walking home if they had a gun in their hand they felt like using? So what did it matter if we found the one who had shot Lena or we found another one?

I knew—even while I was thinking this—that it made me as bad as they were. But was I not entitled to be as bad as they were? Who had decided I had to be better?

The only thing that stopped me from running out of the *Rote Fahne* office was the fact that Lena had not been mine. She had belonged to Pietr. And so I stayed. Stayed in case something on the presses broke down, which of course it did, not long after lunch. But as I stood before the stilled machinery, trying to picture how it was supposed to work inside my head, all I could see was Lena's anarchist hair. Red like something set on fire. Red like the blood the SA man had left her lying in. Lena's untamable hair soaked through with blood. And I could not make myself stop wondering which would be the darker red.

Young men do not have the words for grief, and Pietr did not give himself time to learn them. Three weeks after the SA man shot Lena, Pietr went to photograph a Nazi rally held outside the Communist headquarters on the Bulowplatz. What I heard later was that fifteen thousand Nazi Storm Troopers stood outside the headquarters building chanting, "We shit on the Jew republic." The police, who were supposed to keep order, kept the Communists inside by training their machine guns on the windows.

I heard all this from the reporter who accompanied Pietr. The same reporter who came back to the *Rote Fahne* office alone and told us that Pietr had been killed, run over by a streetcar.

"First he hands me that damned American camera," the reporter said to Herr Brackman, "then he just steps right in front of the thing."

Herr Brackman filled the front page of the following day's paper with Pietr's photographs of the besieged Communist headquarters on the Bulowplatz.

But by then, I no longer worked there. After the reporter had finished telling the story about Pietr and the streetcar, I walked out of the *Rote Fahne* office. I do not know if Herr Brackman expected me back, or if he ever found anyone to repair his unreliable presses, for I never went past that building again, not for all the time I continued to live in Berlin, not even out of curiosity after the Nazis shut down Herr Brackman's newspaper.

I went back to the flat on the Wassertorstrasse and packed the clothes I had arrived with, adding the white shirts Lena had stolen from the factory in the Mitte for me. I packed also my copy of *Das Kapital*, only because it reminded me of Pietr, not because I cared about anything in it. I found a small room in the Kreuzberg, and went door to door fixing things until I had saved enough money to open the shop in Hallesches.

A few months after I opened it, Otto recognized me through the window.

"Comrade!" he shouted, bursting through the door. "You must come back to the Wassertorstrasse and eat lung soup with us!"

"I have had my fill of lung soup."

He glanced at my worktable, covered with the inner workings of a radio.

"Then come and do not eat. Who cares? The revolution needs your talents."

"I think I have had my fill of the revolution as well."

For five years, I went to the shop near Hallesches and fixed things that were broken and stayed away from politics.

And now, after so many years, Rebecca wanted me to play politics with Nazis.

"This game of favors," I said to her, "it will keep us alive?"

"And perhaps more."

I knew she meant it might provide a way for me to leave.

"All right, then," I said, wondering how well I might learn to play it.

The next day I went to the shop near Hallesches and hung a sign in the window printed with the words *This shop is closed*. Then I sat on the stool at my worktable and opened a book. Toward the afternoon, a young Nazi officer came in carrying a music box.

"Can you fix this, Jew?"

I pointed to the sign in the window. "I am no longer in the fixing business."

"I hear that you can fix anything."

I looked up into the officer's blue eyes. "I could, when I was in the fixing business."

The young Nazi set the music box on my open book.

"It would mean much to my wife to have it working. It is a family heirloom."

I studied the music box. It was made of intricate patterns of inlaid wood and trimmed with gold. I could tell without turning the key that you would feel the sound of it deep in your chest next to your heart.

"Your wife is from Vienna?"

"She is from Stuttgart."

"Her family, then?"

"Her family is German. Why these impertinent questions?"

I nodded my head at the box. "The music box, it is Austrian."

The young officer drew back his shoulders. "The Nazi government would consider it a service if you would repair the music box."

"The entire government?"

"Myself, as its representative."

I placed a hand on the top of the box, already picturing the mechanism beneath its inlaid wood. "Come back tomorrow."

The young Nazi officer turned toward the door.

"And perhaps as a service to me," I said to the back of his uniform, "the Nazi government would consider sending you back with half a kilo of stew meat."

Without turning, the officer nodded.

Rebecca was disappointed I had not asked for film for her Leica, and as the weeks went on, I had to promise to make that my request every so often, as well as something more interesting than stew meat and potatoes.

"If I have to live under the Nazis, I want to drink wine and eat chocolate and smoke American cigarettes," she said. "And what about a box of meringues for breakfast once in a while?"

No one except Nazis brought me anything to fix. No one else dared. It was as probable they would be punished if it appeared I was running an unregistered business. I did not pretend this was a good or honorable situation. When Goldman the greengrocer, who had registered his business and then seen it transferred to an Aryan for a minor infraction, called me collaborator on the street, I nodded and agreed with him. I was collaborating with the Nazis by fixing their music boxes and motorbikes in order to save Jewish lives—Rebecca's and mine. Maybe that was not excuse enough for Goldman the greengrocer, but it was all they had left me.

One day toward the end of September, I came home and found Rebecca curled up in a patch of sun like an elderly cat.

"I saw Dr. Bauer for the final time today," she told me. Rebecca had stopped seeing Dr. Lieberman the summer before when it became illegal for Jews to practice medicine, even on other Jews. Dr. Bauer had been a favor called in for a broken oscillating fan.

"Is it because your heart is better?" I asked, stupidly hopeful.

"It is because my heart is not Aryan enough. There is a new law that says Aryan doctors may only treat Aryan patients."

My hands were full of film for Rebecca's camera, and I hurled the package to the floor, wishing now that I had requested a kilo of meat.

"First they take away our doctors, then they forbid us to see theirs. Is this how they will exterminate us?"

"It is one of the ways."

Rebecca pulled me down into her patch of sunlight. "For me, it doesn't matter. Jewish, Aryan, unless he is also a magician, this is not something he will fix."

"But perhaps he can keep it from breaking down so fast."

A week later, Herr Gloeckner parked his shiny Peugeot automobile at the front of my shop and strode to my doorway, filling it and his Nazi uniform the way that sausage meat fills its casing. Herr Gloeckner held a sufficiently high rank in the Nazi Party not to bother with the charade of parking his shining piece of machinery around the back.

"There is a noise, Jakob," he informed me. "I will return at four."

When Herr Gloeckner returned at precisely four o'clock, he instructed me to turn on the Peugeot's engine. He stood in the street with his surprisingly small head cocked at an angle, as if Wagnerian opera was being played beneath the hood of his French automobile. After wasting a quarter-liter of petrol, Herr Gloeckner declared the Peugoet's engine returned to its proper smoothness.

"Of course, as you are forbidden to be in business, there can be no discussion of payment."

"That is true," I said, keeping my eyes on the ground. "Although perhaps Herr Gloeckner's not inconsiderable influence might extend toward granting an Aryan doctor leave to treat a non-Aryan patient?"

I heard nothing but the smooth sound of the Peugeot's engine, saw nothing except my own work shoes. I knew Herr Gloeckner kept a gun holstered at his waist, suspected he had shot more than his share of Jews for only the pleasure of using it. Herr Gloeckner exhaled, and in the sound I believe I heard him contemplating how difficult it would be to find someone else to repair the French automobile.

Herr Gloeckner's boots clicked around to the back of the car. The trunk creaked open.

A packet of coffee landed near my feet.

"Do not overestimate your abilities, Jew."

Two months later, Rebecca and I woke freezing in our bed, wondering how it could be so cold inside our flat, how we could feel so little warmth beneath our blankets. At first, we thought it was the cold that had woken us, then we heard the breaking glass. The sound was coming from everywhere in the city, everywhere at once. And if you did not think about what it could be, what it might mean, it was the most beautiful sound in the world, as if the air was coming together and making diamonds and they were falling from the sky. Because what else could it be? What else could be catching all that light in the middle of the night? That light suddenly appearing all over the city, flickering in the deep dark of November in a city so far to the north.

But this was Berlin, and November nights in Berlin did not give Jews diamonds falling from the sky. What we would get was broken glass, and fire, and revenge for a German embassy official shot in Paris by a Polish Jew who was going to make the rest of us pay for his moment of madness.

We would learn later that it was cold because the city officials had turned off the gas. Turned it off to all the Jewish businesses and Jewish neighborhoods before they went out to break the glass and set the fires. Because they did not want there to be any explosions. Could not risk burning anything that belonged to them. Then they christened the night—Kristallnacht. The Night of Broken Glass.

Rebecca and I wrapped ourselves in the cold blankets from our bed and went to the window. But there was nothing worth breaking on our street and all we could see was the flickering of firelight behind the dark shapes of buildings. All we could hear was the terrible and beautiful sound of breaking glass.

"So much fire and not a single siren," Rebecca whispered. "They are going to let everything burn."

She began pulling on sweaters and woolen pants. I wanted to throw myself on her and keep her inside. It would have taken nothing because she had so little strength by this time. But she would have left me for good the moment I let her up, so I started dressing with her, neither of us speaking, because what was there to say?

Rebecca was stuffing film into the pockets of her coat, all the film she had, which was dangerous. If a member of the Gestapo saw her taking photographs, he would confiscate any film as property of the Third Reich.

"Give me half," I said to her, "in case one of us is luckier than the other."

I do not know how we did not end up beaten or dead, or sent off to Sachsenhausen, the concentration camp the Nazis built in my hometown of Oranienburg, like so many other Berlin Jews that night. Maybe a piece of Pietr's luck was following us, for we roamed the city as if someone had cast a protective spell over us.

In Charlottenburg, the Fasanenstrasse Synagogue was on fire. This temple that had once held seventeen hundred worshippers under its dome, where the Byzantine archways and Majolica floor tiles had made even the undevout feel like God was watching out for the Jews. We stood before it in the cold and watched flames roar into the sky from its arched windows, as if Hell itself had forced its way through those Majolica tiles, Satan coming to claim the famous temple, shut these past two years by the Nazis.

"God has left this place," said a man still in his nightshirt.

"God has left Germany," said another man, who against all wisdom was wearing a yarmulke.

"Why not go with him?" replied a woman in furs. The boy at her side—too young to be awake and out of bed so late at night—was throwing rocks at the temple's windows, though all of them were already broken.

Everywhere we went synagogues were burning—the famous and the small. All with fire licking out of their windows, as if the man in the nightshirt and the man in the yarmulke had both spoken the truth. God had abandoned his temples and Satan had come to claim them, and when he finished, we would be next.

Rebecca and I went west, into Gruenwald, where rich Jews had built big houses they believed would protect them, but had only made them more conspicuous. Outside one of these houses, a woman wearing only a nightgown made of lace against the cold was being pushed out her door by a group of grinning SA men. The woman appeared stunned, as if she was asleep with her eyes open, or as if she wished she was asleep. Her hair, as long and shining blond as an American movie actress, was so knotted at the back, it looked like it was hurting her scalp, and there was blood smeared on her thighs. A man—her husband, maybe—came stumbling behind her. The center of his face was mashed, as if it had been repeatedly punched. More SA men followed the couple out of the house, their arms filled with wine bottles and oil paintings. One SA man dropped a polished mahogany radio on the ground and cursed as he bent to pick it up. I wondered if the radio would turn up in my shop, and what I could ask in exchange for its repair.

Then Pietr's luck—or whatever it was that had been protecting us—ran out. The SA man who had been carrying the radio straightened, glanced into the darkness, and began shouting. And I knew we were no longer invisible.

I pulled on Rebecca's arm, because she was still shooting pictures, still doing what Pietr would have done. "We have to run," I told her.

We went running down the street, but when I heard the SA man's boots behind us, I pulled us off the road and into the yards of the houses the rich Jews had built to protect themselves from all the terrible things that have happened to Jews throughout history. The terrible things they did not realize they could not protect themselves from. Not by money. Not by staying away from politics. Not by anything except not being a Jew.

On the soft dirt in the yards of those doomed Jews, I could not hear if the SA man was close behind us or some distance away. If he was close, he would have known exactly where we were by Rebecca's breathing, which was hoarse and ragged and asthmatic-sounding. And according to both of her former doctors, not doing her much good, as her heart had lost much of its ability to push air into her blood. I knew that if I made her run for much longer, it would kill her before the SA man did. I cut around a row of hedges and pushed Rebecca into the dirt behind them. Then I threw myself on top of her and prayed that the SA man would be too deaf to hear Rebecca's wheezing.

Maybe Pietr's luck had found us again. Or it is possible that the SA man decided that catching two Jews with nothing more valuable than a camera full of photographs was less profitable than paying more calls on the big houses of the rich Jews of Gruenwald. Either way, we lay behind the hedges until Rebecca's breathing quieted, with nothing to disturb us except the cold and the distant shouting of SA men.

From Gruenwald we went to the center of town, where the big windows of the Jewish-owned department stores on Tauentzienstrasse and the Kurfürstendamm had been shattered and all the glass counters and display cases inside smashed into a thousand pieces. It was deserted now, and we peered through the empty windows to see headless mannequins scattered among the shards of glass like the victims of a bomb blast, their dismembered limbs lying in the wreckage far from their torsos.

On the sidewalk, Rebecca and I stood ankle-deep in broken glass and it was cold enough to believe we were standing in ice crystals. I know I wanted to believe we were standing in ice crystals. She was shooting pictures—the mannequins, the looted display cases. I put my hand over the lens of her camera, and she gazed up at me.

I moved the Leica away from her face and took her hand.

"You should have worn gloves," I told her.

Even in the colorless light of the moon, her fingertips were blue. I put her hand in my pocket, all the film that had been there now shot.

"I want you to marry me," I said. "Even if it's only for a short time, I want one thing that feels permanent."

She shook her head, but she left her hand in my pocket.

"It will be easier to talk about a dead girl you once knew," she said, "than a dead wife."

I wanted to break something, but of course, everything around me was already broken.

"You cannot let me have this?"

She touched the side of my face. It was like being touched by ice. "I am letting you have something."

A few months later, when the Nazis passed a decree requiring Jews to turn in their gold and silver, Rebecca said, "See, I was right about not marrying. Now they cannot make us give up our wedding bands."

Rebecca was right about all that was happening in Germany. More right than I was. I do not know if it was her bad heart that gave her this clearer sight, as if her limited time in the world granted her a sharper sense of it. Or if it was only my willingness to ignore what was going on around me, as if I wished to prove Herr Brackman correct when he claimed some people will refuse to see the truth, even if you put it on the front page.

The news that the Nazis had marched into Czechoslovakia appeared on the front page of every newspaper still being printed in Berlin that March. Rebecca had read the entire story to me when I returned from the shop, whether I wished to hear it or not. It was the first springlike day of the year, but she had lit the stove and was wearing a heavy sweater and a woolen shawl.

"Hitler claims he has gone into Czechoslovakia only to protect the Germans who are living there." She wrapped the shawl closer around her shoulders. "But you know he intends to have the world."

"The world will stop him."

"So far, no one has tried."

She did not say it, but I knew Rebecca meant it was time for me to leave. That it was only a matter of weeks before the Führer did something that would at last wake up the world, force England, or France, or possibly the Soviet Union, to declare war on us, making it too late for anyone—Jewish or not—to get out of the country.

But Czechoslovakia was far away and the newspapers—under the control of the Ministry for Enlightenment and Propaganda—insisted that Hitler was not preparing for war.

Although the celebration of Hitler's birthday—five weeks later—

might have looked like preparation, if we could have seen what we had been told were tanks and soldiers marching up Unter den Linden, the street where I had fixed Rebecca's bicycle in a pouring rain. But we could not see them. Since Kristallnacht, Jews had been forbidden to walk on that street. Just as they had been forbidden to walk on Wilhelmstrasse, and Hermann-Göring-Strasse. Just as they had been forbidden to enter any theater, movie house, concert hall, museum, swimming pool, sports arena, and exhibition hall.

But Hitler would not allow anyone to ignore his birthday—even Jews—and he filled the April sky with Messerschmitts. Still I did my best to ignore it, shutting the window against the spring air, putting a Duke Ellington record on the gramophone and playing it as loudly as the machine would go, trying to drown out the roaring of those engines in the sky above Kruezberg. But Rebecca pulled me from my chair, dragged me to the window and flung it open, made me stand in front of it. And when I wouldn't look up, she put her hands on my face and tilted my head, forced me to stare at the blue April sky being blocked out by the dark underbellies of bombers, rows of them making it look like the sky itself was moving and we were being left behind.

Then she took me outside, made me walk until we were a block from where Unter den Linden joined Universität—which was as far as Jews were allowed—where we felt the rumbling of Hitler's tanks moving up the tree-lined street we used to think of as ours, felt it deep in our bones, as if the Führer was demonstrating his power over us from a distance. The blocks around us were filled with people waving red flags with black swastikas, but I do not believe any of them were Jews. All the Jews of Berlin were hiding in their houses—our birthday present to the Führer. I wanted to be one of them, but Rebecca was moving through the side streets toward the forbidden Unter den Linden, and I could not let her go alone.

We squeezed our way through the cheering crowds on the wide avenue. On the ground, Rebecca found one of the red and black flags, and put it in my hand so I wouldn't seem conspicuous. She kept her camera in front of her own face. All around us, happy Germans threw flowers and waved flags, and shouted, "*Heil Hitler,*" too preoccupied with the miles of rolling tanks and soldiers on horseback to notice the Jews in their midst—the pale woman in the sweater taking photographs, and the man who could no longer ignore what the Führer had in mind for his birthday celebration next year.

The next day when I returned from the shop, the flat felt as if a hole had opened up in it and I knew Rebecca had left me.

She had taken everything that had belonged to her. The wool felt beret I had never told her was too big for her head and all of her photographs. All except one print of the old woman with the shriveled leg. That she had left on the kitchen table next to my passport.

"So this is how you will do it. You will leave me first." I sent the words echoing into the hole that had opened up in the flat.

Rebecca had left me one other thing, although she had probably forgotten about it. A photograph of herself.

I had taken it the summer I began collecting favors from Nazis. It was a warm day, and Rebecca and I were picnicking on one of the yellow benches in the Tiergarten, sharing a quarter-kilo of French pâté—courtesy of a motorcycle with a temperamental engine that belonged to a high-ranking SA officer. I am certain it was a trick of the sunlight, but for once, Rebecca looked flushed, as if there was blood running beneath the flesh of her cheeks, and I wanted a photograph of it, proof maybe that she would be with me longer.

I had had to make her swear to develop it, and even then, she would print me only one copy.

"Hide it somewhere, or I will throw it out."

I had hidden the photograph between the pages of *Das Kapital*, because Rebecca would never search for it there. She thought Karl Marx was tedious.

I could have looked for Rebecca, but I did not think I would find her. I could have turned one of my favors into having the Gestapo search for her, but even if they found her, I knew she would leave me again. Instead, I sent a message to Herr Gloeckner letting him know that a Peugeot engine of his automobile's exact make and model had recently turned up in my shop—actually, I had had it for months—and that while it was in poor repair, I was confident I could get it into even better condition than the one presently inside his vehicle. I then mentioned that the SS *St. Louis* would be departing Hamburg for Havana in three weeks' time, and that it would be carrying approximately nine hundred Jews lucky enough to be in possession of one-way tickets and Cuban visas.

Herr Gloeckner sent a message back that he would like to test this new engine before going to the inconvenience of troubling the Cuban embassy. I replied that as I did not wish to overestimate my abilities, I would wire him the location of the new engine once I was safely in Hamburg with my ticket and Cuban visa, reminding him that if I failed to deliver on my promise, it would be no inconvenience for someone of his standing in the party to have me arrested there.

Fortunately, Herr Gloeckner's fondness for his French automobile exceeded his dislike of Jews. A first-class ticket for the SS *St. Louis* and a Cuban visa arrived within a week of my message.

I took the last possible train to Hamburg before the *St. Louis* was set to sail, thinking maybe Rebecca would change her mind, even when I knew she wouldn't. Still, at the railroad station, I stood on the platform until the conductor stopped to ask me if I was getting on or not, and if I was, then I had better hurry up and do it.

. . .

In Hamburg, we were made to wait in a big wooden building known as Shed 76 that sat at the end of the docks. It was a building of no windows, and it was damp. And the way it was bleak, and how the Gestapo officers looked at our Jewish passports made me think that when we were finally let through the door, we would not be walking up the gangplank of a pleasure boat bound for Havana, but into a boxcar headed toward one of the concentration camps we had only then begun hearing about. Concentration camps with the names Dachau and Sachsenhausen and Buchenwald.

The St. Louis *is a lie*, were the words going through my mind, while a square-headed Gestapo officer examined my documents. *It is only another way to make the Jews pay for their own extermination*. For why would the Nazis send nine hundred Jews on a one-way pleasure cruise to the Caribbean?

"This is a first-class ticket." The square-headed Gestapo officer took in my frayed woolen trousers and no-longer-white shirt. It had seemed a waste to turn a favor into new clothes.

"It was arranged by a ranking officer of the Nazi Party."

"First class?"

I stood myself straighter. "Are you questioning Herr Gloeckner's judgment?"

The square-headed officer made me open my suitcase and rifled through my belongings—shirts, trousers, socks, underwear. He found Rebecca's photograph of the woman with the shriveled leg and held it close to his small eyes.

"I know this place."

"It is the plaza outside the Dietrich-Eckart-Bühne amphitheater."

"This is government property."

I let him have it. Let him, because I still had the photograph I'd taken of Rebecca that warm day in the Tiergarten. It was folded in half and tucked into my sock because I had noticed how Nazis were reluctant to make Jews take off their socks, as if they believed the rumor that we possessed hooves like the devil.

When he gave me back my suitcase, I went to sit on the wooden benches beside the other Jews who were hoping that the *St. Louis* was not a lie. It was not much after that the shouting started.

The person shouting was a dark-haired man of close to fifty who appeared to be wearing a larger man's suit, or maybe he had only been shrunken and put back into his own. He was standing before the desk of the square-headed Gestapo officer who had taken Rebecca's photograph of the woman with the shriveled leg, and spit was flying from his mouth as he ranted. "I am telling you this was no accident! No random mishandling of luggage. This was the deliberate work of the Gestapo!"

What I heard in the shrunken man's voice was something I had never heard in a human voice before—the sound a mechanical thing makes when it is near to breaking. When all the other parts of the machine are compensating, so it is functioning in a fashion, but you can tell it will not be for long. I am thinking that the man's wife heard it as well, for she had her hand on the man's knobby shoulder and was whispering into his ear, like that might be a kind of fixing.

"Herr Loesser," the square-headed officer was saying, his tone full of condescension. "The Gestapo takes no interest in your family's luggage."

"Yes, yes, yes, yes." The shrunken man moved his head up and down as if a spring in his neck had come loose. "That is what you always say. The Gestapo has no interest in you, Herr Loesser, but we will put you on our watch list. The Gestapo has no interest in you, Herr Loesser, but we will put you on our arrest list. The Gestapo has no interest in you, Herr Loesser, but we will put you on our death list."

Herr Loesser's wife turned pale and gripped the sleeves of his too-large suit, bunching them like curtains. Beside her stood a thin-shouldered boy of twelve or so. But it was the girl at his side—Herr Loesser's daughter, I supposed—who caught my attention. She was a dark-haired girl of sixteen or seventeen, and there was something about the clear-eyed way she was watching the interaction between her father and the square-headed officer that made me think of Rebecca. *This,* I thought, *is what she was like when she still believed in the dream of Paris, in the time when she knew nothing about her heart.*

"Why do you bring up arrest lists, Herr Loesser?" the square-headed officer asked. "No one has said anything about arrest lists. I have only informed you that one of your family's trunks has been mistakenly sent to Shanghai."

"My husband has been unwell," Frau Loesser murmured to the officer.

The square-headed officer gathered all of the Loesser family's documents in one large hand and rose. "We will look into this mention of arrest lists."

Herr Loesser's daughter stepped close to the square-headed officer and gazed up at him with dark eyes. "My father was a lawyer before the Reich Act." Her voice was low. "I fear he sometimes forgets himself."

The officer looked down at the young Jewish girl. She held his eyes, then only slightly lifted the corners of her mouth—not enough to be called a smile.

The square-headed officer set down the Loessers' documents.

Later, when I saw the family sitting on the wooden benches, I noticed Herr Loesser's daughter wiping her hands on her skirt, as if she had touched something unclean.

The Germans made us wait inside the dim dampness of Shed 76 long enough for us to stop believing in the *St. Louis*, to grow certain we had done them the favor of traveling to Hamburg to prepare for our own deaths. Only then did the doors at the front of that bleak building slide open to reveal—like a floating city—the beautiful ship. Its hundreds of windows sparkling in the sunlight, its flags—covered in swastikas—snapping in the wind off the ocean.

A man in the spotless white uniform of the ship appeared in the open doorway.

"Might I have your attention, ladies and gentlemen?"

We sat stunned, for it had been so long since anyone had called us anything but *Jew*.

"You may now board the SS *St. Louis*."

Then, as if to stun us further, the man in white gave a small bow.

Music began to drift through the open doors—"Vienna, City of My Dreams"—and as we stepped through the open door into the light, we saw that it was coming from an orchestra playing on the ship's deck.

First up the gangplank was a tall woman whose traveling clothes consisted of a fur wrap and beneath it, an evening gown. It was the kind of gown a Hollywood actress would wear, made of shimmering fabric that caught the light as she stepped through the doors, reflecting it back into Shed 76, into the eyes of the Gestapo officers examining the documents of the latecomers, letting them know that Jews could dress like Hollywood actresses. But this woman—Babette Spiegel, the wife of a doctor—was more interesting than any Hollywood actress, for above the shimmering gown and the fur wrap, she wore a perfectly round monocle tucked into the crease of her left eye.

Babette Spiegel began to walk up the gangplank as slowly and grandly as any Hollywood actress. She did not turn her head to see if her husband, handsome in a white dinner jacket, or her young daughters, dressed identically in dresses I recognized from the shops on the

Kurfürstendamm—where Jews had not been allowed to shop for some years—were following her.

A photographer stood beside the gangplank, and spotting him, Babette Spiegel stopped walking and rested one long-fingered hand on the metal railing, and put the other on her shimmering hip. She lifted her chin, as if she knew how the sunlight would catch the golden edge of her monocle.

But the photographer moved the camera away from his face.

"Is the light not quite right?" Babette Spiegel asked him.

The photographer did not answer her, and before she could ask him anything else, a small and disheveled man pushed his way through the crowd and came running up the gangplank behind Babette Spiegel.

I had smelled him before I saw him, and he smelled like a hundred dead animals, like rot and decay and death. His face looked bruised and the back of his hair was matted with blood. His clothes were shabby and it appeared that he had slept in them, but worse, they seemed to be stained with entrails, as if he had come to the dock straight from butchering animals.

Later, once we were at sea and away from Germany, he would tell me that his name was Aaron Rosner, and that for the nine days before boarding the *St. Louis*, he had hidden himself from the Gestapo among the animal hides outside a tannery yard near Hamburg. When I knew him better, he would tell me that he had been arrested a block from his house during Kristallnacht and sent to Dachau.

"Every morning after roll call, they hung somebody and made us watch," he would tell me. "And every night after evening count, they drowned somebody in a vat of water and made us watch that, too."

After six months, with no explanation of why he had been arrested or why he was being let go, the Nazis released him and told him he had fourteen days to leave Germany. His wife and family sold everything they had to buy him a tourist-class ticket on the *St. Louis*. They could not raise enough money to buy tickets for her or his two children.

"I try not to think about them anymore," he told me.

But on this day, Aaron Rosner—smelling horrible and with blood in his hair and the guts of animals on his coat—was so eager to leave Germany, he was rushing the gangway, pushing ahead of Doktor Spiegel and his daughters, stepping on the train of Babette Spiegel's shimmering gown.

The photographer put the camera back to his face and waved at Babette Spiegel to move out of the way. But the sight of the long lens of the camera being aimed at him halted Aaron Rosner, made him hunch his neck into his shoulders and shift from one side of the gangway to the other.

"Keep still!" the photographer snapped.

"What are you doing to this poor man?" demanded Doktor Spiegel.

"I am from the Ministry of Propaganda," the photographer said without removing the camera from his face.

These words stopped us all as surely as if that camera had been turned into a rifle. Babette Spiegel was so still, her dress had ceased to shimmer. Her husband and daughters appeared as if frozen on the gangplank. I stood behind the Loesser family, not daring to take a breath. Only poor Aaron Rosner, who had shut his eyes and clenched his fists, could not stop himself from shaking.

The photographer shot several pictures of Aaron Rosner, the clicking of the shutter sounding in the crisp air like gunfire. Then he waved his hand and released us.

Herr Loesser began the climb up the gangplank.

In the bright of day, I saw how unwell the man looked, how deep-set and haunted his eyes. The photographer could not have missed it either. He stopped Herr Loesser with a raised hand and put his camera close to the man's face, shot two or three pictures. As the camera's bulbs flashed—bulbs which seemed unnecessary, as the day was so bright—Herr Loesser flinched as if he had been struck across the mouth.

Herr Loesser's dark-haired daughter—that girl so much like the Rebecca I had never known—had gone ahead, but seeing what was happening, she turned and came down the gangplank, put her hands on her father's shoulders and spoke softly into his ear.

"Ruth," Herr Loesser said, in that voice of something near breaking.

"Another," the photographer demanded. Again he brought the camera close to Herr Loesser's face. Again the bulbs flashed.

Herr Loesser, like a cornered animal, began to back into me.

"Be still!" the photographer said.

But Herr Loesser would not be still. The back of his too-large suit was pressed against my chest, and I knew if those bulbs went off again, he would run, or worse.

Herr Loesser was shaking his head, saying, *"Nein, nein, nein, nein, nein,"* although everybody knew you did not say *nein* to the Ministry of Propaganda. Not if you wanted your family to keep walking up that gangplank, not if you didn't want to end up in one of those camps we had only recently learned the names of—Dachau, Sachsenhausen, and Buchenwald.

"One more for the Ministry." The photographer brought the lens of the camera within inches of Herr Loesser's face.

The gangplank beneath my feet began to vibrate with footfalls. A man in a white uniform had come out of the ship and was walking toward us with deliberate steps. He pushed himself between Herr Loesser and the photographer's camera, as if stepping between a firing squad and its victim.

"Get away from my ship," he demanded.

The photographer did not move from his spot at the side of the gangplank. "These photographs are to be rushed to Berlin at the request of Minister Goebbels."

"I do not care if Adolf Hitler wishes to view them. I will not have my passengers harassed."

The photographer smirked at the man in the white uniform. "I do not believe the captain of a pleasure vessel has the authority to override an order from Minister Goebbels."

The photographer again pointed his camera at Herr Loesser.

With one quick motion of his arm, the captain knocked the camera out of the photographer's hands, clattering it to the dock.

"If you do not immediately remove yourself," he said, "I will kick you and your camera into the sea. And I believe we have just emptied the bilge."

The photographer looked from his empty hands to the foamy water at the base of the ship.

The captain turned toward Herr Loesser and made a small bow. "I am Captain Schroeder, and on behalf of Hapag Cruise Lines, I apologize."

Herr Loesser, the Loesser family, and I stood on the gangway without moving.

Captain Schroeder put his arm out. "Madam," he said to Frau Loesser.

Herr Loesser's wife placed the very tips of her fingers on Captain Schroeder's white sleeve and allowed him to lead her onto the ship. Ruth Loesser took hold of her father's arm in such a way to make it look like he was leading her. I gave Herr Loesser's back a nudge. "Maybe we should follow," I said to him quietly. "Before anybody has his mind changed."

. . .

The St. Louis sailed from Hamburg harbor on May 13, 1939. Germany was not yet at war with any country, and even we Jews did not know for certain what was happening in the camps. Not unless we had been in them ourselves, and very few of the people who went into the camps came back out to tell their stories.

In 1939, most of the world did not know about the camps, or very much about what was happening to us in Germany. But the photographer who stood beside the gangway and insisted on photographing Aaron Rosner with entrails on his clothes and Herr Loesser hunted and shrunken in his suit—choosing them to represent us rather than Babette Spiegel in her shimmering dress—made me understand why the Nazis would allow nine hundred Jews to board a pleasure boat bound for Havana.

Joseph Goebbels wished to turn us into the real-life representations of the Eternal Jew—the exhibit Rebecca had read to me about on that unusually clear autumn day. We were to be the exhibit's hook noses and thick lips made into flesh and blood. The personifications of the Jew who had mocked Jesus and was condemned to wander the earth until Judgment Day. The Jew who would have considered it a favor to be put out of his misery.

Goebbels would show the world the photographs of Aaron Rosner and Herr Loesser—and a hundred other miserable Jews boarding the *St. Louis*—the Jews the Nazis in their compassion were permitting to sail away from Germany in the luxury cabins of a pleasure boat. And once he had shown us to the world, who in it would criticize Germany for not wishing to keep us? Who in it would criticize them for anything they decided to do with us?

I understood all this before I had reached the top of the gangplank, had absorbed this truth before I watched the Loesser family—with that daughter so like Rebecca—disappear down the ship's corridor. Yet once I was shown to my first-class stateroom, I forgot everything that had happened on the gangplank and fell into a kind of dream world, a spell cast by the sparkling ship itself.

I did not think Herr Gloeckner had bought me a first-class ticket because he valued my services so highly. I believe he bought it because it did not occur to him to buy any other kind. I had never seen luxury of this sort before. Everything in my stateroom gleamed and shone with a brilliance that spoke of money. The bed linen was an unnatural white and had been pressed to the smoothness of marble. Even the air inside the cabin seemed softer, as if the staff of the ship had whisked it, so it would be easier to breathe. I could not think of hanging my rumpled trousers and frayed shirts on the shining wooden hangers, certain the closet would spit them out the second I turned my back.

This dream world persisted when I left my stateroom, for I walked on polished mahogany decks and thick carpets, ate at tables draped with starched cloths. And even if this luxury had vanished, if my stateroom were magically turned into my flat in the Kruezberg, I—and every passenger on the *St. Louis*—would still have imagined we had entered a place of fantasy. For as long as the white-uniformed staff—the *German* white-uniformed staff—continued to call us *sir* or *madam*, continued to bring us cold drinks and warm tea and fresh linens for our rooms, for as long as they did not suddenly stop and put a gun to our heads and call us *Jew*, and demand we begin waiting on them, we would remain in this dream state.

Thus for the first days of our two-week journey, I—and the other nine hundred Jews—floated about the *St. Louis* like people under a spell. Mornings, we played shuffleboard under an open sky on A deck. Late afternoons, we waltzed across the checkerboard floor of the *tanzplatz* on B deck. Evenings, we toasted each other with champagne in the Schanke Bar on C deck. We traded our real money—what little we had of it—for shipboard money, buying postcards with photographs of the glittering ship. I do not know what the other nine hundred Jews wrote on theirs, or to whom they addressed them. I wrote, *I am well, but somehow I think that you know that. Come and find me.* Then I tossed it into the sea.

Under the spell of the *St. Louis*—and maybe also the presence of Herr Loesser's daughter, whose existence alone seemed to promise a second chance for Rebecca—I invented a future I knew better than to believe in, but believed in anyway. On the afternoon Doktor Spiegel said over a game of cards that he had heard the Nazis intended to move Jews into ghettos for the purpose of making it easier to round them up—Doktor Spiegel always knew a lot about what the Nazis were planning, I do not know how—I dreamed up a story in which Rebecca did not fall into their hands. If I had not done this, it would have been the same as if the Nazis had sent me to one of their camps and were exterminating me piece by piece.

I leaned against the bright brass railings of the *St. Louis* and saw Rebecca's story inside my head as if it was an elaborate machine I intended to fix. She would use her French to fool the Nazis and stay out of their ghetto, meet instead some French journalists traveling in Berlin, drawing them to her with her Leica. Journalists who would help her get to France, take her all the way to Paris. Because this was a dream, and where else could I send her?

Beneath the spell of the *St. Louis*, this story seemed plausible. More than plausible, it seemed true. Something that had already happened. And I passed days wandering the sparkling ship, my head filled with pictures of Rebecca in Paris, doing all the things she had told she would do those many evenings in our flat in the Kruezberg.

. . .

There was only one of us nine hundred Jews who was not seduced by the dream world of the *St. Louis*. And I did not think of him until one evening, when his voice—sounding like the thing inside him had moved closer to breaking down—startled me from behind a low wall near the ship's swimming pool.

"They are here, but they will not find me. They are here, but they will not find me."

Herr Loesser was repeating this phrase in the cadence of davening, as if the narrow space behind the wall where he had hidden himself was a synagogue, and he was there to petition God for protection.

One of the white-uniformed crewmen was at the far end of the deck, coming toward us with his arms full of towels, and I feared that if the crewman came upon Herr Loesser crouched behind this wall, davening like a madman, he might change his mind about all of us, maybe change the minds of the rest of the crewmen, and they would stop treating us like passengers and begin treating us like the refugees we were.

"Herr Loesser," I whispered, leaning over the wall.

Herr Loesser grabbed onto the front of my shirt, pulling me close. His breath was vile, a decay nearly as bad as that of Aaron Rosner when he'd first entered Shed 76. But also worse, in its way, for the decay inside Herr Loesser was still working on him.

"You cannot tell them about this hiding place. You cannot let them know anything about it."

"Of course. Of course." I attempted to remove Herr Loesser's hands from my shirt. "Why not come and walk with me? The sunset is lovely."

"Cannot you see?" Herr Loesser breathed his evil breath into my face. "That is how they trick us, with sunsets and swimming pools. Then it is off to the death camps."

The man's eyes were burning and at first I thought it was the reflection of the low-lying sun. Then I understood the sun was on the other side of the ship, and it was his madness I was seeing.

I glanced up. The crewman with the towels was closer now.

"Herr Loesser, the Nazis and the death camps are days behind us."

Herr Loesser started laughing—a maniacal laugh that nudged the thing inside him closer to collapse.

"What if I take you to Frau Loesser?" I said. "To your family. They must be alone."

This mention of his family diluted some of the burning in his eyes.

"Come."

Herr Loesser's hands still had hold of my shirtfront. I took him by the elbows and helped him to his feet.

"All is well here, gentlemen?" asked the crewman with the towels.

I nodded, placing my hands over those of Herr Loesser.

When we reached the Loessers' stateroom, Herr Loesser stumbled through the door, past his wife, and threw himself onto the bed. Frau Loesser stood in the doorway a moment looking me over, then she told me to wait. After a minute or two, her daughter, Ruth, returned with one of her father's suits.

"You do not think your father will need this himself?" I asked, remembering the trunk that had been sent to Shanghai.

"Maybe one less suit will force my father to spend more of his time in our stateroom," Ruth Loesser said with a half-smile.

"Thank you," I told her, and began to go.

"So that you know," she said. "The Gestapo have been trying to arrest my father for the past month. I do not know how he managed to get us onto this boat."

. . .

After I had been on the *St. Louis* for one week, the dream I had drifted into began to be interrupted by a twitching in my hands. I would be sitting in one of the wood chaises on A deck, practicing the phrases from my German/Spanish dictionary, and I would glance up and see my hands in the air above my lap, my wrists turning one way and then the other, as if I was tightening the bolts on an invisible engine. Later, I would be in my stateroom, looking at the photograph of Rebecca—which the spell of the ship had lulled me into taking out of my sock and tucking into the corner of my gleaming mirror—and I would catch the reflected motion of my fingers plucking at something in the air, like I was pulling at the wires of a radio's speakers.

I had never gone so long without having anything to fix, and I wandered the ship, searching for something—anything—that was broken. But long before we had come aboard, the Nazis had taken everything we owned that might need fixing—even our watches—for the small amount of gold they contained, and except for a suitcase with a sticky latch that belonged to a Herr Bergmann, there was nothing.

As the days went by, the jumpiness in my hands grew worse. I could not shave myself without my fingers jerking so violently, my face began to look as bad as Aaron Rosner's had the day he arrived in Shed 76. One afternoon at lunch, I caught Babette Spiegel squinting at me through her monocle and realized that my hands were twirling in the air above my schnitzel. That evening, Doktor Spiegel knocked at my door with a bottle of sedative in the pocket of his dinner jacket.

The next day, I sought out Purser Mueller and told him I had worked in shipbuilding in Berlin and was curious to see the engine room of the *St. Louis*. It was, of course, a lie, but I imagined that being surrounded by so much machinery might soothe me enough to stop my hands from flying through the air. Purser Mueller suggested that after dinner I go down to D deck and seek out First Officer Closterman.

First Officer Closterman was a short man with rounded shoulders and a small head, as if he had been bred to work in the tunnel-like hallways beneath the passenger decks. He did not seem especially happy to see me in his domain. He took me downstairs and led me through a door that had been painted with the words *NO PASSENGER ENTRY*, and did not once look back to see if I was keeping up with him.

The deck down here belonged to the crew, and smelled of cigarettes and piss and seawater. But beneath those smells was the scent of machine oil and metal, and the familiarity of those eased the restlessness of my hands, which by that time had begun to travel up my forearms. It was the scent of machine oil and metal that kept me moving behind the hunched figure of First Officer Closterman, even as I heard the singing—the kind of drunken singing that is generally accompanied by spilled beer and fist-banging and somebody being beaten.

We turned the corner and came upon the singers. Six crewmen seated at a wooden table, all with beer foam on their lips. I recognized Steward Schiendick, a thick-set man with black eyebrows, whom none of us knew very well, as he nearly never spoke to the passengers. I recognized also Assistant Purser Reich, bland and blond beside him. The other men's faces were familiar from my days aboard the ship, although I was used to them looking less drunk.

Beer was puddled on the wooden table and fists were being pounded on its scarred surface, and I was certain that soon someone was going to be beaten, and equally certain it would be me. Because I knew the song Steward Schiendick and Assistant Purser Reich, and now First Officer Closterman—for he had left me in the doorway and joined the others at the table—were singing. I had heard it many times—this favorite anthem of the Nazi Party—could recognize it despite the fact that the men singing it were so drunk, their words were running together on a river of beer.

It was the *"Horst Wessel."* Named for a man who had been elevated to the status of a martyr by Joseph Goebbels himself. A man who had done nothing more heroic than write a Nazi poem, and then get himself shot in the mouth by a Communist for refusing to pay his half of the rent.

And now this song—this Nazi anthem—was being sung two decks below nine hundred Jews who had been seduced by the spell of this sparkling ship. Nine hundred Jews who had been lulled into believing they were passengers and not refugees, who had been called *sir* and *madam* and fed cold drinks and warm tea until they had ceased being wary.

I stood before the table of drunken crewmen, my hands twitching, and raised my voice above their drunken singing.

"I am only here for the engine room," I said, meaning, *I have not come here as a Jew.*

But how could they see me as anything else—no matter how many times they were forced to call me *sir*, to carry fresh towels and cold drinks to my stateroom?

"Purser Mueller has given his permission," I added.

They ignored me—Steward Schiendick, Assistant Purser Reich, First Officer Closterman, and the others, whose names I did not know, whose names I hoped I would never know. They pounded their fists on the table and continued to sing. Louder now. Because you sing louder when you have the object of your hatred before you. You sing as if you have only just thought of the words of the song yourself, as if you have only just come to understand their meaning.

I considered going into the engine room without their permission. Walking past the table of drunken Germans and through the door not more than a dozen feet away. But I had lived too long under the Nazis and had forgotten how to act with such independence. I considered also turning around, retracing my steps back down the long hallway smelling of cigarettes and piss and beer. But I needed to get inside that engine room, needed it so badly that even if one or more of those men rose from the table and beat me, it would be less than my own body was doing to me now.

I remained in the doorway and absorbed their hatred, stood silent while the crewmen sang every verse of the *"Horst Wesse,"* verses that boasted of streets filled with brown battalions, of millions gazing upon Hitler's swastika. When they were finished and sat around the scarred table with beer-bleared eyes, too exhausted by the energy they had put into their singing to rise to their feet and beat me, I said again, "The engine room?"

First Officer Closterman raised his head and regarded me. Then he waved a weary hand at the door behind the table.

I hurried through it.

The familiar sound of machinery—that low and constant rumbling like something alive—surrounded me. I dropped to the floor, getting grease on the trousers of Herr Loesser's suit, and breathed deep, wanting to coat the inside of my lungs, the inside of my whole body with the comforting smell of motor oil and metal—a smell that could make you believe there was nothing in the world except things that could be fixed if only you could see them inside your head.

But all I could see inside my head was Herr Loesser, trembling behind the wall near the swimming pool. Herr Loesser, who had not succumbed to the dream of the sparkling ship, who had understood that there was something broken inside the *St. Louis*. I think because he had something broken inside himself, something that had been broken by the same people.

I pushed myself upright and sat back against one wall. My hands were twitching in my lap, the creases of the fingers stained black from the grease of machinery—the result of so many years of fixing things—a black that never washed out, that made me look, I sometimes thought, guilty of something.

I needed something to fix, and I wondered if it might not be Herr Loesser. If not fix him, maybe keep him from breaking down, the way I had kept the ancient printing presses of the Communist newspaper from breaking down. For I was worried what would happen to his daughter—who was so like what I'd imagined Rebecca had been before the knowledge about her heart broke some part of her—if the thing inside her father, the thing that had set him to davening behind the pool wall, continued to misfunction.

I thought, too, that if I could keep Herr Loesser from breaking down, even if it was only for the single week we had left aboard the ship, it would mean that the story I had invented for Rebecca—the story of the French journalists, of Rebecca going to Paris—would be real. That is how strong the dream world of the *St. Louis* was for me. A world in which Germans called me *sir* and brought me drinks. A world in which we used different money and spent our days playing shuffleboard and dancing waltzes. A world in which I could believe that keeping one man from breaking down would keep Rebecca alive.

The next morning, I went to the Loessers' stateroom and asked Herr Loesser to walk with me on A deck.

Herr Loesser cowered behind his half-open door.

"No, no, no. There are Gestapo on this ship."

I did not want to tell him something I was not certain of myself, so I said, "I have dealt with them before. I promise you will be safe in my company."

Herr Loesser looked me up and down, then asked me to wait. He closed the door. When he opened it, he was wearing a heavy overcoat and had a fedora pulled low on his forehead.

"The morning is warm," I told him.

Herr Loesser merely shook his head and pushed past me.

We walked the polished wood of the deck, Herr Loesser flinching each time a seagull came cawing too close to his head. When I asked how he had come to be on a Gestapo arrest list, he told me he had been a lawyer in Berlin until the Nazis made it illegal for Jews to practice law.

"After that, I prepared briefs for German lawyers."

"For money?"

He nodded.

"You should have done it for favors."

"My family couldn't eat favors."

I was about to tell him otherwise, then realized the explanation would not matter now.

It was one of Herr Loesser's German clients who had told him the Gestapo had learned what he was doing and were on their way to arrest him.

"I had already bought our tickets for the *St. Louis*," he said, "so I only had to stay out of their hands for a month."

"A month is a long time."

"You cannot know. I left my family and slept in the streets, sometimes in worse places. I knew the smell Aaron Rosner brought with him into Shed 76."

Herr Loesser told me about the Germans willing to hide Jews for a price, and equally willing to give them up when the Gestapo came offering more. "One night I woke to the voice of the woman hiding me counting marks. When she got to a number higher than the amount I had paid her, I went for the window. Do you know these

Germans nail their windows shut so that the Jews they're hiding can't escape? Fortunately some of them are not smart enough to hide the hammer."

I coaxed Herr Loesser into telling me every detail of the month he had spent in hiding. And the next day, I did the same. It was, in my mind, like grinding down the rough edges of a gear to make it turn more smoothly, and I believed that if Herr Loesser—Max, as I came to call him—repeated these stories enough times, they, too, would lose the rough edges that were catching inside him.

But it seemed that the *St. Louis* was against me, for after we had been at sea for ten days, the ship killed one of us.

The dead was Morris Weitz, a man in his seventies. He had died in his bed and his wife claimed that what had truly killed her husband was having to leave their home in Germany. Still, the old professor had walked onto the *St. Louis* in what had seemed good health, and now ten days later, he was dead.

Max Loesser claimed it was the Gestapo. During our morning walk on A deck, he ranted about the Gestapo's secret tactics, talked of poisoning, predicted he would be next, and it seemed all the wearing down I had hoped to accomplish had only sharpened the rough edges inside him.

Captain Schroeder wished to keep the news of Morris Weitz's death as quiet as possible. But as we were still four days from Cuba, and with no refrigeration facilities to keep a body that long, he was forced to order a sea burial. He arranged it for eleven o'clock that evening, when few passengers would be wandering the deck.

It was a strange thing, a funeral on the deck of a pleasure boat. Morris Weitz had been stitched into a piece of sailcloth weighted with iron bars, then laid on a plank a few feet from the swimming pool. Those of us who had heard came with the sleeves and collars of our shirts torn in grief, though none of us had shirts to spare.

A rabbi was found from the passenger list. He stood beside the sailcloth-covered body of Morris Weitz and spoke the service in Hebrew. He had shortened the committal service by half, for Captain Schroeder did not want to keep the ship stopped for very long.

"May he come to his place in peace," the rabbi intoned.

Without a moment's breath, Purser Mueller tilted the plank and Morris Weitz slid into the sea with an insignificant splash.

"Remember God, that we are of dust."

At these words, we went in a line to a children's sandbox—the only dirt on the ship—and scooped up handfuls of sand to throw over the bobbing shroud of Morris Weitz.

Only then we heard the footsteps, running toward us through the darkness of the deck.

Max Loesser, dressed in his overcoat and fedora.

I had tried to keep the timing of Morris Weitz's funeral from Max, but I think maybe his obsession with death made him more attuned to it. He rushed toward the children's sandbox, pushing aside those still waiting to fill their hands, and grabbed up big handfuls of sand himself, leaving a trail of it on the polished deck as he staggered to the railing.

"Herr Loesser," Captain Schroeder said. But even the imposing captain made no impression on Max Loesser.

"Max." I tried to put my hands on his shoulders.

But no one could stop Max Loesser. He leaned far out over the railing and with a terrible sound that was like choking, hurled his sand into the wind, which blew it all back onto us. And while we were wiping the sand out of our eyes, Max Loesser shouted, "This is for all of us! For soon we will all end up like Morris Weitz, dead and in shrouds."

I heard in his voice how close to breaking he was. How little I had done to fix him. I wrapped my arms around Max Loesser and dragged him away from the ship's railing.

"Come, Max," I said. "Frau Weitz does not need to hear any more."

It seemed that the death of Morris Weitz—as well as Max Loesser's outburst over his sailcloth-covered body—unleashed something in the ship, set it free to prey on us. For that night, one of the *St. Louis* crewmen, a kitchen hand named Leonid Berg, leapt to his death in the exact spot where we had committed Professor Weitz to the sea.

Captain Schroeder tried to keep the news of Leonid Berg's suicide from us. But this was not the type of news he could keep quiet on a ship of nine hundred Jews. Most of us had been awakened in the early hours when the *St. Louis* turned around to search the black water for the kitchen hand's body. We had been awakened again when the ship resumed course, after the sea refused to yield it up.

All of us had lived too long under the Nazis not to question the notice Purser Mueller tacked onto the message board on B deck describing crewman Berg's frequent attacks of depression.

"Someone discovered he was a Jew," Herr Schiller said. And most of us agreed. What we were divided on was whether Steward Schiendick had thrown him into the water or merely hounded him into doing it himself.

The death of the kitchen hand woke everyone from the spell of the *St. Louis*. It was as if we all knew that beneath the polished and gleaming decks there were men with beer on their lips who were singing the *"Horst Wessel."* As one, we ceased acting like passengers, and began acting like what we were—nine hundred Jewish refugees fleeing with everything we owned. We no longer moved about the sparkling ship as if we had a right to be there, commanding the white-uniformed Germans to bring us drinks and towels. We hesitated before asking for another cup of tea, for fresh sheets for the bed, afraid that such a request might get us tossed into the churning waves beneath the ship. A ship that had begun to feel less like a pleasure boat and more like a floating death camp.

As for Max Loesser, the death of Leonid Berg was wearing on the fragile machinery inside him. When the news came to me of Berg's leap into the sea, I had run to the Loessers' stateroom and found Max cowering behind the bed.

"Last night, when the ship turned," Frau Loesser said, "he declared it was because the Gestapo had discovered he was on board. He was certain Captain Schroeder had turned it to take him back to Germany."

Ruth Loesser was standing at the room's porthole, looking as if she wished she might jump out of it.

I knelt beside Max and told him about the kitchen hand in a gentle voice.

"He was a Jew and they threw him into the sea," Max said.

"That is the speculation."

"And who will be next?"

I shrugged. "There are nine hundred of us, and we are scheduled to arrive in Havana in three days. Your odds of staying dry are good."

After Weitz, after Berg, every one of us was desperate to get off the *St. Louis.* No member of the crew could appear without being asked when he thought we would arrive in Havana Harbor and did he believe there was the chance we would get there early. Barring the hottest hours of the day, there was always a line of us standing at the railings, scanning the horizon, as if we could make Cuba appear only by wishing for it.

The day the purser announced he would be handing out our landing cards, I joined the crowd that filled the narrow hallway outside his office, pushing and shoving each other no matter how many times he reminded us there were enough landing cards for all nine hundred. Because I was not the only one who had convinced himself that having a landing card might somehow protect him from the evil that lived beneath the *St. Louis*'s polished wooden decks.

On the last full night before the *St. Louis* was to dock in Havana—Thursday, May 25—a fancy-dress costume ball was held for the entire ship in the enormous Social Hall of the *St. Louis*. This, Doktor Spiegel explained to me, was the custom aboard pleasure boats.

"Have you not brought a costume?" he said to me.

I shook my head, marveling at the notion of a Jew who would think to pack a fancy-dress costume while he was fleeing the Nazis.

"Then you shall have to improvise something."

After dinner, when everyone was getting ready for the ball, I returned to my stateroom and opened the suitcase I had not touched since accepting the loan of Max Loesser's suit. Raising its cardboard lid released the scent of the flat in the Kruezberg into my gleaming stateroom—the bitter smoke from the tiled stove, the air of mothballs and lanolin from the blanket Rebecca wrapped around her shoulders, her cinnamon-flavored tea. Rebecca always smelled of that blanket and that tea, and under them both, of the chemicals she used to develop her film. I grew to hate the smell of those chemicals, because she made me use up favors on them, turning the small water closet in our flat into a darkroom.

Rebecca does not smell like these things anymore, I told myself, even as I put my face deep into the case. *She smells of French cigarettes and strong coffee, and whatever scent the wind carries when it blows across the Seine*. It is possible I believed this as surely as Max Loesser believed the *St. Louis* was filled with agents of the Gestapo sent to hunt him down.

I put on the oldest of my woolen trousers and the most frayed of my white shirts. As I entered the Social Hall, Herr Bergmann, who was dressed as a pirate with a patch over his eye, asked me what I was supposed to be.

"A Communist," I told him.

Silver streamers cascaded from the ceiling and hundreds—maybe thousands—of balloons floated above our heads. The black and white squares of the marble floor were so highly polished, the floor itself appeared like a great expanse of ice. All the many tables and chairs had been pushed against the walls to make room for dancing, and the ship's orchestra was perched high above us on a platform. As I entered, they were playing American swing music.

It seemed all nine hundred of us were here—everyone in fancy-dress costume. Pirates and Roman gladiators and Japanese geishas circled beneath the silvery streamers. Some, who had been forced to improvise, had turned their bed linens into Arabic-style clothing from British Palestine, or converted the fronds from the palm trees on A deck into Hawaiian hula skirts. Babette Spiegel was wearing a sea green evening gown with a pair of black riding boots. None of us could say who or what she was supposed to be, but it did not matter. Babette Spiegel only needed to be Babette Spiegel.

The mood should have been festive, but there was a desperate quality to the party, a foreboding that floated amidst the balloons and streamers. Everyone appeared in a frenzy to spend his shipboard money, as if we believed the sooner it was out of our pockets, the sooner we would be free of the *St. Louis*. And the only thing to spend it on now was drink—champagne and rum and schnapps and whiskey.

As the evening wore on, the pirates and Roman gladiators, the Japanese geishas and Palestinian Arabs became more and more intoxicated. No one could walk without stumbling, without having to hang onto someone else for support. The ship's orchestra switched from American swing to Cuban rumbas and tangos, and the dancing on the treacherous marble floor grew more abandoned.

I attempted to get just as drunk as everyone else. But the more whiskey I drank, the more sober I felt. Finally I gave up, sat on one of the chairs pushed against the wall, and watched my fellow passengers fling themselves around the dance floor as if they didn't care whether they broke every bone in their bodies.

I began to think the *St. Louis* had put us all under a new spell. That it had convinced us to dress like someone we were not—like something we were not—and then forced us to drink until we were drunk. So drunk we could no longer think, no longer remember who we were. And soon, very soon, we would look down at ourselves in our pirate and gladiator and Palestinian Arab costumes and run to the upper deck, to the spot where the crewmen had dropped Morris Weitz's body into the sea, and we would hurl ourselves into the ocean, just as Leonid Berg had done.

Then, as if he had been the one putting these thoughts into my head, I spotted Max Loesser on the platform with the orchestra. He was not wearing a fancy-dress costume. He had come as himself, as Max Loesser in his overcoat and fedora, and he was waving his arms at the musicians to silence them.

As the music ceased, the drunken revelers on the dance floor gazed up. We were all suddenly sobered, I think, by the fear of what Max Loesser—dressed as himself—might say or do from that platform high above the marble floor.

Max came close to the edge of the platform.

I left the chair at the edge of the dance floor, calculating how difficult it would be to catch a falling man.

"I have just seen the Bahamas," Max Loesser shouted down to us.

The crowd below gasped as loudly as if he had jumped.

"A small light," he continued, "from a lighthouse, probably. You can see it from the upper deck."

We went—all of us in our fancy-dress costumes—to the upper deck and stood at the railing, looking into the darkness at a small light shining from a country where there weren't any Nazis. And for the first time since Leonid Berg jumped into the ocean, the first time since we had stepped foot on the *St. Louis*, the first time in years, we believed we were saved.

Two days later—at 4 AM on Saturday, May 27—the *St. Louis* arrived in the waters outside Havana Harbor. The clanging of the ship's klaxon woke me, and I threw Max Loesser's suit on over my pajamas and went to the upper deck to stand peering out in the darkness with the others. We were still some way out from the harbor, but close enough to see the headlights of the cars moving along the shoreline and the silhouettes of the domed buildings behind them.

After breakfast a small launch sputtered out to the ship carrying a man with a well-waxed mustache. Not long afterward, Steward Schiendick's voice came through the ship's loudspeakers, directing us to assemble in the Social Hall for an examination meant to ensure the Cuban government that none of us were "idiot, insane, or suffering from some loathsome or contagious disease."

I brought Max to the Social Hall myself, arriving late, so we would be at the back of the line. My hope was that the Cuban doctor with the well-waxed mustache would be so eager to get off the *St. Louis* by the time he got to us, he would not notice the existence of anything breaking down inside Max Loesser. But from what I could tell, the Cuban doctor did not seem interested in whether any of us were idiots or insane or suffering from any type of disease. When it was our turn to be examined, he barely raised his heavy-lidded eyes from our paperwork to look at us.

An hour or so later, another launch came, this one filled with Cuban policemen and men wearing elaborate uniforms we were told were immigration officials. These men relieved us of our landing cards, though none of us wanted to give them up.

"They must be stamped," Purser Mueller explained to everyone.

"Stamped for Buchenwald? Stamped for Dachau?" Max Loesser murmured.

"Stamped for Havana," I whispered, pulling the landing card from his grasp.

Hours later, the launch returned and we were given back our landing cards. I opened mine and saw that it had indeed been stamped with the word *Habana*. But when the launch left, the immigration officials in the elaborate uniforms went with it, and the Cuban policemen remained on board.

The sun moved overhead and it grew hot. We were dressed in our traveling clothes, standing on the open deck with our packed suitcases. Everything had been prepared for landing, the swimming pool drained, the wooden chaises folded and stored. And yet the *St. Louis* remained anchored outside the harbor.

To raise our spirits, Captain Schroeder assembled the ship's orchestra and asked them to play a song. The orchestra chose *"Freut euch des Lebens"*—"Be Happy You're Alive." I do not think it lifted anyone's spirits.

After some time, smaller boats motored out to us, mostly fishing skiffs. These were loaded with bananas and grapefruits, and people willing to sell them to us if we threw down a few pesos. A bit later, other boats came carrying the relations of some of the nine hundred stranded on the *St. Louis*—Jews who had emigrated to Cuba in the earlier years. When they shouted up the question of why we had not docked, none of us could answer it.

At dinner, Max Loesser insisted the reason was because Captain Schroeder was hiding him.

"It has nothing to do with you," I told him, "and everything to do with the corruptibility of the Cuban government." For these were the rumors being whispered within earshot of the Cuban police standing guard on the ship. "Governor Brú only wants a bigger bribe for accepting nine hundred Jews the Germans didn't want."

"That is what they are telling you. But the moment the Gestapo comes on board and offers Captain Schroeder more money than I have given him, I will hear Steward Schiendick counting."

I placed my hand on Max Loesser's shoulder to comfort him, and felt his insanity vibrating like a combustible engine beneath my fingers. I willed it quiet, for it seemed the engine that was driving Rebecca's doom.

"We will be off this ship tomorrow," I assured him.

But Sunday came and we stood again in the hot sun with our suitcases. Now the Cuban policemen stood with us, making certain, I think, that none of us jumped into the sea and swam for a shoreline that had begun to look not so far away.

"They are not letting us land because it is their Sabbath," somebody said. "They do nothing on their Sabbath." But all of us could see other ships sailing past us to the dock.

Max Loesser remained below in his stateroom, waiting for Captain Schroeder to hand him over to the Gestapo. I went to see him in the afternoon, sitting with him on his sour sheets—the crew had been given leave to go ashore and there were no more services being performed. I repeated for him the theory about the Christian Sabbath, but he believed it as readily as if he had watched the other ships sailing by with his own eyes.

On Monday the complaints began. *Why are we being held here? Why have we not docked yet?* This complaining prompted First Officer Closterman, the round-shouldered man who had taken me down to the engine room, to insist that Captain Schroeder order Steward Schiendick—and five crewmen of Schiendick's choosing—to search our staterooms for weapons and explosives. As First Officer Closterman explained it, we were making the crew nervous for their safety, because "you never know how many of these Jews are Communists and anarchists."

The crewmen of Steward Schiendick's choosing were the men I had seen singing the *"Horst Wessel"* with beer foam on their lips outside the engine room. They burst into random staterooms, opening trunks and suitcases without permission. They ransacked Aaron Rosner's room, all the while threatening to send him back to Dachau. "I cannot understand how they even knew that about me," he told me later. Before they left, they smashed a framed photograph of his family. "Why would they do something like that? Did they think I had hidden explosives behind a picture of my wife and children?"

Steward Schiendick and his friends went into the stateroom of Morris Weitz's widow, whom we had not seen for days. When she appeared later on the scorching deck, looking pale and disheveled, we believed we were seeing a ghost.

"They blew out Morris's candles," she said in a shaking voice. "Called them a fire hazard." Tears were running down her wrinkled cheeks. "How could they be a fire hazard when I never left the stateroom? When I always watched them and never slept?"

While the searching continued, I sat in the Loessers' stateroom with Max—I had sent his family, including Ruth, to the deck, so they would not have to watch him cowering. We sat on the bed and waited for Steward Schiendick and the other men to burst through the door, but they never came. Maybe they understood that the anticipation of their coming would be harder on Max.

When I returned to my own stateroom, my suitcase had been unpacked and my clothes tossed about the room. I suspected that Steward Schiendick had understood, too, that draping my worn trousers and frayed shirts on these gleaming surfaces would shame me more than any beatings would. As I put my clothes back into the suitcase that smelled of the flat in the Kruezberg, I was grateful that since the night I'd come upon the men singing the *"Horst Wessel,"* I'd returned Rebecca's photograph to my sock.

At sunset, several Cuban police boats sailed out to us and spent the night circling the *St. Louis*, shining their searchlights into our portholes while we tried to sleep, finally banishing any illusion that we were passengers on a pleasure ship.

Tuesday came and brought no change, except that it was hotter. By midday, it was nearly impossible to stand in the sun at the railings on the upper deck. My shirt was stuck to my skin as if with glue, and my tongue was dry and thick in my mouth. Still I forced myself to remain. *If I stand at this railing until two o'clock*, I told myself, *we will get off this ship tomorrow. If I do not wipe this drop of sweat from my eye, the thing inside Max Loesser will not break down before he sets foot in Cuba. If I do not drink water, Rebecca is safe in Paris.*

I had decided the Germans had brought us to Hell. That all the fine linen and the glasses of champagne and the calling us *sir* and *madam* had only been to trick us, to keep us from suspecting. Because if we had suspected, we would have escaped the way Morris Weitz had escaped, the way Leonid Berg had escaped. Because that was the only way you could escape this particular Hell.

It was just after three o'clock and the domed buildings of Havana were shimmering in the heat, or maybe I was only dizzy, when a door slammed hard at the end of the deck. I turned. Coming toward me in the blinding sunlight was Max Loesser. He was running, and his arms were covered in bloody sleeves.

"They cannot get me now!" Max shouted.

As he ran, the sleeves turned to liquid, as if melting in the heat, leaving a trail on the hot deck behind him. But as quickly as they sloughed off, new sleeves appeared, thick and red and running to his elbows.

I shook my head, trying to clear it of this delusion caused by heat and despair. But as I did, Max Loesser rushed past me, moving the air in a way a delusion never could, spattering blood across the bottom of my trousers.

"Murderers!" he shouted. "Try to get me now!"

Max threw himself onto the railings, staining them red. He paused there a moment, waving his red-coated arms as if he was signaling to someone, then in one motion he tumbled into the sea.

The water foamed where he landed. And then the blood came up—thick and red—floating on the surface of the water. Max's head floated up next, a dull black island in the center of all that blood.

My ears filled with the wailing of the ship's siren, or maybe it was me making the sound. Because as I looked down on Max Loesser's black head bobbing in an ocean of his own blood, I knew that despite all I had tried to fix him, the thing inside Max Loesser was well and truly broken. I had failed him in the same way I had failed Rebecca. And while the sun beat down on my head, I built a new—and more terrible—story of her future, one filled with pictures of Rebecca drowning in a vat of water before breakfast, hung from a rope before a line of horrified Jews before the evening count.

It was not that I had not known Rebecca would die before her time. I had learned to live with that knowledge. What I could not live with was the idea that it would be the Nazis who would kill her.

I wrapped my hands around the burning railings, set a foot onto their top.

Herr Bergmann—who had come from where to stand beside me?—grabbed me by my shoulders. "It is a dangerous distance. And crewman Meier has already gone."

I looked down into the sea. Crewman Meier surfaced through the bloody water, his head and shoulders stained red.

Herr Bergmann pulled me back from the railings.

Max Loesser thrashed about in the bloody water, fighting crewman Meier's efforts to save him. One of the circling police boats had to come and help, the Cuban policeman pulling Max into the boat, working with crewman Meier to tie tourniquets above his wrists. But the moment he was let go, Max Loesser clawed at his wrists to open the wounds, bit at the tourniquets with his teeth. It required two policemen to hold Max inside as the boat sputtered toward Havana Harbor, the rest of us watching from the sunstruck deck, wondering if we, too, should slit our wrists and throw ourselves into the sea.

Some hours later, Captain Schroeder informed us that Max Loesser was in a Cuban hospital and was expected to live. He had radioed for permission for Herr Loesser's family, or at least for Frau Loesser, to be allowed ashore to visit. No such permission had been granted. When I later saw Ruth Loesser standing at the railing before sunset, she did not offer me even a half-smile.

On Wednesday, Josef Joseph—a lawyer from Berlin I had hardly spoken with the entire voyage—asked me to be on the Suicide Patrol. The Suicide Patrol was the idea of Captain Schroeder, the consequence of Max Loesser's bloody leap into the sea, and the fact that the ship's doctor had run out of sedatives. That night, as I took my two-hour shift, walking the upper deck in the roving light of the police boat search beams, I wondered what I would do if I encountered one of my fellow passengers teetering on the railings. Push him, most probably, then follow him into the black water.

On Thursday, the reporters and news photographers came, ferried out in fishing boats. We had been anchored outside Havana Harbor for nearly a week, and news of the nine hundred Jews nobody wanted had begun to spread. A few of these boats held sightseers who wanted to see for themselves what we eternal wandering Jews looked like up close.

On Thursday, too, we saw the notice, placed on all the boards where before had been placed notices about concerts and fancy-dress costume balls.

> *The Cuban government has ordered us to leave the harbor.*
> *We shall depart at 10 am Friday morning.*

Captain Schroeder ordered the full Suicide Patrol on watch for the entire night.

By the time Friday, June 2, dawned, bright and hot, the whole world knew our story. Knew how Captain Schroeder sailed the *St. Louis* three miles out from Havana Harbor, and then for two days sailed us in circles while a Jewish humanitarian organization in New York negotiated with the Cuban government—a government that was now demanding a sum of five hundred dollars for each of us.

Once it became clear that raising such a sum for Jews nobody wanted was not possible, the negotiators turned their hopes toward America.

Captain Schroeder turned the *St. Louis* toward America as well, sailing us on Sunday near enough to the Florida coastline, we could see the hotels lining the beaches of Miami. American fishing boats carrying news photographers skidded across the waves to shoot pictures of us. I stood at the railings, trying not to look like a miserable, wandering Jew as the photographers shouted at me in a language I didn't understand. Their clicking cameras were Speed Graphics, which reminded me of Pietr, and made me wonder what kind of truth I represented.

But Jews, it turned out, were not very much more popular in America than they were in Nazi Germany, and Franklin Roosevelt did not wish to have nine hundred of them spilling onto the beach in Florida.

On Monday, we got word that Governor Brú had again changed his mind. He would grant us permission to land in Cuba if we remained on the Isle of Pines. Captain Schroeder turned the *St. Louis* back toward Havana.

But on Tuesday, after reading the morning newspapers, which revealed Cuban sentiment to be against this plan, Governor Brú had yet another change of heart. Captain Schroeder informed the Hapag Cruise Lines of Governor Brú's decision. The cruise line sent the captain a three-word message.

Return Hamburg immediately.

At eleven-forty on Tuesday, June 6, we turned from Cuba and set a course for Germany. Max Loesser was still in the hospital in Havana. His family remained aboard the *St. Louis*.

What the whole world does not know is how different the journey back to Europe was from the one we had made leaving it. "For the safety of the crew," Steward Schiendick ordered a ban on all social intercourse between the crewmen and the passengers. A ban which did not prevent the crewmen from buying up the bits and pieces of jewelry we had hidden from the Nazis—things we sold for money to send cables begging President Roosevelt to reconsider taking us in.

None of us played shuffleboard on A deck. None of us drank champagne in the Schanke Bar. The ship's orchestra, when it played, played to an empty room, for none of us wished to waltz across the checkerboard floor of the *tanzplatz*. Once, one of the crewmen left a shortwave radio tuned to a German station and a few of us heard the voice of Joseph Goebbels telling the rest of the country, "Since no one will accept the shabby Jews on the *St. Louis*, we will have to take them back and support them."

But none of us believed the Germans meant to support us for very long. Indeed, one afternoon as he passed me, Officer Closterman mumbled something that sounded very much like, "These are your last free days."

On Saturday, after we had been heading back for four days, helmsman Heinz Kritsch was found hanging from a beam in the locker room, another suicide. Some of us found comfort in the fact that the ship had started killing Germans. Others imagined Kritsch had had some hidden Jewish blood. For a brief instant, I wished that I had had the courage, but by then, I had repaired the mechanism of the story of Rebecca saved in Paris. Maybe it was that it had been too long since I had fixed anything. Maybe it was that I could not bear to look at Ruth Loesser, sitting on a deck chair that never faced in the direction from which we had come, as if that tropical place no longer existed. Maybe it was only that I was a doomed Jew on a boat full of doomed Jews, and I had already lost too much.

. . .

But Joseph Goebbels would have to wait a little longer to take back the shabby Jews nobody else wanted. Due to the efforts of the Jewish humanitarian organization, on Wednesday, June 14, the *St. Louis* was allowed to dock at Antwerp. I was put on the freighter *Rhakotis* along with more than five hundred other passengers of the *St. Louis*. The *Rhakotis* possessed cabins for only fifty-two passengers and I spent the night on a wooden chaise on the upper deck. Even after it began to rain, I stayed on the upper deck. It did not matter how soaked I got. I was off the *St. Louis*.

The *Rhakotis* arrived in Boulogne at dawn. I stood at its rusted railings and gazed at the French coastline, telling myself I was looking at the country where Rebecca lived.

Two hundred and twenty-four of us were to be chosen for France. I pleaded with the official issuing visas, did my begging in French, imagining that would sway him, telling him I had a connection in Paris, a fiancée.

"Do you have some proof of this person?" he asked me.

I dropped to the floor in front of his desk and removed my shoe, peeled off my wet sock.

The official did not touch the photograph in my hand.

"Do you have evidence that this person is in Paris?"

In the end, I went with the group that was sent to England.

Kitchener Refugee Camp was situated in the green Kent countryside. It held close to five thousand Jewish men, all of us hoping to emigrate to Palestine or South America or the United States. We slept in crowded barracks and worked in the piggery or on the land, and if we were lucky, we were taken on supervised outings to Ramsgate and Margate and Sandwich.

But we were not free, and as I had no money and no relations in any of the places the British government could send us, I knew I would stay in Kitchener until England went to war with Germany, and I was declared an enemy alien and imprisoned in a more obvious way.

But high-ranking officials everywhere have a fondness for temperamental vehicles. I repaired the misfiring engine of an MG Magnette Coupe that belonged to a mid-level official in the London Home Office, who occasionally visited Kitchener. Mr. Simeon was much like Herr Gloeckner, except that he hid his dislike of Jews behind better manners.

At first, I considered asking Mr. Simeon to help me cross into France. But after I had been off the *St. Louis* for some weeks, I began to think more clearly and remembered my promise to Rebecca to leave Europe. In the end, I asked for an American visa.

"The Americans have had their fill of Jews," Mr. Simeon said. "Best I can do is Canada, and that will be temporary. When it runs out, make yourself invisible."

I went to Quebec, but could not blend in with my German-accented French. When the time came to make myself invisible, I slipped into the United States at a spot in the woods where nobody knows or cares where the border is. I went to the Lower East Side because I speak Yiddish, and because everybody there is from someplace else.

One of the first things I bought was a radio. A broken one I found in a pawnshop—like the shortwave radio I had found in the shop in the Kreuzberg to bring France into our flat in Berlin. I fixed it, then spent as much time as I could listening to it, repeating everything that came out of its speakers. Between that and a German-English dictionary, I learned to speak English.

Later, I fixed a printing machine for a man whose name I never learned in exchange for some papers that would allow me to work.

They could be better, but now that it is wartime and so many men are off fighting, nobody looks too close at the papers of someone who can fix things.

I changed my name also, but only my last name. My first name I kept the same. Maybe that was not a good idea, but I could not bring myself to change the name Rebecca had called me.

Twelve

Over the past hour, I'd begun to see Jakob, the chalky blue light of dawn near the ocean seeping through the open doors, lightening the space between us. At some point during his story—I couldn't remember when—the clanging of metal on metal had stopped, the electrical hum whirring down. And now that he'd finished, there was only the distant card-shuffling sound of the tide coming in.

Jakob looked at his watch. "We are between shifts."

In the blue light, his face was full of shadows, as if all the sorrowful parts of his story had settled there.

"The picture in your code-o-graph. It's Rebecca?"

He pushed a piece of hair out of his eyes. "*You* took it?"

"I also let your pigeons go."

He shrugged. "They came back. It is what they do."

"Who are you sending messages to?"

He stood, wrapped the scarf back around his neck.

"Her."

"But where do the birds go?"

"That is a good question."

"And you put them in code?"

"What I have to say is only for the two of us."

I considered asking him whether he believed his pigeons could fly to France, or whether he'd ever gotten a message back; instead, I asked him if he wanted to come uptown with me and get his code-o-graph.

"I would," he said. Then I got up, and Jakob helped me climb out from under the subway car.

In the flat blue light of the dawn, the floating subway cars looked dreamlike, almost as magical as I'd first believed them to be. Jakob stopped to pick up a green metal toolbox, and the two of us walked out into the salted cold.

The wind cut right through my T-shirt. I wrapped my arms around my ribs, and Jakob asked me if I'd had a coat.

"Lost it," I said.

He set down the toolbox and unzipped his jacket, dropped it over my shoulders. It held the warmth from his body and smelled like cloves and the bottom of the subway car, the black grease from the wheels, maybe.

We walked through the still-sleeping streets of Coney Island. Only the gulls and the factory workers were moving, only the restless ocean and the wind from it, blowing onto us, stiff with salt and brine. I'd been awake all night and everything had the sheen of unreality—the pale salt-blasted houses, the poster-ed fronts of the sideshows advertising the *Real Human 2-Headed Baby*, the *Georgia Peaches*, two normal-sized girls with heads the size of baseballs.

From the elevated subway platform, I watched the light at the top of the Parachute Jump wink out—the only light left on at Coney Island since the war had started. A light at the top of an amusement ride, too small to be of any use to the German U-boats floating off the coast, but bright enough to warn ships at sea where the shore was.

Jakob and I stood in the ocean-chilled wind waiting for the train to open its doors.

"I'm sorry," I said. For taking his code-o-graph, for thinking he was a Nazi, for keeping his jacket in all that biting wind.

Jakob shook his head as if it didn't matter, as if so many regrettable things had already happened to him.

When the doors opened, we got onto a Manhattan-bound subway train along with a couple of people on their way to factory jobs. Once we started moving, time seemed to shift onto icy tracks, speeding up and slowing down of its own accord. It was probably the lack of sleep, but the journey from Coney Island to Dyckman Street—which should have taken an hour or more—was over in an instant, and I had no memory of it, except the warmth of Jakob's clove-and-grease-smelling jacket.

Sunlight was slanting across Broadway when we came aboveground, making it feel later than I wanted it to be. I tugged Jakob's shirtsleeve, pulling him through the tide of winter-bundled people pouring down Dyckman Street, dragging him to our building.

I gave him back his jacket and left him in the hallway with the rows of mailboxes. Told him I'd only be a minute.

I ran up the stairs, telling myself I would only be a minute. Because surely it was still early, surely my mother was still asleep. But the moment I creaked open the door to the apartment, my mother was on the other side, pulling me against her, her collarbone pressing against my cheek, her heart beating beneath my ear—a steady fluttering, the most steady thing about her now.

The point of her chin rested on the top of my head, and here time must have hit a slow section of track, because I cannot remember my mother ever holding me for so long.

When she did finally let me go, she said there was a man waiting in the kitchen to see me.

I looked around her. A man wearing some kind of uniform was sitting in one of our kitchen chairs.

My mother has sold me to the Gestapo, I thought. *That is why she stood here and held onto me so long.*

It was a ridiculous thought, but my head was still filled with bits and pieces of Jakob's story.

"Go on." My mother put her hand on my back.

I stood in the hallway, thinking about Jakob downstairs with the mailboxes. Jakob waiting for me to return the code-o-graph with the photograph of Rebecca he'd managed to save from the Nazis, but not from me.

"I have to do something first," I said.

"I think you'd better go see about this." My mother's hand pressed more firmly into my back.

I let her lead me into the kitchen.

The man at our table was older, maybe fifty. And once I got closer, I saw that his uniform was nothing more than a gray suit and a badge. A badge that had the words *New York City Truant Officer* pressed into it.

My mother pulled a cigarette out of her pack and used it to point to the seat across from the truant officer. I sat in it.

"Tell my son what you told me," she said to him.

The truant officer looked at me and smiled. His teeth were yellow. "Our records indicate that Jack Quinlan has been absent from P.S. 52 for forty-six consecutive school days."

He shifted his gaze to my mother. "You do know," he said, "that in the State of New York, it is illegal for a child to miss school?"

"She didn't know anything about it," I told him.

The truant officer turned back to me. He leaned across the table, brought his face near to mine. I smelled licorice and whiskey on his breath.

"You then," he said, "do you realize that truancy is against the law in the State of New York?"

He was so close, his breath was fogging up my glasses.

The truant officer and I sat face-to-face across the red table, staring at each other. I was trying to decide if it would be better or worse to admit I didn't know truancy was against the law. Trying also to figure out how to get back downstairs with Jakob's code-o-graph.

In a puff of smoke, my mother's voice drifted over us. "Are you planning on arresting my son?"

I had not heard this tone—the tone of a bootlegger's daughter—in a long while. I took my eyes away from the truant officer. My mother was leaning against the sink, the cigarette between her fingers, the gap between her front teeth visible.

"Because if you are," she continued, "I'll go pack him a suitcase now."

The truant officer sat back in his chair, waved his hands around as if trying to erase something that existed in the air in front of him.

"No, no," he said. "I'm only here to take him back to P.S. 52."

My mother blew smoke into the air above his bald head.

"Then why don't we let him go change out of his Mass pants?"

When I came back into the hallway with the mailboxes—the truant officer so close on my heels, he was in danger of stepping on the backs of my Thom McAns—Jakob was nowhere in sight. I tried looking for him on the street, but the truant officer kept me moving toward P.S. 52 with one of his surprisingly big hands on my shoulder.

Now that he was out in the daylight and not sitting in my kitchen, the truant officer looked bigger, more barrel-chested, as if he might have been a boxer at one time, and I had the feeling that if I ran, he would have no trouble catching me and making me sorry I'd made him exert himself.

He stayed close to me all the way to P.S. 52, all the way across the empty macadam of the yard—everybody already called inside—and into a classroom that was very much like Miss Steinhardt's, except that the Visible Man and his colorful organs had been replaced by the Periodic Table of Elements, and Miss Steinhardt had been replaced by an older, paler version of herself called Miss Milhaus.

"I've got Jack Quinlan here," the truant officer announced. He made this sound as if we were characters on *Gang Busters* and my forty-six consecutive days of truancy had earned me the status of Public Enemy Number One.

Miss Milhaus pointed at a desk in the front row. The truant officer poked me in the back. His finger felt like the barrel of a gun.

I walked up the aisle, expecting to have that sense of everyone's eyes crawling over me. But it was as if someone had cast a spell on the entire class, fixing their gazes on their social studies books.

It took me a second to figure it out. To understand they weren't concentrating on social studies. They were thinking about my father falling under the uptown A, and how I was now some kind of bad luck.

I stepped over Declan Moriarity's polio brace and took my seat. Rose LoPinto was on my other side. She was wearing a red sweater, and it looked nice against her black hair. Francis D'Amato, still wearing the flesh-colored patch, was on her left. I wondered if Francis had been repeating things for Rose while I'd been out looking for Nazis. The thought of Francis's wet-looking lips next to the RadioEar microphone at Rose's throat made me want to punch him in his good eye.

The day felt like a dream. I hadn't slept in more than twenty-four hours, and the books on my desk changed subject without me knowing how it happened. One moment, I'd be standing on the freezing macadam with a ball in my hand, and a second later, I'd find myself inside the overheated classroom staring at the Periodic Table of Elements, trying to turn the boxes of letters and numbers into some kind of sense.

I came to as Miss Milhaus was explaining something about the weight of oxygen. She was standing at the board with her back to us, sending her words into the chalked letters, sending them in a direction I believed Rose would miss.

I bent my head toward Rose's throat.

"You don't have to do that," she whispered.

Until she spoke, I'd had no idea how much I'd missed her blurred consonants, her out-of-focus vowels.

"It's okay," I said, leaning closer. But Rose stopped me with a hand on my chest.

"No," she said. "Really."

I froze, everything I was about to say about the weight of oxygen trapped beneath her fingers. I couldn't pull my eyes from the small microphone box pinned to the neck of Rose's sweater, now banned to me the way swimming pools and theaters and certain streets had been banned to Jakob and Rebecca. In that instant, it didn't matter that everyone now believed I was bad luck. It only mattered that Rose LoPinto would rather not know anything about the weight of oxygen than let me whisper into the smooth skin of her throat.

What I wouldn't learn until much later was that sometime during the summer—the summer I'd been wandering the marble halls of Pennsylvania Station, making my coconut custard pie last inside the coolness of the Automat—Rose had breathed ether and let a surgeon work inside her ear with tiny instruments. The surgeon hadn't cured Rose's deafness, but he had made it less profound. Enough that she no longer needed anyone to speak into the microphone box pinned near her throat.

And then, somehow, time shifted, and I looked up and the room was almost empty, only a few people left, their coats already on, the backs of them going out the door.

I grabbed my own coat, was putting it on as I bolted out the door and into the cold of November, the weight of Jakob's code-o-graph in my pocket urging me to hurry.

But when I came through the chain-link fence, Moon Shapiro was leaning against the sad, little tree. He was wearing a new corduroy jacket with wooden buttons and had the same light blue yarmulke fastened to his red hair with a circle of bobby pins.

And I very much needed him to punch me in the head.

Even now, I am not certain why I needed this so badly. I only know that I believed something would be set right by that punch in the head, or set back. Something that had to do with Rose. And my father.

I stood before Moon Shapiro, stood within reach of his big fists and waited for the loose-fisted punch to the center of my body. But the spell of Miss Milhaus's classroom had been cast on Moon as well. He would not look at me, only stared down, as if transfixed by a frozen puddle of dog pee at the base of that sad tree.

I stepped closer, my glasses level with the top row of buttons on his jacket.

"Marvin," I said in a low voice. Then I shut my eyes and readied myself for the punch.

When I opened them again, Moon was still studying the layer of ice floating on the surface of the dog pee.

I looked up into Moon's round face.

"Jewboy," I said in a whisper.

Out of the corner of my eye, right at the edge of my glasses, I saw Moon ball his hand into a fist. But the fist did not rise more than a few inches from Moon's side.

I said the word again, and Moon made a sound like a bark. But his fist stayed exactly where it was.

Desperate, I grabbed hold of Moon's arm with both of my hands and yanked his fist toward my face.

But Moon fought me. Each time I brought his fist close to my face it bounced away, as if there was a force field around my head, as if I was trying to push two magnets together.

Francis D'Amato came to watch, staring at us with his lazy eye. Bobby Devine came, too, exhaling the scent of Juicy Fruit into the wintery air. Also people I didn't recognize, people who stopped to stand in the cold, people who couldn't resist watching somebody beat himself up with Moon Shapiro's big fist.

I kept shouting, "Hit me, you bastard," and Moon kept grunting with the effort of keeping his fist away from my head. At last it occurred to me to try Moon's weaker hand.

I let go of his right wrist and before he could figure out what I was doing, I grabbed the other one, folded his fingers into a fist, and drove it into my nose, knocking my glasses onto the ground.

It was like hitting myself in the face with a flesh-covered stone, an arm-shaped baseball bat. Bright pain exploded from my nose outward, and for a second I couldn't see anything except black. Then I was sitting on the sidewalk, listening to a sound that was like pressing seashells hard against both of your ears. Something warm gushed over my mouth and chin. I wiped at it with the back of my hand, and it came away red.

I felt around the cold ground for my glasses, but all I could find was a crumpled-up pack of Lucky Strikes and an empty paper bag. The edgeless figure that was Moon was making a motion like wiping his hand on the front of his corduroy jacket. When he was finished, he turned and disappeared into the general blurriness of Academy Street.

"Here." Declan Moriarity's polio brace clicked next to my ear. "They were behind you." My glasses fell into my lap.

By the time I'd dropped their weight on my nose, Declan—and anyone else who'd stopped to watch—had vanished up Academy Street. I pushed myself to my feet and wiped my sleeve under my nose. It didn't seem to be bleeding anymore, but the skin around my mouth felt stiff, like it had frozen in the cold.

Being punched in the face had disoriented me. Once I stood, the sidewalk shifted under my feet, and the air felt thick and hard to breathe. At the corner of Vermilyea Street, the back of my neck itched with the feeling of being followed, and when I spun around, I saw the small man with the cigarette I believed I'd spotted those first weeks I stopped going to P.S. 52. The man I'd convinced myself wasn't there, because he was much too small to be a man.

I waited on the corner for him to catch up with me, and when he got into my three-foot spot I realized I'd been right. He was too small to be a man, because he wasn't a man. He was a boy. No older than I was.

His hair was almost black, and his skin was pale, and he had purplish half-moons under his eyes as if he stayed up nights worrying. He carried his books in an old-fashioned leather book bag covered with straps and buckles. But the most remarkable thing about him was the cigarette. It balanced on his lower lip as if glued there, sending a curl of smoke into his squinted brown eyes.

"Albie Battaglia," he said, putting out a skinny arm. His voice was raspy, worn out before its time.

I shook his hand. The two of us—kids, one smoking a cigarette—shaking hands on Vermilyea Street as if we were men in suits.

I started to tell him my name, but he said he already knew it. Because of my father. But also because nobody at P.S. 52 had ever gotten away with missing forty-six days of school.

I told him I had someplace I had to be.

"Maybe you might want to wipe off your face first," he suggested. "Unless you want to scare some lady on the subway."

I felt the stiff skin under my nose and around my mouth.

"I live just over there." He pointed to a brick apartment building ahead of us on Vermilyea.

Albie took me to his apartment, where a bald-headed man in a sleeveless undershirt was in the kitchen, stirring something in a big pot. I was so tired and disoriented that for a second I thought he was Otto from the flat in the Wasserstrasse. But then Albie called him *Pop* and shook a can that had a picture of a tree and a Star of David on it.

The two of them stood listening to the sound of one coin rattling.

"That's all you could get for the Jewish Homeland?" Albie's father asked.

"Everybody's buying war bonds." Albie shrugged. The cigarette was gone from his lower lip, though I had no memory of how or when he'd gotten rid of it.

Albie's father noticed me standing in the doorway.

"Whoa, kid, you want to clean that up." He reached across the sink and threw a sponge at my head.

I wiped it around the lower half of my face. It was warm and smelled like garlic and Palmolive.

Albie led me to his room, and the two of us sat on the bed, which was covered with a cowboy and Indian bedspread that was exactly like mine. He told me his parents worked at the Navy Yard in alternating shifts, and that it was his father's dream to move them all to the Jewish Homeland in Palestine.

"My mother says it's because my father is a convert," Albie explained, "because all converts are crazy Zionists."

Albie told me these things in a rush, as if he'd been waiting awhile to say them to me.

When he stopped for a breath, I pointed to his wall.

There was an enormous map of Europe taped there, and someone—Albie, I assumed—had stuck what looked like a hundred different-colored thumbtacks into it.

Albie stood and swept his sticklike arm across the map. "These are all the places my brother Mordy dropped bombs on the Nazis."

I got up and pushed the glasses onto the top of my head, took a closer look. There were thick clusters of tacks around cities in

Germany—Hamburg and Mannheim, Bremen and Kassell. There were also clusters of tacks in places outside of Germany—in Gdynia and Crete and Lorient.

"What about the different colors?"

"It's a code. For when he bombed a place more than once."

"And your brother did all these?"

"Let's say he *might* have done all these. The army doesn't let Mordy get too specific in his letters."

Albie swooped his hand in the air above the tacks, like it was a bomber.

"I put in the tacks from newspaper stories. When Mordy comes home, we'll pull out the ones that aren't his."

He went back, sat on the bed, opened the old-fashioned book bag. "He sent me this."

I pushed the glasses back down. It was a leather flying cap. The kind Captain Midnight wore, with goggles and fur inside.

I went and sat next to him. Albie placed the flying cap into my hands. I buried my hands in the softness of the fur lining.

Again, I felt Jakob's code-o-graph in my pocket, and I was about to tell Albie I had to go. But then I noticed something. Maybe it wasn't real, maybe it was only a piece of Jakob's story snagged on my consciousness. Still, in the light coming through the window, Albie's lips had taken on a bluish color and instead of telling him I had to leave, I asked him why he smoked.

"I have a heart murmur."

"And smoking is good for that?"

"Who knows? But nobody ever got punched in the head for not being able to run because he smoked too much."

I looked at Albie, at the purplish half-moons under his eyes, his small size.

"Moon Shapiro has never beaten you up?"

"Moon Shapiro once asked me to show him how to blow a smoke ring."

"You're a genius," I told him.

Albie lifted his bony shoulders. "*I* didn't get away with forty-six days of truancy."

"Yeah," I said. "Well."

I smoothed the lining of the flying cap.

"Try it on," Albie told me.

I slipped the cap onto my head. It was soft and warm. Comforting.

"What were you doing all that time?" Albie asked me.

Sometimes I think I told him because he slept under the same cowboy and Indian bedspread that I did. Other times I think it was because I'd been awake all night listening to a man tell his story under a floating subway car. Mostly, though, I believe it was because I'd spent too much time keeping too much of a secret on my own. But maybe it was the cowboy and Indian bedspread after all.

Whatever the reason, after Albie Battaglia asked me the question, I sat on his familiar bedspread wearing the flying cap that had come straight out of the radio world, and said, "I was looking for Nazis."

And then I told him why.

The words came tumbling out of my mouth in a rush—the way Jakob's must have all night—and it was like riding the Parachute Jump. The way your body feels after you've climbed to the top and suddenly you're falling through the bright salt-tinged blue of sky and sea, certain you are going to smash into a thousand pieces like glass on the boardwalk, and then your chute catches air, pulling you upward, and every single muscle lets go, every muscle you didn't realize you'd been holding tight.

As I talked, Albie kept nodding his head, as if he was making room inside it for everything I was saying. And when I finished, he asked me if I'd found any Nazis.

"I thought I did," I told him. "But I didn't. That's why I have to go."

I stood and handed back the flying cap. My head felt cold and bare.

I walked to the door of Albie's bedroom.

"Hey," he said.

I turned, and he tossed me the flying cap the way his father had tossed me the sponge.

"It's cold out there," he said.

I was halfway down the dark hallway of Jakob's tenement when I heard voices coming from inside his apartment. At first I thought they might be coming from the radio. But they were too ringing and bright to be radio voices. And they were speaking in German.

I pulled off Albie's flying cap and pressed my ear to the door. I made out the sound of two men shouting, and beneath them, the quieter sound of Jakob's voice. I had no practice with deciphering the undertone in foreign voices, but even through the layers of paint on Jakob's door, there was something threatening in that loud German.

I heard more shouting, and then a flurry of footsteps heading for the door.

I ran for the stairs. Behind me, Jakob's door clicked open. *Down? Up?* I ran up half a flight, then turned and slowly came down. Just somebody on my way out.

Two men in dark overcoats stepped onto the landing below me. One was tall, and one was short. And if I'd seen them on the subway, I might have followed them. Because now that they weren't shouting, they were very good at not being noticed.

I lingered on the stairway until I heard the two men leave the building, then I ran back to Jakob's apartment and once again pressed my ear to the door.

Nothing except silence. He hadn't even turned the radio on, and for a terrible moment I imagined him lying inside there—dead—killed by the two men in one of the terrible ways still swirling around inside my head. Hung by the neck, drowned in a vat.

I began pounding on the door, shouting his name into its thick-painted surface.

A man came out of an apartment across the hallway.

"Hey, boychik," he said, "what's with the ruckus?"

Then there was nothing under my pounding fist, and Jakob was pulling me by the front of my jacket into his apartment.

He slammed the door shut behind me and put his hand over my mouth—the second time he'd done that in twenty-four hours.

"You are finished with the yelling, yes?" he said.

I nodded, and he dropped his hand.

"Who were those men? The ones who were shouting at you in German?"

"It is better if we do not talk about them."

"Are they Nazis?"

"No," he said. "They are Jews."

"Why is it you say everyone I think is a Nazi is a Jew?"

Jakob sighed. "Maybe they are getting more difficult to tell apart."

He turned and walked into the apartment, which was no more than two rooms. A smaller one that contained an unmade bed, and the slightly larger one we were standing in. Jakob moved to stand before an unpainted table covered with bits and pieces of machinery—grease-covered bolts and cogs, and something that might have been a small engine—as if he might be hiding it. Open on the floor was the green metal toolbox he'd brought back from the Coney Island Yards.

"Are you in danger?" I asked him.

He smiled, and though I had not known him long, I realized how rare that was.

"Ah," he said, "the intrepid Nazi-hunter is here to protect the defenseless Jew."

There are many ways a man could have said this to a boy. Ways that would have mocked him, even gently. But the way Jakob said it to me that late November afternoon was none of these. The way Jakob said it to me was meant to make it clear that no one, not in a long while, had asked him such a question, or cared to know the answer, was meant to tell me that perhaps it was the best thing I could have asked him.

He pulled out a chair and sat in it. Then he pushed another one out with his foot, using the toe of his heavy factory shoes.

"Come and sit."

"Are you going to tell me about the men?"

Jakob rubbed his face. He looked tired, and I realized that he, too, had been awake all night.

"I do not suppose any of it matters now."

I crossed the room and took the chair he'd pushed out for me.

He said the two men had come to see him a couple of months ago, knocked on his door in the middle of the day, saying they'd recognized him on Delancey Street, that they knew him from his shop in Hallesches. They told Jakob they remembered his shop very well, remembered how he had fixed things for everyone until the law that required Jews to register their businesses. Then they remembered how he had shut his shop and only fixed things for Nazis.

"They asked me if I felt any guilt over having repaired so many phonographs and motorbikes and automobiles for Nazis while refusing my own people. If I believed I owed them something to make amends," he said.

"I only did what I had to do to keep myself and the people I loved alive, I told them."

The two men asked Jakob what he thought might happen if somebody went to the authorities and told them his true name, suggested they look into how he had turned up in New York with no visa.

When Jakob demanded to know what they wanted, they asked if he remembered the saboteurs who had landed on Amagansett beach last summer, if he had ever wondered what happened to the submarine that brought them here.

I assumed it went back to Germany, he'd told them.

That is what everybody assumes, they'd said. But it only got as far as Montauk when its engine gave out and it had to surface. That was shortly before dawn, the same time two of our colleagues on Civil Defense patrol were scanning the coastline with binoculars.

These colleagues had a boat, some guns, and the element of surprise, and before the sun broke over the water, they had captured the German captain and his first mate, and were towing the stranded submarine toward a private boat basin in Montauk.

I bet you are wondering what we did with the German captain and his first mate, one of the two men asked Jakob.

No, he told them, I am not.

But they had told him anyway.

They tied the men's wrists and ankles together, and then they drove them to a deserted garage near the Montauk pier and locked them in the backseat of a running car.

We gassed *them*, the taller of the two men kept saying. Isn't that perfect?

When the men had stopped laughing about what they had done to the Germans, they told Jakob they wanted him to fix the submarine.

Jakob said he did not have the tools for such a job. They suggested the tools were likely much the same as those used to repair subway cars, and that Jakob would have no difficulty getting his hands on those. Then they reminded him of his reputation for being able to fix anything.

Two days later, they brought Jakob the pigeons and the code-o-graph, and the first piece of the submarine's engine in the green toolbox.

We are going to communicate using a child's toy? Jakob had asked them.

If your neighbors are curious about what you're doing, you can tell them you are playing a child's game.

It had taken a couple of weeks before Jakob had worked up the nerve to ask one of the men—the shorter one—what they were planning to use the submarine for.

Children, the man had said. Refugees from a camp in Marseilles. Our people worked with the Vichy government for months to get approval for one hundred visas. One hundred visas for Jewish children. Then the Allies invaded North Africa and those approvals vanished like a wisp of smoke.

And you can fit one hundred children in this submarine of yours? Jakob had asked him.

The man shook his head. No, but we can fit twenty-three.

But what you did to the captain and the first mate?

Germans are not the only ones who know how to pilot a boat, the man had told him.

"Why do you say it doesn't matter now?" I asked.

Jakob looked over the bits and pieces of machinery on the table.

"They cannot save them, the twenty-three."

"Why not?"

"The submarine must leave for Marseilles tonight."

He explained it to me the way the shorter man had told it to him.

Aid workers in Marseilles had chosen twenty-three refugees who would be taken to the harbor in Marseilles in a supply truck, then slipped aboard the submarine under cover of night. Twenty-three children whose names the workers had seen on the list of those from the camp who were scheduled to be put on trains for Germany.

The submarine would leave Marseilles and cross the Atlantic until it reached a spot twelve miles off the coast of Long Island at exactly the same time a New York–bound cargo ship would arrive at the same location and develop ten minutes' worth of engine trouble. Once the cargo ship had resolved its engine difficulties—and picked up some undocumented cargo—it would resume its journey into a secure loading dock in New York Harbor, where it would be met by fifteen American families, eager to retrieve their newly acquired personal possessions.

"But the submarine cannot leave tonight." Jakob nodded at the thing that looked like a small engine on the table. "Because I cannot fix this final piece."

"But I thought you could fix anything?"

"Perhaps I am too tired. But all day I have sat here and tried to picture how this should work inside my head, and all I have been able to see is Rebecca's face flushed with cold at the Christmas Market, how she looked the day we met, her hair soaking and dark, the two of us standing ankle-deep in broken glass and pretending it is ice."

"You just need to sleep," I told him. "You'll fix it tomorrow."

"Yes, but even if I do, it is too late."

I leapt out of the chair and paced Jakob's small apartment, asking him the questions he'd already asked the two men from Hallesches. Why couldn't the submarine bring the refugees back to the boat basin in Montauk? Because the coastline was too heavily guarded now, and it would be dangerous enough getting a German submarine out with its two pilots. Why couldn't they arrange another cargo ship to break down twelve miles out? Because it had taken weeks to find a captain willing to take the risk this time.

Still, I wouldn't let it rest, couldn't let it rest. I felt responsible for those twenty-three refugees. For surely if Jakob had not spent the night telling me his story under that floating subway car, that final piece of the submarine would be in possession of the two men from Hallesches and on its way to Montauk this very minute.

But there was something else.

Something else that drove me to the green metal box to pull out tool after tool and place it in front of Jakob, as if I could by sheer wanting, produce the one required to bring together all the bits and pieces of machinery on the table. Drove me to keep talking, keep pacing the small apartment. I believe that deep down, I was certain that everything depended on this. Not only the lives of the twenty-three refugees. But also something important about my father. And Rebecca, too. Although I couldn't have explained to you what. Certainly not then. I can barely explain it now.

At some point, I began to tell Jakob how it would work, how *we* would rescue the refugees. Because of course he *would* fix that final piece. There had never been anything he couldn't fix—except that one thing—and this would be his chance to make up for that.

The words tumbled from my mouth as if I were the battered Philco sitting in the corner—a radio Jakob must have bought broken and fixed. And as I talked, I saw the whole thing inside my head. Saw it perfectly clear.

The saboteurs' submarine with the twenty-three refugees safe inside, moving along the dark coastline, its periscope skimming the black surface of the water, searching for a single bit of light. Less than a mile off the coast of Coney Island, the submarine breaks through the waves, silent except for the sound of seawater running down its smooth sides. With a gasp, the top opens and one by one the refugees step out into the starry night. They toss inflatable boats—exactly like the ones the saboteurs used to land at Amagansett—into the dark water, boats big enough to hold four or five of them. And then they begin to paddle, heading toward shore, following that single light shining at the top of the Parachute Jump.

I cannot say how this plan—so clear and fully realized—turned up inside my head. It might have been because there were so many stories already living there, and I had only just seen the light at the top of the Parachute Jump that morning. Or perhaps my father put it there. Perhaps he sent it to me as a message. If you had asked me then, that is what I would have told you.

Jakob listened as I described the rescue I'd seen inside my head, and then he said, "And one of the men from the submarine will go with them, yes?"

"No," I told him. "That would be noticeable. But kids, kids are always fooling around on the beach at Coney Island."

"So nobody waiting on the beach either?"

"I will be there," I told him. "I will wait."

"But these refugees, they speak only French or German. Perhaps a little Yiddish if we are lucky."

I looked down at Albie's flying cap. "I can bring someone who speaks Yiddish," I told him.

"But still," Jakob said, "children on the beach at night. That would be noticeable."

"It's November," I reminded him. "It's dark by six."

Jakob shook his head. "Children alone in rubber boats being met by other children."

"It will look like any other day at Coney Island."

"It is too dangerous."

"Better than the train to Germany," I told him.

"Maybe."

I stopped pacing and stood before him. "Send the men a message."

"I am sure they have already thought of another plan."

"Tell them about this one."

"I am afraid they are too likely to say yes."

I reached into my pocket and set Jakob's code-o-graph on the table with the pieces of machinery.

"We cannot leave them there," I told him.

He stared down at Rebecca's face in the little window. The face with the expression that reminded me of my mother before my father and I went down into the 42nd Street subway.

Jakob picked up the code-o-graph and slipped it into his pocket, then he pushed his chair closer to the table.

"Come back tomorrow," he told me. "I will tell you what they say."

When I got home, my mother was filling the apartment with the smell of meat and spices. The piece of lace had disappeared from the top of her head, and when I sat down at the red table and spooned up some of the stew, there was less of the undertone of trying. But I was so tired that beyond that, I couldn't have told you much more about what my mother's meal tasted like if it had meant the end of Hitler.

When I finished, my mother asked me if I wanted to talk about any of it, and I said not if I don't have to.

"You don't have to," she told me, blowing smoke at the ceiling. "Only please, no more men with badges in my kitchen."

She half-smiled then, which was half more than I'd seen in a while.

After that she got up and left the kitchen. But before she did, she let her hand rest on my head for a moment.

I got up as well, went to my room and spread my father's messages over the cowboys and Indians riding across my bedspread. I knew he was waiting for me to answer the last message, the one that said

ARE YOU SURE.

And I knew I needed to let him know that Jakob wasn't a Nazi, that he was something else. Something more. But I didn't know how to put all of what Jakob was into a coded message.

It was a while before I remembered something my father had told me, a story from when he still lived in Ireland. He'd been seventeen, a year out of St. Brendan's and working in a Dublin pub cleaning up after drunks. My father had boarded a Grafton Street tram and found himself sitting next to Michael Collins. At the time, Collins was the most wanted man in Ireland, but the British had never seen a photograph of him, so he went about the city as if he was its Lord Mayor.

"I knew it was him the second I sat down," my father had told me. "Not by looking, but by the way he changed the air. Charged it in some way. It kept me from reading the man."

The way my father described it, it was like he was reading himself. But a more heroic version of himself.

My father said he never forgot that tram ride. Said if Collins had turned and asked him to take up a gun and join the IRA, he wouldn't have hesitated, would have followed him right off that tram.

It was Michael Collins's death that made my father want to leave Ireland. The fact that after all the bounties the British had placed on his head, he'd been killed by another Irishman.

"It was like the country had lost a piece of itself," my father had told me.

Now, in my room, I ripped a piece of paper from the composition book and wrote

KU YL SYHU XYVKGUS VTSSYRL

which meant

HE IS LIKE MICHAEL COLLINS.

Someone who wasn't Irish, who wasn't my father, might think I meant the person at 165 Ludlow was a spy, a traitor of some kind. But my father, who would have followed the man off a tram, who had left his own country because Michael Collins was no longer alive in it, he would understand what I was trying to say about Jakob.

I slipped downstairs and put the folded paper in the mailbox. Then for the first time in nearly two days, I slept.

The next morning, the message was gone.

Thirteen

I went looking for Albie the next day, thinking I would find him in the sunless sliver of playground formed when the city built an addition onto P.S. 52 in the 1920s. This little alley was dank and cold, and smelled of cat spray. No teacher had been known to have set foot in it, which made it the perfect place for smoking.

But when I entered the rank darkness, flying cap in my hand, the only person there was Elliott Marshman, a pale fifth-grader who wore orthopedic shoes.

"Out sick," Elliott said, pushing what were probably Albie's old cigarette butts into a pile with the thick sole of his shoe. He glanced up at me. "Though I hear there's a lot of truancy going around."

"Yeah," I agreed. Though when I turned to leave that sunless place, I put my hand over my own beating heart.

I wore Albie's flying cap down to the Lower East Side, liking the way its weight on my head and the fur lining made me feel as if my thoughts were safe from the world. At Ludlow Street, I knocked on Jakob's door for a long time, then I went to look for him on the roof.

As soon as I pushed open the door, I could tell the pigeons were agitated. They were flapping their wings against the chicken wire, darting back and forth inside the coop, turning themselves into gray blurs like the snow clouds piling up in the sky overhead. Perhaps it was Jakob agitating them, sitting on the roof with his back against a leg of their coop. Or maybe it was the pale gray thing in his hands.

My feet crunched across the gravel toward him. Something white blew by my face. Something too big to be snow. Another whipped past in a gust of wind, catching on my jacket. It was one of the narrow strips of paper Jakob used to write his messages, and it was covered with tiny writing.

Not in code. In what even I could see was French.

The wind picked up and a dozen—no, two, three dozen—strips of paper flew across the roof, swirling up from the knocked-together shelves near the pigeon coop. White papers covered in tiny black script. I walked through this paper blizzard toward Jakob, came close enough to know that the thing in his hands was a pigeon, its body seeming boneless, as if it had melted despite the cold.

"What happened to it?" I asked him.

"Exhaustion," he told me. "I kept shooing it away, but it kept coming back."

This close I could see that buckled onto the pigeon's sticklike leg was a metal capsule.

I sat on the tar beside him.

"Did you fix the last piece?"

He lifted his eyes from the pigeon to me. "Did you doubt that I would?"

"And the men from Hallesches. You told them?"

Jakob looked into the sky, where the clouds were gathering.

"I was not going to."

"But?"

"In the end I did."

"Of course," I said, "because it's a good plan."

Wind ruffled the feathers on the limp bird in Jakob's lap.

"I told them because it would have been Rebecca's idea of

perfection." He ran his hand over the gray feathers, putting them back in order. "A master plan for rescue dreamed up by a boy."

He looked back at me.

"I only told them the plan was mine."

"Why?"

"I did not think the men from Hallesches would have appreciated the perfection."

"What did they say?"

"They will try this plan of yours, if two problems can be solved."

The first problem was clothing. The refugees would have left their homes in a hurry when the Germans invaded, and not taken many clothes. They also would have spent a long time in hiding, and when you are a child, you continue to grow, even when you are running from the Germans, so nothing they had taken would still fit.

"They will not look like American children when they land, and that will make them not so unnoticeable."

The second problem was where to take the refugees once they had landed. If the families would draw too much attention on the beach at Coney Island, they needed someplace else to meet. Someplace private, yet public enough so that fifteen families coming and going wouldn't attract too much notice.

"And if we solve these . . ." I began.

"If *you* solve them."

A batch of papers blew off the shelf, spinning like a cyclone across the roof and disappearing over the edge. I felt as if I'd gone with them out into the empty air.

"A master plan for rescue dreamed up by a boy," he repeated. "It cannot happen any other way."

I nodded, pulling the flying cap closer about my head.

In all the time since, I have not once wondered why I didn't stand on that roof and argue with Jakob, beg him to help me with these problems, which were so much for a boy. I understood in the way that he did how the plan was meant to work. Believed in it the way that he did. For neither of us were strangers to all the leaps of logic and imagination in which grief can make you believe.

Jakob gathered the dead bird into his hands and got to his feet.

"You cannot take too long," he told me. "They will not let the submarine leave for Marseilles until every part of the plan is in place. And they believe it is soon that the twenty-three will be put on the train for Germany."

I stood and nodded at the bird cupped in his hands, the empty cigar box that had once contained the strips of paper. "And that?"

"You have not read the papers?" he said. "You do not know what Hitler is planning for France?"

I shook my head.

The coming darkness cast a slate-colored light on Jakob's face. He looked weary, as if he'd been up here all night.

"He intends to occupy the entire country." He raised the limp bird closer to his face, as if he were trying to breathe life into it. "If that happens, there will not be a Jew left alive in France."

I turned my back on Jakob and the dead bird, walked across the roof. My head was full of the problems I had to solve, and my hand was on the freezing edge of the door before I realized what I was hearing.

Wheezing.

The sound an asthmatic might make on a cold, snow-threatening day like this one.

It's only the wind in your ears, I told myself.

I lifted one of the flaps of the flying cap and leaned forward. After a moment, I heard it again. Whoever it was, he was close, standing right on the other side of the roof door, with only its width between us.

I made some noise with my shoes on the gravel, and the wheezing was replaced by the sound of footsteps hurrying down the stairs into the building.

I turned toward Jakob—thinking I would say something to him, tell him what I'd heard—but he was still standing under the darkening sky with the lifeless bird spilling between his fingers. I turned back and pulled the door open.

I chased after the wheeze, listening for it beneath the usual noises of the building—the shouting and door-slamming—as if it were the tenement's own faulty breathing. I followed it to the fourth floor, the third. When I lost it on the second, I picked up speed, racing down the rest of the stairs and out through the door.

I stood at the top of the metal staircase and squinted up and down Ludlow Street, looking for somebody running—heading toward Stanton, or maybe Houston. But all I saw was the usual blur of fur-hatted men, and packs of kids, and women tugging on grocery carts.

And the sound of the wheeze had vanished, as if it had never been there, as if it had only been the wind in my ear.

As the subway took me back uptown, I invented elaborate theories about who might belong to that asthmatic wheeze. An FBI G-man who had discovered Jakob had been on the *St. Louis.* Somebody who had seen me following people and had decided to follow me. A Nazi who wanted to send Jakob back to Germany.

I pushed these elaborate theories into every corner of my brain so there would be no room for the more logical one—that it had been

Uncle Glenn hiding behind the roof door. Uncle Glenn, who didn't believe I would come to him if I found a Nazi. Uncle Glenn, who might have been following me ever since I'd shown him how I could hear the undertone in voices.

Still, if it had been Uncle Glenn behind that door, all he would have heard Jakob and me talking about was children and a submarine and the beach at Coney Island. He would know that Jakob wasn't a Nazi. And he certainly wouldn't have run away from me.

Unless, said some part of my brain I hadn't been able to fill with theories, *Uncle Glenn wanted to be a hero so badly, he would turn in twenty-three Jews who weren't supposed to be here. Twenty-four, if you counted Jakob.*

I yanked off the flying cap, as if trying to release the thought from my head. Not Uncle Glenn. Not the man who'd rescued me at my father's wake, who'd pulled me from the depthless dark of the Keener's mouth.

It was somebody else. Somebody dangerous.

Somebody I couldn't tell Jakob about, because he might tell the men from Hallesches, and they would call off the plan. And I couldn't let that happen. Not to either of us.

It was my mother who solved the problem of the clothes.

She'd just come in from five o'clock Mass and was standing in the entryway of the living room, unbuttoning the blue overcoat she always wore once it got cold. Seeing her in it let me believe she was back to wearing normal clothes, that when she slipped the coat off, she'd be wearing a plaid skirt and a red sweater—a color that looked nice with her black hair falling loose around her shoulders. Watching her made me wish she'd stop unbuttoning the coat and put her hands in her pockets, and let me imagine something other than the dead-leaf thing

I knew she was really wearing, because you could never tell what somebody had on underneath a coat.

It was that quick, as though somebody else had put the idea into my head.

I didn't need twenty-three sets of clothes, I only needed twenty-three coats.

And I knew where to get them. Knew from the winter almost no one had paid my father for their portraits, and we had picked out coats for ourselves from the poor box Father Barry kept behind the confessionals. Every Catholic church had a poor box, and the neighborhood around Dyckman Street, being so Irish, had a lot of Catholic churches.

I figured out the solution to the second problem—where to take the twenty-three refugees—while I was changing into my pajamas. I'd just taken the code-o-graph out of my pocket and was looking at the picture of myself in the little window, that picture of my whole face without glasses, remembering the day I'd seen it for the first time, when it had still been a negative, the reverse of me. Suddenly, the words appeared inside my head like a photograph developing.

Paradise Photo.

Where people were always coming and going. Where there were always a hundred kids on the sidewalk. Where I knew exactly where Harry Jupiter hid the key.

Where, once we were all inside—Albie and me, and the twenty-three refugees, and the families who have come to take them, and Jakob, because of course he will be there—the door to the darkroom will open and a man wearing a belted overcoat and a hat pulled low on his forehead will come out and everyone will turn to look at him. But he will be looking only at me.

"You did all this?" he will ask in an accent that still has enough Irish in it to push around the American, an accent I am beginning to forget.

I will nod, and walk over to him, get so close he is no longer in focus. And then I will put my face into his chest, into the spot where his white shirt is showing between the lapels of his belted coat. The white shirt he still wears, though we don't see each other anymore. And by now, it will have taken on the smell of the developing chemicals from all the pictures of Nazis he has taken. And I will smell, too, the Wildroot Cream-Oil he uses on his hair—spiky, like mine. And though he is wearing the hat pulled low, and his face is blurred, I will know it is him.

When I returned to Jakob's apartment the next afternoon, I told him my idea about the poor box coats and about Paradise Photo. He sat and listened at the wooden table, which had been cleared of all the bits and pieces of machinery, turning the code-o-graph with the picture of Rebecca over in his hand, the way the boys eager to play skully turn their bottle caps over in their hands.

"What do you think the men from Hallesches will say?" I said when I'd finished.

"I think they will say I have come up with an excellent plan."

"So what do we do now?"

"You should begin collecting the coats. These men are not ones to waste time. They are like the Nazis in that way."

He told me to get fourteen boys' coats and nine girls' coats. "Your size, or perhaps a little smaller."

I nodded, and then I got up and headed toward the door. I was halfway out when he spoke to my back.

"We will do this?" he said. "Rescue them?"

I turned. He had folded his fingers over the code-o-graph and was gripping it tightly.

"We will," I said. But I had to put my hand in my pocket and touch the thin edges of my own code-o-graph to make my voice steady.

The next day, I found Albie in the sunless alley, surrounded by a half dozen sixth-grade boys who were watching him smoke as if he was a vaudeville act. I said I had something to tell him, and he dismissed the boys, saying that we had private business. They filed out, trailed by Elliott Marshman, who dragged the thick soles of his orthopedic shoes in case Albie decided to call him back.

As I explained the plan—the submarine, the refugees, Coney Island—the lit end of Albie's Lucky Strike bounced in the dim light like a winter firefly. I gave him only the parts of Jakob's story he needed to know, and told him nothing about the wheeze I'd heard behind the roof door. Albie's father—the convert—had insisted he learn Yiddish as well as Hebrew. We made plans to start collecting poor box coats later that afternoon.

I was halfway home when I heard the wheeze again.

Or thought I heard it. For the first time since my eyes had gone bad, I couldn't be certain of something I was hearing. It was possible it had been the bus wheezing up Broadway, or heat escaping through the subway grates, or a hundred other things. Since that afternoon on Jakob's roof, I'd been listening for the wheeze, and I'd started to hear it everywhere.

I reeled around. But there was no one there.

At least, no one I recognized, no one close to me. Because there was never no one on a New York City street in the middle of the day. And with my eyes, twenty people I might have recognized could have been standing just beyond my three-foot zone, and I wouldn't have known it.

A master plan for rescue dreamed up by a boy, I thought. *Who had believed that was a good idea? A man who had tried to make a pigeon fly across the ocean to deliver a message to a dead girl?*

A chill wind blew up the street, turning me cold. Cold as those refugees would be if their submarine was sunk by a battleship, if their inflatable boats were capsized by a coast guard cutter. If somebody with a wheeze had them sent back to Germany.

I felt the weight of those twenty-three lives settle on me. Lives that were depending on my plan. A plan that, perhaps, I'd dreamed up for my own reasons.

I took off, ran all the way back to Dyckman Street, and down into the basement of our building.

I tore through the shelves where everybody stored the things they couldn't fit inside their apartments—glass ornaments and camping equipment and clothes that were wrong for the season we were in—until I found the shoebox my father had labeled *Tax Receipts*. There was so much duct tape wound around the top, I had to get a screwdriver from Mr. Puccini's toolbox to cut through it.

After I did, after I'd taken off the top, I was looking down at my father's gun.

He'd shown it to me more than a year ago. We'd been to see a Charlie Chan movie at the Alpine Theater—*Murder Over New York*—and on the way out, I'd asked him if he still had his gun from when he'd worked as bodyguard to the Duke's illegal alcohol. I remember asking him if he'd ever shot anybody.

"I shot over a couple of people's heads a few times," he'd told me. "That was about the extent of it."

I took my father's gun out of the shoebox.

There were five bullets rolling around in the bottom of the box, and I loaded them into the gun. My father had taught me how the afternoon we'd gone to see *Murder Over New York*. I can't say why. Maybe he thought it was a skill I could use.

I raised my arm and aimed the gun at the coal-burning furnace in the corner—the furnace that was breathing fire like a mechanical dragon, making a wheezing sound like a person with asthma. For a small gun, it felt heavy. No, not heavy, substantial. The feeling traveled up my wrist and into my body.

I made a firing noise with my mouth. Then I lowered my arm and dropped my father's gun into my jacket pocket. My pockets were stretched out from me forgetting my gloves and the gun fit inside perfectly.

Looking back, I don't believe I had any intention of firing the gun at anything more animate than that furnace. It is only that the reality of what Jakob and I were attempting had finally become clear to me, as if it had come and stood in my three-foot zone. And the weight of my father's gun in my pocket made me feel safe.

I went upstairs to our apartment then and got Albie's flying cap—the cap I'd forgotten to bring back to him today. I folded it in half and tucked it into the shoebox labeled *Tax Receipts*. Then I wound several layers of Mr. Puccini's duct tape around the top of the box and put it back on the shelf.

I believed Albie had loaned the cap to me for luck, and now I wanted it someplace where nothing could get at it. If he asked me about it, I would make some excuse, tell him I forgot it.

I didn't plan to remember it until those inflatable boats landed at Coney Island.

When I met Albie on Vermilyea Street, I was pulling my old Radio Flyer wagon. I'd fitted the wooden slats into the sides, and then taped a sign to them that said *ALUMINUM FOR NATIONAL DEFENSE*. I'd also thrown in a couple of my mother's old pots.

Albie asked why the sign and the pots, and I told him part of the plan was making sure nobody knew we were collecting poor box coats.

"Nobody like who?"

"Just nobody," I said.

We were tossed out of the first church we went into—St. Jude's—by a fat priest, after Albie strolled past the bowl of Holy Water as if it were a drinking fountain.

"Don't you know how to make the sign of the cross?" I asked him.

"Why would I?"

"Wasn't your father Catholic at one time?"

"Not since before I was born."

The two of us stood in the wind on the corner of Nagle Avenue, while I made Albie practice the sign of the cross until he could perform it as haphazardly as anyone who'd been born to the faith. Then we headed over to Holy Trinity. As we were entering, Albie turned his face up to the weak November sun and asked me if he looked too Jewish to pull this off.

I recalled what Jakob had told me about the Wandering Jew exhibit, the hooked noses and thick lips made out of rubber. To me, Albie only looked like himself—a smallish boy with pale skin and violet half-moons beneath his eyes.

"You look fine," I told him.

We started out by asking for the coats. Hiding our own jackets in the bushes, claiming to be coatless. We told the priests we had a sister at home who also needed a coat. They told us to have our sister come in and ask for herself.

After that first day, we realized it would take too long to collect twenty-three coats by asking. That's when we began stealing them. We'd wait in the back until the priest disappeared into a confessional, then slip up the aisle to the poor box and rummage through it, tossing the stained shirts and moth-holed sweaters—all the clothes that smelled like other people's closets—onto the floor, until we'd found every coat that was our size or smaller.

Sometimes whoever was confessing only had a few sins, and the priest came out before we were finished. Then we grabbed whatever coats we'd found and ran, the echoey sound of our footsteps bouncing around the church, disturbing the old ladies on the kneelers, their rosaries dangling from their fingers.

Because of my eyesight, because nothing was truly clear unless it was three feet away from me, I was always running into the unknown. This made everything feel hazardous. Still, I liked these flights from the dim churches into the clear November light, my arms full of coats, a cassocked priest nipping at my heels. I liked the companionable sound of Albie's shoes keeping time with mine, the reassuring weight of my father's gun in my pocket tugging on my shoulder.

At some point, we remembered we'd have to take the twenty-three refugees on the subway, so we also began stealing nickels out of the wooden offering boxes from the side altars. The boxes where people paid for the candles set before the statues of saints—Joseph, Mary, Francis of Assisi. When Albie asked me if we were allowed to help ourselves to the money from these boxes, I told him they were only another kind of poor box.

When we pulled the Radio Flyer up to Good Shepherd, I sent Albie in alone. I couldn't bring myself to step inside that ocean-y blue light, couldn't make myself walk into the church I'd run out of only a few months before.

I waited outside with the wagon, praying Father Barry would not sense me there, the way he sensed any minor transgression—chewing gum, daydreaming—during a Catechism lesson. Albie was back out in less than a minute, his gloveless hands empty.

"That priest didn't take his eyes off me for a second. It was like he knew what I was doing there. Like he could tell I wasn't Catholic."

"Not much happens in Good Shepherd Father Barry doesn't know about." I picked up the handle of the Radio Flyer.

Albie stepped in front of the wagon.

"There were coats in that poor box."

"Forget them."

I wheeled the Radio Flyer around him.

"We only need to distract that priest."

"Let's go to Blessed Sacrament."

I began walking up Isham Street.

"You could go in and confess."

I shook my head and kept walking, but I didn't feel him following me. I turned around. Albie was standing on the sidewalk, half-turned toward Good Shepherd.

"What are you going to do?"

"The bowl of Holy Water in there? It's very unstable."

"Don't," I told him.

"It wouldn't take much to knock it over."

I pictured my mother walking into Good Shepherd for five o'clock Mass—less than an hour from now—and seeing that bowl of Holy Water smashed into a hundred pieces on the tiled floor. Imagined what terrible sign she'd take it for.

I turned the wagon around.

"All right," I said. "But be quick about it. Because I'm going to make this short."

The inside of Good Shepherd smelled the same as Father Barry's suit the day they'd waked my father with an empty coffin, the same as my mother's clothes smelled every day now. Like Mass incense. Like candy you believe will taste better than it does.

I dipped my fingers in the Holy Water and moved them to my forehead, heart, shoulders in the sign of the cross. Then I put them in my pocket and pressed them against the barrel of my father's gun to keep them from recalling the rough feel of my mother's mouth.

Father Barry was standing in front of the confessional booths, as if he knew I'd be coming. He said my name, and then he clapped his hands one time, like that was all the applause I deserved.

I pointed to the confessional, and Father Barry nodded. He spun and went through the door, the hem of his cassock swirling around his ankles.

It was stuffy inside the confessional, the atmosphere full of other people's sins. Father Barry's hair shone white through the holes of the mesh screen that divided his side of the booth from mine.

I confessed to lying to my mother, and to not having attended P.S. 52 for forty-six consecutive days. Then I sat on the wooden bench and waited for Father Barry to ask me if I was sorry and tell me how many Hail Marys it would take for my sins to be absolved.

"And why did you not attend school for forty-six days?" Father Barry asked me.

His voice floated through the holes in the screen, clear and distinct. It was the voice he used when he wanted to accuse us of something—not contributing enough to the building fund, or eating meat on Friday. In his tone, which filled the stuffy atmosphere of the confessional, thickening the air, making it difficult to breathe, I heard that my mother had told him everything. Everything I had told her about my father not being dead, everything she hadn't believed.

I gripped the edge of the wooden bench, my arms twitching with fury. First, my mother had given Father Barry all of my father's clothes, let him send them to darkest Africa, then she had poured the story of what had really happened in the 42nd Street subway station into his hairy ears.

"I asked you a question," Father Barry said. "Why you did not attend school for forty-six days?"

"I was looking for Nazis," I told him.

"I should counsel you that lying to a priest is as great a sin as lying to God."

"I am not lying."

"And why were you looking for Nazis?"

"Because we're at war with them."

I heard rustling from Father Barry's side of the confessional. "And that is the only reason?"

I was gripping the bench so tightly my arms were shaking.

"Or perhaps the reason has something to do with your father?"

All the holes in the mesh screen turned flesh-colored as Father Barry brought his face closer.

"You know that your father is dead, don't you, Jack?"

There was a smooth layer of solicitousness floating in Father Barry's undertone like oil, but beneath that hummed the pure pleasure the priest would take in telling my mother that he had been the one to make me see reason.

Alone in my side of the confessional, I shook my head.

"Say it, Jack. Say it instead of a Hail Mary."

Though I tried to stop them, Father Barry's words wormed their way inside my head. That thing he wanted me to say. That lie. It pounded and echoed, making pictures. The way the radio made pictures. Clear and perfect. My father arcing off the subway platform, over and over again. Each time Father Barry's words echoed—*You know your father is dead*—a new picture appeared on top of the old one. My father falling. And then falling again. And again.

It didn't seem my head could hold all these pictures. I was sure that any minute, the bones of my skull would blow apart.

"Say . . . I know my father is dead," Father Barry repeated

My hands—out of my control now—flew to the mesh screen. The screen filled with the flesh color of Father Barry's face. I slammed my fists against the flesh-colored holes, over and over, until the screen began to give, and then cut into my knuckles—a thin, sharp, satisfying pain. I only stopped when the light changed on the other side of the confessional, when it was clear that Father Barry had opened the door and fled.

I bolted back into the ocean-y blueness of the church, ran down the aisle, skirting a pile of clothes spilling out of the poor box. When I reached the bowl of Holy Water—a bowl made of porcelain that truly did look unstable—I wrapped my hands around its edge and gave a sharp tug. The bowl tilted, and then crashed to the floor with a hollow sound that echoed through Good Shepherd.

As I burst through the door onto the street, I pictured my mother having to step over those sharp-edged pieces of porcelain scattered on the floor, her Mass shoes slipping on the oily water in which she had placed so much faith.

Each night, when I brought the poor box coats we'd collected back to the basement, I sat on the floor with the furnace breathing fire behind me and counted them. Often, I'd take out the coats we'd collected the days before, the ones I'd stuffed between the rusted frames of the broken bicycles and old baby carriages, and count them together, see how close we were to the twenty-three. When I was finished, I'd imagine the refugees, try to picture what they were doing at the exact same moment.

When the count was six, I pictured them at the camp in Marseilles, all of them wearing clothes that were a little too small, all of them sitting at a long table set outside a barracks, none of them knowing that a submarine was on its way to rescue them. When the count was twelve, I pictured them in the supply truck trundling over unpaved roads toward the harbor, the clanging of bottles in their ears, the rumble of the engine under their feet. When the count was seventeen, I pictured them deep beneath the ocean, stretched out on bunks that hung from the curved sides of the U-boat. They were listening to *The Lone Ranger* and *Jack Armstrong the All-American Boy*, learning English the way Jakob had—although I was sure the sound of the radio waves wouldn't carry through the water. Still, I liked thinking of the refugees listening to the same things I listened to. I liked thinking we would have this in common when they floated ashore at Coney Island.

The night the count was twenty, I'd stuffed the last of the coats between two bicycles with flattened tires and then heard footsteps coming down the stairs behind me.

"What are you up to down here?"

It was Uncle Glenn in his spying clothes, barely visible in the dim light of the basement.

I stood, the coats behind me.

"Are you going out on Civil Defense patrol?" I said.

"That would be what your aunt May believes."

Uncle Glenn reached the bottom of the stairs and headed toward me.

I tried to step back, but there was nowhere to go. My legs were pressed up against the hard rim of a flattened bicycle tire.

Uncle Glenn came closer, near enough for me to see the silver chain of his Civil Defense whistle disappearing into the neck of his new black overcoat. And then he kept going, past me to a teepee of ski poles leaning against the wall. He reached behind them and took out a long, narrow case.

"I sometimes find it convenient to keep my pool cue down here."

He hefted the case, then turned and came back to where I was standing, pressed up against the rusted bicycles.

"You still didn't say what you were doing down here."

I pointed to the Radio Flyer.

Uncle Glenn glanced at the wagon. "*Aluminum for National Defense.*" He read the sign on the side. "Just doing your part for the war effort."

The furnace clicked on, sounding as if something inside had caught on fire. It was keeping me from hearing his undertone.

Uncle Glenn lifted his foot, placed the front of his shoe on the wheel of the Radio Flyer. He nudged the wagon back and forth a few times.

"I see you and that small kid out with that wagon all the time."

I felt the twenty coats behind me like living things.

"Just doing our part for the war effort," I repeated.

Uncle Glenn pushed the Radio Flyer back and forth several more times.

"That's it?"

My hand found its way into the pocket that held my father's gun.

"That's it."

We stared at each other. Him, with the front of his shoe on the Radio Flyer's wheel. Me, with my hand on my father's gun and the twenty coats behind me. I think in some part of my brain, I believed that those twenty poor box coats were the refugees, and that I was standing guard over them. I don't know what would have happened if he had taken a step forward, reached around me and yanked one of those coats from between the rusted bicycles.

Uncle Glenn lifted his foot off the Radio Flyer's wheel.

"Don't tell Aunt May you saw me."

"I won't."

The next day, after Albie and I had stolen the twenty-third coat from St. Ignatius, I told him that things would go more smoothly when the refugees landed if we buried the coats at Coney Island.

The day we went to bury the coats was gray and drizzly. I'd divided them between the Radio Flyer and an old baby carriage, and even then, no matter how hard I pressed on them, woolen sleeves kept trailing out the sides, as if the coats were trying to escape. I hid two of Mr. Puccini's snow shovels in the bottom of the wagon, and thinking that the sand might be damp, I emptied out some burlap bags of dirt I'd found in the basement and stuffed those in there as well.

Albie and I had to make two trips down the stairs to the subway to get the wagon and the baby carriage to the platform. While we were carrying down the carriage, I asked Albie if he thought the coats we'd left at the top of the steps would be okay, if he thought anybody would take them.

He squinted at me across a corduroy jacket. "Who except us would want to steal poor box coats?"

We sat in the crowded subway car, hanging onto the baby carriage and the Radio Flyer, both of them overflowing with old coats, and nobody looked at us twice. People had begun collecting clothes for European refugees by then, and I supposed everybody on the subway believed Albie and I were just kids helping with the war effort.

It was more drizzly out at Coney Island. We rumbled the Radio Flyer and the baby carriage over the planks of the boardwalk, past old couples bundled up in so many layers they looked stuffed, couples walking with their hands clasped together, as if afraid one of them might disappear in the mist.

We chose a spot beneath the boardwalk directly below the Parachute Jump—closed today because of the bad weather. To help us find it in the dark, Albie carved a Star of David into one of the wooden pilings. He used a pearl-handled pocketknife that was as good as the flying cap.

"This is Mordy's, too," he told me.

When he'd finished the carving, I flattened my palm over it, read it like Braille.

"Perfect," I said.

Then we started digging.

It took much longer to dig a hole in the sand deep enough for twenty-three coats than I'd imagined. Sand slid back into the hole nearly as fast as we shoveled it out, and Mr. Puccini's snow shovels were big and unwieldy. The day was cold and damp, but before long, we were so warm, we'd thrown our own coats onto the sand.

It was a quiet day. Only the sound of the ocean breaking on the shore, and the footsteps of the old couples passing overhead, and the occasional seagull laughing in the rain. And over it all, our snow shovels biting into the sand with a soft grinding.

We lined the hole with the burlap bags, then dumped in the coats. I topped them with another bag before I shoveled the sand back in, flattening it with the backs of Mr. Puccini's shovels. The sky was a much darker gray when we'd finished.

We carried the Radio Flyer and the baby carriage up to the boardwalk, where the wind was whipping the cables of the Parachute Jump, clanging them against its steel base. I was anxious to get back on the subway, to get the wagon and the baby carriage back into the basement before anyone noticed they were missing. But Albie was leaning against the railing, looking out at the dull gray sea.

"Where do you think they are right now?" he said.

The waves were choppy, as if a storm was brewing.

"Coming toward us," I told him.

Then I said something about the rain and dinner, and we headed toward the subway.

When Albie and I came out of the subway on Dyckman Street, the sky was black and the rain had turned to sleet.

"Do you want help with this?" Albie held up the handle of the Radio Flyer.

"It's not far," I told him.

I was partway up the block when I saw Jakob leaning against the stoop of our building. I knew it was him despite the darkness and despite my eyes. Knew it from the way he was huddled into himself, taking up so little space. Knew it from the way he was doing the one thing to guarantee Uncle Glenn would notice him the instant he stepped outside, the instant he stepped through the door that was right above Jakob's head—which, judging by the dark, would happen any second.

I began running up the block—even as I was asking myself why, why I was so worried that my uncle would discover me talking to Jakob—tilting the baby carriage crazily, yanking the Radio Flyer off its front wheels.

"How long have you been here?" I asked him.

The shoulders of Jakob's jacket were soaked black and his hair hung wet in his eyes.

"Twenty minutes."

"Did you ring my bell?"

He nodded.

"My mother doesn't answer it." I glanced up at the door. "Why did you come?"

"You have not been down to see me."

"We've been busy, collecting coats."

"You have them all?"

I nodded.

"Good. Because they will arrive in three days."

I counted in my head. "Wednesday."

"They will come ashore not long after it turns dark."

I pictured it—the boats on the beach, my father stepping out of the darkroom.

There was a sharp bang. The door to our building had been flung open, and someone dressed all in black hurried out. It was Mr. Carbone from 2F, running down the stairs with a newspaper over his head.

I exhaled.

"Is that it?"

"Well," Jakob said, "I suppose there is one thing you should know."

"Yes?" I was already pushing the baby carriage toward the basement stairs.

"The refugees, one of them is deaf."

Fourteen

This is the story I didn't know the afternoon I followed Rose LoPinto home from P.S. 52 with the intention of asking her to come to Coney Island and translate for the deaf refugee. The story Rose wouldn't tell me until much later, until it was almost too late.

The first English word Rose's father learned on his arrival from Sicily as a ten-year-old boy was *wop*. The second was *dago*. And the third was *slow*, which was what the teacher called him when he couldn't learn to read any of the textbooks in the farm town of Newburgh, New York. After a year, Anthony LoPinto traded his desk in the schoolhouse for an upturned bucket in the blood-soaked yard of the local butcher, a man named Colson Gammon, who had once cut up a whole hog while blindfolded.

Anthony LoPinto might have been bad with a book, but he was good with a knife. Gammon claimed the boy possessed an ability for it, as if he could see the tendons and muscles of the animal inside his head. "That slow wop kid?" the other men laughed.

"You have to watch him," Gammon told them. "He'll stand in front of a side of beef, the thing hanging there twice his size, staring at it like he's seeing through the hide to each cut. Haunch, flank, shoulder. Then when he's got it all pictured inside his head, he'll take the knife and start cutting. Never makes a wrong move."

The men didn't believe Gammon. They came to the blood-soaked yard with the trickiest cutting jobs. Goats and spring lambs. Even a hare. They strung each up on the hook and sat on the upturned buckets as if at a show, waiting for the slow wop kid to butcher the meat. Whatever they brought, he could always do it.

Anthony's ability with a knife eventually earned him enough money to open his own butcher shop in Yonkers, away from the town that knew him as the slow wop kid. Enough to marry. Lucia, a girl just arrived from his hometown in Sicily, a girl with hair black as a winter's night and almond-shaped eyes of such an impossible darkness, you were in danger of falling into them.

Rose would tell me that as a child she'd spend hours staring into her mother's eyes, that her mother was the kind of person who'd sit quietly still while you did such a thing.

But Lucia was shy in a way even her beauty couldn't compensate for. In the evenings, Anthony sat with his new wife practicing the simple English phrases she would need to buy food or talk to the neighbors. But Lucia never used those phrases. She was too shy to set foot in a shop that contained even one person she did not already know, too shy to answer the women who hailed her from their apartment windows as she clothespinned Anthony's shirts to the line outside her own.

After Rose was born, Anthony hoped the little girl would bring enough English into the apartment to entice her mother to learn it. But as his daughter grew older—certainly old enough to begin talking, he thought—she remained as quiet as her mother.

One evening, Anthony arrived home from the butcher shop earlier than usual and heard Lucia's voice coming from the kitchen. His wife was speaking in a rush of Sicilian, more words strung together than he'd heard her say in all the years he'd known her, and he wondered who she was talking with. He listened, but the only reply was the knocking of the wooden bobbin Rose liked to play with against the floor.

Lucia was talking about the elementary school she'd attended in Sicily. How they always seemed to be studying Garibaldi, but to this day, she knew very little about Garibaldi because she'd always been thinking about the boy who'd left to go to America. Sometimes, she told her daughter, she'd pretend the dust on her shoes—dust that had come from the lemon grove outside the window—was the same dust he walked on, dust that had seen the feet of wild Indians and buffalo.

Anthony came around the corner, thinking how disappointed his wife must have been to arrive in New York, a place that was nothing like the Wild West. Lucia was still talking, the Sicilian pouring out of her mouth so effortlessly, he might not have recognized her if she hadn't been standing in her own kitchen. Rose sat on the floor with the wooden bobbin, not listening to anything her mother was saying. No, Anthony thought as he watched his daughter roll the bobbin around her shoes. Rose wasn't *hearing* anything her mother was saying. Which, he realized, was what was giving his wife the courage to keep talking.

I always believed, Rose would tell me later, that this was the day my father stopped loving my mother.

If I had known this story the gray-sky afternoon I followed Rose LoPinto's camel-colored coat up Academy Street and onto Sherman Avenue, I might have known sooner how to convince her to help me. But all I knew then was that Rose could talk with her hands. I'd seen her do it once, with a boy on the playground at P.S. 52, the two of them speaking in that secret language that was like a code you kept inside your head. A code that seemed better than anything you could send away for from the radio.

Rose's building was nicer than ours. The mailboxes had locks that worked, and there was a glass door between me and the stairs to the apartments. I pressed the button next to the piece of cardboard that said *LoPinto*, and after a moment, Rose's voice came out of the little holes in the wall.

"I need to ask you something," I shouted at the wall.

I had an image of Rose standing on a chair so the microphone box at her throat would be level with the speaker.

"Jack?"

"It's important," I shouted. "And secret."

The glass door buzzed and I lunged for it.

I ran up the steps to Rose's apartment and knocked on the door. Rose opened it and stood there looking at me.

I realized then that I'd never seen her from straight on. I was always sitting next to her, looking at her from the side. She was wearing a plaid wool jumper that day—a pattern I think was called black watch—and a white blouse, and I'd never noticed before how from straight on, her black curls exploded around the metal headband she wore to hold the RadioEar receiver. I might have stood in the hallway noticing that for a while.

"Is this something you have to come in and ask me?"

"Yes," I said. "Yes, I do."

She led me into the living room and we sat together on a green sofa. Across from us, where other people might have hung a family portrait, were framed pictures of Fiorello La Guardia and Franklin Roosevelt.

"Those belong to my father," she told me.

"Is anybody else here?" I asked her.

"Only my mother, but she's in her bedroom. She won't come out until you leave."

"My mother's like that now," I told her.

"My mother's always been like that."

Rose sat and waited for me to say what I'd come here to say. I sat wishing I could tell her all about my father. But I didn't have any experience telling secrets to girls, and I didn't know how much you could trust them.

What I ended up telling her was that Albie Battaglia and I were helping a friend bring in some refugees, and that one was deaf, and that I needed her to come to the beach at Coney Island at night and translate everything I said into the secret language I knew she could speak with her hands.

It was the first time I'd said so many words in a row to Rose. The first time I'd said so many that had come from my own head and not from the lips of a teacher. And when I was finished talking, I sat on the green sofa all out of breath, as if I'd been running.

"Why are they coming into Coney Island?" she asked. "And why at night?"

From the far wall, the unblinking eyes of Fiorello La Guardia and Franklin Roosevelt bore into me.

"It's possible they don't have visas."

"So, they're not supposed to be here?"

"They *were* supposed to be here. Until the Allies invaded North Africa."

Rose's dark eyes flicked across the room, and for the first time I noticed the blue star hanging in her front window. I tried to remember if she had a brother.

"You and Albie Battaglia are sneaking in Jewish refugees and you want me to help you?"

"Only with the deaf one."

She folded her hands in her black watch lap and shook her head. "I can't."

"Why not?"

"Do you know where my father is?"

"At work?"

"North Africa."

I glanced back at the star in the window. "Your *father's* in the army?"

She nodded. "So I can't be doing anything treasonous."

"It's only talking with your hands."

"It's called signing."

"Signing," I repeated. "How can that be treasonous?"

"Is what you're doing illegal?"

"Your part won't be."

Rose shook her head again, her dark eyes glued to that blue star.

"It'll be dark," I told her. "We might lose the deaf refugee on the beach."

"I can't," she said. "Not as long as my father is in North Africa."

I could have taken Rose at her word, could have figured we'd hang onto the deaf refugee by the sleeve of the poor box coat, make gestures in the dark. But by then, I'd looked straight at Rose for too long, said too many words to her that had been born inside my own head. By then, I wanted her on that beach.

The following afternoon, I ran after Rose's camel-colored coat as it headed up Academy Street and asked her to come with me to Bickman's Fountain.

"An ice cream soda isn't going to change my mind," she told me.

"Then no danger in coming."

I had no actual plan, no words ready to convince her. But I believed I had a better chance away from the twin stares of Fiorello La Guardia and Franklin Roosevelt.

Bickman's Fountain was bright and sugary. Fluorescent light bounced off the chrome edges of the stools, and the air was full of the scent of ice cream, a scent so sweet it made your skin feel sticky. It was a cold day for ice cream. The only person inside Bickman's—except Mr. Bickman scowling behind the counter—was an old man in a hat eating a chocolate sundae.

Rose sat in one of the pistachio-colored booths and unbuttoned her coat. When I asked her what she wanted, she told me a glass of water.

"It's my treat," I told her. I'd taken thirty-five cents out of my mother's wallet that morning.

"Just a glass of water," she repeated.

"Ice cream doesn't mean you'll come to Coney Island," I said.

"I know." Rose slipped off her coat. "I'm just not eating any sugar."

I pointed to the wall behind the counter where Mr. Bickman had taped up pictures of ice cream sodas and sundaes. "You don't have to use your ration coupons here."

"I know that, too." Rose pulled a napkin out of the dispenser and began folding it into perfect squares.

I wanted to ask her for more explanation, because nobody came to Bickman's and ordered water, but there was something about the way she was folding that napkin that stopped me.

I went to the counter and got a black-and-white for myself and a glass of water for Rose. In the time I'd been away, she'd folded three more napkins into perfect squares.

"Do you want a sip?" I asked her. "Since I'm the one who ordered it."

"No, thank you."

I sucked on the straw. The black-and-white was cold and sweet and tasted oddly of Fascism.

"Do you think I could have the money you would have spent on my soda?" Rose asked.

It was such a startling request, I couldn't think to do anything except reach into my pocket and empty all the change there onto the table between us. The coins made a metallic racket, the dimes twirling around on their edges before flattening and going silent.

Rose glanced at the wall with the pictures of ice cream sodas and sundaes, and—I now realized—how much they cost. She slid a dime over to her side of the table.

"What would you have gotten?" I asked her.

She nodded at my half-empty glass. I smiled around my straw.

She opened her schoolbag and took out a *My First War Bond* book. It was exactly like mine, except that hers was nearly full instead of entirely empty. She slipped my dime into one of the half-moons.

I pointed to the war bond book. "Is that your first one?"

"Fourth," she said. Then, "No, fifth."

I looked at the perfectly folded napkins in front of her. Six of them now.

"And when exactly did you stop eating sugar?"

She took a small sip of water.

"When my father got his orders."

It came to me in a sugary rush along with my black-and-white. And why wouldn't it? It was the kind of thinking that made perfect sense to me. Rose believed that if she didn't eat sugar, if she filled enough *My First War Bond* books, her father would come home safe from the war.

I looked at her across the scattered coins.

"You know," I said, "what your father is doing in North Africa isn't any different from what Albie and I are doing."

"It's entirely different." She drank a swallow of water as if it was something she actually wanted.

"Your father is fighting the people who are killing Jews."

"How do you know that?"

"How do I know the Nazis are killing Jews?"

She nodded.

"From my friend. He was in Germany. He talked to somebody who saw it."

Rose stared at me with her dark eyes. I tried not to sink into them.

"That means your father is saving Jews. Just like we are."

I sipped my black-and-white.

"You're doing something illegal," Rose said. "My father would never break one of this country's laws."

"Unless," I paused for emphasis, "following that law meant you were acting the same as the Nazis."

Rose stared at me over her glass of water, her folded napkins.

"I don't believe your father would do that, would he?" I took another sip of my soda. "I don't believe *you* would do that either."

I put my elbows on the table covered with my mother's change and directed my words at the microphone box pinned to the collar of Rose's blouse—navy blue today.

"Because you have to do everything you can *here*, to help your father *there*."

Rose was looking right into my eyes. I held onto the edge of the table to keep myself focused.

"Which makes helping us with the deaf refugee pretty much the same as filling that war bond book or not having an ice cream soda."

I sat back and sucked up the last cold drops of the black-and-white.

"At least that's how I would think of it."

Rose stared down at the stack of perfectly folded napkins.

The man in the hat finished his sundae and walked out of Bickman's.

Then she raised her head.

"Where exactly at Coney Island?"

. . .

That night I left a message for my father that said

VTXU OT WGNGBYLU WKTOT OTXTNNTP 22 WX

which meant

COME TO PARADISE PHOTO TOMORROW 9 PM.

After I put it in the mailbox, I stood with my hand pressed against the door, feeling all the small holes that had been punched into it under my fingertips. *The next time I have something to tell my father*, I thought, *I will say it out loud to him.*

Fifteen

On Wednesday morning—the day the refugees were to land—I told my mother I had to stay late at P.S. 52. "We're rehearsing the Thanksgiving pageant," I said. "The Landing of the Mayflower."

"Will you be late?" she asked. She was buttoning her coat over one of her brown outfits.

"Yes," I told her. "Very."

I left the apartment with my father's gun in the stretched-out pocket of my jacket. All day it hung from a peg in the cloakroom of Miss Milhaus's classroom.

At three o'clock, Albie and I collected the snow shovels from the basement. We walked to the subway with them propped on our shoulders, as if we expected a blizzard to come tumbling out of the cloudless blue sky.

When we arrived at Coney Island, the sun had already gone down behind the buildings. It was dark and cold under the boardwalk. We walked from piling to piling in the deepening dusk, pressing our fingers into the splintery wood like blind people reading a stranger's face. At last I felt the Star of David under my hands, my fingertips slipping into its outline the way they'd slipped into the notches and valleys of my father's film sheets.

We began digging.

The moon rose. It was only a quarter full, but the sky was clear and it cast a pale white light on the sand.

Rose arrived, appearing in a spot where nothing had been a moment before. She was wearing the camel-colored coat, and even standing beneath the boardwalk, she reflected moonlight.

Not long after Rose's arrival, my shovel caught on the burlap covering the coats. We stopped digging and Albie jumped into the hole, began tossing the coats up to me. Despite the burlap, they were damp and sandy in my arms.

The first boat came as a scraping sound. Something being dragged over the sand and small bits of broken shell at the water's edge.

I sent Albie, who could speak Yiddish, and Rose, who could speak that secret language. I jumped into the hole to toss out the rest of the coats.

I carried as many of them as I could to the water's edge. Four people who were not Rose or Albie stood shivering on the moonlit sand. Beside them in the darkness sat the rounded shape of an inflatable boat.

I wanted to touch these people, press my palms against their beating hearts, feel the rise and fall of their breath beneath my hands, prove to myself they were real. But my arms were full of coats.

Albie said something in Yiddish, and the four refugees came and pulled the coats from my arms. My nose tingled with the sharp yeasty smell of people who haven't bathed in a while.

A second scraping sound came from farther down the beach, and I ran back for more coats.

Six more refugees stood dripping seawater on the sand when I returned. The pale light of the quarter-moon turned everything on the beach black-and-white, made the refugees into one of my father's photographs. Seven boys wearing pants that were soaked dark to the knee. Three girls, all in dresses that hung wet to the beach. The girls pulled the coats from my arms with small hands, holding them up to their shoulders. The boys looked out at the water. I wanted Albie to ask these people if they knew the Lone Ranger, or Jack Armstrong the All-American Boy, but another boat was scraping across the wet sand, and they would need coats.

It was while I was gathering these coats into my arms that footsteps sounded above my head. One person in hard shoes, walking slowly, then stopping right over me, right in front of the Parachute Jump. I dropped the coats and went to the end of the pier, squinted toward the water's edge. Even with my eyes, I could see them. A bunch of kids on the beach, bits of their clothing catching white in the moonlight.

I held my breath, listening for the scraping of another boat. Listening for the hard shoes on the steps that led from the boardwalk to the beach. Waves broke on the sand, wind blew the cables of the Parachute Jump against its steel scaffolding. The footsteps shifted from side to side, then moved away, heading down the boardwalk.

When I returned with the last of the coats, the deaf refugee had landed. She and Rose stood apart from the others, surrounded by darkness yet catching the moonlight, as if they were magnets for it—Rose's camel-colored coat and the deaf refugee's dress.

The pale light caught their hands as well, fluttering in the black night. But this was not like watching Rose and the boy in the playground. The deaf refugee nodded at only some of the words Rose made in the air. The rest made her shake her head, sent her own hands flying in interruption, smaller birds driving away bigger ones from a nest. It was as if Rose and the deaf refugee had sent away for code-o-graphs but had each received different versions, versions where a few of the letter codes were off, rendering every message half-understood.

What we didn't know was that American Sign Language wasn't

universal. The deaf refugee had learned a French version, and it was a kind of miracle that she and Rose found any common words in the language their hands made in the moonlight. Or perhaps it was no miracle, perhaps it was only the luck that had attached itself to this master plan for rescue dreamed up by a boy.

And so far, it was lucky. The five rounded black shapes of the inflatable boats sat at the water's edge, reflecting white in the places they were wet. And on the beach, twenty-three refugees—fourteen boys and nine girls—stood shivering in damp coats, cold and wet, but alive.

I counted them—this time putting my hands on them. Touching the damp wool front of each poor box coat, my fingers pressing firmly enough to feel the resistance of breastbone, the solidity of a person who for weeks had been living inside my head. The last one I counted was the deaf refugee. She'd just finished buttoning up her coat when my hand fell on the front of it. She raised her head and studied my face, as if my touch was somehow part of the secret language she and Rose shared. Then she smiled. There was the black gap of a missing tooth on the left side of her mouth.

"Let's go to Paradise," I said.

We walked away from the inflatable boats, our footsteps silent in the sand.

We came up onto the boardwalk between the curved tracks of the Tornado and the Wonder Wheel, white and round like a moon fallen to the earth. The amusements were dark and shuttered because of the war and winter, but still there were people walking along the boardwalk, looking out to sea. None of them paid us any attention. Not the old couple bundled like sausages against the cold. Not the soldier and his girl, kissing against the side of Stauch's Dance Hall. Not the man with the Civil Defense armband just like Uncle Glenn's, squinting out at the shoreline as if maybe he saw something reflecting white out there. We were only kids—twenty-three of us with coats wetter and sandier than the others—fooling around at Coney Island.

We wove our way through the rides and shuttered arcades and came out onto Surf Avenue, crossing the street near the entrance to Luna Park, passing beneath the giant pinwheels, which—had it not been for the Dim-Out—would have been lit up with a thousand tiny lights, would have been spinning and dazzling the refugees. We were a block from the subway and we might as well have been invisible. None of the factory workers hurrying past us with their hair tied up in turbans and their metal lunch pails in their hands glanced at us. We were only kids—twenty-three of us paler than normal from a week under the ocean—walking past the Sodamat and Bushman Baths and Bernstein's Penny Arcade.

Inside the grimy light of the Stillwell Avenue station, Albie and I handed each of the refugees a nickel for the turnstile. Those nickels that had been spent as offerings for saints—Joseph and Mary and Francis of Assisi. Then we all went up to the platform and got onto a Manhattan-bound train, sitting together in the last car.

In the better light of the subway car, I wished Albie and I had stolen some hats. Some of the refugees looked as if they'd cut their own hair. Chopped-looking bangs fell unevenly across their foreheads and stuck out above their ears. I glanced around the subway car to see if any of the factory workers or soldiers or women sitting with bags of groceries on their laps were looking at us. But this was wartime, when people had other things on their minds—sons and lovers who were off where somebody was shooting at them.

Around DeKalb Avenue, I heard a sound like a waterfall and looked down. The refugees' coats were raining sand, small steady streams of it falling onto the floor of the train. And still not one person on the subway paid attention to us. New York City was full of kids with bad haircuts, kids who'd been playing at the beach, kids roaming the city on their own. We were only more of them. Only kids—twenty-three of us who were supposed to have been on an entirely different kind of train.

We came aboveground at Times Square, stood in the artificial smoke drifting down from the soldier's cigarette on the Camel billboard. The neon was dark, the top half of every headlight blacked out, yet the streets were crowded with soldiers and girls and people dressed up in good clothes, all rushing to the shows that went on behind their unlit signs.

We headed west into Hell's Kitchen, where there were always a hundred kids on the street, most of whom were usually wearing somebody else's coat. Rose walked behind me, her moonlit presence shining on my back. Albie was beside me, the top of his wool cap at the edge of my vision.

When we were a block from Paradise, I told him my father would be there.

"Your father?" he said. "Why would he be there?"

"I left him a message."

Albie stopped walking.

"Where?"

There was something in his voice that made me not want to say any more. I tried to keep us moving down 43rd Street, but now that Albie had stopped, I had to as well.

"Where did you leave the message?" he repeated.

"In our mailbox."

"And somebody took it?"

"He did," I said. "My father."

Rose came to stand beside me.

"Tell me what the message said." Albie sounded as if he was holding his breath.

I looked at the twenty-three refugees standing in a quiet line down 43rd Street.

"It said, 'Come to Paradise Photo at nine.'"

Albie exhaled, then he and Rose stared at each other, neither of them saying a word.

"But it was in code," I told them. "They're always in code." I took out my Captain Midnight Code-O-Graph and waved it around in the dark. "And anyway, why are you asking me these questions?"

Albie pulled off his wool hat and held it in his hands, as if what he had to tell me couldn't be told wearing a hat.

"Because," he said, "your father is dead."

I have wondered how it was that Albie could destroy the world I'd so carefully built with only five words. Destroy it as instantly and irrevocably as our bombs—in less than three years—would destroy those Japanese cities. Herr Brackman had once told Pietr that if people don't want to know the truth, you can put it on the front page and they will find a way not to see it. But perhaps there is something different about *hearing* the truth. Or perhaps it has more to do with who is doing the telling.

Whatever the explanation, the moment I heard those five words, the world in which my father had rolled out of the way of the uptown A in the nick of time, the world in which he would come back when the war ended needing his white shirts and his hats smelling of Wildroot Cream-Oil, collapsed in on itself. It seemed as if my eyes had gone entirely bad, as if I had turned blind. I was surrounded by darkness, and entirely alone.

Cold water—freezing water—rushed into my lungs, filling them up, choking off my breath, stopping me from grabbing any new air. I stood on the corner of 43rd Street with my mouth open and gasping and the world gone dark, drowning on dry land.

Fingers, warm from the pocket of a shining coat, slipped around mine.

I drew a breath. The downward-casting streetlights of 43rd Street blossomed back into my vision.

Albie was studying the sidewalk as if he was looking for those five words, perhaps to take them back.

"I always thought you believed me," I said.

He glanced up. "I thought it was like Mordy."

"Your brother?"

"He was shot down the first month."

Details clicked into place, and I realized I should have guessed it. The old-fashioned schoolbag. The map with more colored tacks than anyone could fly. The pocketknife. The flying cap.

"I'm sorry," I said. "I really am."

Albie shrugged.

The deaf refugee tugged on Rose's sleeve, probably wanting to know why we had stopped. Why we were all standing on 43rd Street.

"We can't go to Paradise," Albie said. "We don't know who's waiting there."

"What about the families?" Rose asked.

"Without them," Albie nodded at the refugees, "the families haven't done anything wrong."

I pulled my hand out of Rose's warm one and took a few steps in the direction of the corner, as if the solution was up ahead on Ninth Avenue. The movement rustled my father's messages against my chest.

Except they couldn't be my father's messages.

"What about Jakob?" I said, turning back. "He's there."

Albie, Rose, and I stood quiet on the cold street.

I slipped my hand into the weighted pocket where I kept my father's gun.

"You go back to Times Square," I said to them. "Meet me later under the Camel sign."

"You're sure?" Albie said.

I nodded, but I was wishing I had his flying cap.

He said something in Yiddish to the refugees and turned them back up 43rd Street. I stood on the sidewalk watching them go. Rose was at the end of the line, her coat the one shining thing in the whole of Hell's Kitchen.

I watched Rose's coat wink out like a dying star, then turned and ran down 43rd Street, barreling around the corner onto Ninth Avenue, telling myself it wasn't as late as it felt, that the boats had come ashore early, that the subway had traveled faster, that Albie hadn't taken as much time telling me my father was dead.

Paradise Photo sat quiet, the window of brides dark and the door open a crack. I hurried through the dark front office, past Harry Jupiter's desk with its bottle of rye whiskey and tumbling piles of negatives, past the girlie calendar perpetually opened to May 1936.

A dim light was on in the photo studio, shining a narrow strip on the floor beneath the thick curtains. I ought to have hesitated, taken the time to look first, considered everything I should have seen coming, but instead I pushed my way through the dusty curtains, blinding myself as I went from dark to light.

When my eyes adjusted, I saw Jakob sitting on Harry Jupiter's desk chair. Somebody had placed it in front of the backdrop of the Roman Coliseum, and he looked as if he was waiting for the lions to come roaring out of the archways behind his head.

Next to him—dressed in his black spying clothes—was Uncle Glenn.

I suppose that someplace inside—someplace I could keep myself from looking at—I'd known it all along. Known the he had been the one who belonged to the wheeze.

Known, too—I realized as I stood with the curtains at my back and my heart hammering—that he had been the one sending me the messages.

"Why?" My voice bounced off the backdrops of Mount Rushmore and Niagara Falls, like I was trying for an echo. "Why did you pretend to be him?"

My uncle took a step toward me, then seemed to think better of it.

"At first I thought you would know it was me."

"And when you saw that I didn't?"

"I thought it would be more kind to let you keep believing."

A picture came into my head of all the nights I'd sat pressing my hands against those pieces of paper, certain I could feel my father's magnetism on them, feel the electric tingle. All the weeks I'd walked around with those messages tucked inside my shirt, all the times I'd pressed them against the skin of my chest, thinking how they had only recently been touched by my father, thinking how now they were touching me.

I lunged for my uncle. To do what? Beat my hands against him? Make him pay for all those nights and weeks? Probably.

But before I could get halfway across the room, a man I hadn't seen stepped out of the shadows. He was big and barrel-chested, and had the kind of thin-lipped mouth that looked as if it had long ago decided smiling wasn't worth the time.

"Where are the refugees?" he said to me.

"He will know by now there are no refugees," Jakob interrupted.

It was the first thing he'd said since I'd entered the room. He pushed himself to the front of Harry Jupiter's chair, and though he was talking to the barrel-chested man, he was looking at me.

"He will know by now that there *never* were any refugees."

"I'll bet they're right outside," Uncle Glenn said.

He strode across the room past me and disappeared through the curtains.

Jakob, the barrel-chested man, and I stood in the photo studio, listening to Uncle Glenn's footsteps echo past Harry Jupiter's desk. I kept my gaze on Jakob's face, trying to read what he wanted me to do. I could feel the barrel-chested man's eyes moving over us.

Uncle Glenn's footsteps rushed back.

"Where are they?" he said to me.

"They are nowhere," Jakob told him. "Because it was not children that got off those boats."

"Who was it then?"

"It was men."

What was Jakob thinking? Men getting out of those inflatable boats would not save him from the barrel-chested man, who, though he had said very little, was clearly in charge and dangerous.

"You're lying," Uncle Glenn said. "I heard it myself. Twenty-three children landing on a beach."

Jakob gave him a sick smile. "Do you actually think anyone would trust the lives of twenty-three refugees to a rescue plan dreamed up by a boy?"

Uncle Glenn began to say something more, but the barrel-chested man raised his hand, and Uncle Glenn closed his mouth.

The man began to walk toward me, taking his time. He stopped three feet away, as if he knew by instinct how my eyes worked.

"Did men get out of those boats?"

His voice was gentle, but his undertone told me he was turning it that way.

They were children, refugees. What could they do to them?

But they had no visas. And after my night under the floating subway car, I knew too well what could be done to them.

"Was it men?" the barrel-chested man repeated.

I looked around his bulk at Jakob.

"Yes," I said.

"How many?"

I recalled the five inflatable boats reflecting white in the moonlight.

"Five."

The man swiveled his head around. "Why would you involve this boy?"

"He involved himself," Jakob said. "I decided to make use of him."

"How?"

"Someone had to show them where the subway was."

"But children?"

"They are a good disguise. There are always children at Coney Island."

The barrel-chested man turned back to me.

"Where did these five men go?"

"Pennsylvania Station."

It was the first place I could think of that wasn't Times Square.

The man walked back across the room and stood above Jakob's chair.

"Who are these men? Why are they here?"

Every trace of the gentleness had disappeared from his voice.

Jakob shrugged. "They do not tell me such information."

"And you don't ask?"

"I no longer care for politics."

"And if they are here to work for the Germans, you don't care about that?"

"You think I should care because I am a Jew?"

Jakob stared into the face of the barrel-chested man.

"You think being a Jew means I should be on the side of this country? I was once on a boat of nine hundred Jews, nine hundred refugees who sailed up and down the coast of Florida hoping for a place to land. And do you know what we were to this country? A tourist attraction."

Jakob's dark hair was hanging in his eyes. For some reason I remembered him telling me how Lena would cut it for him. I wondered who cut it for him now.

The barrel-chested man shook his head. "You are making things worse for yourself."

Jakob gave an unhappy laugh. "After the worst has already happened?"

Uncle Glenn pushed himself between Jakob and the man. "If there were no refugees, why did you come here?"

Jakob nodded toward me. "I knew he would come. And I knew he would need to hear some kind of explanation. I did not know you gentlemen would be waiting for me."

"This is all an elaborate lie," Uncle Glenn said.

"If I were lying, I would tell you no one landed," Jakob told him.

"We need to look for those refugees."

"You cannot find what doesn't exist."

"Twenty-three children," Uncle Glenn said to the barrel-chested man. "They can't be far. And they can't be hard to find."

"I have given you myself," Jakob said quietly. "Can that not be enough?"

The pleading in Jakob's voice was clear—even Uncle Glenn had to have heard what Jakob was asking of him. But Jakob hadn't heard the story of Camp Siegfried and the swimming meet, he didn't know about the Cauet hand and how hard it could strike in that soft place between neck and shoulder. He had never heard Uncle Glenn's father speak to his pigeons in the soft German he never used with his son. Jakob couldn't know that Uncle Glenn would not consider one sacrifice enough if he believed there were still twenty-three more opportunities to be a hero wandering in the night.

Only I could stop him. Only I could keep what Jakob and I had told the barrel-chested man from turning worthless. Only I could keep what Jakob and I had done from turning worthless.

I pulled my father's gun out of my pocket and aimed it at my uncle.

"You do not want to do this, Jack," Jakob said.

But I did want to do it.

And for so many reasons. To save the refugees. For making Jakob and me tell a story we both knew would not end well for him. For the messages that were now scratching at the skin of my chest like I'd shoved a nest of spiders inside my shirt. And also, for the part of me where reason had not yet reached, the part that kept looking at the door that said *Knock or die* and expecting my father to step out.

The barrel-chested man did not move. I don't think he believed me capable of shooting at anybody.

Uncle Glenn, on the other hand, began wheezing. It sounded louder and more rasping than it had behind the roof door. Louder than I had heard—or imagined—it these past weeks.

He waved his hands in front of himself—perhaps asking me not to shoot him—but he couldn't force any sound past his frantic gasping for breath.

In the seconds before I pulled the trigger, I wondered if my uncle carried his code-o-graph in his pocket, if he wrote the messages that were supposed to be from my father on Aunt May's ruffled place mats.

The gun went off with a loud bang.

My shoulder jolted from the kickback, and my ears rang as if there was a bell clanging inside my head.

Uncle Glenn fell to his knees. Harry Jupiter's desk chair with Jakob in it toppled over.

The barrel-chested man lunged for me, and I ran.

I went through the front office, spilling out into the blackness of 43rd Street, my ears too deafened by the noise of the gun to know if the barrel-chested man was behind me. I headed toward Eighth Avenue, remembering I had a gun in my hand only when I caught one of the Hell's Kitchen kids staring at it. I shoved it into my pocket and fled down the war-darkened street, pieces of the torn and discarded messages—still warm from my body—flying out behind me like snow.

I ran all the way to the 42nd Street subway station, stood at the edge of the platform looking down at the garbage trapped between the tracks—cigarette butts and the wrapper from a Mounds candy bar that would have smelled exactly like the skin at Rose LoPinto's throat—until an uptown A rumbled deep in the tunnel, blowing warm, mouse-scented air into my face, ruffling my hair.

I forced myself to keep my eyes on the narrow space between the tracks and the third rail as the train came screaming into the station. Calculated the type of speed it would take to roll out of the way, the amount of space it would require to fit between track and rail. I made myself stand on that platform as train after train slid into the station, keeping my eyes fixed on that impossibly narrow space until I was positive I would never again convince myself that anyone would be able to survive a tumble into it.

Then I went back up to look for Albie and Rose and the refugees.

I found Albie in the drifting smoke under the Camel cigarette sign.

"Where's Rose?"

"She waited awhile, but it got late."

"And the refugees?"

"We found the families."

"Where?"

"At Paradise." The edges of Albie's smile disappeared into the earflaps of his wool hat.

"When?" I said. "How?"

Because it was too cold to wander Times Square, Albie and Rose had taken the refugees to the Loews movie theater on 44th Street, sneaking them in through the side exit. They'd sat in the front row, away from everyone else, while Albie translated the dialogue into Yiddish.

"It was *Pride of the Yankees* with Babe Ruth and Gary Cooper, but I still don't think they have any idea how baseball works."

When the movie was over, they came back and stood under the Camel cigarette sign and waited for me. After half an hour, Rose suggested they go to Paradise and see if I was all right.

"Rose suggested that?"

But when they arrived, Paradise was dark and empty.

"No police cars?" I asked him. "No ambulances?"

Albie was explaining to the refugees that they would go back to Times Square—talking in Yiddish—when a man stepped out of the shadows and tapped him on the shoulder.

"He asked me if we'd been to Coney Island lately."

The man told Albie that earlier that evening, as he and his wife were about to enter Paradise Photo, three men had come hurrying out. Something didn't seem right, so the man sent his wife to wait in a bar on Ninth Avenue while he kept watch. When the other families arrived, he sent them to wait on Ninth Avenue, too.

When Albie told the man that yes, as a matter of fact, they had just come from Coney Island, the man ran around the corner. In less than a minute, he was back with the families, fifteen men and women dressed in dark clothes to blend with the night.

"They stood on the sidewalk in two bunches. Refugees on one side, families on the other. And nobody knew who belonged to who."

Then the man who'd tapped Albie on the shoulder said a name into the dark, only a first name, because that was all they had, and one of the refugees, a tall boy, one of the few in a coat that was too small for him, crossed over to the side with the families.

"That's how they found each other, the families saying the name of a refugee into the night, a name they had learned by heart, and then waiting for the right one to walk into their arms."

Except for the deaf refugee. The deaf refugee's mother spoke her name with her hands, spelling it out in that secret code.

"Did anybody see you?" I said.

"It's Hell's Kitchen. The only people around are stumblebums and drunks. They probably believe they dreamed the whole thing."

I stood in the artificial smoke drifting down from the Camel soldier, seeing the refugees fade into the night.

"And Jakob?" Albie asked.

"Tomorrow," I told him.

For tonight I didn't want Albie to have any story that wasn't the refugees walking into the arms of their families.

Sixteen

The next morning, I retrieved the flying cap that had belonged to Albie's brother from the shoebox labeled *Tax Receipts* and replaced it with my father's gun. Two artifacts of the dead exchanging places with each other.

I arrived in the sunless alley before Albie had had time to light up his first cigarette, before Elliott Marshman or anybody had come to watch him smoke it. I returned the cap and gave him an account of everything that had happened the previous night at Paradise, everything except the detail of firing my father's gun at Uncle Glenn.

"It was your uncle writing the messages?" he said.

I nodded.

Albie stuck a cigarette to his lower lip.

"I would have wanted to shoot him," he told me.

"It's a long story," I said.

"It's always a long story," he replied.

For the whole of that day, Rose's desk sat empty next to me.

As soon as I was let out of P.S. 52, I went down to Jakob's tenement and banged on his door. A woman coming out of another apartment told me that three men in suits had come and taken away most of Jakob's things. That the super had just let them in.

"Guess you can't trust anybody," she said.

I wasn't sure if she meant the super or Jakob.

The pigeons, though, were still on the roof, softening the cold air with their cooing. I gave them water and more feed. When I looked inside the Garcia y Vega cigar box, I saw only the metal capsules rolling around. I suspected Jakob had started carrying his code-o-graph in his pocket the way I carried mine, and I wondered what the barrel-chested man would make of it, if he'd let Jakob keep the picture of Rebecca.

I did not see my uncle Glenn—not that I went looking for him. But I was sure that if I'd killed him, I would have heard about it.

Rose didn't return to P.S. 52 on Friday, and I began to be worried that something had happened to her on the way back from Times Square. I went to her building and rang the bell, hoping for her voice to come out of the little holes in the wall. When it didn't, I walked into the street and looked up at her windows. The blue star was gone.

On Saturday, I returned to Jakob's tenement with the Radio Flyer and a hammer and knocked the legs off the pigeons' coop. I tied the coop to the wagon with twine and paid a kid in Jakob's building a quarter I'd taken from my mother's wallet to help me carry the whole thing to the street.

I could have taken the Radio Flyer and the pigeons onto the subway. I'd seen stranger things. An organ grinder and his monkey. Two men moving an icebox. Albie and me and a baby carriage full of poor box coats. But I didn't. I wanted to walk. To pull the wagon loaded with Jakob's pigeons all the way up Broadway from the Lower East Side to Dyckman Street—more than two hundred blocks.

It was a freezing day, but at 23rd Street I took off my jacket and threw it on top of the coop. By 50th Street, my palms were so sweaty I kept losing my grip on the handle. When I stopped to wipe my hand across the front of my shirt, it left a red trail across my chest.

As I passed Lou Brown's Pool Parlor, Uncle Glenn came out carrying the leather case he used for his pool cue. In the frail winter sun, he looked pale and chubby. It was the first time I'd seen him up close since I'd shot at him, and I think that if I'd still had my father's gun in my pocket—and if pulling the wagon hadn't made my fingers so stiff I couldn't bend them—I might have shot at him again.

My uncle set his leather case on top of the coop and took the handle out of my blood-sticky hand. I would have stopped him, but I couldn't lift my arm above my waist.

Uncle Glenn pulled the wagon the rest of the way to our building, then talked Mr. Rubini from 2D into helping him carry the coop up to the roof. Two days later, when I got home from P.S. 52, it was standing on four new wooden legs.

It was a week before my uncle and I spoke, an early December day with a chill that lets you know winter is setting in for good. Uncle Glenn had come to the roof with a bag of feed and as he turned to go, I stopped him with the question that had been keeping me up at night.

"Jakob," I said. "I didn't shoot *him*, did I?"

My uncle said that the bullet from my father's gun had sailed across Harry Jupiter's photo studio, neatly dividing the air between him and Jakob before piercing the backdrop of the Roman Coliseum, leaving a perfectly round hole above one of the painted archways.

"Where is he now?" I asked.

"In a jail in Washington," Uncle Glenn said. "They plan to try him for treason."

The two of us stood and watched the pigeons scatter seed onto the black tar.

"It would go better for him if you told what we both know."

"It was men," I said. Because you cannot find what doesn't exist.

Rose did not come back to P.S. 52. And I began to believe I'd invented her. That she had been part of the world in which my father was alive, and now that it was gone, she'd vanished with it. I was afraid to ask anyone about her, afraid of what they'd say, *We never knew such a girl. A girl who wore a microphone box called a RadioEar pinned close to her smooth olive-colored throat.*

As that winter turned into rainy spring, I believed I had lost everything. My father. Jakob. Rose. Even my uncle Glenn. I would have imagined this would make me feel lighter, hollowed out. Yet I sat beside Rose's empty desk day after day and could barely lift my head. I dragged myself to the roof and stood before the fluttering coop feeling as if my body was made of cement. At night, I lay in front of the Silvertone like someone knocked out in a fight, trying to fill my head with pictures of horses' hooves or the shining fender of the Green Hornet's automobile. But all I saw was Jakob being led out of Paradise by the barrel-chested man.

After a while, I couldn't listen to the radio. I stayed in my room with the door shut. Lay on the bed and stared at the ceiling, much like my mother, but without the cigarettes. When I couldn't drive the picture of Jakob and the barrel-chested man out of my head, I began to tell Jakob's story to myself, out loud, as if I was a kind of radio.

Each night I began a little further back. From when I found him on the subway. From the day he boarded the *St. Louis*. From the day he met Rebecca on the streetcar. But always ending in the same place, the night he gave himself up for the twenty-three refugees.

I told Jakob's story to my walls, to my luminous-face alarm clock, to my cowboy and Indian bedspread. But all this relentless telling and retelling of Jakob's story, all this talking into the emptiness of my room, made me no less heavy. Each time I told Jakob's story out loud to no one, the weight of all those words seemed to fall onto me, burying me deeper, like poor box coats in sand.

I began to believe that the only way to dig myself out from under the weight of the story was to tell it to someone else. Someone to whom it would matter.

And there were only twenty-three of those people in the world.

"Can you remember any of the names the families called out that night?" I said to Albie.

He told me twelve names, and though I followed him all day, I couldn't make him remember any more.

But these were first names and not much to go on.

I asked him if the families had said their own names.

"They said as little as possible," he told me. "I think that was the point."

Could he remember what they'd been wearing? Perhaps one of the fathers had been in a bus driver's uniform? Maybe one was dressed like a waiter and had the name of the restaurant on his pocket.

"They were wearing coats, just like the refugees."

Had they all headed for the subway? Had anyone gotten into a car with a license plate? Had he seen which direction they'd gone?

"They just slipped away into the dark."

I questioned Albie every day, sure there was some detail he'd forgotten, some detail he'd remember if only I asked him enough times. I questioned him until I couldn't anymore, because he was never alone. He was always either in the sunless alley surrounded by boys watching him smoke or walking toward Vermilyea Street in the company of three or four people I didn't know, talking about subjects that had nothing to do with refugees.

I believe I wore away any satisfaction Albie took from what we'd done that night with my ceaseless questions. I do know those questions ended the friendship between us. Knew it the morning I turned up early in the alley hoping to ask him if he thought any of the families had seemed to know Paradise, if any of them had acted familiar with the neighborhood. Only Elliott Marshman was there, using the sole of his orthopedic shoe to scrape Albie's cigarette butts into a corner. Elliott had looked up when I entered, then quickly turned away. But before he did, I'd seen pity behind his pale lashes.

I memorized the twelve names Albie had given me. Learned them by heart the way the families had. Then I roamed the streets of the city, repeating them to myself as I studied the faces of everybody who was near to my own age, looking for traces of the people who'd scraped ashore in those boats.

Once on Essex Street I put my hand on the shoulder of a pale, dark-haired boy I believed I recognized and said all eight of the boys' names Albie had told me. The boy stared back, then shoved me in the chest with both hands, knocking me to the sidewalk.

"Go back to Hell's Kitchen, Paddy," he told me.

In late March, Uncle Glenn came to see me on the roof. It was one of the first warm days of spring, one of the first that wasn't raining, and I was flying the pigeons, a gray swarm circling in the blue sky. I'd been doing this more and more—flying Jakob's birds—though not once did I consider writing a message and tying it to their legs.

"They're sending Jakob back to Germany."

"What about his trial?"

"They don't really have anything against him," Uncle Glenn said. "Besides what he says against himself."

"And what you say."

Uncle Glenn stared at his shoes, pushed a few feathers around with the toes.

"I'm no longer very sure what that is anymore." He rubbed a hand over his thinning hair. "They've managed to convince the Germans he's worth trading for a real spy. One of ours."

"And what do you think will happen to him when they find out he's not?"

"I don't think he much cares."

I stared into the sky, watched Jakob's birds spinning in the clear blue. Then I walked away from my uncle, across the roof to the coop.

"I went to see him," Uncle Glenn said to my back.

I turned. "You?"

I faced back to the coop, rested my hands on the chicken wire. It was sharp and cold, holding all the chill of winter.

Uncle Glenn's footsteps crunched up behind me.

"He gave me this for you."

Uncle Glenn was holding a piece of paper with what looked like a coded message written on it.

"Jakob has a code-o-graph?"

"He said he wrote so many messages he memorized the code."

"How do I know you didn't write it?"

Uncle Glenn shrugged. "You don't."

Wind fluttered the paper in my uncle's hand like pigeons' wings.

I took it from him, wondering if I was feeling Jakob's magnetism, humming beneath Uncle Glenn's like an undertone.

"They didn't try to decode it?"

"The men from the FBI?" Uncle Glenn shook his head. "I'm pretty sure they don't think you're a spy."

I sat on the roof with my back against a leg of the coop and deciphered Jakob's message. Because I needed to know what it said, and because I, too, had memorized the code.

Jakob had written

ONE DOOMED JEW FOR 23 WHO HAVE THEIR LIVES AHEAD OF THEM. IT IS THE SAME AS THE PHOTOGRAPH OF THE WOMAN WITH THE SHRIVELED LEG STANDING BEFORE JOSEF WACKERLES CONCRETE THIGH. THINK HOW MUCH REBECCA WOULD HAVE LIKED THAT.

Uncle Glenn's shoes shifted on the tar, and I knew he was waiting for me to show him the message, knew he wanted more than anything to see it.

I wanted to slide that piece of paper inside my shirt, let it rub against the skin of my chest until it wore away to nothing. But as long as that message existed in the world, the twenty-three who had climbed out of those boats onto that moonlit beach, the twenty-three Jakob had sacrificed himself for, would never be safe.

I pressed my palm to Jakob's message one last time. Then I tore it into pieces, opening my hands and letting the March wind blow them across the roof like so much spring snow.

Uncle Glenn watched the bits of paper fly into the sky.

"Will you tell me now?" he asked.

"Tell you what?" I said. "That it was men who got out of those boats?"

I got up and went back into the building, then out onto the street. Stood in the wind and scanned every face for something I might recognize, Jakob's story still caught in my throat.

Seventeen

The day I saw Rose LoPinto again, she was standing on the Observation Deck of the Empire State Building, and at first I believed I was imagining her.

Ten years had passed since she'd walked away from me, her pale coat shining in the darkness, and yet I recognized her in an instant. Felt the familiarity of her hands moving against the unobstructed sky on this tallest building in Manhattan.

She was surrounded by a group of men in dark suits, speaking to them in that secret language. Her dress was filmy and apricot-colored, and much too light for the weather—it was the kind of spring day that begins fine, but by noon is threatening rain—and her black hair was as wild as it had ever been. But the metal headband that had held the RadioEar receiver was gone, and there was no microphone box pinned to the neck of her filmy dress. When I moved closer, I saw beneath a curl of dark hair, a flesh-colored disk tucked inside her ear and a thin wire hugging the side of her smooth neck.

Of course, I thought, *it is the Atomic Age, filled with the wonders of science. There is no longer the need for speaking into girls' throats.*

I followed Rose across the Observation Deck as she led her dark-suited men on a silent tour of the city's skyline, naming for them the silver spires outlined against the darkening sky. If I had known that secret language, I could have given the men the tour myself. For I had spent nearly every lunch hour for the past four years on this windswept deck. Though I had spent little of that time gazing at the view. Instead, I'd been scanning the faces of the people who came here to point out landmarks, the people who stood holding their hats on their heads against the breeze.

When Rose took her dark-suited men to wait for the elevator, I went to stand before her.

"Rose," I said.

She looked at me with the same depthless dark eyes.

"Jack."

We were both twenty-two years old, and for a second, I wondered at the fact that she'd recognized me. But then, how unrecognizable can a person become who wears the kind of glasses I do?

Rose escorted her men down to the street and put them into a taxi, then she came back, and while we stood at the top of the tallest building in Manhattan, she told me the story of why she'd disappeared.

She said that at the same moment we were standing on that beach at Coney Island, the same moment the first boat of refugees scraped ashore, halfway around the world, her father was walking into a U.S. Army base in Agadir, Morocco, with an expertly amputated left hand and no memory of how it had gotten that way or where he'd been the past two months.

Neither Rose nor her mother had had any idea her father had been missing. The army had sent a telegram, but her mother, who had never learned to read English, had stuffed it in the kitchen drawer where she was keeping all the correspondence until her husband's return.

The telegram saying Rose's father had been found arrived the morning after the refugees landed. She answered the door and learned that her father was missing and found in the same instant.

Once she'd figured out what had happened, after she'd gone through the piles of letters and unpaid bills in her mother's kitchen drawer, she knew that what she'd done on that beach was responsible for her father's miraculous return from the dead.

"It was an even exchange. One deaf refugee for my father."

And the sign of this was the missing hand. A symbol of the secret language of the deaf.

I believe everything that happened between Rose and me that afternoon can be put down to one fact: I was the one who placed her on that beach.

The next telegram was from her father. The army was sending him home. He instructed Rose and her mother to close up his butcher shop in Yonkers, pack his knives, and meet him at the family farm in Newburgh, where they'd stay until he could teach himself to cut meat one-handed.

"The army would have paid for a prosthetic hand," she said, "but my father wanted a hook, said it would be better for holding onto meat."

As Rose told me this story, her slippery consonants slid into my ears, stirring up the cold stream that ran beneath the surface of my skin. The stream that hadn't run in ten years.

When she finished, I told her I had something to show her. We took the elevator down and got into a taxi. I suppose we just walked away from our jobs. Rose was the City Hall interpreter for the deaf, the city's official speaker of that secret language. I worked as a sound engineer for a radio station that broadcast from that tallest building. We didn't think about our jobs for one second.

The taxi driver took us through Central Park, where the air was filled with unsettling blooming. Once going around a curve, our hands touched and I felt an electric shock that was like lightning from the storm that kept threatening but never came.

When we arrived at Dyckman Street, I took Rose to the roof. Together, we stood in front of the coop and watched the pigeons fluttering behind the chicken wire, filling the newly warm air with feathers.

"They were Jakob's," I told her. Though I supposed they weren't Jakob's anymore, and also I'd replaced a few.

The pigeons flapped their wings in time with the wind moving the skirt of Rose's light dress.

"I wish I'd met him," she said.

Rose picked up the Garcia y Vega cigar box on the shelf beside the pigeons' coop and shook it. There was the sound of the metal capsules rolling back and forth.

I took the box out of her hands. "Just some old things in there."

I did not tell her about the afternoon when I was fifteen or so, when I nearly exhausted a pigeon to death trying to make it carry a message to Germany. A message that said

YD ATNNI

IM SORRY.

The clouds above our heads stacked up on each other, and the storm seemed closer. I brought Rose down to my apartment.

I had little experience bringing women home, and did not know what I would do with Rose once she had stepped through my door. But before we'd moved out of the hallway, she turned, swirling the skirt of her apricot-colored dress around my legs, and pressed her lips against mine in a dizzying kiss.

Even I knew better than to take Rose into my childhood bedroom, into the room where I still slept—mostly out of habit, partly because I believed it might be a kind of luck, a talisman for finding those twenty-three.

I took her instead into my mother's old room.

My mother had been gone four years. She left a week after I graduated from high school, the day after I took the job at the radio station. Came out of her bedroom dressed in one of her brown-colored outfits, carrying a small suitcase I didn't know she owned.

"I'm moving to the convent in Poughkeepsie," she said, then stood behind me and rested one arm across my chest. An arm that was so weightless, it rose with no effort on my breath. "You, though," she told me. "You have your whole life."

Rose and I fell into my mother's bed like it was ours.

I had been with other women. Though not, I would guess, as many as Jakob, who had learned which Wassertorstrasse windows were worth whistling up at. And not, I suppose, as many as most twenty-two-year-old men living in New York City in 1952—something I blamed on my glasses, rather than my habit of staring so nakedly at the faces of strangers.

Rose was twenty-two as well. And not long after her too-light dress floated to the floor of my bedroom, I knew I wasn't her first. Anything beyond that was a mystery. Most things about Rose were a mystery to me—perhaps because of that secret language she could speak with her hands.

Still, as a hard rain from the storm that had been threatening all day battered the windows, Rose deciphered the code of her body—and mine—touching me everywhere at once with those hands that could speak a hundred secret languages worth learning.

Only when it was over, only when I was lying next to the full length of her skin, which smelled to me impossibly of chocolate and coconut, only then did I turn my head and put my mouth close to the flesh-colored disk tucked inside her ear and ask for the names she'd heard called out in the dark.

Rose pushed herself to her elbows, her black hair its own spring storm around her head.

"You have been looking for them?"

I pulled her from the bed and wrapped her in a blanket, led her down the hallway into the kitchen. Showed her the table, covered in newspapers.

Rose smoothed the pages of one of the open papers, running her fingers over the names I'd circled.

"'Betrothals and Marriages'?"

"We are of that age," I said.

She looked hard into my face, wound the blanket tighter around herself.

"What will you do if you find one?"

I tried to explain. About Jakob. And Uncle Glenn. And about the story that never grew any lighter, despite so many years of telling it to myself. As I spoke, the storm outside flung hail against the window, as if trying to shatter it, yet Rose never took her eyes from me.

"For ten years, I have been looking," I told her. "Calling strangers on the telephone. Searching the faces of people on the street. But I have never found any of them. Not even one."

Rose put her hand on my face. Her fingers were warm.

"I have," she told me.

Eighteen

RIVKA

Not long after he realized I was deaf, my father invented a secret language for the two of us, a series of gestures that my mother and older brother, Jan, did not share. This was when we still lived in Warsaw, before we moved to Paris so that I could enroll in the Institution Nationale des Sourds-Muets—the National Institution for Deaf-Mutes. Later, when I asked my father why he invented an entire language for only two people, he'd tell me he believed I was like him and that he wanted to know what I was thinking. And it was true that even after we both learned to sign, it seemed we could tell each other more in the language he'd invented.

To help me get along in the world, my father also taught me to read gestures. Every day from the time I was small, he took me out into the city and showed me how to interpret the raising of an eyebrow, the shrug of a shoulder. He taught me what it meant when someone shifted back and forth on his feet, when he dipped his head when telling you something. My father made me understand how much is revealed by the body.

The day the Nazis took him, my father used the secret language he'd invented for the two of us to give me the same instructions he gave to my mother. He knew I was more likely to follow them.

The Nazis did not come themselves—my father was not important enough, only another Jew—but sent two French policemen instead. They arrived on a soft spring morning, pounding on our door so hard, even I heard it. I was eleven years old and not entirely deaf. A year earlier when the Germans arrived in Paris, I'd heard the rumbling of their tanks as they rolled into the Place de la Concorde. I could hear any sound that came with a strong vibration. They say that is why, years later, the surgeons were able to repair my hearing.

We were living in the Jewish quarter, on the Rue des Rosiers in a two-story house with lace curtains at every window. The French policemen stood inside my parents' bedroom, the backs of their uniforms pressed up against the expensive striped wallpaper, and watched my father pack a small suitcase with clothing they probably knew he would never wear. I sat on a small stool at the side of the bed, dressed for school in my skirt and blouse, refusing to leave the house, refusing to leave my father, although my sixteen-year-old brother, always more obedient, had already gone.

As my father folded shirts, I signed to him in our secret language. "Where are they taking you? When will you be back?"

My father was talking to my mother, who kept eyeing the policemen leaning against her wallpaper. By the shape of his mouth, I knew he was speaking in Polish. Each time he set down a shirt, his hands shaped the same words for me. "Go," he was telling her. "Take the children and leave Paris. Leave France if you can."

But my mother had been born into money and believed that every problem—even Nazis—could be solved by it. She hurried from the bedroom, and when she returned with a thick stack of bills, I knew what she'd been doing. She'd taken her sewing scissors with the handle shaped to look like a crane and snipped open the silk lining of her spring coat, pulled the bills from the stack she'd hidden there the day the Nazis marched into Paris.

My mother stood close to one of the French policemen, the taller of the two, a man with a thick mustache. My mother—still beautiful after two children, her dark wavy hair falling down her back—standing so close to the policeman you could barely slip one of the bills in her hand between them. She showed the policeman the money, then ran her fingers along the curve of her throat. My father kept his gaze down, fixed on the shirts in his suitcase, but it seemed to me that his shoulders were shaking.

The policeman looked at the money and at my mother. Then he looked at me, sitting not as out of his sight as I'd imagined. He shook his head. My mother pressed closer to him, but he shook his head again. My mother backed away, the stack of bills still in her hand.

I don't know if it was that the French policeman was so very honest as that it was early in the war, when the policemen were still afraid of the Nazis.

After my father had finished packing his useless suitcase, the policemen led him out into the spring morning. I followed, hiding in the doorways of the still-shuttered shops. It was early, the sun streaming between the buildings of the Marais, but the streets of the Jewish quarter were filled with French policemen escorting men with suitcases, all of them heading in the direction of the Gare d'Austerlitz.

When you learn to see the world through gestures, you learn to see things as they are. And all of Paris knew—even if they pretended they didn't know it—that the trains for Jews at the Gare d'Austerlitz were the trains that went to the camps at Pithiviers and Beaune-la-Rolande.

I pressed myself into the doorway of a shuttered *patisserie* and watched my father walk away. He was wearing his best suit. My father had put on his best suit to be taken by Nazis. His suitcase, tan calfskin, bumped lightly against the side of his leg, and he was leaning a little to the left. My father always walked that way, leaned to the left.

As I stood in the doorway of that shuttered *patisserie* on that soft spring morning, I realized it was because I was usually walking on that side.

It was a long street and I wanted to stay in the doorway and watch until my father turned the corner—my father, the only other person on the earth who knew the language of my thoughts—but my face felt wet and I was afraid I was making sounds, and that alone would have been enough for one of the French policemen to scoop me up and take me to the Gare d'Austerlitz with the others.

I pushed myself out of the doorway and ran home.

Over the next year, I begged my mother to take us south, out of occupied France.

"Your father will be heartbroken," she'd sign, "if he returns and finds no one."

"He will be heartbroken," I'd sign back, "if we die."

Each week, my mother pulled more money from inside the silk lining of her spring coat—money that could have bought our way out of Paris, out of France—and gave it to yet another German officer who promised to look into my father's case.

"You have no case once you are in Pithiviers or Beaune-la-Rolande," I told her. Because I had seen the way people turned away from the Jews who were loaded onto the trains that were headed there, as if they were already dead, only animated corpses.

"You must have faith," my mother told me.

I could see, too, how my mother's faith was feeding off her. She was no longer beautiful, but gaunt and hollow-eyed. I suspected she didn't eat, turning too much of our money over to German officers, saving only what was needed to feed my brother and me. I began to fear that her desire to believe my father was alive would kill her.

I appealed to my brother, but Jan was not interested in leaving Paris unless we could take the Bechstein.

The Bechstein was an upright grand piano that had belonged to our mother's grandfather. It was a beautiful thing, a polished piece of carved mahogany, and my brother loved it like a woman. No, he loved it more than any man has ever loved a woman. For unless he was sleeping or eating, his long-fingered hands were on that instrument.

I might have been deaf, but I understood music from watching my fair-haired brother practice. Although *practice* is the wrong word for what Jan did. Even *play* is not the right word. What my brother did was purposely drown himself in music.

I never watched his hands. I had enough of watching hands at the Institute. I watched how the music took over his body. My brother was tall and made like an athlete. But he wasn't athletic, he was only musical, and when he played his muscles stretched and tightened as if he was running a race. And though I lived in a silent world, I knew the rush of music from the sway and surge of my brother's body on the piano bench.

With the help of my brother, I found a mover—also Jewish, also moving south.

But my mother said she would not hear of her family heirloom being put on a horse cart and taken into the countryside.

When the Nazis ordered all Jews to wear a yellow Star of David, I tried again to persuade my mother to take us out of occupied France.

"It would break my father's heart if he saw us wearing such a thing," I told her. "That is, if his heart is still beating."

My mother slapped my face, then handed me the crane-handled sewing scissors and a pile of yellow stars.

I sewed one yellow star onto a blue sweater, which I wore over all my other clothes, because I could not bear that terrible thing lying too close to my skin.

A month later, my mother disappeared.

Jan and I had spent the night at the home of Monsieur Blancherie, one of my former teachers at the Institute. Monsieur Blancherie had a son and a daughter who were the same ages as my brother and myself, and a lenient attitude toward Jews. Monsieur Blancherie's children were hearing, but because of their father's profession, they both knew how to sign.

When Jan and I returned to the Rue des Rosiers the following morning, we found our house empty.

"Perhaps she has gone to buy something for our lunch," Jan said.

"There is still the food she bought yesterday."

"Then perhaps she has gone again to bribe someone."

"The blanket from her bed is gone. And two pairs of her shoes are missing."

I ran back to Monsieur Blancherie's house to see if he had heard anything, if there were rumors of Jews being taken.

My former teacher stood in his doorway and assured me he had heard nothing. Surely my mother was out on an errand, to the baker's, perhaps. Certainly if I went home now, I would find her there.

Monsieur Blancherie's blunt-fingered hands moved through the air much more abruptly than usual, letting me know he was lying, that the Nazis had come for my mother. His hands did not tell me why he would lie. They did not have to. There was no reason a teacher of sign language should be any less afraid of Nazis than the French police.

I asked Monsieur Blancherie if I might come inside, if I might go up to his daughter's room for something I'd left behind.

Madeleine Blancherie owned a sweater the same shade of blue as mine. I exchanged mine for hers and ran home, wearing a starless sweater that told the world nothing about myself.

I could not make my brother believe that the Nazis had taken our mother, that they would be back to take us as well. He sat with his fingers on the keys of the Bechstein, ignoring me as I cut the yellow star off his shirt with the crane-handled sewing scissors.

"They will have seen our bedrooms," I said, setting down the scissors to sign. "Seen our clothes. Nazis do not like loose ends."

When he turned his head to shut me out, I moved into his line of sight, trying to make him see the truth of what I was telling him.

"Tomorrow," he signed, lifting his fingers from the keys.

"Tomorrow they will have us."

He shut his eyes, which in an argument with me was as good as stopping his ears, and continued to play.

I wanted to stay and watch him one last time, but a pair of French policemen could have been climbing the stairs to our apartment that very moment, and I would not have heard them. I found the rucksack my father and I would take on walks in the Bois de Boulogne and filled it with hard cheese and a sausage and some bread. Dropping the starless shirt on the piano bench next to my brother, I left the house.

It was July, and the day was hot and bright. I forced myself to walk, to look as if I was not running away from anyone. I had only reached the Seine when Madeleine Blancherie came hurrying toward me.

"I saw your sweater and knew you had been to my house," she signed.

I placed my hands on the front of her sweater, not yet sure if I meant to return it or keep it.

Madeleine placed her fingers over mine, left them there for a moment, before she signed.

"I only wanted to tell you that the Germans rounded up more than a thousand Jews this morning. They have them locked inside the velodrome near the Eiffel Tower."

"Where they hold the bicycle races?"

She nodded. "They are going to deport them to Auschwitz."

I turned back toward the Rue des Rosiers, sure this new information would convince my brother.

Madeleine took my hand and dropped a gold cross on a chain into it.

"Do you think it will fool anyone?" I asked her.

She studied my face, my hair, wild and black.

"It's all I have." She gave me a quick hug, wrapping her arms around her own sweater.

I ran through the hot, bright streets, my hands practicing the arguments I'd make for my brother. But when I turned onto the Rue des Rosiers, Jan was stepping out the front door of our building in the company of a French policeman, possibly the same tall man with the thick mustache my mother had pressed herself against a year ago. My handsome brother was carrying the blanket from his bed—ridiculous in this heat—and a pair of shoes. He stopped outside our door and looked up, squinting into the harsh July sunshine at the window of the sitting room where the Bechstein sat. When he lowered his head, he saw me, standing across the street.

My brother's long-fingered musician's hands were hidden beneath the blanket, out of sight of the policeman. He moved nothing else, only those skillful hands, signing the word for *good-bye*. The moment he was finished, the policeman shoved him in the back and the two of them walked away into the harsh midsummer light.

I walked out of Paris wearing Madeleine Blancherie's blue sweater and her gold cross, and for nearly four months, I kept walking. I walked all summer and well into the fall, staying on the smaller roads, keeping to the villages. I ducked into hedges and behind barns whenever my faulty ears sensed the rumbling of trucks, though most of the time it was only a farmer taking wine or cheese or butchered meat from one place to another. And always I walked with my head swiveling because anyone could sneak up on me.

You would think that the worst part of running from the Nazis would be the fear that the Germans, who rode through the parched countryside in open-air vehicles kicking up dust and waving their arms as if they already owned it, would grab me, deliver me to a train station where the local inhabitants would turn away as if I had become one of those animated corpses. But it wasn't the fear that was the worst part, it was the isolation.

I had been at the Institute long enough to learn to sign, but had only begun to learn to read and write in French. At the first village convent I arrived at, showing the elderly Mother Superior Madeleine Blancherie's gold cross hanging around my neck, demonstrating to her that I could perform the sign of the cross—a trick Madeleine had taught me one afternoon because we'd nothing better to do—I could not answer the questions that must have been *What happened to your family? Are you traveling alone?* And when the elderly nun put paper and pen before me, I didn't have the vocabulary to write any kind of satisfactory answer. The sisters there treated me as if I was slow, making their explanations with wide gestures, trusting me with only one direction at a time. Showing me over and over on the map where the next convent was, and looking uncertain as to whether they should allow me to leave at all.

This happened at every convent and chapel where I sheltered. And even when a nun or a priest understood that I was deaf, still it did no good, for none of them knew how to sign.

To have no one you can talk with for such a long time is like being a ghost.

But at least they sheltered me, whether they believed in my Catholicism or not. It was the people in the villages who often looked at me hard when I walked through their streets, stared too long at my black hair, searched my blue sweater for a yellow star they were certain should be there. In a village near Malsherbes, a boy shouted a word into my face I am sure was the French for *Jew*, and when I could offer no more denial than shaking my head, he gave me a beating that left me spitting blood and a molar into the rectory sink.

Even when I reached Marseilles and an aid worker in the camp realized I was deaf, there was still no one there who could sign. No one who could adequately explain why I was woken in the night and slipped into the back of a supply truck, hidden under burlap sacks along with twenty-two others. I didn't know if this was escape or some trick of the Nazis. And when they marched me into that submarine and dropped me into the ocean, it didn't feel like rescue, it felt like being buried alive in a metal coffin.

Then like a small miracle, I was on the surface again. Floating across the water toward a single, bright light. When I stepped out of that inflatable boat into the surf, onto the beach, it was like being reborn. And then, after four months of isolation, four months of silence, a girl in a moonlit coat lifted her hands and spoke to me.

Nineteen

When I open the door to Rose the next day, the woman beside her smiles, and the bulb in the hallway glints on a gold tooth in the left side of her mouth.

"I'm supposed to tell my story to the deaf refugee?" I say.

But the woman laughs, throaty and deep, then catches her dark hair with both hands and pulls it back, showing me the hearing aids—flesh-colored disks that are like Rose's—tucked inside each ear.

"If you do not mumble, I will hear everything."

She has Rose's voice—no hard edges—complicated with the formality of something foreign.

"From what my friend has told me, I do not think you will mumble."

Today it is warm, real spring, and Rose and the deaf refugee are wearing dresses printed all over with flowers. They carry the scent of flowers as well. When they walk in, it's like spring arriving in my apartment.

I think of the twelve names Albie gave me, how I've repeated them over to myself for ten years. And now, here before me is the one refugee whose name was never spoken aloud into the night. The one refugee it would have been the most impossible to find.

I ask Rose how they met, and she tells about the day—four or five years ago now—this dark-haired woman followed her out of the school for the deaf in the Bronx, stood before her signing, *I know you*, over and over.

"I always remembered Rose from the beach," the deaf refugee says. "Because after four months of silence, four months of isolation, she was the first person to communicate with me."

She turns toward me. Her eyes are dark, like Rose's.

"But I remembered you more. I remembered the way you touched us. The flat of your hand on the front of our coats, as if you were feeling for our heartbeats."

When she says it, my fingers remember it, too—the damp, sandy wool, the resistance of breastbone.

I bring them into my kitchen, where the newspapers have been cleared away. And though I have waited ten years to tell my story, I surprise myself by asking to hear the deaf refugee's first.

Perhaps it is because I suspect—know, even—that she is the only one of them I will ever meet. The only one of the twenty-three with their lives ahead of them.

When she finishes, the three of us sit and let the room return to silence.

Then I begin. I start with the moment before my eyes went bad. The moment I would return to. The moment I have always been trying to return to. It is further back than I usually begin. But somehow sitting at this table, which was once too red for a kitchen table but has now faded into something more ordinary, I know that this is where the story starts.

My words travel into the flesh-colored disks tucked into the ears of the two dark-haired women across from me, a broadcast designed specifically for them. And for once—for the first time—as I talk, as I say the words, the weight of them rises up and away from me.

When I come to the end, when I have finished describing how the small pieces of Jakob's final message blew across the roof like so much snow, I ask the deaf refugee if she will do something for me. I ask her if she will let me place my hand on her chest.

She nods, and we both rise from our chairs.

I reach across the table—which I see now has never been very big—and rest the flat of my hand on her breastbone. Beneath my palm I feel the beating of her heart, evidence of what Jakob and I have accomplished.

After Rose leaves to walk the deaf refugee to the subway—saying she will be back, taking the key I press into her hand to make sure of it—I go to the roof.

It has taken a while to tell my story and the sun is setting, streaking the sky over the East River. The soft cooing of the pigeons—a sound like a roomful of babies, like water over stones—carries to me on the April breeze. It's the hour I usually feed the birds, and as I walk toward the coop, they fly back and forth behind the chicken wire, the fluttering of their wings stirring something inside my chest.

I can see the spot where my father placed me the day he shot the picture for the code-o-graph, wanting nothing but the wide, blue sky behind me. Wanting me to look as if I could be anywhere.

The Texas plains.

The Canadian wilderness.

The far horizon of Death Valley.

Places I have never gone.

The pigeons dart about inside their coop in anticipation of being fed, send small feathers floating through the chicken wire. But I do not bend to the shelf where I keep their bag of feed. Instead, I put my hand on the hook that holds their door closed and unlatch it. And then I swing it wide.

It takes the birds some seconds to fly out, but when they do, they come soaring through the door in silvery streaks, spiraling upward like a feathered cyclone.

I stand back and watch them. My birds—though I think they are not mine anymore—spinning up into the orange-ing sky.

"Auf wiedersehen," I say, as if they are German pigeons. As if I am twelve years old, setting them free on a tenement roof on the Lower East Side.

The birds fly into the sunset, out over the trees in Fort Tryon Park, out over the Palisades. Heading west.

All but one. A lone bird who arcs toward the east, in a bright flashing of silver.

ACKNOWLEDGMENTS

The book you are holding in your hands is a much better one thanks to the tireless efforts of my very smart editor, Sarah McGrath. Huge thanks are also due to my agent, the wonderful and generous Ellen Levine, who makes every writer feel like her most important writer.

I owe a bigger debt than the fancy dinner I bought them to the members of my writing group: Lee Kravetz, Cameron Tuttle, and especially, Kirsten Menger-Anderson, Susanne Pari, and Ethel Rohan. An equally large debt is owed to Nona Caspers, who understood what this story was about well before I did.

Thanks go to Peter Orner and Tom Barbash for helping this book see the light of day. And to Chris Hardy for advice on all things photographic.

I am enormously grateful to the Writers' Grotto of San Francisco for giving me a home to write this book. Thanks also to the Jackson family for the use of their retreat at Big Sur for the final push.

I owe thanks to each and every one of my students. Their energy and enthusiasm never fails to inspire me.

As always to Ken, for his unwavering support and encouragement.

And to my son, Alex, for giving me access to the world of boys, and for being himself.

Most of all, to my father, George Cooke, for taking me to a roof on Dyckman Street and telling me his stories with nothing but the wide blue sky behind us.